A Love That Broke Us

Also by Erin Cornia

The Chicago Series

If It Can't Be Us

The Most Perfect Wrong

A Love That Broke Us (Book One of The Broken and Bound Duet)

Book Two of The Broken and Bound Duet – Coming December 2025

Key Characters in A Love That Broke Us

- **Main Couple**
  - Jensen Adams
  - Alley Evans/Adams
- **Jensen and Alley's Family**
  - Matt - Jensen's lifelong best friend; like a brother
  - Megan - Jensen's sister
  - Kevin - Megan's husband; brother-in-law
  - Jeff - Jensen's brother
  - Amber - Jeff's wife; sister-in-law
  - Christy - Jensen's mom
  - Tom - Jensen's dad
  - Michael Evans - Alley's brother; Leo's friend
  - Stella Evans - Michael's wife; sister-in-law
- **Alley's Friends**
  - Scarlett - Alley's best friend in New York
  - Zach - Alley's close friend from work
- **Crossover Characters from If It Can't Be Us**
  - Leo Weston - MMC in *If It Can't Be Us*
  - Vivian Weston - FMC in *If It Can't Be Us*; Leo's wife
  - Adam - Michael's best friend from childhood

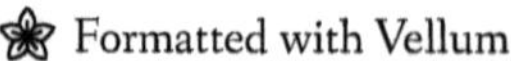 Formatted with Vellum

Content Warning

Your mental health matters.

A Love That Broke Us explores deep
emotions and themes, and contains the following content:

- **Strong Language**
- **Mature Content**
- **Explicit Romance Scenes**
- **Depictions of Drug Addiction and Withdrawal**
- **On-Page Drug Use**
- **On-Page Panic Attacks**
- **On-Page Withdrawal Symptoms**
- **On-Page Anxiety**
- **Drug-Seeking Behavior**
- **On-Page Hallucinations**
- **Emotional Trauma**

If these themes are triggering for you, please read with care.

This book is not intended for public schools or readers under the age of eighteen. **Reader discretion is advised.**

**To anyone touched by addiction—
your own, or someone else's.**
You are not weak for loving.
You are not selfish for leaving.
You are not alone.

This one's for you...

But it's also for me.

A Love That Broke Us Playlist

Music always plays a huge role in the writing process for me, and *A Love That Broke Us* was no different. These songs helped me tap into the heart of the story and feel everything my characters were going through. And with this one, there was a lot to feel.

There were moments I couldn't even listen to certain songs without crying. Sometimes, it was too much. But those chapters? They're the ones that hit the hardest—the ones where the music cracked me wide open and I let it all pour out.

I hope you enjoy this playlist as much as I do.

Playlist:

- *Something Just Like This* – The Chainsmokers & Coldplay
- *Maroon* – Taylor Swift
- *Close to You* – Gracie Abrams
- *Next Summer* – Damiano David
- *Forever* – Lewis Capaldi
- *28* – Ruth B. & Dean Lewis
- *Unsteady* (Erich Lee Gravity Remix) – X Ambassadors
- *Can You Die From a Broken Heart* – Nate Smith & Avril Lavigne
- *Something to Remember* – Matt Hansen
- *Good News* – Shaboozey
- *My Boy Only Breaks His Favorite Toys* – Taylor Swift
- *Exile* (feat. Bon Iver) – Taylor Swift
- *All Too Well* – Taylor Swift
- *You're Losing Me* – Taylor Swift
- *We Pray* – Coldplay, Little Simz, Burna Boy
- *Million Reasons* – Lady Gaga
- *Say Something* – A Great Big World
- *Burning* – Lewis Capaldi
- *All Out of Fight* – P!nk
- *Somebody Save Me* – Eminem & Jelly Roll

A Love That Broke Us

Book One of The Broken and Bound Duet

The Chicago Series
Book 3

Erin Cornia

Chapter One

ALLEY

PRESENT DAY

AUGUST

"HI, you've reached Jensen Adams. You know what to do."

Dammit. His voicemail again. That's the sixth time in twenty minutes.

I end the call, setting my phone next to the leather-bound dinner menu. The white tablecloth beneath it is perfectly crisp and untouched. If I leave now and he shows, we lose our table. But if he doesn't...

I don't even know how much longer they'll let me sit here. This place is reservation-only, and nearly impossible to get into. I booked it weeks ago.

I try texting again.

> Where are you? I'm starting to worry... Please call me.

Two years married. *Happy anniversary to me.*

My fingers drum against the table, heat creeping over my cheeks. I feel ridiculous sitting here alone. I glance down, avoiding the server's stare as he walks past. He probably thinks I've been stood up. How could he not?

I cross my legs, my gaze shifting to the empty seat across from me. *God, where is he?*

I exhale sharply, trying to force a small smile, but it doesn't quite stick.

I'll give him five more minutes.

I close my eyes, letting my mind drift back to the first time I saw him. Just like that, my lips curve up at the memory. Because if there's one thing Jensen Adams has always been good at, it's making me smile.

Chapter Two

JENSEN

THEN—FIVE YEARS AGO

SEPTEMBER

A HOT BLONDE bends over to kiss me, her lips brushing mine. Soft. Warm. *Damn.* I lean into the kiss, chasing the heat, but she pulls back, leaving me with the faint taste of something I don't recognize.

I look around. I'm surrounded by a blur of people. *Wait. Where am I? Central Park?* I blink, the scene shifting. Now she's in the park, laughing as she chats with her brunette friend. There's a dog, too, its leash tangling around their legs.

"Jensen... Jensen."

Her voice morphs into something sharper, closer. A heaviness settles over me as I stir, the park fading to gray. A groan escapes me, my body protesting the idea of moving.

God, I'm so comfortable. Just let me stay here a little longer.

"Hey, Jensen, can you hear me?" The voice cuts through the haze in my brain, pulling me closer to reality. "Jensen. If you can hear me, squeeze my finger."

Something presses into my palm, and my hand instinctively clenches tightly around it. More voices follow, words mumbling into meaningless sounds. My body feels like it's been anchored down, heavy and uncooperative. But one thing stands out: my aching erection. My clustered thoughts spin back to the blonde and her brunette friend. *Where did they go? Come back.*

My eyelids fight against me, cracking open just enough for light to stab through. I wince, shutting them tight again.

"Jensen. It's time to wake up." The voice is soft but insistent, definitely female. *Maybe it's the blonde?* I chuckle, my brain too foggy to care about making sense of anything.

"I have a boner," I blurt, laughter bubbling out of me.

"Is that so?" The same woman's voice responds, amusement in her tone.

My eyes flutter open, adjusting to the blinding brightness. Shapes blur, then sharpen, until I lock onto a pretty blonde standing over me. Her lips twitch, barely fighting back laughter.

"That's pretty normal," she says, patting my arm. "Welcome back. I'm Alley, your nurse. How was your trip?" She winks. "Sounds like you were having some pretty wild dreams."

Is this the blonde from my dream?

"What's your pain level?"

I stare at her as the haziness in my brain clears. *Oh, yeah. Knee surgery. God, my throat feels like sandpaper.*

"Um..." I croak, my voice rough. "Can I have some water?"

"No, sorry. But you can have some ice chips." She hands me a cup filled with ice—the kind that crunches perfectly between your teeth and tastes like childhood summers—red cups, and Dr. Pepper at Pizza Hut. "Do you have any pain?"

I shake my head, distracted by her smile and the one dimple in her cheek. "God, you're pretty," I say, the words spilling out, my drugged brain betraying me.

She grins. "Oh, yeah? Is that why you still have a boner?"

I glance down, the blanket tenting over my lap.

I nod.

"I'm sorry," she says suddenly. "I shouldn't have said that. I hope you're still loopy enough to forget this conversation."

I chuckle. "No chance. I'm going to remember this forever. I have a hot nurse."

She laughs softly, meeting my gaze with amused eyes, then ruffles my hair like I'm her kid brother. "Yeah, well, I'm not your nurse for much longer. You're in PACU. We'll be taking you down to your recovery room in a minute."

"No, don't go," I murmur softly, the words slipping out unfiltered. I'm awake, but still disoriented. I can't hold them back.

She smirks but doesn't reply, helping me sit up as another nurse approaches, an older woman with a kind face.

"How's he doing?" the older nurse asks, her gaze landing on me. "Can you rate your pain on a scale of one to ten?"

I clear my throat, swallowing against the dryness. "A four, I guess. It's not bad."

"That's good. I'm Cindy. We're going to take you down to recovery now. Ready for a ride?"

I nod, then glance at Alley. "Are you coming too?"

Her grin lights up her face. "Slow down, lover boy. I'm coming."

The gurney rolls forward, the ceiling lights blurring above me as I'm wheeled down the hallway. The soft hum of wheels on tile lulls me, and I close my eyes for what feels like just a second. When I open them again, I'm in a different room, surrounded by unfamiliar faces, nurses, but none of them are Alley.

* * *

"I can't stop thinking about that nurse," I say, pulling Matt's attention away from the TV. We're about a month into fantasy football and my team's holding pretty strong.

"So, ask her out," Matt says, as if I haven't considered it a hundred times.

"Yeah, because walking up to the PACU floor like a creep is totally normal." I groan, running a hand through my hair. "Not that it matters, I don't know her schedule anyway."

He glances over, one eyebrow raised. "How hot are we talking?"

"Hot. Like a ten out of ten. But not obvious-hot. More girl-next-door hot." I grin, remembering her teasing me about my hard-on.

"That's the best kind of hot," Matt says, taking a swig of his beer. "Go find her. A hospital unit's never stopped you before. Remember when you stalked that bartender in college? You spent every Friday night at her bar for, what, a month?"

I laugh. "That's different. Waiting at a bar doesn't make you look like a stalker."

"True, but stalking's kind of your specialty," he shoots back with a smirk.

I shake my head, chuckling. "Yeah, but that didn't involve hospital security."

Matt shrugs. "You'll find a way, bro. You always do."

Easy for him to say. If it were Matt, Alley would've handed over her number before the anesthesia even wore off. Hell, he might've even received a handy under the sheets. No need for him to ask, either. Girls throw themselves at him, consequences be damned. Yeah, he'd have walked out with her number and a grin plastered on his face.

Me? I don't have it quite that easy, but I do just fine. I'm not the guy who turns every head when I walk into a room, but I've got enough going for me to keep things interesting: a good face, decent build, great sense of humor, and I can charm my way into just about any opportunity. That's why I've built a solid career in software sales. I don't make Matt-level money, but I've done well for myself. I'm thirty, single, and I've made smart investments.

The main difference between us, though, is that I actually want to find someone to spend my life with. Matt? Not so much. He's more about keeping things casual, and in a city like New York—crawling with women who aren't looking for anything serious—he's thriving.

"Any suggestions on how to do that?" I ask, kicking back against the couch.

"I don't know, man. Do the typical Jensen thing. Stalk her, flash her a smile, and let your charm work its magic. Ninety percent chance you score a date, fifty you get laid."

Matt's attention shifts back to the game, leaving me stuck contemplating my obsession with Alley. I keep asking myself what makes her different. There are plenty of hot girls in New York, and I rarely do a double take, let alone let someone hijack my thoughts for two weeks. Was it her stupid sexy smile and that one dimple? The way she flirted back without trying too hard? I mean, *Jesus*, she cracked a joke about my boner. Made me laugh when I was barely conscious. Not a lot of girls with that kind of sense of humor. And there was something in her eyes. Something honest, and innocent. For some reason, I felt like I could trust her.

Maybe that's why I can't get her out of my head.

Maybe Matt's right. I could go to the hospital, but I don't want to come off as creepy. *Was she even into me? Would she even say yes if I asked her out?* It's been two weeks, and she still lurks in the back of my mind. Every night, I fall asleep thinking about her. Hell, I'll probably rub one out to thoughts of her tonight.

My hand drifts to my knee, mindlessly rubbing the ache. I reach for the bottle of ibuprofen on the side table, pop two into my mouth, and wash them down with a sip of water. It won't do much right away, but in thirty minutes, it should be just enough to take the edge off. Two weeks post-surgery, and I'm ready for this dull ache to leave me the hell alone. At this rate, I'll be limping like an old man forever.

I should've known better than to jump for that rebound. It was way out of reach. One wrong twist mid-air, and my knee gave out like a cheap folding chair. The sound still echoes in my head—like a branch snapping underfoot—followed by the sharp, gut-punch pain that nearly had me seeing stars. I've been playing in an adult basketball league on Tuesday nights for a couple years now. Unfortunately, those days are gone for at least a couple months.

"I should probably wait to stalk her until I'm off my crutches, huh?"

Matt hesitates, glancing over. "I don't know. The whole 'poor me' thing might actually work. Girls love taking care of a man, and she might feel bad about saying no to a guy on crutches."

I laugh inwardly. What a Matt thing to say. He thinks women live to serve him, and judging by his track record, they pretty much do.

We've been best friends for as long as I can remember. Matt and I both grew up on the Upper East Side, lived in the same building, and went to the same private schools together. Even now, we still live in the same building, a building he owns in the West Village.

Matt shouts at the TV, but I'm lost in thought—the past, the present, and what I'm going to do to scratch this itch named Alley.

"Hey, speaking of women... Remember that girl Samantha I told you about?" Matt glances over, pulling me from my thoughts.

And, just like that, we're done talking about Alley. "The one that gave you head at your buddy's birthday party?"

He grins, leaning back with a smug look. "Yeah. She texted me last night, came over. I fucked her against the wall, then again in my room. Best part? She was gone when I woke up. She left a note that said, *'Thanks for last night, call me.'"*

Jesus. He can be such a prick in so many ways, but he'd give me the shirt off his back without hesitation. Matt has some flaws, who doesn't? But he gives everything to the people who matter.

His parents are big real-estate investors, and he followed in their footsteps. He's insanely successful, and, when it comes to women, a total player. I can't really blame him, though. He's always been good-looking, and the ladies have flocked to him since the day he could tie his own shoes.

Growing up, his parents were hardly ever around. His nanny, Gloria, practically raised him. He was an only child, an accident at that, and his childhood lacked the kind of love every kid deserves. He never really had a relationship with his parents. Things are better now, but back then? He was all kinds of messed up. Then again, so was I, and I had no excuse.

My parents were the opposite of his. They were hands-on, which was rare at our school. My dad's a successful lawyer. Not the kind who makes millions like Matt's parents, but enough to live comfortably in New York and send us to private school. Compared to most of the kids I went to school with, our wealth was nothing. My mom stayed home with us, and her whole life revolved around my sisters and me. I always felt seen, supported, and cared for. Everything Matt missed out on growing up.

"So, are you going to call her?" I ask, already knowing the answer.

He glances my way. "Nah, probably not. I like when they come to me."

I roll my eyes. "Of course you do. So... how was she?"

"In the sack? Fucking great. She's a freak—wild, adventurous, hot as hell." He pauses, chuckling. "She slipped a finger in my ass."

My brows shoot up. "Really? She doesn't even know you."

"I know, man, it's nuts. Girls these days are down for anything. Most of the time, they're the ones initiating the crazy shit." He runs a hand through his hair and exhales. "Come to think of it, maybe I will call her."

He leans back, looking at me. "And fuck it, bro. You should go to the hospital and ask this Alley chick out. You've got nothing to lose."

I twist my mouth, nodding. "You're right. I will, as soon as I'm off these damn crutches. I want to feel like myself when I see her again."

* * *

I LEAN my weight onto one crutch, balancing the other against the side of my body, and reach for the heavy coffee shop door. It's not my usual spot, but it's the closest to my building. Still stuck on crutches, I've been settling for shittier coffee in exchange for a shorter walk. I manage to tug the door open, but holding it while hobbling through feels like a cruel joke.

"Oh, here, let me get that for you." A woman's voice comes from behind, and before I know it, she's there, swinging the door open like I'm some helpless old man.

"Thanks," I mutter, glancing at her. My heart practically skips a beat. *It's her—Alley.* She's in dark blue scrubs, her hair pulled back, just as gorgeous as I remember.

"Hey! I know you... Jensen, right?"

Wow, she remembered my name. That has to mean something.

"Yeah," I say, keeping my voice casual. "And you're the hot nurse... Ashley, right?"

"Alley."

I know. I think about you every day. "Oh, sorry."

She waves it off. "You were coming out of anesthesia. I don't expect you to remember my name. I'm surprised you recognize me at all, honestly."

I limp inside with my crutches, and she follows, letting the door swing shut behind us. "Of course I remember you. You're the hot nurse who gave me shit about having a boner. How could I forget that?"

She freezes mid-step, her cheeks flushing bright red. "Oh my God." She groans, covering her face with both hands. "I cannot believe I said that. That was so unprofessional of me! I was making dirty jokes like we were old friends. I prayed you were too drugged up to remember." Her hands slide down her face, and she shakes her head, muttering, "I'm the worst."

I laugh, shrugging. "Why are you giving yourself such a hard time? It's fine, it's *funny*. I mean, I *did* have a boner, and you are very pretty, so..."

She gapes at me, a slow smile spreading across her face. "Well, I'm glad to see your boner has gone away. Or... maybe it hasn't. I mean, I don't actually know if you have a boner right now." Her eyes flick down, and I smack my lips together to keep from laughing. "I'm just assuming you don't." She exhales sharply. "Holy shit." Then she bursts out laughing. "Wow. Okay, I would very much like to start over."

"Oh, you would? Is talking about whether or not I'm hard making you uncomfortable?" I tease, biting back a grin.

"Yes. Very." She nods quickly, then straightens up, extending her hand. "Hi, I'm Alley. I'm a nurse at East River Hospital."

I take her hand, giving it a firm shake. "Jensen Adams. I'm a sales manager for a software company, fancy way of saying I sell techy stuff to businesses."

Her lips quirk into a small smile, and I catch myself holding onto her hand a second too long before letting go.

My turn at the counter comes, and I give the barista my order before turning back to her. "Let me get your coffee."

She waves me off, shaking her head. "No, no. You don't have to do that."

"Come on, I want to. For taking such good care of me... twice now. At the hospital, and just now with the door. You saved my ass."

"Well, when you put it that way, I guess you do kind of owe me." She grins, and damn, it does something to me. She's beautiful.

I pay for our coffees, and we move to the counter to wait.

"This is crazy, seeing you here," she says. "I never come this way, but I was leaving a friend's house this morning."

A friend. Right.

She clears her throat. "So, do you live close by?"

"Yeah, around the corner. I don't usually come here, though." I lean in, lowering my voice. "The coffee kind of sucks. But I needed to get out, and, as you can see, I'm still inept."

Her eyes widen, and she grimaces dramatically. "Oh, crap. The coffee's bad? Will they notice if I bail?" A mischievous smile lights her face. "Technically, I'm not out anything if I leave. It was free." She nudges me lightly.

Shit. I can already feel myself falling for this girl. It's stupid, really. I don't even know her, but she's hot, fun, and jokes as much as I do? This girl might just be made for me.

I chuckle. "You better not leave me to suffer through this shitty coffee alone. The only thing getting me through was knowing I'd have your company."

"Ah, that's sweet, but I can't stay. I'll be late for work." They call my name, and she grabs both coffees before I can even try. "Where do you want to sit?"

She's sweet, saving me from the embarrassment of having to ask for help like I have every morning this week. I gesture to a table by the window and hobble after her, trying not to feel like a total invalid. Hopefully, I'll be off these crutches by next week.

As she sets my coffee down, I try to stall her, even if only for a minute. "Hey, listen. I'll make you a deal. Three minutes of your time, with the world's shittiest cup of coffee, to decide if I'm worth giving your number to."

"I have a better idea. I'll be right back," she says, biting her bottom lip.

She walks over to the counter, and moments later, she's back, holding out a napkin. "How about I don't need three minutes." Her smile is confident as she backs toward the door. With a quick turn, she's gone, leaving me staring at the napkin in my hand, her phone number scrawled across it. Beneath the number, in bold letters, she's written: HOT NURSE.

I can't help but grin as I plop triumphantly into a seat. She's funny, confident, and left me wanting more? Yeah, I'm definitely calling her. Today's already a hell of a lot better than I expected.

* * *

I DECIDE to text Alley after wrapping up a call with a potential customer.

> Hey, I found a napkin on the street labeled HOT NURSE with this phone number… Are you said hot nurse?

I send the text, fully intending to ask her out, but as I reread it, panic sets in. I was trying to be funny, but now I'm realizing she might actually think some random guy is texting her and just ignore it.

Dammit.

I'll give it a couple hours, I decide. She might be working anyway. Let it simmer, and if she doesn't reply, I'll send a follow-up to let her know I'm joking.

I waited a few days to text her because I didn't want to seem overly eager, even though I wanted to message her the second she walked out of that coffee shop. I usually play the dating field by my own rules, but the one rule I always stick to is not coming off too needy. Build the anticipation, make her wait, at least a little.

I glance at my phone for the thousandth time in ten minutes and realize this isn't going to work. I'm going to drive myself crazy.

I start typing.

> Sorry, that was my attempt at being funny and not wanting to come off overly eager. This is Jensen, btw. It was great running into you the other day. You free Saturday night for a drink?

I pause. Do I ask her out here? Or do I wait for her to respond, feel it out?

My thumb hovers over the delete button, but I grit my teeth and hit send. Too late now.

I place my phone face down on my desk, trying to play it cool. But two minutes later, I'm already reaching for it. Nothing. I set it down again. Another glance. Still nothing.

Then, finally, it buzzes.

ALLEY

Jensen? Hmm… sorry, I don't know a Jensen.

My stomach drops, but before I can panic, another message comes through.

ALLEY

Just kidding. Hi, Jensen. Saturday works. Where are we going?

Chapter Three

ALLEY

THEN

OCTOBER

You ONLY COME to Whiskey's for a special occasion, or when you've got money to blow. It's swanky—the kind of bar that says, *I've made it in life.* Brick walls, backlit shelves lined with overpriced bottles, and music just loud enough to make you lean closer. The lighting's dim, and all the chairs and barstools are leather. Before tonight, I would've thought bringing a first date here was a flex. But so far, Jensen doesn't seem like that kind of guy.

We're at the bar top, chairs close, knees touching, angled toward each other. He's grinning, dimples deep, blue eyes locked on mine.

"And that's my family in a nutshell. Things get pretty wild when we're all together, but I wouldn't have it any other way. Tell me about your family," he says.

Damn—his eyes. They're stupid pretty. The kind that make you forget what you were saying.

I thought he was cute at the hospital, and really cute at the coffee shop... But I don't remember him being this hot.

"Well, I can't really top that. My family isn't nearly as interesting. It's just me and my brother, Michael. He's five years older than me." I take a sip of my Guinness. "He lives in Chicago. That's where I'm from. I only see him once or twice a year, but we're close."

"What about your mom and dad?"

There it is—the dreaded question.

I skip over it, flashing a flirty smile. "Do you think people can tell we're on a first date?"

He chuckles. "What's giving it away? The classic *tell me about your family* questions? Or the fact that you're not anywhere near close enough to me?"

He raises an eyebrow, a sly grin curving as he slides his stool a few inches closer, my legs now tucked between his. A warmth sweeps through me and settles in my chest, my pulse picking up speed.

"I mean, look around. You can spot every first date in this place." He nods to my right, and I follow his gaze. "See that couple? First date for sure. She's closed off, her arms are folded, and there's way too much space between them."

I turn back to Jensen. "Maybe she just doesn't like him."

He gestures toward the couple again. "Case in point. You wouldn't go on a second date with someone you weren't into. That girl can't wait to get home."

I roll my bottom lip between my teeth, but it doesn't stop my smile from breaking through. "Okay. Let me find one." I scan the bar, eyes landing on a couple in the corner, sitting close, but not too close. She laughs, touching his arm. "What about them?"

He watches for a beat before letting out a laugh. "Oh, that's a first date for sure. And she is hoping to get laaaaid."

I roll my eyes. "You don't know that."

"Sure I do."

"Oh, you can just always tell when a woman wants to get laid?"

He cocks a brow. "Is it that hard?"

"Well, we're sitting pretty close, Jensen. What do you think people are saying when they look at us? Do we look like a first date ready to jump ship—or jump into bed?"

His grin widens. He picks up his glass and takes a slow sip, eyes never leaving mine. "I think people look at us and think, *that guy is really into that girl... and he definitely wants to take her home.*"

His hand drops to my leg, fingers brushing slowly over the fabric.

Holy shit. The contact is subtle, but my body reacts like he's touching bare skin. Heat pools low in my core, a slow throb settling in as his fingers linger. I don't move. My heart races, and my next breath is shaky.

"And she likes him too," he adds, voice dipping low. "But she's the kind of woman who makes a man work for it. And I'm not mad about that. Not one bit."

He lifts his hand from my leg and reaches for his glass.

"Well then." I drain the last sip of my beer, setting it down with a clink. "Guess you've got your work cut out for you."

* * *

Jensen pushes the door open, and a rush of crisp night air greets us as we leave the bar, stepping onto a busy Chelsea sidewalk.

"You said you live in the same building as your best friend? What was his name again?"

"Yeah, Matt. He's a very successful real estate investor. He owns the building, actually. His parents have been buying up real estate all over the city for the past three decades." Jensen gestures ahead. "Want to walk over to Hudson River Park?"

"Yeah, that sounds great. Are you good to walk that far?" My eyes flick to his knee, remembering how he was still on crutches last weekend.

"I should be fine for a bit. It's not that far."

We head toward the river, and I slow my pace so he doesn't feel like he's holding me back. It's been an abnormally warm day for this time of year, but now, even with my heavy jacket, a chill lingers. I glance up at him with a teasing smile. "Does your friend give you free rent?"

He belts out a laugh. "No, but he gives me a discount. Even then, it's still pretty steep. Matt lives in the penthouse. It's total luxury. I guess I get to enjoy it by association."

"Damn. I need to get myself a rich best friend. What's he like?"

Jensen sighs, gripping the back of his neck as we walk toward the Hudson. "I don't know... he's Matt." He chuckles softly. "If I had to sum him up, I'd say he's fun, confident, loyal, and... kind of a slut."

I can't help but laugh. "A slut? A man slut? Is that even a thing? Sounds more like something he'd win a trophy for."

"Oh, it's definitely a thing. Matt's a player, no doubt. He's had his fair share of girlfriends, but he doesn't stay interested for long. He doesn't like feeling tied down. He loves his freedom, and honestly, he just gets bored easily." He shrugs. "He's always been that way."

"Sounds kind of like my best friend."

Jensen glances over, a smirk tugging at his mouth. "Growing a real estate empire or slutty too?"

A smile tugs at my lips. I appreciate his realness. I've never dated anyone like him. Someone who just says it like it is. He's funny, and I find myself drifting closer to him as we walk. "Well, my best friend at work is Zach. But my ride or die is Scarlett. She's not flipping penthouses, but she's definitely got the freedom-loving, non-committal thing down. I wouldn't call her a slut, but... she loves a good one-night stand." Our arms brush together, and it feels like the most natural thing in the world, being this close to him.

"Okay. Let's agree to never let them meet."

I laugh again, then hesitate before asking, "What about you?"

"What about me?"

"Do you have one-night stands often?" I ask, keeping my tone casual.

I know it's a personal question, and I'm not naive. Most single guys in New York aren't exactly monks. I just want to get a sense of where he stands.

He chuckles, his pace slowing. "Whoa. Putting me on the spot here. No judgment?"

I raise my hands in mock innocence. "Never."

"I mean, I'm a thirty-year-old guy, so yeah, I've had my fair share. But it's not my go-to. If I'm into someone, I'd rather see where it goes. What about you?"

My cheeks heat. "Um... nope. I've never had a one-night stand."

"Seriously?" He stops walking and turns to face me. "Not even one tiny drunken night in college?"

I shake my head, pressing my lips into a thin line. "Nope. Never."

"Wow." His eyes dance with amusement. "I'm completely shocked right now. I don't know many women in this city who could say that."

"I know... It's just not my cup of tea, you know? I like my cup with a side of get-to-know-you first. Scarlett? She likes hers with a side of danger and a possible STD."

He chuckles as he leans his back against the rail, and I follow suit. "You're funny, Alley. And, in my defense, I'm not exactly Matt. So when a woman wants to sleep with me, and it's been a minute... or months, I'm not turning it down."

His smile deepens, his dimples popping, and I catch his eyes on mine. My heart stutters. *Dammit. I like him*—a lot. I haven't had these butterfly feels in so long.

"What do you mean you're not Matt? You're a catch. And you have an incredible personality."

"Ah... personality. The thing that gets me through life."

I nudge him playfully. "Shut up. You know what I mean. You're not just personality, you're hot. Like, stupid hot. But honestly? I'd take a great personality over good looks any day. A hot guy with a bad personality? Hard pass. And by the way, all the nurses are still talking about the blue-eyed hottie who woke up with a boner and hit on me." I smack my lips together, trying not to laugh.

"Oh, we're back to talking about my boner now?"

I shrug, meeting his gaze, a smile playing on my lips. "Seems like it's a recurring theme."

He chuckles, the sound deep and low, sending a shiver through me. "Careful, Alley, or I might end up with another one."

I blink, startled, but try to stay cool because the idea of turning him on stirs something in me. "Yeah? What would you do about that?"

He shifts, stepping closer, his hands gripping the rail on either side of me. I'm caged in, his face inches from mine. "You wanna find out?" he murmurs, his voice teasing.

Yes. Hell yes. I meet his gaze. "Maybe," I say softly.

His eyes flick to my lips, and I suck in a shaky breath as he leans in —slow, deliberate. It's almost torture. When his mouth finally meets mine, I melt. The kiss is everything. Warm. Soft. Sexy.

I feel him smile against my lips before leaning in for more, deepening the kiss. I meet him with equal intensity, his tongue brushing softly against mine, like he's asking for permission.

I give it.

My arms loop around his neck as his hands slide around my waist, pulling me flush against him. We kiss for seconds, or maybe minutes. I lose all sense of time. All I know is I don't want it to end. My stomach flutters with excitement, heat pulsing through me. I'm turned on. In the middle of a public park.

Somewhere in the background, I hear a whistle and a loud, "Get it, bro!" I should care, but I don't. Not when his lips feel this good on mine. Let them look. Let them comment. I'm not stopping.

I barely notice the rest of the crowd, the bustling walkway and the people passing by. I've never been one for making out in public, but right now? It's the last thing I care about. This feeling of newness, of connection, of something just clicking... it's intoxicating.

It's also terrifying, because when it feels this good, this fast—all you can do is hope. Hope that it's real. Hope that he feels the same. Hope he's not secretly collecting toenail clippings or hiding a weird fetish.

Please be normal, Jensen.

And please, please don't break my heart.

* * *

I PULL out my phone to text my brother and sister-in-law.

> Happy freaking birthday, bro! Hope you have the best day ever. Wishing you lots of birthday sex... and Stella, I hope you deliver a top-tier birthday beej.

The door to the break room swings open, making me jump.

"Hey, how's my favorite boo?"

I turn, grinning. "Hey, stranger!" I rise from my chair and pull Zach into a hug. "How was Maui? You guys have fun?"

Zach squeezes me back before heading to the fridge. "Yeah, it was incredible. Joey's sister drove me fucking crazy, but other than that, it was great."

"Oh, no. I thought she wasn't going. What did she do? Or do I even need to ask?" I scrunch my nose, already bracing for the answer. Joey is Zach's boyfriend, and Zach can't stand Joey's high-maintenance little sister.

He lets out an exasperated sigh. "She bought a plane ticket last minute. Can you believe that? Literally made me want to vomit when I found out she was coming. She's such a selfish, whiny little you-know-what. She complained about something everywhere we went. I swear, I can't ever go on a trip with her again."

Zach makes a dramatic face as he places his food in the microwave. He's always been a little over the top, but that's one of the things I love about him. He's fun and never fails to make me laugh. Work is a hell of a lot more enjoyable when he's here.

"God, I'm sorry. That's so annoying." I pause as the microwave beeps. "But I'm glad to have you back. It's been dull here without you."

He rolls his eyes, grabbing his food and sitting across from me. "Yeah, right. Someone told *me* you went out with the blue-eyed hottie from a few weeks ago." His lips curve into a mischievous grin. "Doesn't sound like it was that dull while I was gone. Spill." He drums his fingers on the table, milking the moment for all it's worth.

"Who told you that?" I ask, laughing.

"Mm-mm. I never give up my sources."

"It's not *that* big of a deal," I say, fighting to suppress a massive grin.

He leans back, smirking. "You're such a bad liar."

I let out another laugh. "Fine, fine. I've been dyyyying to tell you. We went out last weekend. I met him at a bar. We talked, laughed, had a couple of drinks. It was a lot of fun."

"Which bar?"

I raise my brows. "Whiskey's," I say, knowing full well why he's asking. He's a total bar snob, and Whiskey's is about as high-end as it gets.

His brows shoot up. "Okay, I approve already. Did you suck his dick to thank him?"

"Oh my God. You're the worst!" I can't help but laugh.

"What? Let me live, Al. You know I love Joey, but come on, I've been ordering the same entrée for two years now. Excuse me for wanting a taste of the dessert you've got on your plate."

This is exactly why work is so much more fun with Zach. We've worked together for three years now, both RNs, and he's easily one of my closest friends, my best friend at work.

"No, I didn't suck his dick. I'm not as easy as you. I like to make them work for it."

"Shame. I forget sometimes that you're such a prude."

"I am not!" I shove at his arm, laughing.

"Al-gal, you've been with, what, two people? You're practically a virgin."

"You're such an ass. I've been with five people, thank you very much. One of whom I dated for three years. I am *not* a prude. I love a good dick as much as the next person."

"Good girl. Me too." He grins. "So, what's he like? What does he do? And since blow jobs are off the table for you on a first date, did you at least kiss him?"

"He's really cute, as you know. He has a great smile, and the sexiest dimples. He's funny—had me laughing all night. It was easy, you know? Like we were old friends just chatting. Never a dull moment." My grin stretches wider as I talk. "He's in sales, something with software. I don't really know the details, but it seems like he's pretty successful. Lives in the West Village, grew up in the Upper East Side, went to private schools. The whole fancy rich kid thing."

Zach's eyes light up. "Oh, he grew up wealthy? Tell me more. Does he have any brothers for me?"

I give him a pointed look. "You gonna leave Joey for a potential rich brother?"

He shrugs, smothering a grin. "What else? Get to the goods. How far did you go?"

I roll my eyes. "It's always about sex with you. We had a really great connection."

"And?"

"And... we kissed at the end of the night."

He lets out a dramatic sigh. "That's it? No rub-rub under the table, in the taxi, at the door?"

I laugh, shaking my head. "No! But we shared a very heated kiss at the park. It definitely left me wanting more."

Zach laughs, folding his arms. "Ahh, how very PG-13 of you."

I shove at his shoulder.

"I'm kidding," he says, softer now. "I'm happy for you. Are you seeing him again?"

"Yes! He's taking me to dinner on Friday. We've been texting all week." I can't help the smile spreading across my face. "I'm really excited about it."

"That's great. I'll look forward to hearing all about it, and how you hopefully ran a few more bases." Zach winks and gathers his things, then plants a quick kiss on my cheek on his way out. "I've got to get back out there, babe. Technically, I'm not even on lunch yet, I was just starving."

I let out a breath, watching him go. I got here way too early. My shift doesn't start for another ten minutes. I glance at my phone and notice new message notifications.

> **MICHAEL**
>
> Jesus Christ. Did you really just text that?
>
> **STELLA**
>
> Don't worry, Al. I take my birthday duties very seriously.

I grin, texting back.

> That's the kind of support system every brother needs. You guys doing anything fun tonight?
>
> **MICHAEL**
>
> Dinner with friends. Wish you were here.
>
> Me too... New Year's?

I try to go to Chicago every other year for Michael's birthday, but this year, I just couldn't swing it. My bestie, Scarlett, and I went to Montenegro and Croatia two months ago, so my time off is tapped out. It was totally worth it, though. I'll see him at New Year's. His friends throw a great party. I've only been twice, but since I'm missing his birthday, I decided to make the trip for New Year's instead.

Michael and I grew up in Barrington Hills, about a forty-minute drive from Chicago. We lost our mom eight years ago, and my dad's a drunk. Hence why it's not exactly first-date material. I haven't been home to see him since Mom died. Michael's always on my case about it, but I just can't bring myself to do it.

It's not that I'm heartless. I honestly can't handle it. Seeing him that way tears at my insides. Dad's always struggled with alcoholism. He went off the rails when I was young, but stayed clean through most of my teenage years. Then Mom got cancer, and everything changed. He relapsed when we needed him most. I think I hate him for that— for checking out when she was on her deathbed, for drowning at the bottom of a bottle while she was dying.

My stomach churns at the memories, a heaviness settling in my chest. Michael's text pulls me from the spiral.

MICHAEL

Can't wait. Talk soon. Thanks for the birthday wishes. Love you, little sis.

Love you too, old man... You too, Stell! Give the kiddos a squeeze for me. Xoxo.

Chapter Four

JENSEN

THEN

NOVEMBER

Thank God it's Friday, and I get to work remotely. I'm spread out on my sofa—laptop open, coffee in hand, the fireplace crackling under the TV. The golf channel's on mute as I prep a presentation for next week.

My phone dings, and the message pops up on my laptop screen. It's from Alley.

ALLEY

Hey, I'm in the area. Want me to bring you the world's shittiest cup of coffee and some stale bagels?

A grin spreads across my face as I grab my phone, sliding it open to text her back. I took her out twice last weekend—Friday night, to a Knicks game, and Sunday for brunch. We text constantly, and I'm falling harder for her every day.

> How could I say no to that? Does it come with a side
> of Alley, or is it just the stale bagels?

ALLEY

Only if you promise not to spill me on your lap. I
know how easily you get boners.

On second thought… maybe I wouldn't mind.

I laugh out loud.

> If that's an offer, I'm not going to say no.

ALLEY

I'll keep that in mind. Now send me your address so
these stale bagels don't get any more stale.

I shoot her my address along with instructions on how to get to my floor. Then, I call down to the concierge desk to let them know she's coming. Jumping up, I take a quick scan of my apartment. I'm not messy by nature, but there are a few dishes in the sink I didn't get to last night. I hurry to load them into the dishwasher.

I'm in loungewear, but I don't think Alley will care. At least, I hope she won't.

Ten minutes later, there's a knock at the door.

I open it to find Alley standing there, looking beautiful, arms full. Her eyes scan me, landing on my head. Her lips curve into a grin.

"Wow. You must be a wild sleeper. That's some impressive bedhead you've got going on."

I chuckle, grabbing the coffees and waving her in. "Sorry, this is about as sexy as I get before coffee," I tease.

She laughs, walking past me to the counter where she drops her purse and the bagels. Shrugging off her jacket, she drapes it over the barstool, and my pulse kicks up a notch. She looks *hot*—tight, low-cut top, heels, flawless makeup. My eyes drop to her chest. I can't help it. Something about her look right now has me floored. Maybe it's the heels. Maybe it's the fact that it's only nine in the morning.

Did she just come from another guy's place?

"Whoa." I wave a hand up and down in front of her. "I didn't know this was a dress-to-impress breakfast. What's with the outfit?"

Her grin widens, mischievous and teasing. "What are you talking about? This is just how I look when I wake up." She shrugs dramatically. "Jealous?"

"More like jealous I'm not the one waking up next to you," I say before I can stop myself. My brows lift. "Did you just come from another guy's place? Who's the lucky guy?"

She narrows her eyes. "What? No. I came from my friend Scarlett's. We went out last night and had a couple drinks. I don't like going home alone late, especially after I've been drinking. I always crash at her place when we go out."

It all clicks.

"Oh, okay. I'm a douche." I grip the back of my neck, sheepish. "All this time, whenever you said you were leaving a friend's in the morning, I assumed it was because you were... uh... seeing someone else." The words tumble out in a rush. "Not that it wouldn't be okay! We're not exclusive, obviously. And we haven't even slept together, so of course you can sleep with other people. I'm not like... weird and possessive like that."

Her lips press together, her eyes sparkling with amusement. I stop myself before I dig the hole any deeper.

She stares at me, clearly entertained. She starts to say something, then smacks her lips shut like she's reconsidering. Finally, she grins. "Is your grave deep enough yet? Or do you want to keep talking so you can make sure you're buried under every awkward thing you've ever said?" She grimaces dramatically. "Because that was pretty embarrassing. I might have to crawl in with you just to stop cringing." She bursts out laughing, and I can't help but join her.

"Okay, okay," I say, chuckling. "I admit, that was not my best moment."

She steps closer, wrapping her arms around my neck. "Didn't peg you for the jealous type, Jensen." Her gaze softens as it drifts over my face.

"I'm not. I swear it." I mean it, too. I've never been the jealous type. I'm confident. Hell, I don't know what that was, but it's not a feeling I can ignore. I like her so damn much that, for a minute, I really was envious. Envious of whoever might be getting more of her than I am.

Before I can even explain, her mouth is on mine, hot and deliberate, like she's trying to prove there's nothing for me to worry about. My hands slide around her waist, pulling her closer, and my thoughts blur as her lips move against mine. Her kiss is all-consuming, a mix of sweetness and urgency that makes my chest tighten.

I haven't had sex in over three months, between the surgery and now dating Alley for the past four weeks. I've wanted to with her, but I've held back—waiting for the right moment, wondering where she stands.

She's not like the women I usually date, the ones who show up in skimpy dresses with flawless bodies sculpted by Pilates and protein shakes. She's thinner, sure, but she has a softness to her, a realness. Her curves aren't exaggerated, but she's got enough for me to hold onto, and I like that. I like that she feels human, not like some unachievable ideal. And I like that she doesn't expect that same ideal from me, that she's kissing me with bedhead, even after I made an idiotic comment.

That's what makes her so great. Everything with Alley feels real. Her laugh, her smile, the way she blushes when she catches me staring too long.

Usually, by this point, I've slept with someone I'm dating, maybe even a few times. But with Alley, it's been slow. Innocent kisses. Public makeouts. And now this. This is so much better than sex on the first or second date.

It's messing with my head in the best way.

My hand snakes to the front, brushing her stomach, inching higher. She's soft in all the right places, and my palm sweeps across her breast. She gasps, her body arching into me. That sound. *That sound alone could undo me.*

Her response ignites a deeper desire in me, and I walk her backward to the couch. We fall onto it, her body sliding beneath mine. Propping myself on my elbows, I sink between her legs. Her hands immediately begin to explore me, gliding up my chest, brushing over my shoulders and down my biceps. The press of her body against mine, the way her hips tilt up to meet me, her breath warm on my neck—it's exhilarating.

My pulse hammers in my chest as her hands drift lower, her touch leaving a trail of fire in its wake. She's made me work for this, made me wait—and somehow, that's made it all the more intense.

Her hand brushes over my hard-on, and I'm ready to lose myself completely in her when my phone rings. At first, I ignore it. There's no way I'm stopping now. But then I remember—I'm supposed to be working.

"Damn it," I mutter, breaking our kiss. My head hangs in frustration as I force myself to pull away. I groan, reluctantly sitting up and reaching for my phone. "I'm sorry, I have to get this."

She sits up next to me, her hand falling to my thigh, and I glance at her apologetically as I answer the call.

I go through the motions, saying all the right things, but my focus is shot. Her hand starts to move, tracing slow circles on my thigh, and it's killing me. She's not even trying to hide that she's messing with me —her smile small, but wicked. My cock aches, and my thoughts are anywhere but this call.

God, she's going to be the death of me.

I end the call, and she's on my lap before I can even set my phone down, her lips crashing into mine. I meet her kiss with a renewed sense of urgency as her hips grind against me, sending a jolt of heat through my body. My hands find the hem of her shirt, sliding it up, her arms lift instinctively, helping me pull it over her head.

I pause for just a moment, my eyes roaming over her, taking in what's been hidden underneath her clothes for the past month.

Damn. She's hot.

My mouth is on hers again before I can even think, my hands finding her waist and pulling her even closer.

"You're fucking sexy, Alley," I murmur, my lips brushing hers as I speak.

She grins against my mouth, her hands sneaking under my shirt, her fingers drifting over my stomach. "So are you."

I chuckle, my voice low. "You haven't even seen me yet."

"I don't need to," she says as her hands move higher. "I like you enough to know I'll like what's underneath."

The way she says it—those innocent words—I don't know if words have ever turned me on more.

Her hands scramble to pull my shirt off, and I let her. She leans back, her eyes wandering over me, taking her time. I'm in shape—I work out, run, play basketball—but I'm no gym rat. I don't have a six-pack or rippling muscles, but I'm lean, tall, and have an athletic build.

A soft smile forms on her lips as her hands trail up and over my chest, her fingertips sending sparks of desire shooting through me. Leaning in, she whispers in my ear, "I like what I see." Her tongue flicks against the shell of my ear, and a shiver runs down my spine as my thumb brushes over her nipple through the thin fabric of her bra.

She presses kisses along my jaw, working her way back to my lips. Her tongue sweeps across them, and I open for her, letting her in. The taste of her lips, the warmth of her body, the way she's grinding against my cock—it's completely consuming, and I lose myself in her.

My phone rings again.

I groan, louder this time, frustration dripping from every sound as my hand grips my hair. "Fuck."

I reach for my phone again, answering it with an effort to mask how pissed off and distracted I am.

Alley's hands don't make it any easier. Her fingers stroke my chest and abdomen, her eyes locking with mine, a fire burning in them that matches the tension coursing through my body. My cock throbs against her, and I already know this call is going to be time-consuming. Resigned, I gesture toward my laptop, and she slides off my lap.

I try to focus, nodding along to the call while she moves around the room. After five minutes, she slips her shirt back on, and I nearly groan again. She leans back against the couch, running a hand through her hair, fully clothed now, but somehow she looks no less tempting.

Another five minutes crawl by, and I glance at her, mouthing an apologetic, "I'm sorry."

She shakes her head, mouthing back, "It's fine," before standing and making her way to the kitchen. She starts rummaging through my cupboards, finally pulling out a glass and filling it with water. An ache tugs at my chest as I watch her. I like seeing her wander through my things, making herself at home.

The call drags on for another ten minutes, and by the time I end it, Alley's purse is slung over her shoulder, and she's lingering near the door, looking ready to leave.

I stride to the kitchen, meeting her halfway. My hands find her hips, her fingers brushing against my bare chest. I lower my head, pressing a kiss to her forehead. "I'm sorry that took so long," I murmur.

"Don't worry about it. I'm sorry I interrupted your workday." Her arms slide around my back, and she presses a soft kiss to my chest. "I just wanted a reason to see you."

"I'm glad you interrupted my workday... Now, where were we?" I lean in, capturing her lips in a kiss. She kisses me back—until she pulls away.

"Jensen," she says softly, her fingers tracing along my shoulders. "I'm going to go, let you get back to work. But thanks for letting me stop by. I had a lot of fun."

"You don't have to go. I don't *want* you to go."

"I know... but you're working, and I have things I need to do. Besides, I don't want our first time to be interrupted by phone calls." Her gaze locks with mine. "When we have sex, I want you all to myself."

Shit. Just hearing her say it—*when we have sex*—sends a spark straight to my dick. I don't want her to leave, don't want to stop what we've started, but knowing that she wants it, that she wants me, and that she wants it to be uninterrupted? It makes me so damn excited for when it happens.

"Okay," I say with a grin. "I can handle that. I want that too." I kiss her again, lingering just long enough to make her smile. "I'll see you tomorrow night for Matt's birthday party?"

Matt's throwing a massive thirtieth birthday bash at his penthouse. His parties are always epic, and tomorrow will be no exception. I invited Alley because I'm more than ready to introduce her to my friends, and if I'm being honest, I'd rather focus on her than fend off the inevitable attention from half the women there. Let's face it, I'm not interested. Matt's probably sacked half the guest list anyway.

She nods. "Of course. I'm planning on it. I'm excited to meet him and your friends."

"Alright, great. Are you sure you don't want me to pick you up?" I ask, even though I already know her answer.

She shakes her head. "That's dumb. Why would you come all the way out to me just to head right back here? I'll meet you here, and then we can go together."

"Okay, if you're sure."

"I'm sure."

I walk her to the door, stealing one last kiss before she goes, leaving me with my cock hard and only one solution to the problem.

Chapter Five

ALLEY

THEN

"Crap," I mutter, glaring at my reflection and wishing for a roommate, or an extra arm. My fingers fumble with the zipper at the back of my dress, one hand reaching awkwardly over my shoulder while the other tries to shove the fabric up. It's the last inch. The one spot that's impossible to reach no matter how flexible you are.

I jump up and down, as if somehow that will magically fix the problem. Desperation makes you do stupid things. Finally, my fingers catch the zipper and tug it into place with a satisfying zip. Relief washes over me as I look at myself in the mirror, the earlier frustration melting away.

Victory.

Slipping on my heels I head over to the full-length mirror in the corner of my studio apartment, working to fasten my earrings as I walk. If I don't hurry, I'm going to be late. I smooth my hands over my dress, pausing to glance at myself. I look good—nothing too flashy, but good enough to feel confident.

The dress code is cocktail attire, and my trusty little black dress never lets me down. It's short, hitting mid-thigh, and paired with my heels, it gives the illusion of longer legs. My hair is having a rare perfect day, styled in soft, messy beach waves that fall just past my shoulders.

I take a deep breath. Damn. I'm nervous.

I'm meeting Jensen's friends—his best friend, at that. From what he's told me about Matt, the party will be filled with wealthy, gorgeous women. The kind who turn heads without trying. I know that. But I can't let it intimidate me.

I may not be model-gorgeous or come from money, but I can hold my own. Jensen is into me, and that's what matters. He makes me feel beautiful. More than anyone ever has.

I smile, giving myself one last once-over before grabbing my coat. I thread my arms through the sleeves, grab my purse, and step out the door.

I called an Uber. I didn't feel like dealing with taxis or the subway from Astoria at this time of night on a Saturday. Plus, it's stupid cold outside, and the idea of walking any farther than the curb to Jensen's building door is a hard pass.

Sliding into the backseat, I'm grateful my driver's in his own world, singing along to the radio. I settle in, my gaze shifting to the window as my thoughts drift to yesterday morning. A smile creeps across my face. Lordy, making out with Jensen was hot. So damn good. And his body? Those abs, that deep V, the faint veins trailing down his hips—holy hell. I get tingly just thinking about it.

I can't even remember the last time I felt this way about someone. It's been a while. This is technically only the sixth time I've seen Jensen. Well, seventh if I count our coffee shop run-in. No, scratch that—eighth, if I also count the day he woke up from anesthesia.

A small laugh escapes my lips, thankfully drowned out by the music. Oh, boy. That moment when Jensen was waking up from the drugs? Hilarious. I've seen my fair share of weird things in PACU, but Jensen coming down from his high was unforgettable. Mumbling about some hot blonde woman and how he wanted to taste her lips again. And then the boner—*oh my God.*

I wasn't lying when I told him it's normal to have an erection after surgery. It happens all the time. But most men don't laugh about it—or blurt out that they've got one. God, me and Cindy were *dying*.

I redirect my thoughts back to yesterday. Was I really ready to go all the way with him?

Yeah.

I think I was.

I trust him. And trust is, hands down, the most important thing to me in a relationship. I'm attracted to him, he makes me laugh, he's kind, and he makes me feel like a million bucks.

My phone buzzes in my purse, snapping me back to the present.

I pull it out, glancing at the screen.

> **SCARLETT**
>
> Good luck tonight!

A string of sexual emojis follows. I roll my eyes, smiling.

> I'm getting nervous.

> **SCARLETT**
>
> Girl... why? It's been a month. You like him. He likes you. If he was gonna bounce, he'd have done it already. Just be your hot-ass self and trust the process.

I like the message just as another comes through. This one's from Michael.

> **MICHAEL**
>
> Did you get your flight booked for New Year's?

> Yeah. Sorry I forgot to send it to you. I'll send it now.

I pull up my flight info, snap a screen shot, and send it to Michael.

> **MICHAEL**
>
> Cool. Stella and I will most likely both be working, but Adam or Leo could probably come pick you up.

I shake my head.

> They don't need to do that. I can get an Uber. It's not even that far—probably be $25-$30. Not a big deal.

Adam is Michael's childhood best friend, and Leo is his best friend from college. He's also a silent partner in my brother's restaurant. Michael's a phenomenal chef.

MICHAEL

Ok. Well, we can talk about it when it gets closer. You still seeing that same guy?

A smile tugs at my lips. I love that he still takes an interest in me, even with his own family to focus on.

> Yeah. On my way to his place right now. He's taking me to his best friend's birthday party.

MICHAEL

Well, have fun… Be safe please… in every way. 😉

> Ew, don't talk to me about that. But yes, of course I'll be safe.

MICHAEL

So you can joke about birthday blow jobs, but I can't tell you to use a condom, even without saying the word? You're so weird.

> It's different. I know Stella. You're my boring, dad-mode older brother. I have to keep your life interesting. But you can't say that stuff to your little sister. It's just weird.

MICHAEL

You make no sense.

The car stops at the curb in front of Jensen's building.

> Oh, I'm here. Gotta go. Love you!

I drop my phone back into my purse and step out onto the curb, the winter chill hitting me immediately. Pulling my coat tighter, I follow the same instructions Jensen gave me yesterday to get up to his floor.

I take a deep breath, calming my nerves before I knock on his door. A moment later, it swings open, and I'm caught staring at the most handsome man I've ever seen. "Wow. You look great," I say. I don't know why I'm so surprised. Jensen's always attractive. But damn, this man can pull off a suit.

"You should talk. You look gorgeous." His hand slips into my coat, sliding around my waist, and he pulls me in for a kiss. And damn it, if it doesn't make my knees go weak.

When he pulls back, his eyes meet mine. "You ready to go?"

"Yeah, but can I leave my coat here?"

"Of course."

He helps me out of my coat, letting out a low whistle as he drapes it over a bar stool.

"Alley," he says, his gaze sweeping over me, lingering. "You look *hot.*"

My cheeks flush, and a smile spreads across my face. "Thank you."

"So, what'd you do today?" he asks, holding his elbow out for me to loop my arm through.

"Nothing exciting—laundry, cleaning, lunch with Scarlett. That's about it." I follow him to the elevator, where we ride down to the lobby before switching to the private one for the penthouse.

"Hey, Mikey," Jensen says to the elevator operator waiting by the doors.

"Hey, Jensen, my man." Mikey gives him a quick fist bump and scans a key card.

Honestly, I've never visited anyone in New York who has their own private elevator access. Butterflies churn low in my stomach, nerves spreading through me. What if Matt doesn't like me? The best friend's opinion matters. A lot.

The doors open, and we step inside just as a woman's voice echoes across the lobby.

"Jensen, hold the elevator!"

My eyes settle on a stunning brunette with long, sleek hair, a glamorous gold dress that's definitely designer, and a flawless face to match.

Her skin is radiant, and her body? Perfect. She's stunning—intimidatingly so.

Jensen presses the "door open" button as she hurries through the lobby, pausing to give Mikey a quick hug. "Hey, Mikey, how are you?"

Mikey's reply fades into the background as my thoughts spiral. She steps into the elevator, her smile widening, before throwing her arms around Jensen in a tight hug. Her perfume—a perfect blend of sweet and expensive—fills the small space, making it feel even smaller by the second.

"Jensen!" she exclaims, squeezing him tighter, like they're good friends.

"Hey, Jordan," he says, his tone calm but friendly.

"How the hell are you? It's been forever!" She pulls back, placing her hand on his chest and giving it a light pat. "God, you look good."

The doors close, and the elevator lurches upward, the tension palpable.

"Thanks, so do you," Jensen says genuinely—because, let's be honest, how could he not?

Her eyes flick to mine just as Jensen's hand slides to the small of my back. "This is Alley," he says. "Alley, this is Jordan."

Her smile doesn't falter. "Oh, my God, hi." She wraps her arms around me. "Sorry, I'm a hugger. It's so nice to meet you." She steps back, looking me up and down. "Alley, you are gorgeous!" Then, turning to Jensen, she says, "I'm so happy to see you with someone." Her attention shifts back to me. "I'm Matty's ex. I know, it's weird, but he's still one of my best friends."

Relief washes over me, though I hate that for a split second, I was nervous she might be Jensen's ex—or that they'd slept together at some point. It wouldn't matter, obviously. Except, *my God*, how could I possibly compete with someone like her? She looks like an exotic supermodel. And, annoyingly, she also seems genuinely nice, which would ruin the whole *I can see why he wouldn't be with her anymore* logic.

"So," she asks, tilting her head with a curious grin, "are you two together, dating, friends?"

Jensen looks to me. "We're dating. Haven't really talked about anything more, but... I'm not seeing anyone else."

My face warms as Jensen's gaze locks with mine, sending a rush of heat through my body. "I'm not seeing anyone else, either." My grin spreads as I say it, happiness filling me as the truth of our feelings settles in the small elevator.

Jordan laughs, light and genuine. "Okay. You two are so cute."

The doors slide open, and she steps into the penthouse first. "I'm gonna find Matty," she says, turning back to me briefly. "It was so good to meet you, Alley." With that, she beelines to the right, leaving me to scrape my jaw off the floor as my eyes take in the space.

"Oh my God," I say, spinning to take it all in. "This is where Matt lives?"

Jensen scoffs. "Yeah. And this is only the first floor."

The penthouse is spacious, with an open floor plan that's oozing with luxury. Glass lines every exterior wall from floor to ceiling, offering breathtaking views of the city. The design is modern with a distinctly masculine edge—flawless decor, sleek surfaces—a true bachelor's pad, and big enough to house a family of eight. The sliding glass doors to the terrace are open, heat lamps glowing in every corner, inside and out.

Jensen grabs my hand, guiding me through the throng of impeccably dressed guests to find Matt. We step onto the terrace, and my mind continues to reel at the level of extravagance. There's a hot tub, multiple fire pits, plush furniture, a fully stocked wet bar, and even a large plunge pool. Who lives like this?

We approach a small group: a strikingly good-looking guy, who I assume is Matt, along with Jordan and another couple.

"Jensen!" the guy calls out, his grin lighting up his face.

"Hey, brother!" Jensen replies as they embrace in a brief, back-patting hug.

As soon as they pull apart, Matt turns his attention to me, his smile warm. "You must be Alley," he says, stepping forward and pulling me into a hug. "I'm Matt. I've heard so much about you."

Feel-goods spread through me as Matt's words sink in, a smile tugging at my lips. I hug him back, pleasantly surprised that he's heard *so much* about me. As I step back, Matt waves over a cocktail waitress. Yes, there are actual cocktail waitresses.

A woman strides toward us, dressed in a sexy number—black bra, high-waisted cheeky bottoms, thigh-high socks, a garter belt, and heels. She's beautiful, and Matt doesn't hold back. His arm slides around her waist, flashing a flirtatious grin. "Hey, gorgeous, mind grabbing drinks for my friends here?"

It's... a lot—cringe-worthy, even. I'm not sure if it's jealousy, discomfort, or just the surrealness of being at a party this over the top, but something makes me shift on my heels. Maybe it's knowing Matt is acting exactly like the player Jensen said he is. Or maybe it's the way I feel so out of place—like a small-town girl who's accidentally wandered into the dazzling, chaotic world of Manhattan high society.

"What are you two drinking?" Matt asks, his eyes flicking between Jensen and me.

"I'll have a scotch, neat," Jensen says easily, glancing at me. "What about you?"

I'm not a big drinker. I only indulge socially, and even then, I have strict rules: a two-drink max and never hard liquor. I'd actually be fine to never drink at all, but I hate the peer pressure that comes with it. People get weird when you say you don't drink, and it doesn't get better with age. So, to avoid the awkwardness, I play along. The truth? I don't even like drinking. Deep down, I'm terrified of turning into my dad. It's a fear that keeps me in check, steering clear whenever I can.

"What beers do you have?" I ask, praying he has a dark beer.

Matt rattles off a list of craft beers, IPAs, and stouts—names I don't recognize but nod along to anyway.

"Any stout will be fine," I tell the waitress. "Surprise me."

"Ah, a dark beer girl. You don't come by that very often," Matt says.

Jensen had the same reaction when I ordered a Guinness on our first date. Stouts are the only alcoholic drink I actually enjoy.

As soon as the waitress turns away, Matt's arm wraps around Jordan, pulling her into him. She responds in kind, sliding her arm around his waist, the other drifting up to rest on his chest.

I try to act natural, like I'm not completely thrown off. What is this? Some kind of modern-day Playboy mansion, with Matt as a young, real-life Hugh Hefner? One thing's for sure—this is definitely shaping up to be a night I won't forget.

"So, Alley, are you from here?" Matt asks, his focus now on me.

"No, I grew up in Chicago."

"Chicago? What brought you to New York?"

I shrug lightly. "I just wanted a change, honestly. New York appealed to me, and I always dreamed of living here when I was a kid."

"Well, good for you. Following your dreams," he says with an easy grin. "I love Chicago. I've got a few friends and business connections out there."

His smile is so genuine, it catches me off guard. I'd pegged him as someone who wouldn't even bother with small talk, let alone ask personal questions. I figured he'd be one of those guys who only talk about themselves, maybe throw in a brag or two for good measure. Turns out, there's more to Matt than I expected.

"Matt has friends everywhere," Jensen chimes in.

"What business takes you to Chicago?" I ask.

"I've looked into investing there a few times. I almost partnered with a buddy of mine I met at a conference a few years back. He's a big name in Chicago, so if I ever do branch out of New York, it'll most likely be with him."

As soon as he says this, my gut tells me he's talking about Leo. I grin, unable to hold it back. "Is it Leo Weston?"

Matt's head jerks back in surprise, his shocked face almost making me laugh. "Shit! You know Leo?"

"Yeah, Leo's basically family to me. He's one of my brother's best friends from college."

Matt laughs, still looking floored. "No way! Who's your brother? I've met a few of Leo's friends."

"Michael Evans. He owns..."

Matt cuts me off, his hand going up like I've just dropped a bomb. "The chef? Get out of here! Michael's your brother? I've met him a few times. Leo's taken me to his restaurant. His food is exceptional. He's an excellent chef."

My smile grows as I glance at Jensen, who's watching us with mild amusement. This is bizarre. "That's crazy! What a small world."

Matt chuckles, taking a sip of his drink. "The world actually gets much smaller the older I get. It's wild how often this kind of thing happens."

Jensen exchanges a glance with Jordan, who's been quietly sipping her drink, then turns to me. "See, I told you... Matt knows everyone."

Matt shakes his head, grinning. "The Chef's little sister. I can't wait to text Leo about this."

I cock a brow. "Well, maybe I'll get to him first."

Matt laughs. "No chance! Come here. We're taking a picture and sending it to him right now." He hands his phone to Jordan. "Babe, can you take a pic?"

I shoot Jensen a look, making a face and shrugging, while Matt wraps an arm around me like we've been best friends for years. Jensen's grinning from ear to ear, and I smile as Jordan snaps the photo.

"I'm sending this to him immediately."

Before I can respond, the cocktail waitress arrives with our drinks, and Matt's attention shifts to someone across the terrace.

"Excuse me, guys. I've got to go say hi to someone."

He scurries off, leaving us with Jordan, whose attention is short-lived when a group of girls approach her.

I turn to Jensen, a smile plastered to my face. He wraps his arms around my waist, pulling me close. "I think Matt approves of you."

I laugh softly. "You think?" I meet his gaze, and my stomach does that stupid flutter thing it always seems to do when I'm close to him. "Your friends are great. I'm not going to lie, I was nervous to meet Matt. With what you've told me... I didn't expect him to be so... I don't know, nice."

He chuckles. "He plays the field a bit with women, but he's honest, loyal, and genuinely a good guy. He'd do anything for me. Hell, he'd probably do anything for you now, too."

I glance around at the people mingling inside and on the terrace. I laugh softly, feeling silly for ever being intimidated, and kicking myself for watching too much TV.

Jensen raises a brow. "What's so funny?"

"Oh, nothing. It's stupid, really."

"Come on, tell me."

His eyes lock on mine, and something about the way he looks at me makes me feel safe, like I can say anything without being judged. "It's a little embarrassing, but... I thought the people here were going to be pretentious assholes. You know, like a real-life *Gossip Girl* party. And while the party is very *Gossip Girl*, the people are not."

He bursts out laughing. "Shit. No, we're nothing like that. I can't say there weren't parts of high school that felt like it, though."

I grin, cocking a brow. "I'm surprised you've seen that show."

His brows shoot up. "Not by choice. My girlfriend in college was obsessed with it. I was forced to endure many episodes."

I laugh. "I actually pictured Matt being like an older Chuck Bass. But he's more like an older Nate Archib—"

I'm cut off by Jensen's lips, his tentative kiss silencing me. One hand cups my face, his thumb grazing my jaw as his tongue softly strokes mine. It's tender and sweet but hot as hell, and it sends butterflies shooting straight through my core.

I kiss him back, not caring, once again, that we're in the middle of a crowd. It's so not like me, but with Jensen, *God*, I feel confident—like I'm stepping into this bolder version of myself.

He breaks the kiss, grinning, his dimples cutting deep into his cheeks. "Sorry, I couldn't help myself. You're too fucking cute, Alley."

Taking my hand, he leads me to a sofa on the terrace, where we lose ourselves in conversation for the next two hours. Occasionally, we're interrupted by friends stopping by to chat or a cocktail waitress offering drinks.

I'm on my second beer, savoring it. The initial buzz has worn off, but it's fine. I don't need it anymore, the nerves of being new have completely faded. Everyone I've met tonight has been great, and I feel at ease.

We've settled under a blanket as the night has gotten colder. Between the fire pit at my feet, the heat lamp beside me, Jensen's warm body next to mine, and the blanket, the crisp air feels refreshing against my face.

The conversation quiets, and I take a moment to soak in the scene. The city lights stretch out from Matt's terrace, the fire glows softly, and Jensen's strong frame presses comfortably against mine. One arm is wrapped around me, and I sink into his chest. His other hand rests on my leg, his thumb brushing soft strokes along my bare thigh. A distracting pulse builds low in my core, stirring a craving that's hard to ignore.

I notice Jordan and Matt through the glass windows inside, locked in what looks like a heated conversation. Her brows are furrowed, and she looks upset. Matt leans closer, trying to console her, his hand sliding to her waist. Before I know it, they're lip-locked, kissing, his arms wrapped around her, hers hooked behind his neck.

I break the silence, nudging Jensen lightly. "What's going on over there?" I ask, nodding toward Matt and Jordan.

Jensen breathes out a chuckle. "Oh, they always do this. Anytime Jordan's around, Matt gets all possessive. They'll end up in bed together tonight. It happens every time. They're sort of friends with benefits, but honestly? I think they're in love with each other."

"Really?"

"Yeah. Matt would probably settle down if she gave him the green light, but he's too damn stubborn to admit that, even to himself. And Jordan plays it off like she's fine being the occasional hookup, but come on—she cares more than she lets on. I think they're both full of shit."

"Hmm. That's interesting." I try to wrap my head around a relationship like that, but it feels so complicated. "I don't think I could ever do that."

Jensen squeezes my thigh, his touch steady and reassuring. "No?"

"No. It would mess with my head too much," I say, grateful Jensen seems so different from Matt when it comes to dating and relationships. At least, I hope he is. It's strange how little I actually know him, yet I feel like I've known him forever.

His fingers inch upward, tracing small, deliberate circles that burn into my skin with every stroke. The warmth of his touch grazes the hem of my dress, and my heart skips a beat.

I'm positive I'm ready to sleep with him, but there's a nervousness

I can't shake. I haven't been with anyone since my ex and I broke up almost a year ago. The thought both excites and unsettles me.

My hand instinctively reaches for his—whether to stop him or encourage him, I'm not sure. A rush of anxiety floods my senses, tingling through me in waves, rising to my throat and tightening my breath.

"Alley," he says softly. My stomach flips as I turn to meet his gaze, his blue eyes intent, his breath warm against my cheek. "Do you wanna go back to my place?"

Chapter Six

JENSEN

THEN

My heart pounds against my chest as her dark brown eyes lock onto mine. She gives a faint nod, and whispers a quiet "Yeah." Relief floods through me, my pulse speeding up in anticipation.

I grin, sitting up and tossing the blanket aside. My eyes follow her as she stands, folds the blanket, then tugs at the hem of her dress. Her fingers brush against her thighs, making it impossible to look away.

I extend my hand, and she takes it, her lips curving into a sly smile that shoots straight to my cock.

We weave through the crowd, my dick straining against my pants. I can't get out of here fast enough. All I can think about is getting her alone in my apartment and tearing off her clothes, touching every inch of her.

Jesus. That thought's only making me harder.

"Don't you want to say goodbye to anyone?" she calls.

I press the elevator button and glance back at her, grinning. "Nope."

Her brows lift, but she's smiling too. "Won't Matt care?"

I shake my head, my grin widening as the elevator dings. "Trust me, he won't even notice."

The doors slide open, and I guide her in with my hand on the small of her back.

As soon as they close, I cup her face and crash my lips against hers. Goddamn, the past few hours with Alley have been both incredible and torturous. That short fucking dress? It's been driving me insane. Under the blanket, I was this close to losing all control, ready to finger her like some horny teenager.

When we reach the lobby, I force myself to pull back, letting her go just long enough to switch elevators. As soon as the doors close on the main one, she's on me—her kiss urgent, demanding, and hot as fucking hell. Her body presses into mine, and we nearly miss the doors opening on my floor, too caught up in each other. I shove my arm through to keep them from closing, and her laugh echoes behind me.

We hurry down the hall, hand in hand, and I punch in the keypad code to unlock my door. It swings open, and I all but drag her inside.

The door slams shut behind us, and we don't miss a beat. I'm not sure who kisses who first, but our mouths collide, a tangle of lust and need. I don't bother turning on the lights; the faint glow from under the cabinets is enough.

Right now, all I care about is her.

We walk together, her moving backward, until we hit the wall. My hand slides up to her breast, giving it a gentle squeeze, and she gasps softly.

"God," I murmur, leaning in closer, my breath mixing with hers.

She tugs at my suit jacket, shucking it from my shoulders and down my arms until it falls to the floor. Her fingers fumble with the buttons of my shirt, undoing the top two, then three. My other hand is gripping her ass, making its way down to the hem of her dress so it can lift it up, desperate to touch her skin.

She stops suddenly, pulling back, her breath heavy and uneven. "Jensen," she says softly, a nervous edge in her voice. "Maybe we should slow down." She swallows hard. "Should we slow down?"

Her eyes search mine with uncertainty and vulnerability. My thumb brushes across her bottom lip, my brow lifting slightly. "Do you want to slow down?" I ask, keeping my tone soft and steady.

She shakes her head swiftly, the corners of her mouth lifting into a timid smile. "No," she whispers, but then she hesitates again, her gaze dropping to my chest.

"It's just that... I haven't been with a lot of people," she admits, her voice so quiet I almost miss it. Her fingers tighten on the front of my shirt as if bracing herself for my reaction.

I give her a reassuring smile. "It's okay. We can slow down. We don't have to do this tonight." But *God,* I want to.

"No. I want to. It's just..." Her hands caress my chest. "It's been a while... for me. I'm nervous, I guess. Aren't you nervous?"

I suppress a laugh because I want her to know she can tell me anything without feeling stupid, but damn, if she isn't the cutest. "No. I'm not nervous." I tuck a piece of hair behind her ear. "I'm excited."

She nods, like she's trying to convince herself it's the same. "Yeah, me too. I'm sorry. I'm overthinking this—I'm in my head." She laughs. "God, I'm so awkward. Let's keep going."

I grin, cupping her face gently. "Yeah? You sure?"

"Yeah. I'm good. Promise."

I kiss her again, slower this time. My hands trail up her arms, pushing the thin straps down her shoulders. My mouth follows, kissing the curve of her shoulder, tracing across her collarbone.

Her fingers work more of the buttons on my shirt, and then I feel the cool air hit my skin, followed by her warm hands on my chest.

I groan, desire crackling through me like electricity hitting water. My hands wrap around her, finding the zipper in the back of her dress. I drag it down, pausing to meet her gaze. As I pull the straps down her arms, her eyes stay locked on mine, and I don't dare look away. The way she's looking at me—like she's trusting me with this moment—has my heart in a goddamn vice. The dress gathers at her hips, and she pushes it the rest of the way, stepping out of it and kicking it to the side.

My gaze drops, drinking her in—her black panties and strapless bra, the way her skin seems to glow in the low light. She tugs at my shirt, and I shrug it off, letting it fall to the floor. It's like time has stopped. We're not kissing, not speaking—just standing here, undressing each other—getting to know each other on every level. And fuck, all I can think about is how good she's gonna feel wrapped around me.

Her hands glide down my torso, finding my waistband. She undoes the button and slides the zipper down. I reach around, unhooking her bra with ease, and it falls away as she drags my pants down. I push them the rest of the way, stepping out of them slowly, letting my eyes trail up her body, taking in every inch of her bare skin.

When I stand fully, I pull her close, her warm body pressing against mine. *God, she feels so good.* The intensity builds, and our kisses turn wild, desperate—almost savage—like she just needed to get past the awkwardness of getting naked, and now she's all confidence, leading the way.

Her hand lingers, teasing the waistband of my underwear. It's torturous. I'm silently begging her to touch me. Finally, her fingers slide lower, brushing over my cock through the thin fabric. My stomach fucking dips. Then she drifts lower, cupping my balls lightly, kneading them softly. My brain short-circuits, every thought drowned out by sensation.

"Fuck, that feels so good."

She grins against my mouth, and I can't stop myself from kissing a path down her jaw, her neck, and lower. My tongue flicks over her nipple, and her hands thread through my hair, pulling me closer. I suck the pink bud into my mouth, and she moans, her hips arching toward me.

"Oh my God," she whispers, her voice a mix of need and surrender.

It's too much—I need her on my bed, splayed out and naked. I kiss her firmly on the mouth before pulling back, our breaths ragged. "Come on, let's go to my room." I grab her hand and lead her toward the bedroom, my heart pounding with pure fucking want.

When we reach my room, I don't bother with any lights. I back her onto the bed, and her legs hook around me, pulling me down with her. I'm lost in her, the sounds she makes, the way her body feels beneath me.

My phone rings loudly from the kitchen.

"Your phone's ringing," she says in between kisses.

"I know."

She laughs softly. "You don't need to get it this time, do you?"

"No. Fuck no." The song cuts off abruptly, and I don't waste another second thinking about it. My fingers hook around her panties, peeling them down slowly, my touch skimming her smooth skin, my focus fully back on her.

My phone rings again, and I'm cursing myself for the volume level I have it set on.

"Okay, but seriously, it's like your phone *knows* when you're about to get laid," she says through laughter.

"Fucking cockblocker," I whisper against her lips, smiling. "Just." Kiss. "Ignore." Kiss. "It." My hand slides between her thighs. "Holy shit. You're soaked." Her slickness coats my fingers, and it's fucking *heaven*. I trace slow, even circles over her clit, savoring every gasp that falls from those beautiful lips.

"Oh my God," she says, her voice breathy. "I'm going to come so fast." Her hands fly to her face in embarrassment.

"That's good, baby," I murmur, my lips brushing her ear. "Come for me. Whenever you're ready." I plunge a finger into her, groaning softly. "Jesus, Alley. You're so tight."

"That feels so good," she whispers, her body arching beneath me.

I keep my rhythm consistent, sucking her bottom lip in-between my teeth. Pushing a second finger in, I go deeper, harder—curling to hit just right.

Her body writhes beneath me, her head tilting back as a moan spills from her lips. It's hot. It's sexy. Fuck, it's euphoric watching her unravel like this.

I don't think I've gotten a girl off this quickly since college. She said it's been a while, but *Jesus*, it's intoxicating. As her body begins to relax, her hands shoot out, grasping at my boxer briefs, tugging and pulling at them. I help her, shoving them down and tossing them across the room. Settling between her thighs, my gaze sweeps over her —naked, beautiful, and I prepare to take my time. Kiss every inch of her. Make this last all night—or as long as I can, anyway.

Her eyes slowly roam over me, and I soak it in. The city lights pour through the windows, casting just enough light to highlight every curve of her body. A smile tugs at my lips. "Alley... you're..." I let out a breath of appreciation. "God, you're sexy."

She smiles softly, biting her bottom lip. "Thank you," she whispers. "So are you."

I lean down, hovering over her, and draw her lips into a kiss.

Her hand travels down, lower and lower, until it wraps around my cock. Gripping me firmly, she gives it a long, purposeful stroke.

My eyes squeeze shut. "Shit," I hiss. The sensation is almost too good.

She keeps going, her movements firmer now, controlled, deliberate. When she takes the tip and swirls it against her wet clit, my abs clench, and a primal need takes over—a hunger to claim all of her, feel her, taste every fucking inch of her.

I kiss down her neck and chest, my lips mapping a path down her body. Anticipation floods through me with every inch closer, my mind already spiraling with the thought of what's waiting for me. Her moans quiet as I approach her pussy, her body stiffening slightly beneath me.

"Jensen..." she says softly.

"Yeah?" I ask, looking up at her as my hands smooth along her thighs.

Her fingers flex in my hair, and she exhales sharply. "You don't have to do that... I mean... it's fine if you don't want to."

I blink. *If I don't want to?*

I prop myself up on my elbows, tilting my head. "Alley..." I say her name slowly, like I'm making sure I heard her right. "You do realize I'm doing this because I *want* to, right?"

Her lips press together, her gaze shifting away. "I just... had a boyfriend who made it feel like a chore. Like something he had to do to get what he wanted after." She lets out a dry laugh. "One time, he literally told me I owed him."

My stomach drops. "Jesus," I mutter. "That's fucked up."

"I just... don't want you to feel like you have to."

I lift myself up further, pressing a kiss to her stomach. "I want to. Really fucking badly." My voice is rougher now, edged with desire. "And for the record, you don't owe me anything. That's not how this works." I kiss my way back down, my voice dropping lower. "So just lay back, baby... and let me enjoy you."

Her laugh is breathy, but it turns into a soft moan as I press a kiss to her inner thigh.

That's all the permission I need.

She comes undone in exactly three point four seconds. Okay, not *that* fast, but damn near close. It's almost instant, like her body's been waiting for this, *needing* this. Her hips jerk toward my mouth, fingers gripping the sheets, soft moans falling from her lips.

Fuck. I'm so turned on I can barely think.

She's so quiet, almost like she's embarrassed by how easily she loses control.

And damn, if that doesn't make me fall even harder.

She's been nervous this whole night, since Matt's party. Reserved, sweet—almost innocent. The two-drink max, the way she hesitated before letting things go further. And now this? She overthinks, worries about everything. But right now, she's trusting me, letting go, letting herself feel this fully. And it's everything.

Her hips move with me now as she relaxes into it, rolling toward my mouth, chasing the next orgasm.

I want to feel her squeezing my cock the next time she comes. I press one last kiss to her hip before sliding up her body, grinning against her skin. Would I love a blow job? Sure, who wouldn't? But the last thing I want right now is for her to feel like she has to reciprocate.

Actually, I don't want her to. I want her to know she can just take. That she doesn't owe me a damn thing.

Things heat up fast, our urgency spilling into every movement. The room fills with the sounds of raw, carnal desire—breathless gasps, low moans, the quiet movement of skin against skin.

I settle between her thighs, my lips trailing over her skin, "You on the pill?"

She nods quickly. "Yeah. And I haven't been with anyone in over a year. I'm good. You?"

"Clean," I say as I nudge her thighs wider. "Tested before my surgery. Haven't been with anyone since."

Her eyes search mine for a second before she tugs me closer, wrapping her legs around my waist. "Okay, then."

Sweat slicks our bodies, and when I finally slide into her—*dear God,* it's everything. She's warm, wet, and so fucking tight, gripping me in a perfect storm of unrelenting pleasure. A low groan rumbles in my chest as I sink deeper, savoring the way she gasps beneath me, her body stretching to take me in.

I start slow, letting her adjust, letting myself feel every inch of her. But when she tilts her hips, urging me on, a switch flips. My thrusts deepen, slow and measured at first, but soon turning desperate, driven by the way she moves with me. Her body meets mine in perfect rhythm, her hands clutch at my back, nails dragging, breathy moans filling the air.

The sounds she makes? They're enough to make a believer out of me. I don't even know if I believe in God, but right now? I'll preach whatever sermon you give me, because she feels like pure heaven.

"God, Jensen," she gasps, her voice wrecked, her body trembling beneath me.

"I've got you, baby," I murmur, my lips brushing her jaw, my hands gripping her hips as I pull her closer, needing more, needing all of her.

Her legs tighten around me, pulling me deeper. The pressure coils inside me, winding so tight I feel like I might break apart. And then— she shatters, her body arches, and her cries muffle against my neck as she clenches around me, dragging me right over the edge with her.

My body tenses, pleasure crashing through me in waves as I drive into her one last time, an eruption of pure fucking bliss as I spill into her.

I shudder as I pull out, collapsing onto the bed beside her. Reaching into my nightstand, I grab a few wipes, handing them to her before cleaning myself up. When she's done, I pull her close, her head resting on my chest.

I press a soft kiss to her hair as a grin spreads across my face. That wasn't perfect—far from it, with the interruptions, the laughter, and the nervousness—but I wouldn't change a thing. Because it was Alley.

It was us. And that might just be the most memorable sex I've ever had.

Chapter Seven

ALLEY

PRESENT DAY

I WAITED forty minutes for him. Twenty minutes too long. Twenty minutes past embarrassment settling in. Twenty minutes more than anyone deserves. Forty full minutes of hope crumbling. Forty minutes of fear sinking into my chest, of anxiety tearing through the walls I've carefully built around my heart—opening old wounds that never fully healed.

Tears sting the backs of my eyes, but I refuse to let them fall. Not here. Not now.

I walk out of the restaurant into the pouring rain, not caring that I'm getting soaked. At the curb, I raise an arm, hailing a cab. Moments later, I slide into the backseat, giving the driver my address. *Our* address.

Goddammit. Where is he?

The knot forms in my stomach, anxiety swelling, rising through my chest, closing off my throat.

I'm going to be sick.

I pull out my phone, swiping up to my text thread with Christy. My fingers hover over the screen as I reread the last text she sent over a month ago.

CHRISTY

> I don't want to argue anymore, Alley. He's my son.
> You don't know how hard this is for me, and you
> won't understand until you have kids of your own.

My chest constricts, and my hands tremble. I take a deep, steadying breath. Christy is the *last* person I want to text right now.

I blink rapidly, resisting the urge to cry. *Dammit. This hurts. And it sucks.* How did things get so messy between us? I remember the first time I met her. It was instant love.

I text Megan instead.

> Hey… Have you seen or heard from Jensen today?
> He was supposed to meet me for dinner forty-five
> minutes ago. It's our anniversary… I'm starting to
> worry.

MEGAN

> No… I haven't talked to him for a few days. You
> okay? Need me to come over?

> No, it's fine. Just lmk if you hear from him.

I drop my phone in my lap as the screen lights up again—another message from Megan. With effort, I force my gaze out the window, watching the rain pelting against the glass as we pass Madison Square Garden.

I don't have the energy to respond right now. I bite my bottom lip hard, fighting back tears. Resting my elbow against the door, I let my head fall against my hand as I lose the battle against myself. Tears slip silently down my cheeks, and I sob quietly in the backseat of the cab.

Chapter Eight

ALLEY

THEN—A LITTLE LESS THAN FIVE YEARS AGO

WE'RE all gathered in Jensen's parents' spacious living room, the fireplace blazing warmly behind us, the Christmas tree twinkling in the corner. And currently in the middle of complete mayhem.

"Harry Potter!"

"Santa Claus!"

"Dobby the elf!"

"Oh my God, Dad!" Megan yells, chucking a pillow at him. "Not everything is Harry Potter!"

"Voldemort!" Jensen's dad shouts triumphantly, completely ignoring her.

"Is he even trying?" someone mutters under their breath.

I can't hold back my laughter at the ridiculous chaos. It's beautiful.

Amber throws her hands in the air, shaking her head in frustration. "You're all hopeless!" she shouts, exasperated.

"Bellatrix!" Jensen's dad guesses—still stuck on Harry Potter.

"Dad! Shut up!" Megan throws another pillow at him.

To be fair, Amber is continuously making an exaggerated flicking motion with her wrist, it looks like she's casting a spell.

Lightbulb. "The Fairy Godmother!" I shout.

Amber throws her arms up in victory. "Finally! Thank God, Alley's here to save all of you degenerates!"

Charades is the game—and proceed with caution, because Jensen's family? They're competitive.

It's Christmas Eve, my first time meeting Jensen's family, and I'm having an absolute blast. His mom and dad are most definitely drunk, Megan has a ruthless competitive streak, and Jensen... well, let's just say charades is not his calling in life. He sucks at this game.

My team consists of me, Jensen (yes, unfortunately), his sister Megan, his dad Tom, and his sister-in-law Amber. We're up against his mom Christy, Matt—who apparently spends every Christmas Eve with Jensen's family—his brother Jeff, and brother-in-law Kevin.

We're getting our asses handed to us, and we even have an extra person. Jeff, Matt, and Christy are surprisingly good at this game. Like, weirdly good.

Jensen's hand grips my thigh. "Nice job, babe," he says, leaning in to kiss me. Something so simple, yet it spreads a warmth and tingly sensation through my entire body.

We've been seeing each other for three months now. We had the official *"let's be exclusive"* talk a few weeks ago, and while it's moving fast, it doesn't feel rushed. We spend so much time together—talking all day, every day via text, and after work, it's either my place or his. When we're apart, we're on the phone. I'm falling for him—fast and hard.

I haven't been this fully happy in so long. Jensen fills my cup in every way, in ways I didn't even realize I needed.

His family only solidifies what I feel for him. They're kind, hilarious, and have a love for each other that I didn't know existed in families. They're so close, and they genuinely enjoy spending time together. I never had this growing up. Michael is amazing, but this? This feels like a gift.

Jensen's the baby of the family, his sister Megan is two years older, and his brother Jeff is four years older. Each of them has two kids, and the oldest, Grace, who's twelve, is being paid to watch the three littler ones so the adults can drink and play games in peace.

Matt's up, and Megan groans. "Isn't it Kevin's turn?"

"Hey! I resent that, babe," Kevin says, gesturing to his crotch. "See this? It's off-limits tonight. Don't even try to get some because this shop? It's closed."

Megan rolls her eyes, laughing. "Oh no, whatever shall I do?"

"Shut up, both of you, and pay attention!" Matt yells. "Also, Kev, don't ever gesture to your dick again. That was weird." He flips the timer over and immediately begins. He mimes stepping into pants, pulling them up over his waist, then drawing back a bowstring.

"Robin Hood!" Christy shouts.

"Dammit!" Megan cries. "That was way too easy. You guys always get the easy ones."

"It's called skill, Megan," Matt says with a smirk. "I'm telling you, Hollywood is missing out. I should've gone into acting."

He bows dramatically and takes a seat.

Crap. It's my turn, and while I'm thoroughly enjoying myself, I'm not exactly thrilled about making a fool of myself in front of Jensen's entire family.

I draw my paper, and relief washes over me. *Rose, from Titanic.* Easy peasy. I flip the timer, spread my arms out wide, and tilt my face to the ceiling.

"Jack! Rose! Titanic!" Megan shouts triumphantly. "Yes!" She pumps her fist in the air. "Suck it, bitches!" Laughing, she jabs her hands toward her crotch in a mock *suck it* gesture.

Jeff and Matt simultaneously flip her off, grinning.

This goes on for another hour, until everyone has had three turns. We lose, but my hell, I feel like a winner just sitting here with Jensen and his family.

His mom disappears for a moment and reappears in the living room, holding a handful of prizes.

"What's this for?" I ask Jensen, raising an eyebrow.

"Oh, we now have the charades awards ceremony. MVP, best guesser, and the cutest—which is basically the person who sucks the most but looks cute doing it."

I burst out laughing. "You're joking."

Jensen grins, his dimples on full display. "Never. This is serious shit, Al. I'd never joke about something like this."

"Oh my God. Be honest, how many times have you won?"

He leans in, chuckling. "Oh, I win every year, babe. There's a reason I suck at this game." He winks, and dammit, I fall a little harder for him.

"Okay, ladies and gentlemen, listen up," Christy announces, taking a generous sip of her wine. *Good Lord, this has to be her fourth glass. How is she still standing?* She holds up a small basket, neatly wrapped in cellophane. "Cutest player goes to... drum roll, please!"

Everyone literally drum rolls, and for a moment, I swear I'm not in a room full of adults but at a middle school assembly.

"Jensen!"

A chorus of boos erupts from everyone, laughter following close behind. Megan chucks a pillow at him and shouts, "I refuse to be on your team next year!"

"You suck!" someone else calls out, and everyone doubles over laughing.

This is, hands down, the best thing. Ever.

Jensen plops back down beside me, holding his gift basket like a trophy and grinning like a fool.

Christy raises her voice over the commotion. "Alright, alright! Best guesser goes to..." She pauses for dramatic effect. "Drum roll!"

Again, everyone drum rolls.

"Alley!"

I blink in surprise, then grin, but before I can even process the moment, Megan calls out, "Well, no shit. We have Jensen on our team, and she sees his dick!"

Megan is, without a doubt, both the best and the worst.

I stand to accept my prize, whistles and catcalls filling the room. Between all the attention and Megan's comment, I'm certain my cheeks are blazing red. I give an exaggerated curtsy, earning a fresh round of laughter, and quickly sit back down.

"And last but not least, our most valuable player," Christy announces.

Jensen leans in, his breath warm against my ear. "It'll be Matt. Mom has a soft spot for him."

"It was a close one this year," Christy continues, drawing out the suspense, "between Jeff and Matt... But the winner is... drumroll, please!"

Like clockwork, nine adults drumroll, and Christy beams. "Matt!"

Matt makes absolutely no effort to be humble. He leaps up, flexing his biceps like he's on a bodybuilding stage, then kisses each one for good measure. He bows dramatically, over and over, before mock-holding an invisible microphone.

"First and foremost, I'd like to thank God," he begins, pointing upward, his grin so smug and charming it could make any woman weak in the knees.

It's over the top, ridiculous, and the verdict is in—I absolutely love Jensen's family.

* * *

"So, Alley, has Jensen told you what a spoiled little shit he used to be?" Megan asks, her eyes darting toward Jensen with a mischievous grin.

"Oh, God. Here we go," Jensen groans, shaking his head.

"What? You were!" Megan says, doubling down without hesitation.

"You really were, buddy," Jeff chimes in, earning nods and murmurs of agreement from the rest of the table.

My eyes flick from Jensen to Megan, a laugh already bubbling up. "Whaaat? You were?" I tease. "No, he has definitely managed to keep this little tidbit from me." I nudge him playfully. "What did you do to earn this kind of reputation?"

It's almost midnight, and all the siblings and in-laws are gathered around the kitchen table. Jensen's parents went to bed about an hour ago, along with the kids. I learned earlier that it's tradition for everyone to sleep over on Christmas Eve. Santa comes to Grandma and Grandpa's house for the kids, which means waking up together as one big family. It's a concept I'm still wrapping my head around, but one I absolutely adore. The idea of choosing each other—of sacrificing individual Christmas mornings for this—blows me away.

Jensen's parents live in Scarsdale in a spacious six-bedroom home.

They weren't weird about Jensen and me coming, or even about us staying in the same room. In fact, they've been nothing but welcoming and accommodating. Before heading to bed, Jensen's mom pulled me aside and told me how much they liked me, adding that Jensen hadn't brought anyone home in years. Her words meant the world to me, but they also hit me in a way I wasn't prepared for.

I missed my mom so much in that moment, I almost cried. God, I hadn't realized how much I needed this—a family's love. I ran from home the second my mom passed away, leaving behind the only family I had left. And I haven't looked back. But this? This makes me wish I lived closer to Michael.

Thankfully, I'll get to see him in just a few days.

"You guys are assholes," Jensen says with a grin, pulling me back to the present.

"Hmm," Megan muses, looking around the table. "Where should we start, guys?"

"How about the time Mom caught him with a stash of weed, and he blamed it on me?" Jeff says with a smirk.

My brows shoot up.

"Yeah, or the time he said the box of condoms were mine and Will's." Megan turns to me, rolling her eyes. "Will was my high-school boyfriend junior year, and this little shit"—she points at Jensen—"was hooking up with Summer Barker and wrote on the box with a Sharpie, *'Megan's—touch these and you die.'* Like I'd ever be dumb enough to write my name on a box of condoms. But sure enough, Mom believed everything her *'baby boy'* said."

Jeff snickers. "Classic Jensen. Mom's golden boy. He could do no wrong."

"But he literally did everything wrong. And to Mom? Whatever he said was truth. Gospel even," Megan says, exasperated.

Jensen shakes his head. "Stop. You two exaggerate so bad."

"Did I or did I not get in trouble for having a box of condoms?" Megan asks.

Jensen grins sheepishly. "Yeah, but come on, it's not like you weren't having sex. Not only were you sleeping with Will, but you were totally messing around with Nathan Humphreys at the same time."

Megan opens her mouth to protest, but Jensen cuts her off, pointing a finger at her. "Don't even try to deny it. I saw you two at a party."

Megan's hands fly up in mock innocence. "Fine. Maybe I was. But I wasn't an idiot. I hid my condoms on my bookshelf behind the Bible."

We all burst out laughing.

"Don't forget the time he rammed Tom's car into the curb driving home from a party drunk," Matt says, lifting his glass. "That one actually wasn't funny," he adds, his tone serious.

"Oh my God, how did I forget about that?" Megan laughs. "Dad was so mad he wanted to call the cops to teach Jensen a lesson, but Mom shut that down real quick."

"Wow." I gape at Jensen, shaking my head in disbelief. "I had no idea you were such a bad boy!" The thought is almost comical. I've only ever seen him as put-together and practically perfect. This doesn't match the image I've built of him at all.

Jensen shrugs. "I had a wild streak for a minute."

Megan scoffs. "Ha! That's the understatement of the year. A rebellious stoner is more like it—drugs, alcohol, girls... you name it. He was always one bad decision away from ending up in juvie. Slept his way through half the girls at our school, probably some of the staff too." She looks at Matt. "Wait, but Matt was way sluttier than you. Still is. Just a thirty-year-old fuckboy now, aren't you, Mattie boy?"

Matt and Jensen both laugh it off.

"You were all assholes," Jeff says, shaking his head. "I was the only one who didn't party, cheat," he says pointedly at Megan, "take drugs, or sleep around."

Megan rolls her eyes. "Yeah, you just came out of the womb as a boring adult." She turns to me. "Jeff and Amber met in middle school and have been together since."

"Aw, that's sweet," I say genuinely.

"Thank you, Alley," Amber replies, her tone sharp but playful as she narrows her eyes at Megan. "And we think you're sweet. Seriously, we all really like you."

"Yeah, don't fuck this up, Jensen. Really, Alley, you're way too good for him," Megan adds with a grin.

"Stop trying to scare her off," Jensen says, tossing a carrot stick at Megan.

I smile, warmth spreading through me. "Thank you. That means a lot. This has been so much fun. Honestly, I'm jealous you all have each other. It's incredible."

Jensen wraps an arm around my shoulders, pulling me close. "Don't listen to anything they say about me. I'm crazy about you."

Oohs and ahs echo around the table as Jensen leans in, his lips meeting mine in a sweet but heated kiss. My heart races, and I know, without question, that I'm one hundred and ten percent smitten.

Absolutely falling.

In.

Love.

With.

This.

Man.

Chapter Nine

ALLEY

THEN

I WHEEL my suitcase through the swarm of people at Chicago O'Hare. It's December thirtieth, and the airport is packed. I make my way toward passenger pickup, relieved I don't have to deal with finding a ride. Michael insisted someone come get me. He texted this morning to say Leo would be here.

Leo's great company. He's easy to talk to and fun to be around. I've always gotten along with him.

Michael's five years older than me and moved out when I was still in middle school. Even then, he always made an effort to stay close—coming home on weekends, sometimes with friends in tow. He was so good about keeping our relationship strong, even when he could've easily ignored his bratty little sister.

He'd take me to breakfast or lunch, invite me to games in his dorm, or bring Leo and Adam over for dinner. Nothing big, but it meant the world to me—especially after Mom was diagnosed with cancer and Dad started slipping in his recovery.

Michael stepped up, hardcore. I was too young to fully appreciate it then, but now I know how lucky I am to have him. Michael is the best brother anyone could ask for.

I dig through my purse for my phone to tell Leo which passenger pickup I'll be at. When I pull it out, he's already texted me.

LEO

Hey Al, I'm here. Black BMW. Let me know where you'll be.

I quickly text him back, pausing by the door to pull on my coat. I take a deep breath before heading outside, bracing myself for the Chicago cold.

The air smacks me in the face, stealing my breath. You think you know cold—then you come to the Midwest and realize you don't. *Please hurry,* I silently beg. My fingers already feel like they're going to fall off, and I've only been outside for fifteen seconds.

Leo's car pulls up just as I reach the curb. He pops the trunk and hops out, rushing to grab my bag.

"Go get warm, love. I've got this," Leo says, effortlessly picking it up and tossing it in.

"Thanks, Leo." I'm already sliding into the front seat before he even shuts the trunk. My hands fly to the heat vents, the hot air blasting my tingling, frozen skin.

Leo slides in and adjusts the vents toward me. "Is it warm enough? I turned the seat heater on for you." His charming British accent carries a familiarity I didn't realize I'd missed. It's comforting, nostalgic. And it's been a while since I've felt that.

"It's perfect, thanks. You'd think I would remember how cold it is, but I always seem to forget."

Leo chuckles. "I don't blame you for trying to forget." He flashes me a grin. "How the hell are you? It's been a long time."

"It *has* been a long time. I was bummed I couldn't make it for Michael's birthday. I'm good, though." I pause, letting that truth sweep through me. "Really good, actually."

"Yeah? Michael told me you're seeing someone. Wait—it's Matt's friend, right?" Leo glances over. "Tell me he's a good one. Because you know I'll go big brother and kick his ass if he isn't."

"Yeah. It's Matt's friend." I laugh softly. "I'll be sure to let him know. But yeah, he's a good one. The best, really."

"And?" Leo lifts a brow. "Are you going to tell me about him or just leave me to guess?"

"You sure you wanna know?" I ask, already smiling. "Once I get started, there's no stopping me. You'll have to shut me up. I get all giddy when I talk about him."

He chuckles, the soft wrinkles around his eyes starting to set in. "Go on, then."

"Well... he's funny. He always knows how to make me laugh. And he's nice—like overly thoughtful. He works in software sales. His company does SaaS—software as a service, or something like that. I don't totally understand it, but he's a sales manager, and he's really good at what he does. He grew up on the Upper East Side. Rich kid, private schools, the whole shebang. But you know all about that life." My smile grows as I keep talking. "I don't know, he's just... really great. Treats me well. Puts me first. And I love his family. Honestly, it's almost been too good to be true."

Leo's grinning when I turn to look at him, his dimples deeply set—just like Jensen's. "He sounds great." His eyes flick to mine. "I'm really happy for you. Not that I was ever worried. You've always had a good head on your shoulders."

"Thank you," I say, soaking in his words. I appreciate that more than he knows. "How's your love life going? Find anyone to settle down with yet?" I ask with a teasing grin.

A chuckle rumbles deep in his chest as he shakes his head. "You had to go there, didn't you?"

I've always given Leo shit about his dating life—or lack thereof.

"Same old, same old," he mutters, amusement in his eyes.

I laugh, pulling out my phone as we settle into a comfortable silence. All this talk about Jensen has me itching to text him, but he's already beat me to it.

JENSEN

Hey, babe. Did you get there safely?

Hi! I'm here. On my way to Michael's. What are you up to?

He responds immediately.

JENSEN

Glad you're safe and sound. I'm just headed home from work. Gonna pick up some sushi and call it an early night since tomorrow will be a late one.

Sounds like you've got a relaxing night ahead. You planning to relive one of those wild high school stories tomorrow night? Ha.

JENSEN

The only wild stories I want to recreate are with you… and you're not here. So I'll do the best I can with my imagination and my hand. Maybe we can FaceTime tonight?

A pulsing builds between my thighs, butterflies swirling in full force. I've never done anything sexual via the phone… I don't know if I'd actually be brave enough, but the thought of it totally turns me on. And if there was anyone I'd be comfortable enough to do that with— it's Jensen. He has this way of making me feel more confident than I really am.

I'm grinning as I text back.

I'm here for all of that… and more! Call me later?

JENSEN

You bet your ass I will.

I try to wipe the ridiculous grin off my face before tucking my phone away. I wish he could be here. He was invited, obviously, but New Year's falls on a Tuesday, and he just couldn't swing the time off. We were both bummed; it's our first New Year's as a couple. That's kind of a big deal. You always remember your first New Year's kiss. I would've stayed, but I'd already booked my flight and made plans with Michael.

"So, what time is everyone planning to go to the party tomorrow night?" I ask as we turn onto Michael's street.

"I usually try to get there around nine. Most people roll in between nine and nine-thirty."

He pulls into the driveway, and I unclick my seatbelt. "Well, I guess I'll see you tomorrow then. Thanks for the ride, Leo." My hand grips the door handle.

"Just run inside, love. I'll bring your bag."

"Fine, be a gentleman," I reply with a smile. "I won't argue that." I push the door open, run to the garage, and enter the code. As soon as it's high enough to slip under, I bolt for the door and slip inside.

* * *

THE NEW YEAR'S Eve party is in full swing. The theme this year? The Great Gatsby. Once again, my trusty little black dress came in handy, and Stella worked her magic on my hair—finger waves, a flapper headband, the whole nine yards. She's a magician with hair, and honestly, the only reason I look even half as put-together as this glamorous rooftop bar.

The decorations are straight out of a movie: a bold balloon installation cascading from the ceiling, feather centerpieces, a sparkling dance floor. Live jazz music fills the room, and cocktail waitresses in fringe dresses carry trays of champagne.

My eyes briefly catch Leo across the room, chatting up a gorgeous brunette. He's charming her, no doubt, with the same effortless ease Matt uses on women. In fact, they're so similar I can't believe I ever prejudged Matt. A small grin tugs at my lips as my thoughts shift to Jensen. He's so different from them. He wants to settle down. He wants a family. The same things I hope for.

I take a slow sip of my beer—the one I plan to nurse all night—and walk across the room to the windows that overlook the river. I never tire of this view.

A moment later, Adam and Michael make their way over.

"What are you doing over here all by yourself?" Michael asks.

"Stella went to talk to a friend, so I figured I'd take in the city while I waited. I forget how beautiful it is at night."

Adam chuckles. "Even better when you actually know what you're looking at."

I turn to him, brows furrowing. "What's that supposed to mean?"

His eyes flicker with amusement as he nudges Michael. "Do you remember when we took her on the architecture riverboat tour?"

My stomach drops. "Shut up. I already know what you're going to say." I turn fully toward Adam just as Michael bursts into laughter.

"Art Deco?" he laughs, harder now, Adam joining in.

Michael and Adam took me on an architecture riverboat tour when I was seventeen. They talked a lot about the design, structure, and history of the buildings. *Art Deco* kept coming up, and finally, I turned to them and asked, *"Who's Art Deco, and why do they keep talking about him?"*

They both lost it—laughed for hours—and never let me forget it.

"Hey," I say in teasing defense. "At least I learned something that day. And at least it was you two, not years later on a date or something. It could've been so much worse."

We all laugh together, an old familiarity settling in. I really love New York, but sometimes I miss these kinds of moments. The ones with the people I grew up with, who helped shape me—who remind me of who I used to be, and how far I've come.

Michael glances at his phone. "Excuse me, guys. I'll be right back." He shuffles off, leaving Adam and me alone.

Adam's gaze lingers on mine, his smile reaching his eyes. "It's good to see you, Alley Cat."

I groan. "Oh God, are you *still* calling me that?"

"Seems like you're still answering to it," he teases as I playfully shove him.

"You're such a jerk." I roll my eyes. "I can't believe I ever liked you."

He chuckles. "Ah, but you did. Remember when I found your notebook?"

"Please. Don't remind me," I say, burying my face in my hands.

A smirk tugs at his lips as he takes a sip of his drink. "It was cute."

I had a crush on Adam for as long as I can remember. He moved across the street when he and Michael were in fifth grade. By the time they were seniors and I was in seventh, that crush had spiraled into an obsessive infatuation. I scribbled my name with his last name on every notebook I owned—Alley Iverson. It was pathetic. But it was harmless... until I left one of those notebooks out and he found it. He teased me for an entire year, and it honestly made me hate him a little.

If by hate, I mean *love.*

Because let's be real—middle school crushes don't die easily. But to him, I was always just Michael's little sister—until Michael's thirtieth birthday party.

"Cute? And what about you? What about when you got drunk and kissed me two years ago?"

The look of shock on his face is both satisfying and a little embarrassing. "Didn't see that one coming, did ya?" I stick my tongue out—because, yes, I still fight like I'm twelve. And he started it.

"Yeah, that backfired real quick, didn't it?" he says, laughing. "Do you remember how awkward the next morning was?"

"Um, yeah. I've spent the last two years trying to forget. Turns out Adam and Alley? Just friends." I hold up my fist, and he taps it with his knuckles.

It's funny. For so many years, I thought Adam was *the one,* back when I was too young to know what love really meant. I used to dream of him kissing me. It wasn't that the kiss wasn't good—it *was* good. But the energy was all off. We both felt it. Like it wasn't meant to be. And standing here now, bantering and laughing with him, I feel nothing beyond the friends that we are. He's safe. Familiar. But he doesn't make my chest tighten or my pulse race. Not like Jensen. Jensen always gives me that fluttery feeling, the kind that tells you something good is about to happen if you just stick around long enough to find out.

Our laughter quiets, and after a beat, I say, "Michael told me about Andrea... how your engagement fell through. I'm really sorry. How are you holding up?"

He takes another sip, his Adam's apple bobbing as he swallows, his mood shifting somber. "I'm doing alright. It sucks, but it's for the best. It really is." He nods, like he's trying to convince himself. "Way to kill the mood, by the way."

I laugh softly. "Yeah, sorry. I'm a lame-ass. I just haven't seen you, and... I wanted to tell you that."

He glances past me, then grins. "But look at you. Michael says you've got a new boyfriend. Tell me about him."

My eyes light up. "I do. His name is Jensen. He's funny, hot, successful—"

I pause, Adam's grin growing as he looks past me, eyes fixed on something behind me, like he's trying not to laugh.

Before I can turn around, arms wrap around my waist and a deep voice sends chills down my spine. "Who's funny, hot, and successful?"

My breath catches. *That voice.*

I whip around, practically squealing as I sling my arms around Jensen's neck and he pulls me into a heated, gotta-have-you-right-now kind of kiss. *Did he really just do this?*

My heart bursts wide open, making all the room in the world for everything Jensen. He can't be real. He tugs on my bottom lip before pulling back, and suddenly, I couldn't care less about New Year's or parties. I just want him. All to myself.

"You're the best," I whisper, tightening my grip around him. "Seriously, I can't..." I stumble, shaking my head in disbelief. "How?"

Jensen chuckles, the sound reverberating off his chest. "I stole your phone for a second and got Michael's contact info. He's known for weeks."

I gape at Michael, who's now standing next to Adam and Stella.

"What? You knew?"

Michael laughs. "We all knew. Even Leo, when he picked you up yesterday. It's been fun keeping this from you."

My eyes land on Stella. "I can't believe *you* were able to keep it a secret."

"Oh, Stella didn't know," Michael says, still laughing. "I only told her twenty minutes ago."

Stella shoots him a look that could kill.

"C'mon, babe! You're awful at keeping secrets. You would've told her."

"No, I wouldn't have."

I turn back to Jensen while Michael and Stella continue to bicker.

"I'm so happy you're here." A smile is permanently plastered to my face—seriously, my cheeks actually hurt from grinning. It's him. He's here. And somehow, he just keeps getting better. "You're making me feel a lot of things right now, Jensen Adams. And now I kind of want to get out of here and thank you properly for being the best surprise I've ever had."

"Oh yeah?" he replies, one brow raised. He leans in for another kiss. "Well, I won't say no to that... but I did just fly across the country to party with you on New Year's Eve. And if we leave now, you might regret it later."

I shake my head. "Uh-uh. Nope. I wouldn't."

He presses a kiss to my forehead. "Why don't you introduce me to your friends, and I promise you can make it up to me later." Then he leans in, whispering against my skin, his breath hot. "After I really give you something to thank me for."

Heat spreads through my core. *Holy hell. How does he do this to me?* My whole body melts, and it takes everything I have not to drag him out of here right now. I have to literally give myself a mental pep talk just to chill.

With a deep breath, I turn back to the group and officially introduce Jensen to my friends and family. Jensen naturally charms everyone, and I savor every second of having him here with me.

The night is absolutely perfect, everything I could've wanted and so much more. Jensen and Leo hit it off, their shared connection through Matt making conversation easy. They chat for a bit, but he spends most of the night with me, his hand in mine, making me feel like the luckiest girl in the room. And when midnight comes, Jensen's lips meet mine—fierce and all-consuming, like he's claiming me for the year to come.

And I don't know if I've ever wanted anything more.

Chapter Ten

JENSEN

THEN

JANUARY

"Babe, come on!" I shout from the couch. "You're gonna miss kickoff!"

What's she doing? She was just in the kitchen two minutes ago, putting wings in the air fryer, and now she's vanished. "Babe!" I call again, glancing over my shoulder, keeping one eye on the TV.

She appears seconds later, padding down the hall in nothing but one of my Jets jerseys.

I raise a brow. "I can't believe I'm saying this—but I'm gonna need you to put some pants on. This game's important for my fantasy team, and if that's all you're wearing..." I scoff under my breath. "I'm gonna spend the whole game thinking about fucking you instead of watching my quarterback."

She just laughs and flashes me a wicked grin, then grabs the charcuterie board and brings it over to the coffee table. "You say that like it's a bad thing."

I lick my lips. "It's distracting."

My eyes rake up her bare legs as she leans forward to make herself a plate. She always wears one of my jerseys—it's sexy as fuck. But no pants? That's another level.

We've been dating for four months now. She's been coming over every Sunday to watch football, and she goes all out—buffalo wings, charcuterie boards, little smokies, you name it. It's not just impressive; it's super cool. I've never had a girlfriend who actually liked football, let alone made it an event. It's quickly becoming my favorite part of the week.

Sometimes Matt or a few other friends join, but today? Today, it's just us.

Her eyes flick to mine, and I smother a grin. *Busted*—I was staring. Hard.

A sly smile tugs at the corners of her mouth. "Don't worry... I'm wearing underwear."

She plops down next to me, curling into my side, and weaves her fingers between mine.

I shift uncomfortably, adjusting my dick with my free hand. "Is that supposed to make you less fuckable?" I ask with a smirk.

Her bottom lip rolls between her teeth as she tries to suppress a grin. I press my lips to her temple as the kicker lines up. A few seconds later, his foot connects with the ball and the game begins.

"Which guys are yours again?" Alley asks.

"The quarterback and the tight end. Numbers seventeen and thirty-seven."

"Okay. Cool."

This is one of the best parts. She asks questions about my fantasy team. Cheers for my guys. She actually *watches* the game with me. She cares. It's such a fucking turn-on.

It's like I found my soulmate. We're so incredibly different, but we want the same things. We have so much fun together.

We've been home from Chicago for about a week and a half. New Year's was a whole different ball game. It made every other year feel like a joke—kissing some random at midnight or dragging a girl to Matt's party just so I didn't have to go alone? What was the point? I'd been playing the dating game without even knowing the rules. Just showing up because that's what you're supposed to do.

But this New Year's, it was like I finally saw the whole picture. Finally understood what matters. What it means to win. The whole damn meaning of life. When you find someone like Alley, you don't take the easy pass. You don't half-ass it. You *cling* to it. *She's* the touchdown. The game-winning point. Girls like her don't come along for everyone. So when they do, you run for the goal.

You fucking show up.

Alley's family and friends were cool. Easy to talk to, welcoming—but you could tell they're protective of her. They love her. And honestly... how could you not?

She shifts beside me, my hand dropping to her thigh, fingers skimming her smooth skin. My gaze follows, thoughts of dragging up the hem of that jersey taking over, pushing football to the side.

"Oh! Your guy has the ball!" she says, nudging me with her elbow.

My head jerks up, focus snapping to my quarterback. My grip tightens on Alley's thigh as he makes a pass—a *crucial* one—resulting in a touchdown.

"Yes!" I jump out of my seat, whooping and clapping. Alley cheers right along with me.

I sink back into the couch, and she kisses me—hot, celebratory. It takes everything in me not to keep going.

"So how many points do you get for that?" she asks.

It's so damn cute how she wants to learn about fantasy football.

"Passing touchdown gets me four." I rub my hands together. "Jake better buckle up. I'm coming for that win." I'm in the finals against a buddy of mine at work.

"Hell yeah!" She puts her hand up for a high-five, and I meet it enthusiastically.

During the next commercial break, Alley heads into the kitchen to finish the wings.

"Babe, you want another beer?" she calls out.

"Yeah. That'd be great."

I watch her move around my kitchen like it's her own, rummaging through the fridge, my Jets jersey rising with every lift of her arms. I like it. *Damn, I wish she never had to go home.*

Whoa. That's a thought I didn't see coming.

She pops the top off my beer, tossing the opener back into the drawer where it came from. It does something to me, watching her like this. A grin spreads across my face, and my chest tightens—but not in the bad way. Not the aching kind. The good kind. The kind that says I can't get enough of her.

She brings my beer and the wings over to the coffee table. And yeah, I know, she's serving me like I'm a fucking king. But trust me, I've offered to help a hundred times. This is *her* thing. She loves cooking. And she keeps telling me how much fun it is to make football Sundays special for me.

Like I said—she's the best.

By the time the second quarter's nearly over, I'm two beers in and full of buffalo wings. One of Alley's arms is looped around mine, while the other traces light strokes up and down my forearm, gliding over my fingertips before trailing back up. It's sensual as hell, and I'm torn—between wanting to fuck her right here on the couch and not wanting to miss the game. Not only am I in the fantasy finals, but the Super Bowl's coming up. It's a big deal.

I *try* not to think about Alley naked. I force my eyes to the screen, but my cock's already throbbing inside my joggers. I know she sees it. She knows exactly what she's doing. She loves to fuck with me—always ready to crack a joke about my boner.

It's almost halftime. I can make it five more minutes.

Well, five minutes in football time. *Fuck. That's like twenty.*

The game breaks for commercial, and Alley glances up at me. "Hey... will you explain how this game works?"

"What?" My brows pull together. "What do you mean, explain how it works?"

Her one dimple sinks deep into her cheek as she grins. "I don't know anything about football." She giggles, and it's the cutest fucking thing. "I honestly have no clue what's going on. I never watched it growing up."

My heart stutters, my eyes locking on hers with more adoration than I've ever felt for anyone. "Are you serious?" *The fuck?*

"Dead."

Her cheeks blush, like they always do when she's embarrassed—

her admission shooting straight to my heart. All this time, she's been pretending to love this—for me. She's made it my favorite part of the week because she cares that much.

"Oh my God, I love you." The words slip out before I know what I'm saying. Panic surges, and my pulse spikes. *Did I just screw up?* I meant it, but shit, that hadn't been part of the plan today.

But she doesn't miss a beat—a huge grin spreads across her gorgeous lips. "I love you too."

She leans in and kisses me, heated and urgent. My hand slips under the jersey, and before I know it, we're naked on the couch—breathless, sweaty, snuggled under a blanket.

This has by far been the best Sunday football afternoon to date.

My fingers trail down her arm as she rests her head against my chest—and I explain the game of football to her.

Chapter Eleven

ALLEY

THEN—FOUR AND A HALF YEARS AGO

MARCH

WE HAUL the last of the boxes into the apartment. I set mine down on the kitchen table and lean against it, trying to catch my breath. *God, I'm winded.*

I inhale slowly, blinking as stars flash behind my eyes, a pounding starting to build in my head.

"Babe, you okay?" Jensen asks, his brows knitting together. "You look a little flushed."

I wince. "Agh, I'm not feeling great."

"Really? What's going on?" He crosses the kitchen toward me, concern etched across his face.

I press my palm to my forehead. "I don't know. I just... I feel like I'm gonna pass out all of a sudden. And my head's pounding. Feels like I'm getting the flu or something."

Jensen wraps his arms around me, and presses a kiss to the top of my head. "Why don't you go lie down?"

"Because this is all my shit."

I'm officially moving in today, even though I've practically lived here for the past three months. Jensen asked me to move in a few weeks ago, and my lease is up, so I finally made the leap. I sold off most of my furniture, and Jensen did the same. It was his idea to get new stuff that reflected both our tastes. Not many men in their thirties would be willing to ditch their manly decor, let a woman move into their space and take over—I know how lucky I am.

"Leave it. I got it, babe."

"But... you won't know where to put my things."

He chuckles softly. He knows what an organized control freak I am.

He kisses my forehead, amusement dancing in his eyes. "How about this? You lay on the couch and tell me where everything goes. And when we get to the bedroom boxes, you can order me around some more." A grin spreads across his face. "I'll even let you boss me around in bed later while you're being a pillow princess."

I try not to laugh, but it's hopeless.

"Seriously, babe. I got this."

"Really? You swear you don't care? I feel bad."

"I swear. The hard part's done, we got all the shit here. This part's easy." He grabs my hands and tugs me toward the couch. "Plus, I can't wait until you fall asleep so I can fuck everything up."

I laugh again and my hand flies to my forehead. "Ow. Stop making me laugh. It hurts."

His warm lips meet mine.

I push against him, weakly. "You don't want to kiss me. You're gonna get sick."

He replies by crushing his mouth to mine, firmer this time, slipping in some tongue. Then he pulls back, his lips hovering over mine. "Don't tell me what I want," he whispers, then nips at my bottom lip. "And if I get sick? I get sick."

He kisses me again, slower this time, taking his time. A half smile breaks across his face, one dimple popping as he finally releases me from the hot torment of his mouth—a mouth that makes me wish I felt better, just to finish what he's starting.

He meets my gaze. "Worth it," he says, voice husky. "Now lie down and rest. That's an order."

I raise an eyebrow. "I thought I was supposed to be giving the orders."

He laughs as I lie down on the couch, then grabs a nearby blanket and tucks it around me.

"Now," he says once I'm settled, "what do you need? Ibuprofen? Tylenol? Whiskey? An orgasm? Your wish is my command."

"Stop... making me laugh," I groan through a breathy chuckle. "Some ibuprofen would be great."

I close my eyes for a moment, the tension and bright light making my head throb even more. He's back two minutes later with the pills and a glass of water.

"Thank you," I whisper. "Will you turn off this light?"

"Sure. Get some sleep. I got this. I'll start with the kitchen. I can't screw that up too badly. There's only so many places this stuff can go."

* * *

My eyes crack open, and I blink the sleep away. I don't even remember closing them.

I'm in bed now—*our* bed. The soft light from my nightstand glows across the room. I must've been really out. Jensen moved me here, and I didn't even notice.

He moves about the room quietly, pulling something from a box, then sliding open a drawer. I smile to myself, gratitude swelling in my chest. *My stuff is going to end up in the weirdest places.*

My gaze lands on the dresser, and a weak laugh slips from my lips. "Oh my God. What did you do?"

He turns around, a wicked grin stretched across his face. "What do you think of our new decorations?"

I have these heinous dolls from all over the world—souvenirs my grandma used to bring back every time she traveled. They're ugly as sin and creepy as hell, but I cherish them. I usually keep them boxed up, but once a year, I'll get them out just to look at them. I would've preferred that not be today. And definitely not around Jensen. Looks like he found the box and lined them all up on our dresser.

"Okay, but seriously. We gotta talk about these," he teases. "Should I be concerned?"

I shake my head, laughing, and he joins in. Every time I look at the dolls and imagine him finding the box, I laugh harder. I wish I could've seen his face. I'm laughing so hard, tears sting my eyes—until suddenly, without warning, the laughter turns to crying. Real tears. My chest tightens. My throat burns. And before I can stop it, I'm sobbing. My face contorts into what's probably the worst cry face imaginable, and I'm instantly mortified. But I can't help it. That ache —the one that misses my grandma—punches me in the gut. And it hurts.

And then I think of my mom, and I can't breathe.

No. No. No. I've never cried in front of Jensen before. This is new. He hasn't seen this side of me, and I'm not ready for that.

"Babe!" Jensen rushes to my side. "God, babe. It was a joke. I'm so sorry."

He pulls me into a hug, and I sob like a baby in his arms. "Hey," he says softly, kissing the top of my head, patient as ever.

Who cries the first day they move in with someone?

Eventually, my tears slow, and the room falls painfully quiet—just the sound of my quick, uneven breaths.

"Are you wishing you hadn't asked me to move in?" I ask, breaking the silence.

"It'll take a lot more than a few tears to scare me away." He pulls back, his hands cupping my face. "You wanna talk about the dolls?" His lips twitch into a smile.

"They were from my grandma."

His brows furrow. "Well, hey, I've never been a doll guy, but we can leave them up if you want."

A laugh bursts out of me. "You're so sweet. And I love you for that —but no. They're so creepy. But I love them at the same time. It just made me sad for a minute." I blow out a breath, still a little shaken. "I'm sorry. That was... different."

"Hey." His hand finds mine. "Don't be sorry." A soft smile touches his lips. "I'm just glad they can go back in the box... How you feeling? Aside from the doll fiasco?"

"Not great," I say, my voice thick, nose too stuffed to breathe properly. "Turns out crying's not great for a head cold."

His lips press to my forehead in a lingering kiss, and I close my eyes, sinking into the safety of him. It's the kind of tender moment where sometimes, what he doesn't say says more than anything he ever could.

"Can I show you what I did with all your stuff?"

My eyes go wide. "Oh boy. I'm not gonna lie—I'm a little worried."

"Nah, babe. You're gonna be impressed. I paid attention when we were boxing up your stuff." He stands, making his way over to the new dresser. "You get all six of these drawers. I just took the three on the left."

He pulls one open. "Underwear's in here." He glances back at me. "And don't worry, I kept it in that little cube box thing you had it in." He closes it and opens the next. "Socks. In the cubes, and color coded. Just like before."

He keeps going, pulling each drawer open and giving me the full rundown.

I hug my pillow tight to my chest, resting my chin on top, a smile planting itself on my face—even though my head's pounding and I feel like crap.

He finishes his presentation, then slides into bed next to me, flipping on the TV. He finds the sports channel and turns the volume down low.

I close my eyes, sinking deeper into the mattress, soaking up the comfort of our new bed. *Our* new bed.

"Are you picturing me naked?"

My eyes snap open to find Jensen watching me, grinning.

"What?"

He laughs. "You had the biggest smile on your face with your eyes closed. Figured you were imagining me naked."

"You're so dumb." I reach out to smack him, but he dodges it, laughing.

"I wouldn't blame you, you know." He smacks his lips together, his gaze settling on mine. There's so much love in his eyes, so much adoration, it tugs at my chest. No one's ever looked at me the way he does.

My smile deepens. "I was thinking about how comfortable this bed is... and how cool it is that it's *ours* now. Not yours or mine."

A small smile pulls at his mouth. "Yeah. It is cool." His voice dips low and gravelly—sexy. His eyes sweep over my body, awakening all my senses. *I wish I wasn't sick.*

Then his gaze returns to my face. "Tell me more about your grandma. You've never really talked about her."

My eyes go misty at the mention of her. "Well... she was the best. She loved to travel. She'd go with her best friend. They were both widowed pretty young, in their fifties. I never knew my grandpa." I pause to swallow, a sore throat setting in. *Great.* "Anyway, she'd always bring me back these weird dolls. I kind of hated it when I was little because I was like, *what am I going to do with these?*" I laugh, and Jensen's smile grows wider. "I just wanted her to bring back some cool candy or chocolate or something. Something normal, you know?"

That pulls a laugh from him. "I mean..." He gestures toward the dolls. "I get it."

My smile's not going anywhere. "Anyway, as I got older, she started inviting me to her Pounce parties—it's a fast-paced card game you play with a partner. Every Thursday night in middle school, I'd hang out with my grandma and her friends. There was always a buy-in, she'd cover mine. And when we won, she'd split the pot with me."

"She sounds like a good time."

"She was. She could hang with the best of them."

His expression softens. "When did she pass?"

"A year before my mom." I purse my lips. "That was a tough year. My grandma died, my mom was sick, and my dad... spiraled. I feel like I lost all three of the most important people in my life in the span of twelve months."

I blink, forcing the tears back, and shift to a lighter note. "She left me her travel scrapbooks and all her romance novels and of course, my collection of creepy dolls."

He pulls his pillow down flat and turns, lying onto his side to face me. "I was wondering about the box of books, especially when you always use your Kindle."

"Yeah." My lips break into a grin. "Turns out my grandma loved a dirty book."

"No way!"

"Oh yeah. Some of the smuttiest books I've ever read came from that box. I basically learned everything I know about sex from Grandma's dirty little library."

Jensen belts out a laugh. "Grandma's dirty little library... Hey, is that a business idea?"

We laugh together, and I wince as the laughter spikes the pressure behind my eyes.

"I think I like Grandma," he says, still grinning.

Our eyes lock, and even though we've slept in this room together for months, it feels different now, like we're starting something new. Something permanent. Something forever.

"She would've loved you," I whisper.

"Come here," he murmurs, closing the space between us. He shifts, pulling me in, and our lips meet. My nose is stuffed, my head is pounding, and somewhere in the back of my mind I'm worried about getting him sick. But it doesn't matter. It's healing—physically, emotionally. The past, the present, all the broken pieces coming back together beneath Jensen's mouth.

"Do you want me to stop so you can get some sleep?" he whispers against my skin.

I'm already shaking my head when he grins against my lips. "Or do you want to be a pillow princess so I can help you forget all about this cold?"

"Pillow princess," I whisper, pleading softly.

He leans in, voice husky. "Is that a command?"

I nod.

"Good."

He trails slow kisses down my jaw and neck, his hand sliding under the blanket to cup my breast, palming it gently.

I gasp, heat flooding my core and surging through my veins. Suddenly, I'm *hot*—and I pray it's from him, not a fever. I reach for the hard length beneath his joggers, but he swats my hands away.

"No way, baby. You're sick. I'm taking care of you tonight."

His hand slides down my stomach and dips into my sweats, and I arch into him. He circles his fingers against my clit, drawing out a soft moan. "Babe," I whisper, my eyes squeezing shut.

"Hey," he says softly. "Open your eyes."

So I do.

He meets my gaze. "I love you."

Then he's kissing me again before I can respond, filling me with the best remedy in the world.

Don't they say that food is the best medicine?

Bullshit.

Jensen is.

Chapter Twelve

ALLEY

PRESENT DAY

THE CAB PULLS UP to our building, and I step out, the rain hitting instantly, soaking me in the fifteen feet it takes to reach the entrance.

Inside, the lobby blurs—familiar people, familiar space, but I barely see any of it. My feet carry me to the elevator, my brain blanking the moment I step inside. The doors close, but I don't move. I just stand there, staring.

My phone rings. I yank it from my purse, pulse spiking. *Jensen.*

No—Adam.

I send it to voicemail, a lump forming, tightening my throat. The weight of why he's calling pressing on my chest, constricting my goddamn heart until I swear it might explode. Of all nights for something else to go wrong. Why tonight?

A text dings.

I slump against the elevator wall, my fingers sluggish as I swipe up.

ADAM

I just talked to Michael. How are you holding up?

The tears come faster now. I squeeze my eyes shut, gripping the phone tighter.

God, this is the worst night ever. Opening my eyes, I realize I'm still in the lobby. I fumble for the button, pushing for the sixth floor.

I don't even remember walking down the hallway. But when the door to our apartment slams shut behind me, my cry rips through the empty space. Rain and tears soak my face as I drop my stuff in the middle of the entryway and drift toward the living room, numb.

I collapse onto the sofa, a guttural moan tearing from my throat—one I've been holding in since the cab ride home. I fold my arms over my knees and press my forehead against them.

Holy shit. I can't breathe.

The weight of it all—Jensen, Adam's call, life. It's crushing me.

I force myself to sit up, dialing Jensen one more time, knowing he won't answer. I'm sent straight to voicemail.

"Hi, you've reached Jensen Adams. You know what to do."

I scream. A raw, monstrous sound shreds out of me as my phone flies from my hand, crashing into the wall.

"FUUUUCK!"

The voice isn't mine. It's unrecognizable—angry, broken, shrill. And most definitely crazy.

I gasp for air, but my lungs refuse to work. My heart pounds, hammering in my ears. I slide off the couch, onto the floor, and lie on my back. Panic grips me, sinking its claws in, and my chest tightens. My body forgets how to work, every muscle locked, nerves firing with no sense of direction, wild and out of control.

I shudder as the sobs wrack my body. Everything feels like it's slipping away—noise, touch, my surroundings.

Jensen.

Chapter Thirteen

JENSEN

THEN—THREE YEARS AGO

OCTOBER

I slide my arms into my shirt jacket, rolling the sleeves up a couple times before heading to the guest bedroom closet where the small box is hidden. I pick it up, its weight nothing compared to the enormity of what it represents—our future.

I open it one last time, giving it a long look. A lump forms in my throat, emotion rising as I picture slipping it onto Alley's dainty finger. The love I feel for her—it's overwhelming. I always wanted this but never truly imagined it happening until now.

My mind flashes back to the first time I told her I loved her. How it hadn't been planned and it just slipped out. I asked her to move in with me after that. Now, here we are, eighteen months later, two years since we met, and everything is about to change in the best possible way.

Grinning, I snap the box shut, the sound echoing off the bare walls, pulling me back to the afternoon ahead.

"Jensen?" Alley's voice carries through the house.

I shove the box into my pocket. It bulges slightly, but not enough to be obvious.

"There you are." Alley says, stepping into the guest room as I walk out of the closet. "What are you doing in here?"

"Oh, I was just looking for something, but I can't find it," I lie.

My gaze travels down her body, my grin giving away every thought of how goddamn beautiful she is.

I'm taking her to a football game today, her first ever. Matt hooked us up with the suite. Honestly, I don't have a detailed plan for the proposal. I didn't want it to feel staged or rehearsed. Alley's so chill; she'd hate some big, cheesy production. She'd want something real, something meaningful.

And football? Fuck, football is what proved how much Alley loved me. It's what made me fall even deeper in love with her. It doesn't sound romantic, but for us, it is.

"You ready?" She slides her arms inside my jacket, wrapping them around my waist, and kisses me.

"Yep. You look hot." Our lips meet again, then again, and before I know it, my hands are raking through her hair, kissing her like she's the air I need to breathe. That thought borders on insanity, but it's true. In a way, I do need her to breathe. I'd do anything for her. Sometimes I think God put me on this earth simply to worship Alley. To make her laugh. To please her.

Damn, that's good. I'll have to remember that.

I didn't prepare a speech either. She'll appreciate a raw, vulnerable moment. Nothing is sexier to her than honesty. So I'm going into this blind. I only need to know one thing today: I love Alley, and I can't imagine a single day without her—because that would be my personal hell.

I grin against her lips. "Damn you, babe. We don't have time to have sex right now, but I really want to."

She laughs against my mouth. "Who says we don't have time? We can miss the kicking thing."

I chuckle. She still has a lot to learn about football.

Gripping her hips, I deepen the kiss, knowing damn well we'll barely make it out of this house on time—if at all.

But fuck the game.

Alley's the only win I care about today.

* * *

My phone dings, startling me awake.

Then it dings again.

And again.

"Hell," I mutter, reaching blindly for it. I squint at the screen, groaning when I see the time—ten minutes before my alarm was set to go off.

Another ding.

It's my sibling group chat, lighting up at six-fucking-thirty in the morning. *What a bunch of overachievers.*

Well, sibling chat—plus the in-laws. And Matt.

> **MATT**
>
> Bro, did she say yes?
>
> **JEFF**
>
> You were supposed to text us last night. How did it go?
>
> **MATT**
>
> The suspense is killing me...
>
> **MEGAN**
>
> What the hell is wrong with you, Matt? It's six in the morning. I'll have your balls for this.

I couldn't stop grinning if you paid me. I probably look like the damn Cheshire Cat right now. Silencing my phone, I glance at Alley—still fast asleep. My heart lurches, my grin widening when I take her in. Hair a mess, mouth open, heavy, even breaths. She's always been a deep sleeper. She can pass out anywhere. I have dozens of pictures of her sleeping in random places—mouth open, catching flies. She hates them. I tell her it's the ultimate blackmail.

She said yes.

She wants to be mine. And I'm going to be hers.

Damn. When did I become this guy? The one lying in bed, grinning like a lovesick puppy over a group text and having a *fiancée?* Never thought I'd be the type.

My fingers hover over the screen. I punch out a reply, feeling giddy—like a goddamn schoolboy.

> She said YES!

Matt sends a GIF of someone fist-pumping the air, and Megan replies instantly with about a hundred excited emojis mixed with party-themed ones.

I chuckle softly.

MATT

> So when's the bachelor party? I vote Vegas. And I'm your best man, right?

Kevin finally makes an appearance.

KEVIN

> He has two brothers, bro. Why would you be best man?

JEFF

> But I'm the only REAL brother, so obviously that position goes to me. It's like royal succession.

MATT

> I believe marriage disqualifies you from succession. It naturally falls to the next eligible bachelor. AKA Moi.

MEGAN

> Eligible bachelor my ass. Hahahahahaha.

> I wanna go to Vegas. What do I have to do to get in on this? I'll shove a rubber dick in my pants for a bro weekend. This mom needs a fucking vacation.

KEVIN

> Jesus, Megan. Have a girls weekend or go to brunch. No need to be stuffing your pants with dicks.

MATT

Yeah, I won't recover from that image… ever.

MEGAN

Why are you texting me, Kev? I'm literally in the next room.

KEVIN

Needed everyone to know I do not approve of you stuffing dicks in your pants… unless it's mine.

JEFF

Good God. I've gotta get ready for work. Congrats baby bro, happy for you both. Give Alley a hug from us.

Thanks, Jeff, I will. Matt—I just proposed last night. Can we talk about Vegas later? No best man. I love you all equally. Megan—there are no words. But if you need a vacation, why don't you go to Chicago with Alley next week for her brother's birthday?

MEGAN

Kev, can I go to Chicago next week? I'll suck your dick.

KEVIN

Your mom watching the kids? And gonna have to be more than once for me to say yes.

MEGAN

Fine. Three blow jobs in the next week, and I'll ask my mom. Final offer.

I shake my head. I know how these group chats get, they'll go on forever. Dragging my ass out of bed, I head to the bathroom and start the shower.

MATT

Christ, you two. Ever heard of a separate text? I don't tell you about my sex life, and we don't need to know about yours.

MEGAN

We don't need you to tell us. Friday night? Fucked
Jessica. Saturday night? Fucked Jordan. And lemme
guess, last night? Brought home some girl from a
bar who gave you the best blow job of your life.

How close am I? For real, I wanna know.

I laugh. She's spot-on, I'm sure of it. Megan is possibly the most
vulgar woman I know, and I'm damn proud to call her my sister.

MATT

Nailed it, Megs. Except Friday night was a girl I met
a few weeks ago. Her name was Shannon.

MEGAN

WAS? What, did she change her name for you? "Oh,
Matt, I'm yours. Call me whatever you want.
Anything for you." Insert dick in her mouth and a gag
in mine. #PUKE

MATT

You're so funny Megan.

I peel my shirt off and step out of my pants, brushing my teeth
while the shower heats up. These two are always the comedic enter-
tainment. They've bantered like this since we were kids. Megan used
to kick Matt's ass, until he outgrew her. She was a mean older sister
when we were little.

K guys, getting ready for work too. Thanks for being
excited for us. Megs, I'll have Alley text you when
she wakes up… if you're serious about Chicago.

MEGAN

Serious as a coroner.

Deeply unsettling, but okay.

MEGAN

Love you. Happy for you.

MATT

Yeah, love you both, brother. Give Alley a hug for
me too.

Come give her one yourself. She doesn't go into
work until noon today.

I set my phone down and step into the shower, closing my eyes as the hot water streams over my face. I relish the heat pelting against my skin, soaking in the joy of the moment. I've got my dream girl, my best friend and siblings hyping me up, and a hell of a lot to look forward to.

Damn, life is good.

When I open my eyes, Alley's staring at me through the glass, grinning. She lifts her shirt over her head and slides her shorts down her legs. Desire surges through me, my cock instantly hardening. I've seen her naked hundreds of times, yet she still has this effect on me. She hooks her thumbs into her underwear, dragging them down, and as she steps into the shower, it feels like this next chapter is going to be the best goddamn one yet.

Chapter Fourteen

ALLEY

THEN

Our patient, David, gasps for air and shoots upright, arms outstretched like he's in a zombie apocalypse.

"Holy shit," Zach mutters as we both brace our hands around his back and chest, trying to calm and stabilize him. He fights us, his body thrashing—he's freakishly strong. He's also a very large man, and my small frame struggles to manage someone his size.

"David, you're okay. You're in recovery," I reassure him firmly, but he's disoriented, arms flailing.

His hand whips back, connecting hard with my cheekbone before I can dodge it.

"Ow! God." I wince, leaning into him, pressing my weight against his shoulder as we help lower him back down again.

"Cindy?" Zach calls out urgently. "We need a third over here!"

Cindy rushes over, and between the three of us, we manage to settle David. Wild moments like this happen in PACU sometimes.

"You okay, Al?" Zach asks.

"Yeah, I'm fine," I say, forcing a smile. But damn, my cheek throbs. That's definitely going to leave a bruise.

95

A few minutes later, David is fully coming to, no longer fighting us, and Cindy leaves to attend another patient.

Zach turns to me. "So, when's the engagement party?"

I shrug. "I don't know. Is that something we have to do? I'd rather just have close friends over to celebrate."

"Call it whatever you want, babe. But there has to be a celebration of some kind."

A slow smile spreads across my face. "Yeah, okay. Let's do something. Does Friday work for you and Joey? Everyone can come over to our place. We'll order food, have drinks, play some games. Keep it chill."

Zach snorts. "Is Matt coming? Because you know 'chill' isn't in his vocabulary." He shakes his head. "Friday works for us, but I guarantee the second Matt finds out, this is turning into a party at his place."

"No. No way in hell am I letting Matt take over. I don't want a big thing, just an intimate celebration. Something I don't have to get dressed up for."

Zach grins. "Yeah, good luck with that. So, how does it feel to be engaged?"

"It feels... surreal. Exciting. Jensen's amazing."

"He really is. You did good." Zach pauses, then smirks. "Speaking of good, has Matt decided to play for both teams yet? Because that is an ass I wouldn't mind tapping."

A laugh bursts out of me. "Oh my God! You and everyone else. Get in line." My hospital pager interrupts before Zach can respond. It's Cindy asking about a patient. I answer quickly, then turn back to him. "You can't say stuff like that. What would Joey think?"

"Please. You've seen Matt. Joey's seen Matt. Trust me, Joey's thinking the same thing. Hello, threesome?"

I shake my head in utter disbelief. "You're unbelievable."

By now, my friends and Jensen's have all met plenty of times, plus I tell Zach almost everything. Of course, my friends are obsessed with Matt, and they never let me forget it.

Zach's expression shifts, turning serious. "All joking aside, if you need any help for Friday, Joey would love to be of service."

I give him a playful shove. "I don't know how Joey puts up with you."

It's Monday. Yesterday, Jensen took me to my first football game—and proposed. I know, it doesn't sound like the kind of proposal that would make a girl swoon, but trust me, it was. It was so damn swoon-worthy, tears threaten just thinking about it.

The only thing I might've changed, had I known beforehand, was my outfit. No woman dreams of getting engaged wearing a football jersey. But then again, Jensen loves that Jets jersey on me, so maybe I wouldn't change a thing after all.

It was halftime. The stadium buzzed in the background, the TV was muted. Just another Sunday—except it wasn't.

I sat back against the arm of the suite's sofa, legs draped across Jensen's lap, his hand resting on my thigh, thumb brushing lightly over my jeans. I'd been laughing at something he'd said when suddenly his expression turned serious. He just watched me, his eyes bright with admiration, his gaze burning straight through to my soul. The way he looked at me stole my breath away.

"Marry me," he blurted out.

I laughed, thinking it was a joke. "Ha. Okay. Maybe if they win." I nudged his arm.

"No, I'm serious, Al." He reached into his pocket and pulled out a ring box. No theatrics. No kneeling. Just Jensen, grinning, opening the box, and asking again. "You and me. This. It's my favorite thing in the world. I knew I was going to ask you, I just didn't know when. But sitting here with you, watching football, just us... I don't want that to ever change. I don't ever want to watch another game without you. Will you marry me?"

I didn't even look at the ring. I didn't need to. It could've been tinfoil twisted into a circle, and I still would've said yes. Because it was Jensen. The guy who loves me even though we're complete opposites. The one who'd rather go out but stays in because he knows I'm an introvert. The one who makes me feel sexy even in my ugly hospital scrubs. The one who doesn't care that I'm obsessive about cleaning or that I won't let him come in my mouth.

The guy who doesn't just love me despite my flaws—he *loves* my flaws.

The one I share everything with. The one who makes me laugh until it hurts. The one who carries my burdens as if they're his own. My best friend. The guy who took something as simple as football and made it special. Made it ours. Every game from now on would remind us of this moment.

I don't know how he does it, but he always finds a way to turn ordinary moments into once-in-a-lifetime memories.

I looked at him, nodding as a smile spread so wide it stretched my cheeks. "Yes. Yes. A thousand times, yes."

Jensen slid the ring onto my finger. And the kiss that followed? To die for. Beautiful. Hot. Romantic as hell. I ended up straddling his lap, and we made out right there—a little more than that too.

We never finished watching the game. I couldn't even tell you who won. Eventually, I looked at the ring, and it couldn't have been more me. It was simple, delicate diamonds set into a band—just enough to say, *I'm taken*. It was perfect. It was us: classic, beautiful, and each other's.

Zach's voice pulls me from my thoughts. "So, are you already dreaming up big wedding plans?"

I scoff. "Please. You know me. I don't want a big wedding. What, with my grand total of fifteen people to invite? I'd be fine getting married in Vegas." I laugh, but as I say it, something shifts. It hits me. It *stings*. I don't have parents. No real family. Just Michael, maybe my aunt and uncle, and a few close friends.

I shake it off. "Honestly, I haven't thought about it yet. It's still so new. But maybe end of summer next year? Early fall? I don't know. I'm just excited to marry Jensen. I don't really care how it's done."

Zach gapes at me. "Knock that off right now. You have so many people in your corner who love you, and you deserve the best of the best. And you better be prepared for an elaborate wedding. Jensen has a big family, plus they're loaded. You know how the wealthy do it in New York. I don't see Vegas happening, babe."

I shrug. "It is what it is, I guess. As long as I go home as Alley Adams, I don't care where it happens."

"Okay, fine. At least tell me you've thought about what you want your dress to look like." But before I can answer, he huffs. "Of course you haven't. You don't care about the dress either. Honestly, Al, it's a good thing you have Scarlett and me for these things."

I just laugh. "You know I don't care about that stuff, Zach. And if Jensen's mom wants a whole to-do, then I guess I'm having a big-ass wedding."

"You're crazy, boo. Are you inviting your dad?"

"Why would I? So he can forget to show up?" A self-deprecating laugh slips out. "No. Michael can walk me down the aisle. He's been the only father figure in my life for the past decade."

Zach frowns. "But what about the first sixteen years of your life? Doesn't that count for something?"

"If doing a half-assed job for half my life makes someone a good father, then sure. He was a great dad for sixteen years."

I feel his stare on the side of my face. I know what he's thinking. And there is no way in hell I'm inviting my father.

"Hey, help me move this gurney," I say, interrupting the awkward silence before he can push it further.

He exhales. "Alright. Whatever you need."

Chapter Fifteen

ALLEY

THEN

Conversation and music fill the apartment, empty wine glasses and half-eaten desserts scatter across the countertop. The night is winding down, friends trickling out in pairs. My cheeks ache from smiling, my body pleasantly tired from playing host.

"Ah, thank you both for coming." I give Joey a hug before moving to Zach.

"Of course! We wouldn't miss it," Joey says.

"We're so happy for you." Zach squeezes me tight before stepping back, and I wave as the two of them leave.

Scarlett, Matt, and Jordan remain. An awkward combo, if you ask me. Especially since Scarlett has been flirting with Matt all night, even though she knows Jordan will probably be going home with him. It's brutal to watch.

"Okay, well... I'm gonna head out too." Scarlett moves toward the living room, grabbing her jacket and purse from the couch. I follow.

"Thanks for coming, friend." I lower my voice to a whisper. "Sorry Jordan's here. I know you were hoping to get some one-on-one time with Matt."

Scarlett exhales. "Stop. This night isn't about me. It's about you and Jensen, and I'm so happy for you." She pulls me into a hug. "Does it suck going home alone? Sure. But I can always call someone on the roster. No biggie. Plus, I like Jordan, and I hate that she's so damn likable."

I laugh softly. "I know, right? She's so great."

"And so beautiful. I could never compete with that anyway."

I shake my head. Scarlett is stunning. She has a classic, timeless beauty about her. The kind that makes her look like she walked straight out of a 1950s magazine.

"Hey," I scold. "Don't talk about my best friend like that."

She gives me a small smile. "I love you, Al. I'm really glad you found someone like Jensen."

"Thank you. I love you too." We make our way to the front door. "Alright, shoot me a text when you get home so I know you're safe."

"Will do." She hugs me once more, takes one last, barely concealed glance at Matt, then walks out.

I sigh, shutting the door behind her. My phone buzzes in my back pocket, and I reach for it, swiping up without thinking.

LEO

Michael told me the big news. Congratulations, Alley!

A small smile tugs at my lips as I type back quickly.

Thanks, Leo!

I look up to find Jensen watching me, grinning. He pushes away from the counter and steps toward me, closing the distance between us.

"What are you smiling at?" I ask.

"You." Jensen's arm slides around my waist as Matt and Jordan joke in the kitchen. He presses a quick kiss to my temple. "Just... you." His fingers trace a deliberate pattern against my hip.

I wrap my arms around his neck, grinning. "Is someone getting impatient?"

"You have no idea." His voice drops. "What do you say we get rid of these two so you and I can..." He raises a brow. "You know..."

"Oh, I know." I lean in, my voice a soft whisper. "Yeah, let's get them out of here."

"We can hear you!" Matt calls from across the kitchen. "C'mon, babe. These two wanna get naked." He laces his fingers with Jordan's, tugging her toward us.

Matt embraces me first. "Come here, you!" He pulls me into a tight, brotherly bear hug. I have a special place in my heart for Matt, and I know he feels the same way about me. It's like a sibling bond, unspoken but solid.

He lets go, turning to Jensen, and the two of them clasp hands before pulling each other in. "So happy for you, brother! I fucking love you."

"Thanks, man. I love you too."

Jordan and I exchange amused looks.

"Do you two need a minute alone?" she teases.

Matt turns to her, raising a brow. "Woman. You wanna red ass?"

"Ooh. I don't know, maybe. Is that a threat or an offer?"

"Oh my God. You two..." Jensen groans. "Get out of here."

Jordan laughs as Jensen gives her a brief hug.

Matt points at me. "I'll come down in the morning to help clean up. Don't you dare start cleaning before I get here, Alley. I know how you are, and you shouldn't have to clean up your own damn engagement party."

I hold up my hands in mock innocence. "Okay, I won't. You don't have to beg me not to clean."

He squints at me, unconvinced. "Uh-huh. Sure." His point lingers. He knows I'm full of shit.

"Okay... I'm trusting you." He opens the door, tossing one last look over his shoulder. "Bye, you guys."

"Bye," Jordan says with one last wave.

"Bye," Jensen and I say in unison.

Jensen shuts the door behind them, his attention immediately shifting to me as I instinctively move toward the kitchen before I even realize I'm doing it.

His arm loops around my waist, reeling me back against his chest before I can take another step. "Nope. You heard Matt," he murmurs against my ear.

I groan, my hands resting over his. "I can't just leave it like that. I won't sleep."

"Yes, you can." His teeth graze my earlobe, voice smooth and coaxing. "And you will. Leave it, baby."

His lips skim my neck while his hand slips beneath my shirt, heat building with every touch. My stomach flutters, and I let my head fall back against his chest, melting into him. I close my eyes. *Why does he feel so good?*

His hand slides up, cupping my breast with a slow, purposeful squeeze. A soft hum escapes me as I sink further into him.

He chuckles, his lips grazing my ear. "You're mine now, and I know just what to do with you. I know exactly what you like."

"Mmm. And what do I like?" I ask, eyes still closed, savoring Jensen's touch and the slow, steady rise of my arousal.

"You like this," he murmurs, nibbling at my ear. His fingers glide over my skin, featherlight strokes across my chest, down my torso. My back arches instinctively.

"And this." His mouth moves to the base of my throat, his tongue flicking against my pulse point. He trails kisses down my neck, his hands roaming lower—teasing, exploring—his breath hot against my skin.

I bite my bottom lip, a slow grin spreading as a steady thrum builds between my thighs. *Damn.* He gets me. Every. Time.

"And definitely this." His fingers flick open the button of my pants before dipping beneath my underwear, sliding smoothly down the center.

A soft moan escapes as my body responds instantly, one hand reaching behind to grip his neck, the other curling around his arm, pulling him closer, needing more, craving him in every way.

His voice drops, husky and teasing, lips brushing the curve of my throat. "Did you still want to clean?"

"No," I murmur, tilting my head back as his lips graze over my skin. "I want more of this."

"That's my girl." He presses a lingering kiss to my jaw before fisting the hem of my shirt and pulling it over my head. Then, in one smooth motion, he spins me around, his mouth meeting mine in an urgent, needy kiss.

His lips are warm, demanding, and I soften into him, welcoming the all-consuming desire that always comes with Jensen—the feeling of pure need, like he might actually die if he doesn't have me. Right. Now.

It's the greatest feeling in the world—to be loved like that.

I've never had this before. Never felt this cherished or this desired. Not until him. We have a love that's rare, unshakable. The kind of love they sing about in songs.

The kind that lasts forever.

We make our way into the bedroom, shedding clothing as we go, until we're tangled in the sheets. He moves slowly, savoring the moment—his body pressing against mine, every touch familiar but electric. Our movements sync effortlessly, molding into one, everything else fading away until there's only him, only us, only this.

I roll myself on top, positioning myself to take him deeper, and everything blurs—warmth, ecstasy, quiet. Breathless moans fill the room until my body finally melts into his, sated and spent.

I catch my breath before slipping into the bathroom to wash up and ready myself for bed. When I return, Jensen's already under the covers, his arms immediately wrapping around me, pulling me close.

These are my favorite moments. The sex and orgasms are incredible, obviously. But this—being held in Jensen's arms, drifting off as he spoons me, his hand cupped lazily around my breast—is the best thing in the world. Nothing beats it.

Nothing.

The room is quiet now, just the soft sounds of the city beyond the window and the rhythm of his breathing. His fingers trace lazy patterns over my stomach as I relax into his touch, that familiar content humming in my veins.

His touch slows, and his breath deepens. He's falling asleep.

I grin into my pillow. He always knocks out so fast after sex— sleeps like a damn baby. I turn, pressing a soft kiss to his chest, then roll onto my back. My thumb rubs along the new ring on my finger, a smile creeping as it all sinks in.

I'm getting married.

* * *

WITH MY COFFEE IN HAND, I retreat to the living room, curling into my favorite spot on the oversized chaise lounge. The city stretches beyond the window, a soft haze clinging to the skyline. My legs tuck beneath me as I sink deeper into the cushions.

It's almost ten, and Jensen's still in bed. We rarely sleep past nine, but the party went late last night.

I scan the apartment. It's a mess in here, but I force myself to stay put and enjoy the stillness of the morning. My eyes drift to my ring finger. It's been almost a week now, and my heart still flutters every time I see it. Smiling, I bring my mug to my lips. *I'm engaged.*

The bedroom door swings open, and Jensen pads into the kitchen —rumpled, groggy, hair sticking up in every direction.

My gaze follows him as he moves straight to the coffee pot, his boxer briefs slung low on his hips.

"Hey, babe," he rasps, voice rough with sleep.

My heart lurches at the sight of him, and I can't help but laugh as he opens the fridge to grab the creamer, his underwear doing nothing to hide the raging erection pressing against them.

This is love. Right here. Quiet Saturday mornings, bedhead, coffee in your underwear. These are the moments I live for.

"Good morning," I say, standing and making my way toward him.

He glances at me over his shoulder. "What are you laughing at?"

"You," I say. "Do you ever wake up without that thing?"

Jensen chuckles, setting the creamer on the counter before pulling me into him, pressing a soft kiss to my lips. "I Imm. No. They don't call it morning wood for nothing, babe."

"I know. I just thought it might, you know... taper off with age. But here you are, in your thirties, still rocking morning wood like a champ."

He scoffs. "I'm thirty-two, not dead. Jesus. I don't assume Lola's gonna dry up the second you hit thirty."

I snort. "Okay, morning wood and the ability to get it up are not the same thing. I wasn't implying you wouldn't be able to get an erection."

"Don't call it an erection. We're not at the hospital," he says, laughing. "God, I hate when you use clinical terminology on my manhood. Clark deserves better than that, Al. And after everything he does for Lola?" He clicks his tongue, shaking his head.

I giggle, biting my lip. Yes, he named my vagina Lola. And his dick? Clark—after Clark Kent, you know—Superman. Because, of course he would.

I press a slow, lingering kiss to his chest, breathing him in—salt, musk, and the faintest trace of last night still clinging to his skin. When I look up, he's watching me, that familiar spark in his eyes.

"Oh, you think Lola's a lucky girl?" I ask.

"Psh. I know she is, babe. Clark delivered hardcore last night."

I laugh. "And what about Clark? I'd say he's pretty damn lucky, too."

He cups my face, his thumb grazing my cheek. "Oh, he's the luckiest motherfucker on the planet."

Then his lips crush against mine, warm and insistent, his hand sliding to the back of my neck, pulling me in deeper.

I melt into him, letting his mouth wake me up as all the sleepy parts of me start to perk up, a slow buzz igniting inside me.

A knock interrupts us.

Jensen ignores it, completely consumed by our kiss.

The knock turns into a pound.

I pull back. "It's Matt. He's here to help clean."

"Just ignore him. He'll go away," Jensen mutters, voice low, leaning in for another kiss.

I laugh, wiggling free from his arms. He groans as I make my way to the front door.

I swing it open.

Matt steps inside, grinning way too big for ten a.m., and holds up a bag. "Hey, guys. I brought bagels."

Chapter Sixteen

JENSEN

THEN—TWO AND A HALF YEARS AGO

FEBRUARY

"Alright. I think that's it. I think that's everyone."

My mom's voice pulls me from my list. I look up and reach across the large dining room table as she passes me her stack of papers—as in, multiple.

I flip through the endless names. "Mom. This is way too many fucking people."

She rolls her eyes.

I skim the pages, stopping when I land on the Bennetts. "The Bennetts? Seriously? They hate me. Jack spent my entire childhood making my life hell, and now we're sending him a free dinner invitation?"

"Oh, stop. He doesn't hate you."

I keep flipping, irritation rising with every name. "Who the hell are half these people anyway? There's no way you know all of them."

Beside me, I catch Alley's shocked expression as she scans the list in horror.

"These are our friends, Jensen. Your father's and mine."

I set the list down, shaking my head. "No. You need to cut at least a hundred names, Mom. We don't want a wedding this big."

Honestly? I don't care who my mom invites, but I know Alley would love to keep it intimate. She's already pushing past her comfort zone—one hundred guests max, fifty if she had it her way. But between my list, hers, and now my mom's? This thing isn't just big. It's a goddamn production.

"What do you mean you don't want a big wedding? It's already big. Another hundred won't make a difference at this point," she argues.

Alley meets my gaze, and I see the resignation there. "She has a point," she says, forcing a small smile. "What's another hundred when there are already hundreds?"

God bless her for trying to be okay with this. But I'm not. I take a deep breath, then push back from the table, her list in hand. "I'm hungry. I need to eat before I lose my mind."

I give my mom a look that says, *You better follow me.*

My mom hesitates. "Right... I think I'll join you. Alley, do you want anything to eat?" she asks, standing.

Alley's eyes flick up. "No, I'm good. Thanks."

She goes back to figuring out the ceremony while I head to the kitchen, my mom trailing behind me.

As soon as we're out of earshot, I turn to my mom, keeping my voice low but firm. "What are you doing? You can't just take over like this."

She fires back in the same hushed tone. "I'm not taking over! You asked me to make a list of people we wanted to invite to the wedding. That's what I did!"

"Mom, this list is ridiculous. No one has this many friends. No one cares about this many people. And I guarantee half of them don't give two shits about you, let alone me and Alley."

I flip through the pages, frustration mounting. "Who the hell are Roger and Janice Baker?"

"Oh, that's a couple we met at wine club a few years ago. They're great. You'd really like them."

"Would, as in, I've never even met them?" I shake my head. "Yeah, that's gonna be a no."

She lets out an exasperated sigh. "Why is this such a big deal? We're paying for the wedding. Can't we have a say? We're excited! We want to celebrate you both, introduce you to people who care about us."

"That's bullshit, and you know it." I exhale sharply, gripping the papers tighter. "This isn't about us. It's about status. The never-ending New York game of who had the bigger, better wedding. Who can pack a room with the most people that don't actually give a shit. No. You guys get one hundred and fifty guests. That's it. Pick your favorites."

"What? That's impossible! There are over four hundred people on this list."

"Looks like you've got some work to do." I hold the stack of papers out to her.

"This isn't what we want, Mom. Alley hates attention. Her entire guest list barely fills one page." I sigh, lowering my voice. "Look, I love you, but this day isn't about you. It's not even about me, not really. The ceremony? Yeah, that's ours. But the wedding, the reception? That's for Alley." I hold her gaze, softening my tone, letting her hear how much this matters. "Please. Just make it perfect for her. She deserves that".

My mom's brows knit together as she begrudgingly takes back the list, blowing out a slow exhale. "Fine. I'll cut the guest list. And you're right... It's not about me. I want this day to be perfect for you both."

She pauses, giving me a long look before shaking her head with a small, wry smile. "You know, I guess I should be proud right now."

I frown. "Proud? Of what?"

She lets out a soft laugh, her expression shifting to something more serious. "Because you're a good man. I'm proud of you, son."

I clear my throat. "Thanks, Mom." I pull her into a hug. She's the greatest. She's always had my back, and there isn't a thing she wouldn't do for me. And now she has Alley's back, too. That means more than she probably even realizes.

We walk back to the dining room, and I settle back down next to Alley.

"Where are the snacks?" she asks knowingly.

"Um..."

She laughs. "Ah, busted! Come on, I know you two went in there to talk about me."

Alley looks at my mom. "Christy, I promise it's not a big deal. Does having that many people watching me walk down the aisle make me anxious? Sure. But honestly, I'm going to feel that way regardless of the number of people there. So truly, whether it's one hundred or five hundred, it's all nerve-racking to me." She offers a small smile. "I just appreciate you both helping plan, paying for the wedding, and being there for us. If a large wedding makes you happy, I get it. Invite the people you want to invite."

My mother grins, glancing between us fondly. "You two are so lucky to have found each other, you know that?" Her gaze lands on Alley. "How about a compromise? The wedding is bigger than you both want, but I'll cut the guest list."

Alley's smile stretches wide. "That sounds perfect." She reaches for me under the table, grazing my thigh, giving it a squeeze. My hand instinctively falls over hers.

"Alright. If you two don't need me for anything else today, I'm going to go ponder my guest list and decide who's getting the cut." Mom winks, grabs her dictionary of names, and scurries off.

Alley leans in, brushing her lips against mine. "Thank you," she murmurs. Then she grins. "While you two were off playing secret agents with the guest list, I think I figured out the wedding line."

"Oh, you did, huh?" I kiss her and immediately go in for seconds. "God, I love your lips." My fingers weave between hers.

She smiles against my mouth, parting her lips to let me in. We kiss for several seconds before she finally pulls back, sighing.

"We need to stay on task." She looks down at her paper.

I groan. "Come on, baby." I lean in, whispering in her ear. "Let's go fuck in one of the back bedrooms."

She laughs. "Oh my gosh, you're ridiculous. Not here."

"Why not here?"

"Because... your mom's home. That's weird."

"Why is that weird? It's not like we haven't had sex here before." I smirk. "Remember Christmas Eve? And morning?"

She shakes her head like she thinks I'm joking.

I'm not. Obviously.

"Come on, I never had my snack. And do you know what I'm craving?"

Her lips curve. "Ooh, let me guess… starts with P, ends in Y?"

I nod. "Yep. And I'm really, *really* hungry."

She giggles. "Okay, horndog. I'll make you a deal. Give me ten more minutes of your undivided attention, and I'll sit on your face in any bedroom you want."

"Done. Done. And fucking done." I scoot in closer. "So, what are we looking at here?"

She laughs softly, her eyes locking onto mine with adoration. "I love you." She presses a quick peck to my cheek before turning back to her paper.

"Alright. Back to the ceremony. Jeff and Amber go first, then Megan and Kevin. Matt and Scarlett—which, by the way, she's going to love. Then Zach and Stella, since Michael will be walking with me. Four and four. It lines up perfectly. And the kids will go last, right before Michael and me."

She takes a deep breath.

I sense it—that flicker of doubt. I know what it is. And I don't want to push, don't want to make her sad. But I have to try.

I place a hand on her back, rubbing gently. "You're sure you don't want to invite your dad?" I ask, keeping my tone light, as if I haven't already asked her ten times.

She shrugs.

A shrug… What?

She's never shown even an ounce of uncertainty in all the times we've had this conversation.

There's a beat of silence before she answers. "Nah. He wouldn't come anyway." She goes somber, and it tears at my heartstrings—that look.

Here I am with this massive, loving, overbearing family—so many people my mom can't even narrow it down. And then there's Alley. Her list barely filling a single page.

Front only.

I pick up her guest list, scanning over the names. Michael and Stella. Leo and his girlfriend, Vivian. A few childhood friends. Zach and Joey. Scarlett. Cindy. A few coworkers. An aunt and uncle.

That's it.

No friends of parents. No dad. No other family members.

It breaks me.

"Hey," I say, my voice low, soft. "Thanks for compromising with my mom. I know having a big wedding freaks you out... especially when you won't know half the people there."

"It's not a big deal, babe. She's excited for us. And she *is* paying for it. It's the least we can do." She scribbles something in her notebook. "Besides, I'll have you to hold my sweaty hands and catch me if I pass out." She grins at me. "All that matters is that we're getting married."

Damn. I don't know what I did to deserve her.

If there's a God, I'm pretty sure he messed up because somehow, I'm getting the far better end of this deal. And Alley? She deserves a hell of a lot more than what she's stuck with, and I'll spend the rest of my life making sure she never regrets it.

A soft chuckle slips out. "Come here."

I cup the back of her neck, closing the space between us. Our mouths meet, and I drink her in, savoring the warmth.

Her lips are soft, supple. Her tongue strokes against mine, and I deepen the kiss, pulling her closer before finally easing back.

"Thank you," I murmur, our breaths mingling. "And I'm still hungry." A sly smirk tugs at my lips.

"You craving a side of Alley?" she teases.

"No. I want the whole damn entrée."

I push back from the table, pulling her up with me. In one swift motion, I lift her, her legs wrapping around my waist as she gasps, then laughs, holding onto me tighter.

Her lips find mine again as I carry her down the hall to the back bedroom—the one that's technically ours.

Pushing the door open, I walk her to the bed and collapse onto it, tugging her shirt over her head. She reaches for mine, pulling it off with my help. Her hands move to her pants, sliding them down.

She pauses. "Wait... lock the door."

I groan but obey, dragging myself away just long enough to turn the lock. By the time I face her again, she's sliding her underwear down her legs, watching me with that look. I guess we're skipping foreplay. Not that I ever need it. I'm already hard as hell for her.

My gaze drops between her thighs, and damn—like my cock wasn't already desperate for her. A slow grin spreads across my face, excitement building. "Scoot to the edge of the bed for me, baby."

She shifts closer, anticipation clear in her eyes. I drop to my knees, sliding my hands up her thighs, squeezing lightly before settling between them.

"Fuck, Lola's pretty." I shoot her a mischievous grin, hooking her legs over my shoulders.

She laughs. "Oh my God, that's such a weird compliment."

I chuckle against her skin, trailing my tongue up the inside of her thigh as my thumb circles her clit.

She moans softly, and fuck, the sound alone is such a turn-on— never gets old. I press a kiss against her inner thigh, then another, dragging it out, savoring her. *Jesus.* She's so soft and smooth. Nothing better than feeling bare skin against my tongue.

Her fingers thread into my hair, tugging gently, and I flick my tongue over her clit—just once—before pulling back.

Her legs tense around my shoulders. "Babe," she whines. "Don't tease."

I grin against her skin, then seal my lips around her clit, sucking just hard enough to make her hips jolt. Her fingers tighten in my hair, and I groan against her, the sound vibrating between her thighs.

God. She's so wet. This is the best thing ever. It's better than football. It's better than vacations. And it's a hell of a lot better than wedding planning.

Her hips roll against my mouth, chasing the friction, chasing more. I groan, gripping her thighs tighter. I can feel how close she is, and I fucking love it. I love this. I love her. I work her faster, harder, determined to send her over the edge—and when she finally does, my name leaves her lips in a breathless, desperate moan that shoots straight through me.

Damn.

I love this woman.

Chapter Seventeen

JENSEN

THEN

ALLEY SLIPS into the passenger seat of my Audi as I load our luggage into the trunk. Her giant suitcase takes up half the space, and I chuckle to myself. Three days. That's all we'll be gone for, and she's packed like we're leaving the country. Then again, it's winter. I'll give her that.

I slide into the driver's seat, settling in for the three-hour drive to the Berkshires for a long weekend ski trip with my siblings. By the time we hit the road, Alley's already connected her phone to my Bluetooth.

"What do you want to listen to?" she asks, scrolling through her playlists.

"I don't care, babe. I'll listen to almost anything." I flash her a grin. "Just pick something we both like."

Alley and I have wildly different tastes in music, but I learned a long time ago—always let the woman control the music. If she's happy, everybody's happy.

"Alright." She taps on her screen. "I'll just throw on a playlist with a little of everything."

"Works for me." I lean over, stealing a quick kiss before shifting my focus back to the road.

Matt's parents own an estate in Lenox. The grandkids all stay with Grandma and Grandpa so the adult kids can get drunk and enjoy the slopes. This trip's been an annual thing for years.

Alley's never been. She couldn't get work off last year, and the year before that, Michael was in town. This will be her first time. She's never even stepped into a pair of skis, and I can't wait to teach her.

I know having a newbie will slow me down, but it's not like I'm some pro. I just love skiing, and getting to do it with her? That's what matters. It's going to be great.

We chat about work and wedding planning for the first thirty minutes of the drive. Then silence settles in—the kind that's comfortable but also makes me want to stir shit up.

Time for some fun.

"Hey, babe." I glance over at her.

"Yeah?" She doesn't look up from her phone.

"Would you rather..." I pause, a grin creeping in as I carefully craft the most disturbing scenario possible. "Accidentally text a full-frontal nudie to my mom—wait, no! Changed my mind, my dad... or"— I bite back a laugh—"have to moan, in a real sexual way, every time you make eye contact with someone?"

Alley's head snaps up. "Oh my God." Laughter bursts out of her. "You cannot be serious."

I furrow my brows. "I'm dead serious, babe. You know I love this game."

She rubs her forehead, grinning. "Oh, God. I can't with the moaning. I guess your dad's getting a nudie." She cringes.

"Really?" I'm actually a little shocked she chose that. "My dad?"

"Yeah, it'd be real weird for a minute, but we'd get over it... My turn."

She pauses, thinking. Then her eyes light up. "Would you rather... never have to work another day in your life, or never be able to go down on me again, or anyone, for that matter, ever again?"

I don't even hesitate. "Nope." I glance over at her. "I fucking love your pussy, baby. I wouldn't give that up for anything."

A smile spreads across her face. "Ah, that's so sweet... and honestly kind of disturbing—but very on brand for you."

She leans across the console and presses a kiss to my cheek.

I smirk. "What about you?"

"What about me?"

"Would you give up sucking my dick to never work again?" I bite back a laugh, watching her reaction.

Her brows draw together as she bites her bottom lip, trying—and failing—to smother a laugh. "I... agh, God, I love my job, but..."

"What?!" I whip my head toward her, mock-offended. "You love your job? You don't love my dick?"

She giggles. "No, of course I love your dick, babe. And I love what your dick does to me."

I let out a dry laugh. "Wow. The truth comes out." I glance down. "You hear that, Clark?"

"Babe! Come on." She swats my arm. "Never having to work again? That's hard to pass up. I mean... I'll do anything else you want to make up for it."

I cock an eyebrow. "Anal?"

She presses her lips together, her head bobbing like she's trying to convince herself. "Yeah... maybe. Yep. I think I'd even do anal." She points a finger at me, narrowing her eyes. "But only if I'm also retired."

I laugh as she waves a hand. "Moving on."

She pauses, thinking. Then turns to me, her lips curving mischievously. "Would you rather... have a full-blown orgasm every time someone shakes your hand OR have to bark like a dog every time someone says 'hello'?"

"Full-blown orgasm. Easily."

Alley gapes at me in disbelief. "A full-blown orgasm?"

"Over barking like a dog? Fuck yeah. Give me an orgasm all day, every day."

She shakes her head, laughing. "Your turn."

"Alright, alright. Gotta make this a good one." I rub my chin, thinking. Then it comes to me. "Got one. Would you rather... suck Kevin's dick or Jeff's? If you *had* to." I emphasize with a teasing grin, watching as her face scrunches in immediate disgust.

She bursts out laughing. "I can't answer that. I'm not sucking any of your family members' dicks."

"Of course you're not. But if you had to... who's it gonna be?"

She groans, shaking her head. "I hate you." Then, without hesitation—"Kevin's."

My jaw drops. "Whoa-hoa! Kev's? Why Kev?"

Her eyes gleam smugly. "Oh, now you need to know why?"

I nod, grinning. "Oh, yeah."

She shrugs. "Kev looks like he'd come faster."

Laughter explodes out of me.

"I'm kidding," she says, cracking up. "Jeff looks too much like you, but also not enough like you at the same time. If that makes sense. It'd be way weirder."

Our laughter fades, but the amusement still lingers in her eyes as she leans in close. "But do you know whose dick I do wanna suck?"

My cock twitches at her words, her breath hot against my neck. "Whose?"

"Yours." Her hand slides across my thigh, finding the growing bulge confined in my jeans.

Raising an eyebrow, I say, "Right now?"

I steal a quick glance at her. Her eyes have gone dark, and she nods vigorously.

"Yep. Now." Her fingers pop the button of my jeans, tugging the zipper down smoothly.

Heat floods my veins, excitement crackling through me. *Hell yes,* I haven't had road head in years.

I lift my hips as Alley tugs at my pants and boxer briefs, just enough to free my dick—fully hard now and already aching for her.

Her fingers wrap around the base, giving me a slow, teasing stroke. She leans in, her lips brushing my ear. "I can't wait to have this big, hard cock in my mouth."

Fuck. A shiver ripples through me, my grip tightening on the wheel. "Jesus."

She lowers her head, her breath hot, teasing, maddening as it ghosts over the tip.

Focus on the road, man.

I force my gaze forward, my heart racing as she swirls her tongue over the head, then drags it up the length of me before cradling my balls in her fingertips. My abs flex, a groan slipping from my throat.

She flicks her tongue over the sensitive ridge, then finally—finally wraps her lips around me, lowering down slow and deep.

"Fuuuuck. That feels so good."

She hums around me, the vibration sending a sharp jolt of pleasure straight to my spine. Her hand tightens around my base as she works me deeper, hollowing her cheeks, sucking just right.

My fingers flex against the wheel, vision blurring for half a second. I should pull over, let her do this properly, maybe get her off too.

But is it really *road head* if you stop the car? Feels like cheating.

She does something with her tongue—suction, pressure, a twist of both—and I inhale sharply, my body tensing. Shit. It's so good. Too fucking good.

"Goddamn, baby, you're my fucking queen."

She picks up the pace, her head moving faster, working me with expert precision. My right hand falls to her back, slipping into her pants, gripping her ass—needing to touch her.

I squeeze my eyes shut for a second, my chest rising and falling in quick, shallow breaths. *I have to focus. I have to—*

She flicks her tongue, her lips tightening around me, and she moans as she sucks my length deep, sending a bolt of pleasure straight through me. Then she slips a finger past my balls, applying just the right amount of pressure.

I swear to God, I almost black out.

"Shit, baby, I'm gonna come." My muscles lock up, my grip tightening on her, ready to pull back—

But she doesn't stop. She takes me deeper. Takes all of me.

Holy. Fucking. Shit.

She's never done this. Never let me come in her mouth.

A groan tears from my throat as my climax rips through me like a goddamn hurricane—consuming, destructive—so good I can barely keep my eyes on the road.

When she finally pulls off, she wipes the corner of her mouth with her thumb and grins as she reaches for her water.

I'm still catching my breath. "Al." I shake my head, grinning. "That was incredible. And really fucking cool of you."

She laughs, leaning in for a kiss. "It wasn't so bad, honestly. I expected it to be so much worse."

A low chuckle rumbles in my chest. "Well, for the record, I fully support this new chapter in our relationship."

I weave my fingers between hers, my grip firm, my heart still pounding faster than normal.

The road stretches ahead, and my eyes shift between the highway and the woman beside me—Alley. My beautiful, fucking perfect fiancée. A slow grin tugs at my lips as I lift her hand to my lips.

I'm a lucky son of a bitch.

* * *

Two hours later, we pull into the estate, snow falling thick and heavy, coating everything in white. It started about thirty minutes ago and hasn't let up since. The roads were getting slick as it began to stick, so I'm glad we made it earlier rather than later.

Two cars sit side by side in the driveway—Kevin and Jeff's.

"Looks like we beat Matt and Jordan," I say, putting the car in park next to Kevin's Range Rover.

A few minutes later, we're rolling our luggage into the living room. Warmth hits my face the second we step inside. The fire's raging, and the whole cabin smells like burning pine with whatever candle Megan's lit this time.

Matt's parents come here often and keep this place stocked like they're prepping for the apocalypse. There's neatly stacked logs beside the sleek black fireplace, and I know the cabinets will be full of snacks and supplies.

Kevin's already sprawled in the armchair, one leg hooked over the side like he owns the place. Amber's curled up on the couch with a book, Jeff's in the kitchen mixing a drink, and Megan scrolls through her phone. It's the same setup as always.

Same scene. Same people. Same weekend tradition. Except now, I'm walking in with Alley—my future wife.

"Hey guys!" I call across the room.

Amber looks up, smiling as she echoes, "Hey guys." She starts to get up, while Jeff shouts from the kitchen, asking what we want to drink. Megan and Kev mumble half-hearted greetings from their spots.

"Anything with tequila," I call back to Jeff as I shrug off my coat, shaking out the cold. I turn to Alley, reaching for hers, only to find her still standing there, mouth gaping as she takes it all in.

"Holy crap. This place is phenomenal." Her grin spreads wide, eyes going big as she turns to meet my gaze. "I'm so excited to be here!"

I guess it does have a bit of a shock factor for a first-timer. Huge open space, floor-to-ceiling windows framing nothing but trees covered in snow. And I'm not one to get all in my feels about scenery, but damn—it's beautiful.

Megan finally peels herself off the couch, coming over to hug us after Amber. "How was the drive?" she asks.

"It was good," Alley and I say at the same time.

"Went by fast," I add.

Alley kicks off her boots and steps onto the wood floor. "Holy shit. The floors are heated."

"Just wait till you take a shit," Kevin calls from across the room.

I chuckle, catching Alley's gaze.

Megan shoots Kevin a look of disgust. "Get your ass off the couch and come say hello."

"All the toilets have bidets with heated seats and warm water," I tell Alley.

Megan turns back to her with a deadpan expression. "It's like a day spa for your ass."

"Can't wait," Alley says with a laugh, her one dimple sinking deep into her cheek. Swear to God, my heart fucking bursts.

"I'm gonna grab my drink. What can I get you?" I ask, kicking off my shoes.

Her gaze sweeps over the kitchen counter, lighting up when she spots the espresso machine.

"Can you make me a coffee?"

"Sure thing, babe." I press a quick kiss to her lips and turn toward the kitchen—

Megan grabs my arm, yanking me back. "Will you make me an espresso martini?"

I arch a brow. "Do we have the stuff for that?"

"Of course we do. You know how I love your espresso martinis. You make them the best." She flashes me a grin. "I brought everything. It's all on the counter."

"Matt makes them better," I say, matter-of-fact.

"I know, but he's not here." Megan gives me a sweet, pleading smile before pressing her hands together in fake prayer. "Pleeeease."

I chuckle, giving in. "Sure. Whatever." I pull free from her grasp and head into the kitchen.

Twenty minutes later we're all gathered in the living room, drinks in hand, catching up. Megan's mid-rant about a woman at her work having an affair with a coworker when Matt's car finally pulls up.

He steps out, grabbing his bag, and I do a double take. No Jordan?

I watch the passenger door, waiting, expecting her to emerge. But she doesn't.

Megan notices instantly. "Where the hell is Jordan?"

I shrug, catching her eye—a look passes between us, saying everything we're thinking but not saying.

I exhale. "Who fucking knows?"

The door swings open, and Matt's voice booms through the cabin. "Hey, guys."

He steps in, stomping the snow off his boots as he pulls off his coat. He kicks off his shoes, barely pausing before heading straight for the kitchen.

We all greet him, but he's already reaching for the whiskey, practically pouring before he even grabs a glass.

Yeah. Something's up.

I make my way over as everyone else falls back into conversation. Sensing something off, I tread carefully. "Hey, man. How was the drive?"

"Good," he says, voice neutral. "Peaceful."

Too neutral.

I study him, but he keeps his gaze locked on his drink, swirling the amber liquid. "Yeah? What happened to Jordan?"

He exhales sharply, dragging a hand down his face. "Bailed last minute. Something about a new guy she's seeing."

I raise a brow. "Really? Damn."

He lets out a bitter chuckle. "Told her she could have her own room. We're just friends. But I don't know, man... some guys just aren't secure enough to let their girl have guy friends."

"Yeah. Hard to say where the line is with that." I don't really know what to say. We all know if Jordan came, they'd sleep together. It's just what they do. And honestly? If she's finally putting her foot down because she's seeing someone, good for her.

But I still feel for Matt. It's not just about sex. He loves hanging out with her, too.

Matt mutters something under his breath in disagreement.

"Sorry, man. Hopefully, you guys can work things out when you get back," I say, taking a sip of my drink.

He scoffs. "Yeah, I'm not holding my breath. She'll push me out of her life—like she always does when she's seeing someone."

I get it. But I can't blame her, either. "Well, you'll deal with it like you always do. But for now, just try to forget about it and enjoy the weekend."

Matt nods, letting out a slow breath. "Yeah, you're right. I'll deal with it later. So, what's the plan?"

"For tonight? Drinking, games... just shooting the shit."

He takes a sip of his Old Fashioned. "Sounds exactly like the kind of night I need."

I clap Matt on the back, then head for the living room. Sinking onto the couch, I wrap an arm around Alley, pulling her close. She leans into me without hesitation, like she belongs there.

The fire crackles, drinks are flowing, Megan's laugh carries through the wide open space—it's the same weekend tradition I've known for years. But it hits different this time.

I give Alley's shoulder a squeeze, pressing a quick kiss to her temple. Yeah. This is gonna be one to remember.

* * *

"Snowplow, babe! Plow! Plow!"

Too late.

Alley flies straight for me, arms crossed over her face like she's bracing for impact. I plant my skis, ready to take the hit—but at the last second, she flings herself backward, landing hard on her ass.

A puff of powder explodes around her as she skids to a stop just inches from my feet.

She blinks up at me, dazed. Then bursts out laughing. "Oh my God. That could've been so bad."

I exhale a laugh as I crouch to help her up. "Jesus, babe. You're gonna take someone out. You okay?"

She takes my hand, groaning as she stands. "Yeah. But I think I bruised my ass."

I click out of my skis, then bend down to unclip hers. "Maybe next time, don't panic-flop."

She lets out another laugh, brushing snow off her pants. "Oh, that's what we're calling it?"

I chuckle. She's a disaster out here. She keeps forgetting how to stop, her turns are a lost cause, and after three hours, we're no closer to getting off the bunny hill than we were ninety minutes ago. But she's a damn good sport. And even though I'm itching to hit a tougher run, I'm having a blast.

Alley has a way of making everything fun. Shit, she could make knitting fun. (Not that I'd ever willingly do that. Jesus.)

She presses a quick kiss to my cheek. "Thanks for sticking with me."

"Always," I say grinning.

She sighs dramatically. "I think I need a break. Wanna grab a beer? Then you can meet up with the guys and hit a few runs."

"That sounds perfect." I pause, frowning. "You sure you're good with me ditching you for a bit?"

She waves me off. "Oh yeah. That fireplace in the lodge is calling my name. I'll be fine, babe. I have my Kindle."

We trudge toward the lodge, skis in tow. She's still a little wobbly in her boots, but managing. And when she stumbles, laughing at herself, I can't help but laugh with her.

She may suck at skiing. But she's still my favorite person to do it with.

Outside the lodge, we prop our skis in the designated racks, then step inside. The blast of heat is instant, thawing my face. *God, that feels good.*

Matt's already at the bar, beer in hand, looking gloomy as hell. This thing with Jordan is messing with his head, but I don't know if it will ever be enough to make him change—make him want more.

As we approach, he exhales, rolls his shoulders, then plasters a smile on his face like nothing's wrong. "Hey, you're alive!" He stands, pulling Alley into a hug. Classic Matt—acting like he's fine, drowning whatever he's feeling in booze and jokes.

Within minutes, I've managed to pull him out of it—or at least, he's letting me think I have. We're all laughing, Matt and I reminiscing about past ski trips, dragging Alley into the stories.

My gaze locks on her as she laughs, the sound ringing out over the bar, her smile lighting up the whole damn room. I could watch her forever. The way her dimple pops when she laughs, how her eyes brighten when Matt teases her, how her voice is so effortlessly cheerful it could make the saddest person feel happy—even if only for a moment.

She's not loving the skiing, I know that. But she'll keep coming, year after year. Just like football. She'll either pretend to love it, learn to love it, or push through. And that thought—the way she does these things for me—fuck. It makes my chest ache.

There's not another woman in the world like Alley.

Not one.

And I'm so fucking grateful she chose me.

Chapter Eighteen

ALLEY

THEN

I DRAIN the last of the champagne in my plastic cup and turn to the mirror again, a laugh bursting out as I take myself in.

"Take that ugly-ass dress off, now!" Megan says, her laughter echoing through the store. The second we make eye contact, I completely lose it.

"Shh! You guys!" Amber scolds, though she's fighting back her own laugh.

"She looks like she's about to become a sister wife from the 1800s," Megan snorts, doubling over.

I bend at the waist, tears stinging my eyes from laughing so hard.

This dress *is* awful. And honestly? I do look like I'm about to join a cult. I don't even know how it ended up in the try-on pile—probably Megan's doing.

Megan and I have gotten really close over the past two years. She and Kevin don't live far from us, and we double-date all the time. The guys wanted to hit the slopes again today, but honestly, I was tapped out. Whether Megan and Amber were too or they're just appeasing me, I'm not sure, but they rallied for a girls' day. We found a little bridal shop nearby and figured, why not? Wedding dress shopping sounded way better than falling on my ass all day in the freezing cold.

We've been at it for a couple hours now, and I can't remember the last time I laughed this hard—though, to be fair, Jensen makes me laugh daily.

I haven't found the one yet, but I'm still hopeful, and I've definitely found plenty of worst-case scenarios.

"Is it time to try another store? Or should we take a break?" I ask, turning to face them.

Amber glances around. "I don't know if there are any other bridal stores in this town."

Megan bursts out laughing again. "I can't even take you seriously in that dress. Let's grab an early dinner, then shop for the wedding night instead. Pretty sure we all need a break. And we can all benefit from some new lingerie and toys."

Amber perks up. "Ooh, I like that idea."

I avoid the mirror at all costs so I don't bust up laughing again. "Alright. That's a great plan. Meg, find us a place to eat, and Amber—help me out of this damn dress."

"On it." Megan holds up a finger, already reaching for her phone.

Amber steps behind me, starting on the tiny hooks down my back. "So... have you and Jensen picked a honeymoon spot yet?"

"Not yet. We've narrowed it down to Thailand or Bali, but we haven't made a final decision. I'm just excited to go somewhere new with warm weather, beaches, and no wedding planning."

"Thailand is amazing," Megan chimes in. "But I haven't been to Bali. I've heard great things though. Either way, you can't go wrong." She glances down at her phone. "Oh! I found a place. It's called The Grove, and it's only a seven-minute walk."

I step out of the dress and reach for my pants. "Seven minutes in this weather is seven minutes of torture."

"Oh, I know. It's actual hell... We'll walk fast." Megan slips her phone into her purse and stands as I tug my shirt over my head. I do a quick sweep of the dressing room, making sure we didn't leave anything behind, then the three of us grab our coats and head out.

And somewhere in those seven minutes, I realize these aren't just my friends—they're my sisters.

* * *

I WALK into the living room wearing leggings and a cozy sweatshirt, my bag of goodies from earlier clutched in one hand, and fall into the couch. Megan's already camped out on the other end with a glass of Merlot, her bag resting in her lap like it's prized treasure. Amber's in the kitchen, dumping popcorn into a giant bowl. She douses it in melted butter, gives it a heavy sprinkle of salt, then grabs the bowl and a glass of wine and joins us—her bag already saving the seat in the middle.

We had an amazing dinner and then hit up this lingerie and sex toy shop called The Cheeky Boutique. Totally cheesy name, but the store was amazing. We all tried on lingerie, laughed our asses off, and made a pact to each buy three things: something to wear, something for him, and something new to try. There was one rule—no peeking. Nobody could see what the others were buying until we got home.

Now we're sitting here, bags in hand like a bunch of kids on Christmas morning, itching to see what's inside. Megan has the movie —*Beaches*—paused and ready to go on the home screen. She and Amber nearly lost it when I admitted I've never seen it, so apparently that's happening tonight because I *have* to see it.

The boys are still out, extending their day on the slopes into a full-blown guys' night. Naturally, that means they'll all stumble in drunk, which might actually work in my favor. I'm a little nervous about some of the stuff in my bag, and part of me is worried I'll feel dumb trying to pull it off. But if Jensen's not totally sober, maybe I won't overthink it. Maybe I'll just let him take the lead and feed off his adventurous energy.

My phone vibrates in my lap.

JENSEN

Hey babe, we just finished dinner. Heading to a bar with live music. You sure you don't want to come out? I miss you and that sweet ass of yours.

I smile to myself, thumb hovering over the screen.

> Haha, I miss you too! I'm sure. We're all cozied up by the fireplace. Just don't be out too late… Got some new toys to try out. 😉

Amber glances over, holding out the bowl of popcorn. "What are you grinning at?"

"Oh, nothing. Just Jensen being Jensen... you know, cute."

Megan makes a face, scrunching her nose. "Ugh, I forget you both fuck my brothers. This suddenly feels like a terrible idea. Do I really want to know what you bought to seduce them?" She mock gags.

We all crack up, and I dig into my bag, pulling out a butt plug and holding it up between two fingers.

"Wait, so do you *not* want to hear about how your brother is obsessed with the idea of doing anal, and I've yet to brave the butt stuff?" I say, half laughing, half cringing at myself. I take a breath, showing off the plug. "Starting small. But... I want to give him that fantasy."

"Hold on." Megan throws her hands up, palms out. "You guys don't do anal?"

Amber's head snaps toward her. "You guys do?"

Megan's jaw drops. "You don't either?" She looks between us, genuinely shocked. "Okay, what the hell? I am *not* the minority here. You two are." She takes a sip of wine, her eyes wide over the rim. "Great, I've officially stepped into an episode of *Sister Wives*. You're both so PG."

"We are *not* PG!" I fire back, laughing. "Give me some credit. I'm trying to be more adventurous. I even gave Jensen road head on the way here. And..." I pause for effect. "I swallowed."

Silence.

Megan blinks, wine glass frozen halfway to her mouth.

"For the first time ever," I add, grinning.

Her mouth drops open. "*Oh. My. God.* Your *first* time ever?"

Amber smacks her leg, shooting her a look. "Atta girl," she says to me, grinning as she holds up her hand for a high five. "That's what I'm talkin' about."

I laugh, giving her a high five, but Megan still hasn't recovered.

"Seriously? First time?" she repeats, like she can't wrap her head around it.

Amber rolls hers eyes. "Yeah, Meg. Calm down."

Megan leans back. "No, I mean... I'm proud, but also, finally! And ew, now I'm thinking about my brother and—" She bursts out laughing mid-sentence, completely losing it. "I'm so glad you're finally swallowing my brother's... spunk," she chokes on the word, dissolving into fits of laughter.

Her whole body is shaking, and despite being the butt of the joke, I can't help but laugh too.

"Oh my God, stop," I say, covering my face, but I'm grinning.

"I'm sorry, I'm sorry," Megan gasps, wiping tears from her eyes. "I've had way too much wine." She takes a deep breath, trying to pull it together, but the second she looks at me again, she snorts, biting her lip to keep from laughing more.

My phone buzzes again.

JENSEN

Do you even know how hot you are? 10/10.
Seriously. And new toys? On my way... haha.

I smile, biting my bottom lip as I quickly type back:

You think? What are you gonna do about that?
Also... your sister is very drunk.

JENSEN

Oh, I've got plans for you and Lola tonight. And
Megan's drunk? What's new? I'm gonna be right
there with her if Matt keeps buying everyone shots.

Before I can respond, Megan turns to Amber. "What'd you get to try?"

I set my phone in my lap as Amber casually reaches into her bag and pulls out a set of nipple clamps. My hands immediately fly to my chest, covering my boobs like that'll somehow protect them. Just looking at those things makes my nipples ache.

"Do people *actually* like that?" I ask, eyeing the clamps like they might bite.

"Oh, Jesus, Alley," Megan mutters, then turns to Amber. "Give her your nipple clamps."

Amber clutches them to her chest, scandalized. "What? No! I bought these for *me*. I've never tried them, but I've always wanted to."

Megan laughs. "Wow. Am I the only kinky one here?"

"Yes," Amber and I say at the same time, grinning at each other.

"Hey, give me a minute to catch up," I add. "Jensen's been... opening my eyes. I mean, my ex before him was seriously vanilla. Like, wouldn't even go down on me. Meanwhile, Jensen wants to set up camp down there."

"Oh my God. Stop. I don't want to picture my brother like that." Megan groans, covering her face.

I lift my brows, smirking. "He's *really* good at it too!"

"Nope. Don't want to know," Megan shakes her head furiously, eyes squeezed shut.

My phone buzzes again in my lap.

JENSEN

I can't wait for you to sit on my face tonight. 😏

I giggle as the text comes through at just the right time.

"Speaking of setting up camp..." I hold up my phone so they can see.

Megan groans, dropping her head back. "Ugh. You guys are still so cute. Where's *my* text?" She picks up her phone, scrolling, then scoffs. "Oh yeah, my husband forgot how to flirt when we had kids."

She sighs. "I swear, I hope they're out getting drunk because Kev needs to loosen the hell up... *live* a little. He's been so busy with work, stressed to the max, and then he comes home with a stick up his ass. But if he's buzzed, I know he'll go down on me tonight. He can't not when he's tipsy."

Amber and I both laugh.

"Excuse me, Kev needs to relax? Hello, I'm married to the king of structure and responsibility." Amber lifts her glass and drains what's left. "I'd kill for Jeff to actually let loose. Sure, he'll have a drink or two, but never enough to really relax. Never enough to just let go and be free."

They both turn to me, expectantly.

"What?" I ask, innocently.

"Come on, you can't bitch about *one* thing with Jensen?" Megan says. "I know you haven't been together for years, but Jesus, you've lived together for what, like a year and a half now?" She raises a brow. "Do you guys even argue? It's like you're fucking perfect. Probably still have sex every day too." She rolls her eyes and takes another sip of wine.

"Honestly? We don't really argue," I say with a shrug. "A few disagreements here and there, but Jensen's easy to get along with. He's good at balancing work and life. He makes time for me, plays basketball to unwind, goes on runs." I reach for more popcorn. "I don't know... we just make a really great team, you know?"

"Yeah, *we* know," Megan mutters, though she's smiling. "And we're jealous as hell."

Amber shoots Megan a playful look. "Give it time, Meg. They won't be perfect forever." She flashes me a teasing grin.

"Stop... You both have great relationships. You're just in a different phase of life than us. I mean, you *do* have kids, for one."

Megan laughs. "We know. We're just giving you shit."

"More like living vicariously through you." Amber says, then turns to me. "Okay, serious question, though. How often do you two have sex?" She leans in close to Megan. "Do you remember when *we* used to have a lot of sex? Before kids came along and murdered our drive?"

"Yes," Megan groans dramatically, before shifting her gaze back to me. "No, but really. I can't believe I haven't asked you this before... probably because I don't want to know about my brother's sex life— but also, I kinda do." She grins. "So? How often? And don't lie. I know Jensen doesn't need to be drunk to go down on you." Her eyes widen. "Wow, that sounded pathetic out loud."

They both stare me down, waiting.

"I don't know. It depends on the week," I say with a shrug. "Just kind of varies with life and work and what's going on."

Megan immediately shakes her head. "Nope. Not good enough. We need numbers, Al. *Details.* We *need* this."

I sigh, my cheeks warming. "Fine. I don't know... probably four or five times a week?"

Megan's brows shoot up, and Amber's eyes go big as they exchange a look. "That's like... almost every day."

"I know," Megan says, glancing back at me. "Okay, but how often does he go down on you?"

I laugh, covering my face for a second. "I don't know... when he feels like it. Which is a lot."

Amber groans playfully. "God, I remember when we used to have sex that much." There's a hint of nostalgia in her voice. "To be fair, we still do it two or three times a week, but I'm not as horny as I used to be, and I wish I was. I probably need to get my hormones checked."

Megan laughs. "And I remember when Kev used to come home on his lunch break just to go down on me. God, I need my kids to be in school full-time. My libido finally came back full force, but now we're never alone." She sighs. "That's why I just wanna get drunk tonight with you ladies, let Kev get drunk too, and let alcohol work its magic. I love drunk sex. It makes me feel like a sex goddess."

I'm about to chime in, when my phone buzzes in my lap.

JENSEN

Babe, come down here. We're having so much fun. Matt's buying shots.

Jesus. More shots?

JENSEN

I fuckin love you, babe. You're the best. Best ass too.

Best road head giver too.

Sorry. Shots are hittin me.

I bite my bottom lip, smiling. He's clearly had a few, but even out with the guys, drunk as can be, I'm still the number one thing on his mind. It's definitely a turn-on.

I hope he gets home soon. Hopefully not *too* drunk, though—because drunk sex hits different when one person's sober. It's good, but it can be a lot.

There was one night, after one of Matt's parties, when Jensen had been pretty drunk. I'd only had a beer, but when we got home... damn. The sex was hot—messy and a little sloppy—but oh, so good. He couldn't finish, though. It just kept going and going, until finally, I had to laugh and tell him, *"Okay, let's pick this up in the morning."*

But even then, he was still so Jensen—sweet, determined, focused only on me. God, when he's had a few? The things that man says in bed—mouth like a dirty poet, and hands that know exactly what to do.

I shift on the sofa, heat winding low in my stomach, pooling between my thighs just thinking of him whispering in my ear. Holy hell. I need him to come home.

JENSEN

I'm so lucky. Like. Luckier than anyone. You're pretty. Also Matt is dumb.

Did I already tell you what a great ass you have? I think your butt is the best. The best butttttttt.

I let out a laugh, and the girls glance over at me. "The guys are drunk. Jensen's probably one drink away from a real shitty tomorrow."

"Typical Jensen. Never knows when to stop." Megan smiles into her wine glass, taking a sip like what she said is nothing more than a harmless observation.

Her comment grates, but I force a smile, my stomach tightening in a way I can't explain.

Sure, Jensen's had his fair share of drunk nights, who hasn't? But he knows when to stop. He's always been good at that. He rarely even gets a hangover.

He's fine.

I cross my arms, trying to shrug off the unease crawling up my spine. "He knows his limits," I say, maybe a little too firmly.

Megan scoffs. "Ah, I forget you never met pre-thirties Jensen."

"Well, he hasn't been in his thirties that long. You're saying three years ago he was just a complete shit show?" I ask, my defenses rising.

Megan glances over at me, brows raised like she hears the edge in my voice. "No... I'm just saying he's been known to overdo it. But I guess we all did before we got married. I didn't mean anything by it. I've just seen him at his worst, but that was a long time ago."

I nod like I'm letting it go, but my chest stays tight—a little seed of something from Megan's words planting itself deep within me. I take a breath, forcing my shoulders to relax. "Okay. Well thanks." I gesture toward her bag, needing a shift in conversation. "What did you buy?"

A grin spreads across Megan's face as she reaches into her bag and pulls out a monster dildo—a full-on, human-looking penis with a suction cup on the back. I blink at it, wide-eyed.

"This sticks to the shower wall. I've got one similar already, but this baby has all the bells and whistles. It vibrates and rotates—the whole works. I'm sooo excited to try it. Kev's been traveling a lot for work, and this is gonna do me right." She smirks so smugly you'd think she already took it for a test drive.

Amber tries to not laugh. "That's a pretty girthy dick, Meg."

"Just the way I like it, Amber."

Amber holds up a fist, motioning upward. "That's basically a fist."

Megan's brows raise. "Which is exactly what I want. No one wants a pencil dick. You've gotta *feel* him enter, you know?" She looks at me, eyes narrowing. "Don't tell me you're both settling for subpar. Are my brothers not bringing the goods?" She pauses. "Wait... actually, I don't want to know that."

"Oh! Too late. You asked." I say laughing. "Just so you know, Jensen's dick is perfect. Good girth, good length. It's just right. Not too much, not too little." I grab a handful of popcorn, tossing a piece in my mouth. "Now let's start the movie."

"Good idea," Amber says, getting up to turn off the lights.

Megan points the remote at the TV and hits play. We all settle in, shifting positions and pulling blankets tighter around us as the movie starts.

We get quiet—no more teasing, no more sex talk—just the three of us, popcorn, a bottle of wine, and a good movie.

It's so cozy here. And as much as I hate winter, I could get used to being holed up here for a couple of weeks a year, especially if Jensen and I had the place to ourselves. I totally get why Matt's parents come here so often. It's snowing again, and with the giant windows and the fire flickering—reflecting in the glass—it's absolutely stunning.

About thirty minutes into the movie, I pull out my phone and text Jensen. Mostly to check on him, but also to see where he is on the drunk meter, and when I can expect him.

> Get home ASAP. I'm horny.

His response is immediate.

JENSEN

> FUUUUUUCCCCK. Cummmmming.

I shake my head, grinning. He always says *cumming* anytime I ask how long he'll be or where he is.

> Hurry.

JENSEN

> K. But have to find guys. I'm ddurnk.

> I know. Just cum home ASAP. Need you.

> And your dick.

A second later, he sends a GIF of a fire hydrant shooting out water, and I laugh out loud.

"Sorry," I say, glancing at the girls.

I silence my phone and turn my attention back to the movie, already plotting how I'm going to take advantage of him when he gets home.

Chapter Nineteen

ALLEY

THEN

A DISTANT NOISE pulls me from my sleep. My eyes crack open, adjusting to the dark. I glance over at Jensen's side of the bed. It's still empty.

Fumbling for my phone on the nightstand, I squint against the sudden brightness as I tap the screen. It's 2:30 a.m.

Where the hell is he?

As the fog of sleep lifts, I realize what woke me—the guys. Laughter and hushed voices echo down the hall from the living room. Something crashes, followed by more laughter and shushing.

"Ow! Fuck!"

Matt... God, are they kidding right now?

Jensen and Kevin's laughter carries down the hallway.

"Help me, Kev," Matt groans. "Fucking walk, man. Move your legs."

More laughter, then a deep groan.

"Keep it down, you guys," Jeff mutters, his voice sharp and serious. More shushing follows.

"Do we just leave him out here? Alley's going to kill us if we bring him to her like this."

Matt again.

"Come on, man, get up." Jeff's voice is quieter, more serious. "Matt, knock it off and help me with him."

Cue me. *Awesome.*

I slip out of bed and pull on the sweats from the floor, making my way to the end of the hall.

Jeff and I lock eyes as I cross my arms, taking in the scene. Jensen's sitting on the couch, leaning back with a lazy grin, laughing at something Matt says.

A little knot tightens in my stomach, but I push it aside, watching as Jeff reaches for Jensen's arm, trying to pull him to his feet.

"Alright, bud, time to go to bed," Jeff mutters, clearly struggling to keep Jensen steady once he's standing.

"Noooo, wanna see my girl," Jensen slurs, grinning wide and sloppy, his eyes glassy.

My stomach twists as the words leave his mouth. He's not just tipsy—he's completely gone.

Jeff glances at me, offering a helpless shrug as he starts hauling Jensen toward the hall. "Sorry, Al. I'll help get him to your room."

"Whoooa, heeey, there she is," Jensen adds when he sees me, his words drawn out, like his brain can't quite keep up.

What the hell happened? Why is he this wasted?

I nod to Jeff, pressing my lips together, trying to shove down the mess of feelings swirling inside me.

When we reach the doorway, Jeff pauses. "You good, buddy?"

Jensen nods, lazily swiping Jeff off. "Yeah, yeah. I'm good, bro."

Jeff blows out a breath, running a hand through his hair, looking to me. "Good luck."

Jensen stumbles forward, crashing into the doorframe before I manage to catch him.

His arms snake around me, too heavy, his breath hot against my neck. "Babe... you're so hot... mmm... love you."

I stiffen, my stomach twisting, throat tight. God, he smells like he bathed in a tub of whiskey.

"Hey, let's get you to bed, okay?" I whisper, trying to stay calm, even as my pulse races and a creeping sense of déjà vu settles over me —familiar and too close to home.

He groans against me, mumbling nonsense as I steer him toward the bed, each step harder than the last.

Behind me, Jeff lingers. "He'll be fine, Alley. Just overdid it a little. He'll sleep it off."

I nod, swallowing hard. "Yeah... yeah, sure."

Jeff turns and heads down the hall.

"Oh fuck," Jensen groans, swaying. "I'm sick. Gonna be sick."

He bends at the waist and vomits. Hot, sour liquid splashes over my bare feet.

I freeze. My breath catches, and my heart pounds in my ears. The sharp stench hits me first. Then the heat, clinging to my skin.

Move, my brain screams. *Move. Do something.* But I can't.

"Fuck." He drops to his hands and knees.

I should be getting him to the bathroom, grabbing a towel, rubbing his back—anything but standing here.

More retching pulls me from my stupor, and tears sting my eyes as Jensen dry heaves and vomits again, splashing across the floor.

Panic squeezes my chest as memories slam into me—my mom with my dad, helping him while he stumbled around, trying to keep him upright as he puked in the middle of the living room.

"Shit." Jensen groans, falling to his side, collapsing in the mess, and I can't tell if the storm tearing through me is fear, anger, or sadness.

I know Jensen isn't my dad. I know I'm not my mom. I know he doesn't do this often—if ever.

Dammit. Do something.

The nurse in me kicks in, and suddenly I'm moving—rushing to the bathroom, grabbing towels and wet washcloths. I rinse my feet off in the tub, scrubbing away the stench of bile, before hurrying back to Jensen's side. I lay the towels over the mess. I'll deal with that later.

"Hey, babe. Can you sit up?" I ask softly.

He grunts, and I slowly guide him upright, just enough to peel his shirt over his head before he slumps back down, groaning. I nudge him away from the worst of it, then take the rag and wipe his face.

I feel like his goddamn mother.

Fifteen straight minutes of working—soaking towels, scrubbing, rinsing, wiping—fighting the urge to gag as the smell clings to everything. My hands shake, my stomach turns. And all I can think about is my mom and how she used to do this. Not just for us as kids, but for my dad.

Don't. Don't go there.

I swallow hard, pushing the thought down as I finally get Jensen to the bathroom. I lay him down gently, resting his head near the toilet, tucking a blanket and pillow beside him like I'm caring for a sick child.

I push my hand through his hair, brushing it down his cheek. "You okay?" I whisper, my voice shaky.

He vaguely nods, and I'm taken right back to the last time I saw my dad, to all the times my mom had to help him to the couch or drag him to the bathroom.

The sharp ache in my chest catches me off guard. I've been around plenty of drunk people since moving to New York, but Jensen like this? It's tearing me apart.

Because this is different.

I *love* him.

A tear falls and I catch it with my hand, swiping at my eyes. I know Jensen isn't an alcoholic. I know this isn't some kind of problem. I've seen him drunk before—laughing, playful, a little tipsy. Even full-on drunk. But this? This is something else. This is past drunk.

I lean back against the bathroom vanity, shutting my eyes because I can't look at him like this. I don't want to look at *anyone* like this. But my dad's image burns behind my eyelids—unwanted and vivid.

He's not my dad.

I take a breath, trying to shove down the fear, but it's shaky, unsteady.

He's nothing like him.

Still, I stand frozen, eyes closed, cheeks damp from the few tears I let fall.

Jensen groans and heaves again, and I'm moving before I even think, back at his side, holding him over the toilet. I rub his back, speaking soft, gentle words to him.

God, I hate this.

I get that people over drink sometimes—I do. But Jensen always knows when to stop. He knows when one more is too many. *Was he upset? Did something happen?*

I get him laid back down and eventually crawl into bed. I squeeze my eyes shut, trying to block out the noise from Matt and Kevin down the hall, and my own thoughts, but it doesn't work. My mind races, cycling through every possible scenario of why. I bounce between worry and anger, then start rehearsing all the things I'm going to say to him.

Eventually, my thoughts slow, just enough, but I can't sleep. My eyes crack open, gaze locked on the empty, cold side of the bed—his side. The side where he's supposed to be next to me. The place that's always been mine to curl into him.

It's something my mom dealt with her whole life.

I take a shaky breath and tell myself it's okay. This is a one-time thing. Jensen is *not* my dad. I am *not* my mother.

We're different.

I won't put up with this shit.

Not like she did.

Not ever.

* * *

I didn't sleep well. I tossed and turned all night.

By the time the sun rises, Jensen's still on the bathroom floor, and I'm sunk deep into the couch, my fingers wrapped around my coffee mug keeping my hands warm.

It's a quiet, peaceful morning. The fire flickers in front of me, and a fresh blanket of snow covers the ground. The sun's out, reflecting off the white, and everything's still. It's beautiful. It *should* be calming. But even this perfect morning can't ease my mind from the conversation that needs to happen.

Maybe I'm overreacting. I keep telling myself that. But seeing Jensen that way last night hit something I didn't even know was there. It brought it all back—the things I've buried so deep I almost forget they exist. Is it PTSD? I'm not sure. But it was a trigger. That's for damn sure.

My mind wanders back to the last time I saw my dad. It was about a month after my mom passed. Three weeks since we'd had the funeral.

I was living in an apartment in Evanston with a few girlfriends, splitting rent, sharing rooms, scraping by while going to school. I was working part-time at a coffee shop in the city, and that night, I had gone home looking for a wig for a Halloween party. My mom always kept our old costumes packed in a bin in the closet.

I knew going home wouldn't feel the same without my mom there. But still, I wasn't prepared, not even a little. The second I walked through that front door, I felt it—it wasn't my childhood home anymore.

It reeked of booze—thick and suffocating. Stale liquor and heavy breath clung to the air. The kitchen was trashed, like my dad had forgotten how to function. The sink overflowed with dirty dishes, beer cans piled high, empty liquor bottles lined up on the counter like collector's items. Red Solo cups, pizza boxes, and random crap were scattered across the table and floor.

I stood there, trying to make sense of it, but everything I knew about my home had been stripped away.

My dad had taken every family photo with my mom and turned them face down. It was like he wanted to erase her. Like in some drunken rage, he thought if he smashed everything that reminded him of her, he could somehow get back at cancer—or her for leaving him.

My dad loved my mom. *God, he loved her.* But walking into that house, it was like she had never even existed.

And then I found him.

He was passed out on the floor, in the middle of the hallway, lying in a puddle of vomit. Like he'd tried to make it to the bathroom but never did.

He stirred when I walked by, groaning, and then mumbled, "Ellen?" He was hallucinating. He couldn't tell what was real and what wasn't. Didn't even know it was me—his own daughter.

I've never felt so much sorrow as I did in that moment, freshly grieving my mom—staring at my dad, broken and filthy, asking if I was her.

That's when I knew I was about to lose him too.

The truth is, I had already lost him months before we lost her. His soul left the day he started drinking again. But standing there, watching him reach for someone who wasn't me—who wasn't anyone—something inside me snapped. Anger seethed through me, hot and sharp, mixing with the fresh sting of tears.

I hated him for leaving us. For leaving her. For not even recognizing me.

I hated him.

And it broke me.

I blink away the memory, moisture pooling, blurring my vision as I swallow the lump rising in my throat. Staring down at my coffee, I close my eyes, willing the tears to stay put, but the heaviness lingers, sitting low and tight in my chest.

Guilt gnaws at me, that familiar whisper creeping in—telling me I should've tried harder. I should've stayed. I should've helped him.

But I didn't.

I forgot about the wig. I saw my dad, heard him call for my mother, and turned, cool and collected, right out the door. Straight to my car. I didn't even look back. Didn't clean him up. Didn't help him. Didn't cry. *Dammit, I didn't even say goodbye.* I just left.

And I haven't been back.

He texted me a few times, even tried calling, at first. But over time, the messages stopped. The calls stopped.

I let him go.

And he let me.

A tear slides down my cheek as a door closes in the distance. I wipe my eyes and glance at my phone. It's still early, only eight. Turning my head, I catch sight of Jensen making his way down the hall, looking like death himself.

His eyes are half-closed, one hand pressed against his forehead, probably nursing a raging headache. His joggers hang low on his hips—like pulling them up took too much effort. And even from here, I can see the way his morning erection tents the front of his pants.

A smile tugs at the corners of my mouth, *dammit,* I can't help myself. He's still sexy as hell, even when he's half alive. I'm still pissed at him, though.

"Morning," he croaks as he shuffles past, heading straight for the kitchen medicine cabinet.

I watch the muscles in his back shift as he sorts through a cluster of bottles. Finally finding the Advil, he pops the lid, dumps a few into his hand, then fills a glass of water and knocks them back like they're his savior.

He's onto coffee next, using the Keurig instead of the espresso machine. Less work, I guess. He leans forward, folding his arms and letting his head rest against them on the counter. A groan slips from his lips, and I catch a low "God" as he waits for it to finish.

A few minutes later, he's standing in front of me, leaning down to press a kiss to my lips.

"Hey, babe." He lingers for a second, then straightens. "Don't worry, I brushed the hell out of my teeth when I woke up. Pretty sure I drank half the mouthwash under the sink." He flashes a weak smile and flops onto the couch, taking a long sip of coffee. "God, that's good. Bring me back to life."

I manage a soft, barely-there smile but say nothing, gathering my thoughts.

He groans again, running a hand down his face. "I feel like hell." His eyes meet mine. "How was your night? Did you guys have fun?"

"Yeah," I say quietly. "It was a lot of fun."

"Yeah?" he chuckles, cocking his head. "Why you being so quiet? Something wrong?"

My brows knit together. Does he seriously have no idea what happened last night?

"Do you not remember?" I ask, working to keep my voice neutral, steady. I don't want to come at him defensive or upset, that's not how we do things. Jensen's always been great at communicating, and he deserves a chance to explain.

His brow furrows, and he glances down like he's searching for an answer. "What do you mean?" His voice dips lower. "Ah, shit." He runs a hand through his hair. "Did we have sex?"

I let out a slow sigh. So he really doesn't remember.

"Well, you came home wasted," I say, the words soft but heavy. "And puked all over the floor... and yourself... and my feet." His face twists as I go on. "Then, I practically dragged you into the bathroom, and you puked some more before passing out next to the toilet."

His face crumples with something close to horror. "God, babe. I'm sorry." He blows out a long breath, rubbing his hand down his face. "I knew I threw up, but... fuck, I barely even remember leaving the bar." He shakes his head, softly chuckling, gripping his neck, sheepish. "I don't even know the last time I got that drunk."

Silence settles between us. My eyes fix on my lap, but I can feel his gaze on me.

I finally lift my face, locking eyes with him. "Look, I'm not trying to pick a fight, and maybe this isn't fair, but I need to say it... Last night really freaked me out. I've seen you drunk before, but not like that. I felt like I was right back in my childhood—watching you, not knowing what to do, not knowing if I should clean you up or just walk away."

I swallow, blinking back the tears that threaten. "Like my mom did for my dad."

My voice cracks, thick with emotion, and I hate it. I feel stupid, because I know this isn't a thing. But at the same time, it is.

"Al... babe, I'm so sorry." His voice drops. "I didn't mean to do that to you. God, I didn't even think. I just... got carried away. And if I'd known, if I'd even thought... you know I'd never want to hurt you like that." He scoots closer, grabbing my hand and pulling it to his lips.

I nod, forcing a tiny smile. "I know you're not my dad. I know that. And I know everyone goes too far sometimes. But... seeing you like that brought back a lot of stuff for me. Stuff I don't want to feel again." I take a shaky breath. "I need to know that's not going to be my life with you. I need to know this isn't gonna be a thing, because I can't do that. I can't live like that."

"I would never do that to you. I didn't realize how bad I was. I don't even remember all of it. But I hate that I made you feel that way."

He runs a hand through his hair. "Things just got carried away. There was a live band, Matt was buying shots, and then I started making friends with everyone at the bar." He gives me a small, sideways glance. "You know how I get when I've had a few. Next thing I know, I'm taking shots with them."

He wraps an arm around his stomach, resting his opposite elbow on top, his head dropping into his hand. "You know I don't usually do that. I'm not that guy." His gaze locks with mine. "I'm not your dad. And I won't be."

I squeeze my eyes shut as tears slip free, no matter how hard I try to hold them back.

"Hey." Jensen's hand cups my chin, gently tipping my face up until my eyes meet his. "Ever."

My throat tightens, emotion rising so fast I can't catch my breath. I'm overwhelmed and relieved all at once. I feel so vulnerable—a wound I didn't know existed ripped wide open. It hurts more than I ever could've imagined.

The pain is still there. I just hadn't realized it. But what I do know is that the thought of Jensen being anything like my dad nearly wrecked me.

"Hey, come here." Jensen pulls me in, his lips brushing mine in a tender kiss—a kiss full of apologies and promises. He tugs my bottom lip between his, deepening it, reminding me we're okay, that we're a team. He's on my side.

His hand slips around the back of my neck, pulling me closer, his tongue brushing mine, soft and slow. Safe.

I melt into him, letting his lips take away all the heavy shit in my chest. My arms wrap around his neck, and I let out a soft sound, a mix between a cry and a moan. He shifts, hovering over me as he lays me back on the sofa. His lips keep moving against mine, and somehow, it makes everything better. Just like that. He fixes it—because Jensen can fix anything. He loves harder than anyone I've ever known.

He loves me.

His hand palms my breast, and he groans. "Hey," he whispers, pulling back just enough to meet my eyes. "Never again." His gaze softens. "I promise. Forgive me?"

I nod, a small smile sneaking across my face. "Yes. Now keep kissing me."

He chuckles, nipping at my bottom lip. "I know I was drunk, but didn't you say something about new toys last night?"

His lips graze my jaw, and I laugh softly, bringing a hand to my forehead—suddenly second guessing my purchase. I bite my bottom lip, embarrassed. "Yeah," I say slowly. "I bought a butt plug."

I laugh, and he grins. "You wanna try it out right now?"

I hesitate, my pulse quickening. "I'm not sure if I'm ready."

His fingers brush my cheek, his smile softening. "That's okay, baby." He presses a kiss to my temple, lingering for a moment. "No pressure. You know that, right?"

I nod, and just as my heart starts to settle, his lips curve into a familiar smirk, the one I can never say no to.

"But, uh..." He drops his gaze, shifting slightly. "Clark's still gonna need some attention, though."

I laugh, rolling my eyes. "Oh, really?"

"Really." He stands, extending his hand. "Come on."

I take it, and he pulls me up with little effort. He starts for the bedroom but suddenly pauses. "Shit!" He reaches for his knee, rubbing it.

"What's wrong?"

"Agh, nothing. I just... I don't know, I fucked up my knee skiing yesterday. It was aching before we went to the bar. It's fine. I just stepped on it wrong." He shakes it off. "I'm sure I'll forget all about it once I get you naked." He cocks a brow, grabs my hand, and pulls me toward the bedroom without another word.

Chapter Twenty

JENSEN

THEN—TWO YEARS AGO

AUGUST

This.

This is a top five moment of my entire life—which says a lot, considering the best happened just six days ago. The day Alley became my wife.

I look around, taking it all in. It's quiet.

My arm's draped around Alley's—no, *my wife's*—shoulder. The corners of my mouth pull upward as that thought settles in.

My wife.

Shit. I'm fucking married.

A full-blown grin spreads across my face. So far, so good. These last few days have been some of the best. But right now? I don't even know how to describe it.

Alley called it *breathtaking and indescribable*. And well, I've never been great with words, but a few come to mind: magical, incredible, unbelievable.

Alley shifts closer, resting her head in the crook of my arm. Colors stretch wide across the sky, clouds hovering just below the mountain peaks. The sun burns low to the left, promising another perfect day.

It's fucking beautiful—almost spiritual, though I'm no expert in that department. But if anything fits the word, it's this. People are talking around us, but only in soft whispers, like we're on sacred ground.

I bring the mug of hot coffee to my lips, savoring the rich flavor as it warms my tongue and slides down my throat. A blanket stretches across our laps, and I sniff against the brisk morning air, my nose running.

The only thing killing the moment is my knee. It's been throbbing for the last hour, despite wrapping it tight before we started the two-hour hike up Mt. Batur.

Setting my coffee down on the makeshift bench, I reach for my phone to snap a few pictures. Moving to use both hands, Alley sits up and stretches, her arms extending toward the sky as she lets out a long exhale, her breath visible in the cold air.

"Not too many," she says, glancing at my phone. "It'll take you out of the moment. You'll blink and it'll be gone."

Grinning, I put my phone down, slide my arm back around her shoulder and pull her in for a kiss. Our lips meet, and the contrast of her warm skin against the cold on my face makes me want to get lost in her mouth right here. Right now. But I force myself to pull back. She's right. We'll blink, and this will be gone.

I slide my hand from her shoulder to her thigh, finding her hand and wrapping it in mine, our fingers weaving together.

"This is the coolest thing I've ever done," I say, voice low, almost a whisper. "Aside from marrying you." I nudge her shoulder with mine.

"I know," she whispers back. "I don't want it to end." She glances out over the view. "I'm actually dreading the hike back down. Do you think we could call a helicopter to come get us?" A soft laugh slips from her lips.

I chuckle, my knee silently agreeing. "God, that'd be great."

The hike was steep. Straight up, and unlike any hike I've ever done. The ground was soft—dirt or maybe volcanic ash, I'm not sure—sinking under your feet with every step. Rocky, too. Half of it was giant steps up jagged rocks, then planting your foot in soft sand that just slides back down. Basically, every goddamn step took twice the effort, and with my knee barking at me, it was fucking brutal.

Now, the thought of going back down freaks me the fuck out. I can only imagine those giant steps, the uneven ground—jarring in the worst way.

I take another sip of coffee, realizing I'm just about finished as coffee grounds start making their way into my mouth. The coffee's different here—delicious, but not what I'm used to. Every cup has grounds at the bottom, and I seem to forget every day until I hit them and have to spit them out.

Bali's been incredible, easily one of the coolest places I've ever been. Totally different from my usual Europe trips or long weekends in the States. The people are amazing—friendly, humble, and easy to talk to. I've never been to a developing country like this before, and honestly, it's been eye-opening in the best way. I could definitely live here for a few months out of the year.

Our morning started dark and early, at 12:30 a.m. Our driver, Wayan, picked us up and drove us to the base of the hike, getting us there by 2:30. So, I'm tired as hell, but worth it.

My stomach flips and rumbles.

Fuck. I have to shit.

I glance around, even though I know damn well there aren't any bathrooms up here. *You're on top of a volcano, dumbass.* And at least two hours away from any kind of relief. *Great.*

This should be fun. The coffee's running straight through me. I've had a few of these moments since we got here—hunting down questionable spots to take care of business. I've even given in and taken a few of Alley's activated charcoal pills she packed after doing all her research. I thought they were hokey as hell, but I'll admit, they work.

"Babe," I say as quietly as possible, breaking the silence.

"Hmm?"

A grin tugs at my mouth. "I have to shit."

A laugh bursts out of her, and she quickly covers her mouth with her hand. "Oh my God. Shocker!"

I glance over, catching that beautiful smile, her dimple deepening. *God, I love her.*

"Yeah, that's not happening," she says, shaking her head before turning to meet my eyes. "Good luck with that. You're gonna have to hold it."

"Yeah, I know." I sigh, rubbing a hand over my stomach. I swear to God, every time we're somewhere without a bathroom, this happens—fast and fucking terrifying.

She unzips her belt bag. "I have an activated charcoal. You want one?"

"Can't hurt at this point." I hold out my hand, and she drops a pill into it.

I look at my empty cup, realizing all that's left is sludge. "Shit. You got any coffee left?" I ask, knowing full well another sip might make this worse—but desperate times.

She hands me her mug, and I gulp down the pill, praying it'll help —because I've got the full-blown shit scaries, and it's a problem.

My hand drifts to my knee, rubbing at the ache.

"Your knee hurting again?"

"Yeah. It's acting up." I wince. "You don't have anything in your bag, do you?"

"No." She frowns. "I left the ibuprofen back at the hotel. You gonna be okay?"

"Yeah. I'll be fine." I wave her off, even though the pain is sharp enough to make me grit my teeth.

"You really need to get that checked out."

"I know. But it only hurts when I overdo it. Hasn't even hurt on basketball nights lately."

Honestly, it hasn't hurt much over the past few months. The last time it was this bad was those few weeks after that ski trip. After I was a complete jackass and got so drunk I made my fiancée question her life choices—made her question me.

I've been careful since then, only having two, maybe three drinks. Just enough to catch a good buzz—never more. I drink to relax and loosen up, not to forget. I'm not like her dad. I've never met the guy though, so I don't really know why he drinks. I guess alcoholics don't always need a reason. They just do. I've never understood it.

She's been talking about her dad a lot this week, bringing him up here and there. Telling me stories I've never heard before. It's like she misses him, maybe even regrets not having him at our wedding. And that makes me sad for her.

I can't imagine not having, or *wanting*, my parents there on the biggest day of my life. It was the best day ever. Not sharing that with them? Not having them see me that happy? I can't wrap my head around that.

Damn. I'd have to hold some serious resentment to do that to them. Which tells me just how deep this cuts Alley, because she's nicer than I am. Better than me, in so many ways.

"Well, we can take it slow on the way down. Just promise me you'll rest if you need a break," she says, concern in her voice.

"Promise," I say, giving her hand a gentle squeeze.

Twenty peaceful minutes pass, with only the occasional quiet exchange between us as we talk about plans for the day.

A trail guide's voice slices through the now chatty crowd, their voices soft and reverent. It's time to head back down. I look around one last time, committing this to memory, and steel myself for the long trek down. Every fucking step is going to suck.

* * *

THE SOUND of Alley's toothbrush muffles through the bathroom wall as I pull my swimsuit up and over my ass.

After that tumultuous hike down this morning and the long drive back, all I want is a lazy pool day. Soak up the sun, swim in salt water, sit in the sauna—rest my fucking knee. Every step was killer, and I grimaced the whole way. Still, it was cool, even with the pain—steam rising from the volcano, and little shithead monkeys everywhere you looked.

I chuckle to myself. The monkeys are assholes. They'll snatch anything loose right out of your hand if you're not paying attention, but they're cool as hell at the same time. Some even look old, wise beyond their years. They're all over the resort grounds, too. If you leave a patio door open, you'll find one inside, digging through your shit.

Alley steps out of the bathroom in her string bikini, turning to bend over her suitcase, shuffling through it for something.

My eyes drop to her ass, zeroing in on the tiny bottoms slicing up her backside. This is more than a cheeky cut, and my dick twitches in my shorts.

I love seeing this side of Alley. She's always been naturally reserved, but slowly, over time, she's gotten riskier with me—braver, trying new things. She's learning not to give a fuck, and I love that I'm the one she lets in. The one who gets to help her feel confident in her skin.

We're perfect for each other. I don't say that lightly, either. We're like a zipper—perfectly aligned, needing both sides to come together to be something. She brings out the best in me. And I'd like to think I do the same for her.

She's always been carefree and fun, but now? She's a little more adventurous, more confident. A few weeks ago, we even had anal for the first time. We'd been working up to it for a while, and guess what? She fucking loved it. My bottom lip rolls between my teeth as I try, and fail, to suppress a grin while my dick hardens—because Jesus, look at her. Thinking about the night we did anal only adds fuel to the fire.

She turns to me and freezes when she catches my grin. Her eyes trail down my body, stopping right at my cock, hard and straining against my swim shorts. A slow smile curls her lips as she reaches behind her neck, untying her bikini top.

The fabric slips loose, sliding down to reveal just enough of her perfect tits to drive me crazy. Her nipples peek out, tightening in the cool air. The strings around her back hold the rest in place.

Her eyes darken, and she cocks a brow. "Wanna fuck before we go?"

My eyes widen. *What the shit?*

I've literally never heard Alley say "fuck." Not once. Hearing it roll off her tongue like that, aimed at me? Jesus Christ. I'm gone. It's hot as hell.

I'm crossing the room before I can even think, practically slamming into her and backing her up against the wall. She laughs as we collide, but her laugh dies when my mouth crashes against hers, hungry and possessive—like I'll die if I don't taste her. Right. Now.

I kiss her desperately, like it's the first time I've ever touched her—like she just offered me her V-card, and I need her more than air.

My hand grips her hip, the other sliding around her back, trailing over her smooth, warm skin. I reach for the strings in the back, tugging until her top falls loose to the floor. My mouth is on her immediately, replacing what I just stripped away. I take a nipple into my mouth, teasing it with my tongue, flicking, nipping, tasting her skin.

She gasps, arching into me, her hand drifting down, finding my cock, and rubbing over me through my shorts. Slow. Deliberate. She knows exactly how to work me.

"God, you get hard so fast for me," she breathes, her voice sultry and low.

I grin against her skin, kissing my way up to her neck. "Who are you, and what have you done with my wife?" I murmur, chuckling softly.

"Mmm. That sweet girl you brought here? She's gone. And this one wants you to fuck her."

"Jesus, baby." I mutter, dragging my lips along her jaw. "If you keep talking like that, I'm not gonna make it to the bed."

My fingers tug at her bottoms, my eyes locked on the fabric as it slides down her thigh and pools at her feet.

I've seen her naked a thousand times, but fuck if this doesn't feel new. Her tanned skin contrasts with her smooth, pale pussy. And she looks good. She worked her ass off before the wedding, counting macros, working out, and while she's always been perfect to me, it's done something for her. She's different. I can tell *she* feels sexy. She's bolder, confident—hell, even a little naughty. And it's making me lose my mind in the best way.

"You're so beautiful," I say, taking all of her in. My gaze shifts to the side, catching the large mirror in front of the chaise lounger close to the patio door.

Perfect.

"Come here." I take her hands, pulling her toward the patio, positioning her in front of the mirror.

She tips her head back, laughing softly. "Jensen..."

I pull her against me, chest to her back, my hands sliding to her hips. "Look at yourself, baby." I press a kiss to her jaw, trailing down her neck. "Look how beautiful you are. I'm the luckiest man alive."

She relaxes into me as my hands come up to cup her tits, thumbs circling her nipples, my gaze locked on her reflection, watching every damn second.

"Touch yourself for me," I murmur, voice low against her ear. "I wanna see you."

She grins, a flicker of hesitation before her hand slowly slides down her stomach. She pauses just above, glancing at me in the mirror.

I cover her hand with mine, guiding it lower until her fingers brush her clit.

Her breath catches, eyes fluttering shut, and I lean in. "Keep your eyes on the mirror." I kiss her shoulder, one hand still teasing her breast.

"Yeah, that's it," I whisper, watching her work herself, her cheeks flushed, lips parted. "God, look at you. Look how fucking sexy you are."

Our eyes lock in the mirror, heat building between us.

"You see what you do to me?" I whisper, grinding my cock against her ass so she feels me, hard and desperate for her. She moans softly, rubbing herself harder.

I slide my hand down between her thighs, brushing my fingers over hers. "So wet already," I murmur. "Ready for me, huh?"

She lets out a breathy laugh, nodding, "Yes."

I take over, circling her clit in slow, purposeful strokes. "Keep watching," I whisper, my mouth at her ear. "Watch me touch you."

Her head drops back against me, body arching into my hand as I work her faster. I watch her in the mirror—brows pinched, mouth parted, completely lost in what I'm doing to her.

"Jensen," she breathes. "I don't think I can—"

I grin against her neck, lips brushing her skin. "Yeah, you can," I murmur. "You're gonna come just like this. Standing here. Watching me love you."

Her breathing grows shallow, and her body tenses. She's right there on the edge. I pull back, removing my hand.

Her head snaps up. "What are you doing? I was so close." The frustration in her voice makes me smirk.

"Bend over, baby. Hands on the chair," I shove my swimsuit down.

She hesitates, but turns and does what I say, glancing back at me over her shoulder.

"God, look at you." I drag the tip of my cock up her slick pussy. "So fucking ready for me."

She lets out a soft whimper, pushing her ass back against me, silently begging for it.

"You want it?"

"Yes."

"Say it."

"I want you to fuck me." Her gaze locks on mine in the mirror, her voice breathless and desperate. "Please."

Holy shit. That. The eye contact. The begging. The *please.* Sweet Jesus, it's a fantasy I've had for as long as I can remember. I'm so turned on. My cock aches, and I swear to God, I'm already seeing stars.

Sliding my hands down her back, I grip her hips and guide myself in—slow at first, short, shallow thrusts, working into longer, deeper strokes.

With every snap of her hips, her tits bounce, and between the way she feels wrapped tight around me and everything I'm watching in the mirror, my head spins. *She feels so damn good.*

I thrust harder, faster, her ass slapping against me, our bodies moving together. My breath turns sharp and shallow, and I'm already teetering on the edge.

Jesus. Are my eyes closed? What the fuck am I doing?

I force them open, needing to see her because I know I won't last much longer. She catches my eye in the mirror, flashing a wicked grin, then suddenly shifts her hips forward, pulling away from me. Before I can react, she spins around, dropping onto the chaise and tugging me down on top of her.

Okaaaay. Not mad about being handled a little. I love seeing this side of her. But damn. I was so close.

Her legs wrap around me, guiding my cock to her entrance, and I sink into her, groaning as I savor every inch. Her fingers slide into my hair, pulling me close until we're sharing breath. Then she grabs my jaw, making me look at her, eyes locked.

"I want to look at you when you fuck me."

I let out a shaky breath. "Fuck, baby." My forehead drops to hers. "I love you so much."

I capture her lips, pouring everything I feel into the kiss. I'm torn between making slow, sweet love to her and fucking her so hard she forgets her own name.

I start slow, touching her like she might break. "Jesus... You feel too good. Every time. So fucking good."

Then she surprises me. She bucks her hips, taking me deeper. Her nails dig into my shoulders as she meets every thrust in the most desperate, demanding way. I groan against her mouth, giving her more, matching her intensity. *Fuck-her-hard it is!*

"You want it like this, baby?" I rasp, pulling back just enough to see her face.

She nods, gasping, her eyes wild.

That's all I need.

I drive into her, hard and deep, our bodies colliding in perfect cadence.

Her legs tighten around me, locking me in. That's my cue. She's close. I keep my pace steady, pushing her to the edge until I feel her pulse around me, her moans spilling into the air.

The pressure builds, hot and blinding, until I explode, emptying into her with one final thrust, my body tensing as I do. Her hands grip my biceps, holding on as I let out a low groan.

As we both come down, I press my forehead to hers, still inside her, our chests rising and falling in sync. Her arms are wrapped tight around my neck, and I swear, I could stay like this all day.

She giggles softly, brushing her nose against mine. "So... you still wanna go to the pool?"

I chuckle, pressing a kiss to her lips. Slow. Soft. Lingering. "Pool can wait. You? You can't."

She hums against my mouth, fingers toying with the hair at the nape of my neck. "I love being married to you."

A grin tugs at my lips "Yeah?" I murmur, kissing her again, fiercer this time—like this one kiss can somehow mirror everything I'm feeling right now. "Me too, baby. Me too."

I shift, rolling us to the side and pulling her close as we both catch our breath. I don't know if my cup's ever been so full. I can't stop grinning.

Well, shit. If this is what marriage looks like, if this is us...

I'll take forever.

Chapter Twenty-One

ALLEY

PRESENT DAY

THE POUNDING at the door yanks me back to reality—slamming into me, sharp and unwelcome.

I flinch.

"Alley!"

There's more banging, but I can't move.

"Al, I'm coming in!"

My eyes lock on the ceiling—smooth, white, empty. I stare at nothing, but it feels like a mirror, like I'm staring back at my soul. Nothingness.

There's nothing left. Nothing more I can give. Nothing more I can do. Nothing left to live for.

I'm helpless.

Alone.

And scared out of my mind.

"Alley! Hey, Al. What's going on? You okay? Come here."

I'm being pulled up, but I don't want to be. I want to stay here. I want to keep staring at the nothing.

Strong arms wrap around me, and gut-wrenching sobs deafen my ears. *Are those mine?*

Hands cup my face, thumbs swiping away my tears. I'm on the couch now, a body beside me.

"Jesus, Al. Talk to me. What's going on? Where's Jensen?"

The soft sounds of shushing fills the air as my head presses against a chest, my tears soaking the shirt beneath me.

Then, slowly, everything calms.

It numbs.

I blink and take a deep, shaky breath—one that feels like my first in minutes. My pulse steadies, and my breathing begins to even out.

Chapter Twenty-Two

JENSEN

THEN—TWO YEARS AGO

SEPTEMBER

THE DOOR CLICKS SHUT behind me, and I make a beeline for the kitchen. My knee's been killing me all day. We've been back from our honeymoon for two weeks, and it's been giving me hell ever since that hike. I took the last ibuprofen I had in my car this morning, and the throbbing's been shooting up my leg like a damn lightning bolt ever since.

I yank open the medicine cabinet and start rummaging through the bottles. Ibuprofen, Advil, Aleve—hell, I'll take a Tylenol, even if it's only going to scratch the surface. I finally find one of those regular strength Tylenol bottles, twist off the lid, and stare inside.

One.

"Shit," I mutter, huffing out a breath.

That's not going to touch the pain.

I take it anyway, chasing it with a swig from the faucet. Then I grab an ice pack from the freezer and limp into the living room. Dropping onto the couch, I kick back against the arm and stretch my leg out, balancing the pack on my knee.

I point the remote at the TV and flip on whatever game's on. College football—don't even care who's playing. I just need something to distract me from the dull, relentless ache that's been dragging me down for three goddamn weeks.

Thirty minutes later, between the ice and the Tylenol, the pain's manageable, but barely.

I pick up my phone, swipe up, and type out a quick text.

> Hey babe, can you grab some ibuprofen before you head out tonight?

Alley's working till eight, and the hospital pharmacy's right downstairs. I set my phone aside, knowing I probably won't hear from her until her shift ends.

By six p.m. the ice pack's lukewarm. I've already done two rounds —twenty minutes on, ten minutes off, but the relief didn't last.

Groaning, I push myself off the couch and hobble to the kitchen, ice pack in hand. My knee barks with every step of the twenty-foot trek. I toss the pack back in the freezer and open the liquor cabinet, reaching for the tequila. Maybe that'll take the edge off.

I pour a shot neat and take a slow sip, exhaling as the burn coils down my throat. *God, I needed that.* But then it hits me—I took a Tylenol an hour ago, and you're not supposed to mix that shit.

I let out another groan. "Ah, fuck."

My hands rake through my hair and stay there, fingers gripping tight. I tug at the strands, frustrated, completely at a loss. I hate bitching about this, especially to Alley. She keeps telling me to go in, but for what? So they can tell me I need another surgery? Prescribe pain pills?

No fucking thank you.

I've got a life. A job. A wife. I can't be popping pain meds like candy. I need to function. That shit never really fixes anything anyway. I just need to manage the pain and give it time. Rest. That's all.

It took a few weeks after the ski trip, but it eased up. This'll pass too. It has to.

I turn to put the tequila back, but the twist in my knee sends white-hot pain shooting straight to my brain.

"Agh, God!" I shout, wincing, eyes squeezing shut as my hands fly to my knee.

The bottle slips from my grip, hitting the floor with a heavy thud.

"Dammit!"

The bottle rolls across the floor—unbroken, thank God. I grip my knee hard, like pressure alone might fix it. Slowly, I push myself up, breathing deep as white and black stars flicker across my vision. I blink them away, leaning on the counter until the haze clears.

"Fuck," I mutter. I didn't even do anything, just stepped wrong.

I limp back to the medicine cabinet. There has to be more Tylenol —*anything*. I can't wait three more hours for Alley to get home. I start tearing through bottles: supplements, activated charcoal, Zyrtec, Senna Plus—yeah, definitely don't need help shitting. None of it's useful.

Two prescription bottles are shoved way in the back. *Jesus, how old are these?* I don't even remember the last time one of us had a prescription. I grab them both to throw away. I hold the first one up— Azithromycin, *whatever the hell that was for*. I toss it in the trash.

I pause, holding the second one over the bin.

Oxycodone.

Oh, shit. This is from my surgery. I didn't even use half of them. I rotated Tylenol and ibuprofen after the first few days. I remember taking one or two the following week when the pain spiked. They worked—really well.

I shake the bottle, eyes scanning the label. They expired six months ago. But painkillers don't actually expire, do they? They just put that shit on the label to cover their asses. It's not like they go bad.

Twisting the cap, I tip the bottle until a single pill drops into my palm.

I stare at it.

I know how this shit works. I know it can be addicting. But I've taken it before, and I was fine. Right now I'm in pain. It's not like I'm chasing a high. I just want to not feel like I'm being stabbed every time I move.

My knee pulses hard, like it's reminding me that this isn't optional. I sigh, open the silverware drawer, and grab a knife. I'll cut it in half. It's safer that way. Not a big deal.

I line the blade up to the score and rock it back and forth. Powder crumbles, but it cuts clean enough. I pick up one half between my thumb and finger, hesitant, staring again. It's just a little white pill—small, *harmless*.

Just half. Just for the pain.

Placing it on my tongue, I take a sip of water and swallow. *Please work*, I pray. *I'd kill for a good nights sleep tonight.*

I limp back to the couch and sink into it, resuming my position—legs kicked up. I grab a few throw pillows, and tuck them behind me, settling in for the next few hours until my gorgeous wife comes home.

Twenty minutes pass, and I'm thoroughly enjoying the game when my phone dings.

I glance down. It's Matt.

MATT

Hey bro, you and Al still planning on tomorrow?

Ah, shit. I totally forgot. One of Matt's clients is throwing some gala for a charity. He told me the name of it, but I couldn't tell you what the hell it's for.

Yeah. You wanna drive together?

MATT

Yeah. I'm bringing a date. We can pick her up on the way?

Works for me.

MATT

K, I'll meet you downstairs at 7:30. How's the knee?

Fucking killing me today.

Matt's one of the few people I can bitch to about my knee. He was there the first time I fucked it up in high school—a drunken stunt gone bad. Then, of course, he helped nurse me back to health after my surgery, back when I met Alley.

MATT

Damn. Have you made an appt yet?

Nah. What are they gonna do? Tell me to take more ibuprofen?

MATT

True.

Found an old pain pill in the cabinet. Took half. It's finally starting to numb the pain.

MATT

Oh shit, nice. So, it's working?

I glance down at my knee. It doesn't hurt. Nothing does, actually—for the first time in weeks. *God, I'm finally fucking comfortable.*

Yeah, I think so.

MATT

That's good. Maybe you'll get some good sleep tonight.

Sleep. That sounds great.
I blink, my eyes growing heavy.

Hopefully.

I drop my phone to my side, my arm following. Stretching out on the couch, I let the tension melt from my body. My knee? I don't feel it. I barely feel anything at all, just warmth and comfort. Like everything is... fine.

My shoulders slump, everything suddenly feeling heavy. The throbbing's dulled—not gone, but numbed enough to ignore it.

I draw in a deep breath and let it out slow, blinking at the TV. It's only 6:45, but damn, I'm tired. My body sinks deeper into the cushions, loose and relaxed, like I just had the best deep-tissue massage of my life. The couch wraps around me like a blanket, and the soft background noise of the football game fades into perfect white noise.

I close my eyes. Just for a second.

* * *

A SOFT TOUCH brushes along my jaw, warm breath skimming my skin. I stir, brows pulling together as I inhale deep, a yawn stretching through my chest. The weight of sleep clings for half a second, thick and heavy. My fingers twitch against the couch cushions.

"Hey, babe."

Alley's soft voice drifts through the quiet. I blink my eyes open to find her sitting beside me, grinning as she leans in and presses a kiss to my neck. Her hand glides across my chest.

I grunt, lifting one arm in a deep stretch before letting it fall to her thigh. "Shit. I fell asleep. How was work?"

"It was fine." She yawns, and the sound pulls another one from me. With a soft laugh, she shifts, moving to straddle my lap.

I cock a brow. "You planning to wake me up?"

"You bet I am." Both hands slide up my chest as she grinds against me, her hips rolling just enough to make my dick jerk in response before stilling. "In a minute... How was your day?"

I push myself up a few inches, then slide my hands up her thighs, my thumbs tracing along the fabric of her scrubs.

"It was good." My voice is low, still thick with sleep. "Busy. Passed the fuck out apparently."

"Well, that's good. You obviously needed it." She pauses before asking, "How's your knee today?"

"Same ol' shit, different day." I huff a laugh. "Took a regular strength Tylenol. It didn't do shit."

"Yeah, that's not gonna help."

"Did you get the ibuprofen?"

She nods. "You want me to grab you one?"

I assess the pain. It's not terrible, just a dull pulse if I really focus on it. I know why it feels better—but I don't want to think about that.

"I'll take one before bed," I murmur, my hands inching higher. "Right now, I'm more interested in the distraction that's making me hard as hell."

My gaze locks on hers as my thumb brushes along the sensitive crease where her thigh meets her pussy.

Yeah. She loves that.

She bites her bottom lip, a grin breaking through. Her eyes drop, then lift again beneath her lashes—dark, alluring.

"Oh, really?" she teases, her hands gliding up my chest. One slips higher, curling around my neck, her thumb brushing my pulse point. "And what distraction is that?"

She hovers over my lips, her breath warm against mine.

I chuckle, low and wicked. My hand slides to her ass, giving it a light slap before gripping the soft curve, firm in my palm. I'm even harder now, pressing up against her. "This hot nurse."

She kisses me, grazing my bottom lip with her teeth and tugging gently.

"I hear she gives good head, and her pussy's like a fine wine," I say, unable to stop the grin tugging at my lips.

She pulls back, locking eyes. "My pussy is not a fine wine. That would mean it's aged."

I chuckle again. "You're right. That wasn't good."

She shakes her head, lips pressed together like she's fighting a grin.

Kissing my jaw, she trails her mouth to my ear, nibbling my lobe. "No," she whispers. "It's young." She kisses that sweet spot behind my ear—one of my favorites. "Tight." She flicks the inside of my ear. "And wet." She grinds into me, sliding back just right, rubbing my dick right where it counts. "Waiting for you and your incredibly hard cock."

"Jesus, babe." I can hardly think straight. She's so hot—knows exactly how to drive me crazy. My arms wrap around her without thinking, pulling her close. I press a kiss to her neck, her skin soft and smooth beneath my lips.

Her mouth finds mine, and I pull her into a heated kiss, one hand cupping her neck, my thumb brushing her cheek.

A low groan rumbles in my chest as her hands slide under my shirt.

Fuck. She's the best.

Even if my knee were screaming right now, I doubt I'd care. She's better than any drug I could buy. She makes everything better—every day. Every. Damn. Day.

Can you be addicted to a person?

Because if so, I am.

I'm an addict.

And my drug of choice?

Alley.

Chapter Twenty-Three

ALLEY

THEN

Slinging my purse over my shoulder, I grab my water jug and push open the break room door.

I nearly run into Zach as I step into the hall.

"Whoa! Leaving without saying goodbye?" he asks, mock offended.

"I was just coming to find you," I say with a laugh. "You working tomorrow?"

"Yeah, but not until noon. You?"

"Seven a.m.," I groan.

I hate the morning shift, yet, somehow it keeps landing on my schedule. I'll have to leave the house by six fifteen and won't see Jensen until dinner. I'd much rather sleep in, have a slow morning—maybe even some sex—drink coffee together before he heads out at eight.

He sticks out his bottom lip in a pout and opens his arms. Laughing, I step into him, wrapping my arms around his waist.

"I'll see you tomorrow," I say as I pull back.

"See you, babe. Enjoy your night."

"I will. You too," I reply, walking backwards a few steps before turning toward the elevators.

Once inside, I press the lobby button and lean against the wall. I reach into my purse and pull out my phone. A missed text from Michael lights up the screen.

I blink at it.

MICHAEL

Dad asked for your number today.

My heart skips a beat, a claustrophobic pressure creeping up my throat, squeezing tight.

Why? What did you say?

The elevator doors slide open, and I step out—distracted, my gaze locked on my phone as I type.

MICHAEL

He wants to talk to you, obviously. I told him I'd ask you.

No. Don't give it to him.

I changed my number a few years after moving to New York. I told myself it was for a local area code, for a clean break from Chicago. But who was I kidding? I know why I really did it.

MICHAEL

He's sober, you know. Has been for a while.

My grip tightens on my phone, but I don't react. I don't let myself. I lock the screen, shove it into my purse, and keep walking.

My pulse picks up—and so does my pace, like maybe I can outrun the anger. The resentment. The hurt.

He stopped calling and texting.

I never gave him a reason to keep trying. I know that. I never responded. Once in a while, I'd get a call out of the blue. A random text—*How you doing?* But after two years, he just... stopped. He gave up.

I can't blame him. I gave up on him long before. But I'm his daughter. Isn't he supposed to try harder? Get on a plane? Make a grand gesture? Keep calling until I finally pick up?

He didn't.

No. It would hurt a hell of a lot less if he couldn't call. If there was a reason for his absence. Because knowing he could, and chose not to? That's what hurt the most. That cut deep.

Yeah, no. It doesn't matter that he's sober. How many times has he actually stayed that way?

He wants my number. After all this time.

My jaw clenches, but I keep moving.

Not my problem.

The walk from the hospital to the subway is short, but it feels like a marathon. I descend the stairs, catch the next train, and slide into a seat, tapping my foot anxiously.

I sniff, holding back the tears that threaten to break through. My breathing is sharp and shallow, and my throat grows tight with every stop the train makes.

Swallowing hard, I pull out my phone, my fingers trembling as I type.

> Good.

* * *

I ʀᴏᴅᴇ the train with my sunglasses on.

I know. It's not sunny on the subway. But after I sent that text to Michael, a whirlwind of emotion swept through me, and I felt like I might cry. I didn't, but I know I looked like I had. I felt stupid.

The sunglasses were the only solution.

My thoughts flip back and forth, circling the same question: *did I do the right thing?*

Michael seems to have no problem letting him in. He never

pushed him away. Never stopped checking in—even when Dad was at his worst.

The smell of New York stings my nose as I pass a sewer, stepping wide over a man passed out in the middle of the sidewalk, like he just decided this was the perfect place to take a nap. I hesitate, slowing my pace, heart snagging in my chest, torn between wanting to help him and scream at him.

My hell. How do people end up like this?

Michael's text lingers in the back of my mind like a ghost, dragging up memories I've tried to bury.

That day crashes into me. My chest squeezes, and my stride slows as I stop, turning around right there in the middle of the sidewalk. Someone cusses at me as they bump into my shoulder, telling me to move.

But I can't. I can't move.

I see my dad. Not lying in a hallway this time, but on this sidewalk.

I left him.

God, I left him.

I won't leave this guy too.

I step closer, my gaze dropping to his pants hanging halfway off his ass, his crack out for the world to see. I stand five feet from him, staring.

He looks to be in his fifties, maybe late forties. Does he have kids? Did he used to have a wife? Did she die like my mom? Did something happen that broke him? Why is he here?

God, I can't breathe.

The dam breaks. Tears spill down my cheeks, and I swipe at them with the backs of my hands.

Someone stumbles over him and gives him a kick, and I feel it like it was aimed at me. That could be someone's father.

Suddenly, everything inside me aches. I don't know if it's because I feel hopeless for this man... or because I miss my dad so much I can't see straight.

Another person bumps into me, this one calling me the C word as they pass. I stumble back, pressing into the side of the building, my breath shaking in and out. My head tips against the firm brick, and I let the tears come. I let them fall. I don't know why it's all hitting me so hard right now. Maybe it's everything—the past, the guilt—the ache of missing people I'll never get back.

I told myself a long time ago it's okay to feel. Healthy, even. So I let myself feel it. My eyes squeeze shut, and I picture the good times I had with my dad... and my mom. The four of us. The family vacations, sometimes with Michael's friends or mine. Sunday homemade ice cream and a family movie.

My dad *loved* Jim Carrey. I can't tell you how many times I've seen *Dumb and Dumber* or *Liar Liar*. He'd laugh every single time like it was the first. Those were the good days. But they were rare. Most of my childhood is haunted by images I've tried to forget—of him being gone or coming home late. Even when he was there, he wasn't. Not fully, anyway.

My body's moving before I even realize it. I crouch beside the man. I don't know if he's drunk or high, but I'm not going to let him get kicked again. At least not today.

He smells of liquor and dried urine, and the dirt under his nails could start an ant farm.

I nudge his shoulder. "Hey."

Nothing. Obviously. I know how this goes. I'm not going to wake him up or talk sense into him. I can't fix this. All I can do is get him out of the way.

I step behind him and put my nursing skills to use, wrapping my arms under his armpits. His weight sags against me, dead and heavy. My feet plant firmly on the sidewalk as I use my legs, pushing with my body to drag him closer to the wall. My palms press into sweat and grit, and the strain bites at my shoulders.

A tear falls.

And then another.

I get him out of the way the best I can, my breath catching in my throat. I whisper a prayer for him, just a few words, soft and shaky, and turn to walk the rest of the way home.

* * *

I'm emotionally wrecked by the time I get home, and all I want is to melt into Jensen's arms. I need a hug.

He's asleep on the couch again. That's the third time in two weeks I've come home to find him passed out in front of the TV. He must be stressed or worn down, because Jensen never naps. And he's always been a night owl.

Weird. It's only six thirty. Maybe he's fighting off a bug.

I walk to the sink, rinse out my water jug, and slide it into the dishwasher. I hover for a second, debating whether to start dinner or wake him.

I really need to talk to him.

Crossing to the couch, I sit beside him and gently brush my thumb across his forehead. "Hey," I whisper.

His eyes crack open, and after a few seconds, his brows furrow. "Hey," he says, his gaze finding mine. "What's wrong, babe?" He reaches for my hand, gripping it tight.

I lose it. All over again.

He sits up, pulling me into him, his lips pressing to my forehead. "Hey. Hey." His hand moves in slow, soothing circles along my back.

"Michael texted me... my dad..." My words come out in sharp, broken sobs. "He's sober... and he wants my number." I shake my head against his chest, tears soaking into his shirt. "I don't know what to do."

Jensen's chest rises and falls with a long breath. "Babe..." He exhales slowly, like he's choosing his words. "That's... a good thing. Right?"

I nod.

He stays silent for a long moment—just holding me, rubbing my back, pressing soft kisses to my hair. He lets me fall apart without trying to fix it. He's just... there. Solid. Steady. Comforting.

And I know I'll be okay. I'll figure this out, not because he's saying the right things, but because I have him. He's my strength when I'm weak. My calm in the storm—my other half. He always knows how to show up when I need him most.

I tighten my arms around him, pressing in closer. I could stay right here with him forever—just the two of us.

I breathe in deep, steadying myself. I already feel a little better just having his arms around me.

The tears still come, though. There's no stopping them, no swallowing the ache back down. I don't know if it's my dad, the guy on the sidewalk, or hormones. Maybe it's everything.

"Do you wanna talk about it?" Jensen says quietly, his voice deep but soft.

"I don't know." I sniff. "I don't even know what I'm feeling, but I just had a full-on meltdown on the sidewalk because of a homeless man." I laugh-cry, because it sounds ridiculous even as I say it. "He was passed out. People were tripping over him. I couldn't just leave him there, you know? So I moved him. Dragged him out of the way the best I could."

Jensen pulls back, cradling my face in his hands. His thumbs brush under my eyes, catching the tears before they fall. The corners of his mouth lift, and he lets out a soft chuckle as he leans in to press a kiss to my forehead. "Of course you did," he says. "You know that's why I love you so much. You're such a good person. You have a heart of gold." He chuckles again, shaking his head as if he's both proud and unsurprised. "No one else would've done that."

"God." I laugh through a new wave of tears, the sound breaking as it slips from my lips. "I feel so stupid. What is wrong with me?"

"Nothing." He shakes his head again, firmer this time. "Absolutely nothing."

He watches me for a moment, his thumb brushing slow, rhythmic strokes across my cheek. "You wanna talk about your dad?"

Fresh emotion rises like a tide in my throat, catching hard just from hearing his name.

Jensen doesn't wait for me to answer. His hand slides down, wrapping around my own, his fingers threading between mine. "I think you need to see him, Al," he says gently. "I know it's not my place, and I'd never push. It's your choice. I'll support you no matter what, but..." He lifts my hand and presses it to his chest, right over his heart. "I think you've been questioning it for a while now. I know you think about the wedding. About him not being there. I know that's been killing you."

I nod slowly, mulling over his words. "Dammit," I whisper,

pressing my forefinger into the corner of my eye as the dam threatens to break again. "You're right." I meet his gaze. "I know you're right. I just... don't want you to be."

"Ah, babe. I know it's hard being married to someone who's always right." He tries to keep a straight face, but the corner of his mouth betrays him.

I laugh through a sniffle. "Jerk."

I nudge him, and he catches me instantly, crushing his mouth to mine—earnest, devout. He kisses me like he's trying to stitch me back together with his lips alone.

God, how does he love me this hard?

His tongue teases mine, slow and deep, and then he nips my bottom lip before pulling back just enough to meet my eyes. "You could see him when we go for New Year's. If you're ready. I'll go with you. You don't have to do this alone."

I nod, biting my bottom lip. "Yeah. Maybe."

I kiss him again, climbing into his lap, his mouth a kind of comfort that always soothes the storm. His arms wrap around me, hands sliding down to my ass, and I break the kiss.

"Promise me you'll never leave me," I whisper, hovering just above his lips. "I can't do life without you. I don't want to."

He cracks a small smile, eyes locked on mine. "I'd never leave you. It's you and me, babe. Always."

The next kiss is harder. Deeper. Hotter. He pulls back just long enough to meet my eyes and say, "For fucking ever," before claiming my mouth again like it's a promise he intends to keep.

Chapter Twenty-Four

JENSEN

THEN

OCTOBER

I ADJUST the ice pack on my knee, the TV casting just enough light to see. Some rom-com Alley picked plays in the background. I couldn't tell you the name. It's had a few funny moments, but I've stopped paying attention.

I take a long sip of my IPA, almost like I'm trying to chase the relief. My knee's been giving me hell. Like always.

I only have eleven pills left.

Eleven.

I've started taking them in the mornings just to get through the day. I'm way more productive when I'm not gritting my teeth through every meeting. My mood's better, too. When the pain flares, my patience thins, and I get irritable. That's not who I am—not normally.

Up until last week, I was able to go every other day. Now it's every day. It's still just half a pill, though. Not a big deal. The dose is hardly anything. I'm still functioning, still working.

The drowsiness I had at first faded after a few. That's when I switched to mornings.

Alley shifts beside me, pulling me from my thoughts. Her head drops to my shoulder, and my arm lifts automatically from her thigh, wrapping around her. I press a kiss to the top of her head, inhaling the scent of her shampoo. I can never quite place what it is, but it smells good—*smells like her.*

Her laughter fills the room, and a grin tugs at my lips, even though I have no clue what she's laughing at. It's a nice distraction. But it's short lived. My mind drifts back to my knee, and the issue at hand.

What will I do when I run out?

I let them run out. Obviously. I don't need them. I can switch back to ibuprofen. I still take it, just after the pill wears off. It's manageable.

I'll wean off.

Same as after the surgery. Every other day, then just as needed.

I do the math. If I time it right, I can be off them by the time I run out. Maybe even stash two or three for emergencies. That buys me two weeks to taper, and still leaves a safety net. Totally doable.

I force my attention back to the television.

Yeah. That's what I'll do. That's a good plan.

I tip back the rest of my warm beer, because I already know the ibuprofen I'll take in an hour won't do shit. At least the alcohol might take the edge off.

* * *

I slam the door behind me, raking a hand through my hair as I pass the kitchen and head straight down the hall to our bedroom. In the closet, I rip off my work pants, tug on a pair of joggers, and throw a hoodie over my head.

I'm tense as fuck.

One day. One fucking day, and I'm about to lose my goddamn mind.

I walk back into the kitchen, dragging a hand down my face, deliberately avoiding the medicine cabinet.

Don't even look at it.

I already took ibuprofen two hours ago. And four hours before that—and when I woke up. I'm way over the limit.

God, I'm gonna fuck up my stomach.

I groan, grabbing a sparkling water from the fridge and the ice pack from the freezer, then park my ass on the couch.

I settle into my usual spot, propping my leg on the coffee table, the other relaxed with my foot on the floor. I flip on the TV, but my eyes don't even register the screen. I just stare, blank and unfocused at the wall in front of me.

Work sucked today. The pain was brutal. Nonstop. All day. I didn't realize how much relief I'd been getting until it was gone. But it's bad. It was hell.

It got so bad that I broke down and called the doctor's office around noon, desperate for an appointment. I don't even know what they'll do—prescribe something, recommend surgery, maybe throw me back into physical therapy. That shit frustrates me more than anything. It's a never-ending carousel of appointments that all lead to the same dead end.

It's not going to get better.

I'll have ups and downs with this for the rest of my life. The knee's been through too much—too many injuries, too much damage. It's compromised.

My jaw tightens, and I drum my fingers against my thigh, trying to stay calm.

The front door opens, and Alley's voice echoes through the apartment. "Hey, babe. You're home early."

Yeah. My knee is killing me.

"Hey," I call out, glancing at her. She's in her gym clothes, hair pulled up, and my eyes drop to her tits in her workout tank.

But only briefly.

My mind's too scattered to linger. I barely register Alley's voice —something about work, her day—blending into the background noise of the TV, muffled beneath the dull, relentless throb in my knee.

I shift, pressing my fingers into the joint, trying to work out a knot that won't let go. The ibuprofen should've kicked in by now. Maybe it's just not strong enough. Maybe it never really worked in the first place.

My eyes flick to the kitchen. The cupboard. Second shelf. The bottle's still there.

Stop.

"Jensen?"

I blink. She's watching me, waiting for a response. I force a nod and reach for my water, taking a slow sip—anything to buy time.

"Yeah," I murmur. "Sorry. Zoned out."

She studies me for half a second too long... then keeps talking.

One day. That's all. One fucking day without it. My knee pulses with a slow, familiar ache. I exhale, rubbing my jaw, forcing my eyes away from the cupboard.

I can do this.

"Babe." Alley's standing in front of me.

My brain stalls for a beat, and I force my gaze to hers. "Yeah?"

Her brows knit. "Everything okay?"

"Yeah." I shake it off. Push it down. "Yeah... sorry. Just a stressful day at work. I guess I brought it home with me. Sorry."

"I'm sorry, babe. That sucks." Her eyes flick to my knee, then back to me. "Have you made an appointment yet? You can't take ibuprofen forever, you know. Even one dose a day isn't good for you."

"Yeah, I know. I called today. I've got an appointment Friday."

Jesus. She's worried about me taking it once a day, and I'm over here counting down the minutes until I can take my fourth dose.

She sits across from me on the coffee table, careful not to bump my leg. Her hand finds my calf, a comforting presence.

"That's good. I'm glad you're finally going in." She leans forward for a kiss, then pulls back with a grin so big it tugs my lips into a smile without even trying. "I have fun news."

I cock a brow. "Yeah? What is it?"

"Zach and Joey got engaged! I'm so excited and happy for them!"

"That's awesome! When did that happen, this past weekend?"

"Yeah. I think they'll get married next summer. You should've seen Zach at work. He was glowing. It was so cute. They'll probably have a big party this weekend or next, just FYI."

"Well, we'll make sure we're there. That should be fun."

"Yeah. It will be... Okay, I'm gonna go hop in the shower. You good? Need anything?" she asks, giving my leg a gentle rub, her eyes flicking to the ice pack.

"Nah, I'm good, babe."

"Alright." She leans in, kissing me softly before standing. As she walks away, she tosses a glance over her shoulder. "You know you can join me... if you want."

My lips curve slowly.

Turns out, my knee doesn't hurt *that* bad. I'll limp if I have to.

"Right behind you," I call, tipping back the last of my water and setting the glass down before rising to follow her. She's already peeling her clothes off as she disappears down the hall.

Funny how the sight of her bare ass works better than any painkiller.

* * *

My eyes open, and I blink a few times. A dull throb pulses up my thigh and into my hip—deep, down to the bone.

Great. Now my whole body's fucked.

Rolling onto my back, I stare at the ceiling, my vision adjusting to the dark. The soft white noise from Alley's phone hums beside her, filling the room.

The pulse sharpens into a pound, and my hand flies to my hip, pressing hard against the ache buried deep in the joint.

"Fuck," I mutter into the dark.

My mind immediately goes to the Oxy on the shelf. Relief, just steps away.

God, relief.

I'm dying for it. I can't keep doing this.

Maybe I'll just take more ibuprofen—or alternate with Tylenol. Something. *Anything.*

I glance over at Alley and almost laugh. Mouth wide open—catching flies, as always. The soundless chuckle eases the pain, if only for a second.

My chest tightens. *Fuck, I've got to get this figured out.* She didn't sign up for a life with a guy who's going to slow her down in ten years.

Hopefully the doctor has answers on Friday. I'll try anything. If not for me, then for her—for my wife. For the future we're building.

She went off birth control before the wedding. We talked about it. We're ready. She'll be thirty next year, and I'll be thirty-three. We've got steady jobs, we've lived together for over two years. We're in love. We're married. It's the next step. It feels right. But I refuse to accept a version of my life where I'm not able to run around with my kids, play basketball with them, walk the golf course. I need to be active, strong and present.

No. I won't fucking accept that.

The ache in my leg grows sharper, and I swing to the edge of the bed, sitting up. I bend and straighten my knee a few times, stretching it, trying to wake it up. My fingers dig into the muscles around it, massaging through the pain, searching for any kind of relief.

I push myself off the bed and shuffle into the kitchen. My palms brace against the counter as a sharp pang shoots through my leg. I grit my teeth, eyes locked on the medicine cabinet.

It's right there.

Relief.

No. I'll take ibuprofen.

Forcing my gaze away, I grab a glass and fill it with water. The bottle of ibuprofen is already on the counter, so I twist the lid off and shake two into my hand.

Alley's words echo in my head—*"You can't take that stuff forever."* I hold them in my hand for a couple of seconds, then toss them back into the bottle. I know they're bad for me. They can fuck up my stomach. And the rate I've been taking them, like they're going out of style? Well, that can't be good. They don't do anything anyway. My knee's too far gone.

I slide the bottle back across the counter and open the medicine cabinet instead. The prescription bottle sits right at eye level.

Reaching for it, I twist the cap, and let one pill fall into my hand. My eyes squeeze shut as the pain explodes through me, like shrapnel after a bomb. It hits every nerve, every thought, until there's nothing left but agony.

God, it hurts so bad. I tell myself again and again, *Don't be a fucking pussy.* But each pulse grows stronger, louder—like music swelling at a concert. The pain radiates through me, along with the voices in my head telling me not to do this.

Put it back. It's not that bad. Take the ibuprofen. Wait until Friday.

Fisting the pill in my palm, my whole body tenses, fighting the urge that's raging inside me.

Friday. That's still three days away. I could just take them until then—after I go to the doctor. They'll give me something else, something for the pain that isn't this. I'll start physical therapy. It'll get better. I won't need these after Friday. Only one a day until then. Just enough to get by, until I have another solution.

Slowly, I open my hand, staring at the little white pill. This small amount *has* to be better for me than all the ibuprofen I've been popping. I went over the recommended daily dose yesterday.

That can't be good.

Why am I even questioning this? Half a pill, or overdosing on ibuprofen every goddamn day? It's not even working. It's a no-brainer.

I grab a knife, cut it in half, and pop it into my mouth. Bitter powder seeps across my tongue from the freshly split pill. Bringing the glass to my lips, I let the cold water swirl around, trying to wash out the taste. I kick it back and swallow.

I drop the other half into the ibuprofen bottle, wipe the counter clean, and carry the bottle to my office. Gripping the zipper on my work bag, I tug it open and drop it inside.

I sink into my desk chair, my good knee bouncing. Sleep's pointless now. I have to be up in less than an hour anyway. I force myself to be productive—flip open my laptop and run a few reports, then open a presentation I've been prepping for the executive team. Each passing minute drags, feeling like an eternity, as I wait for the Oxy to kick in and do its job.

* * *

My gaze flicks to the clock on my laptop. It's only been twenty-five minutes? It feels like it's been an hour. My knee's still throbbing. It should've kicked in by now. *Shit. It's not working.*

183

I lean back, stroking my jaw, my elbow resting on my arm crossed tight over my stomach. My eyes lock on my backpack, my knee still bouncing. I'm restless as fuck.

I don't think. I just move.

Before I know it, I'm unzipping my pack and reaching for the ibuprofen bottle. My fingers close around it, pulse pounding in my throat. I know what I'm doing. I know exactly what I'm doing.

I fish the other half from the bottle, bitter powder dusting my fingertips. There's no hesitation this time. I pop it into my mouth, gather enough spit to swallow, and feel the heat rise across my tongue as it slides down.

And I swear to God—I already feel better.

Chapter Twenty-Five

JENSEN

THEN

THE BREEZE HITS MY CHEST, and my unbuttoned shirt blows open, cold air brushing against my nipples. I scan the crowd, catching a glimpse of Alley inside, laughing with Jordan and a few other girls.

That red swimsuit she's wearing is doing things to me. No way I'm focused on this conversation. It took some convincing, but she finally agreed.

Matt's Halloween party theme this year is famous couples, and I picked Kid Rock and Pamela Anderson. Sure, they were short-lived, but they count. She fought me hard on the Baywatch suit, but I won—mostly. She made me agree she could wear jean shorts with it.

And she's *killing* it.

Seriously, she looks sexy as hell. No question, I've got the hottest wife at this party. Her tits are pushed up with a strapless bra, making them look larger than usual, and it's taking everything in me not to drag her into one of Matt's guest bedrooms and suck one into my mouth.

I adjust my dick as it starts to chub and force my eyes away, turning my attention back to Matt and our mutual friend, Landon.

I shift my weight to my good leg. My knee's okay, for now. Still sore, always nagging, but bearable. I've taken a full Oxy each morning for the past three days, and it's made a huge difference. It gets me through work. Ibuprofen's been enough to manage the pain at night as it wears off. It doesn't take it away, but it dulls the edge.

I took another half about thirty minutes before we left for the party. I knew all the walking and standing would be rough, and I didn't want to be a buzzkill or make Alley leave early. So far, it's helped. The pain's been manageable.

I panicked when I cut that last one in half, though. I've only got two and a half left. I don't have a clue what I'm going to do when I run out.

I just need a few more, enough to get me through next week, after my MRI. The doctor didn't prescribe anything. I didn't expect painkillers, but I need something stronger than ibuprofen and Aleve. He told me to *"Wrap it, ice it, and keep taking those two anti-inflammatories until we can get an MRI."*

The MRI's scheduled for Wednesday. If I don't need surgery, I can get an injection, and start physical therapy. But if I do need surgery... fuck, I don't want to think about that.

I just need to get through next week and get the injection. The last one gave me solid relief for a while.

Still, only three pills left. *Two and a half,* I correct myself.

Out of the corner of my eye, I spot Seth mingling with a group of guys I don't really know. *Seth.* He went to college with Matt and me. He always had connections. The kind I'm in desperate need of right now. But that was years ago, back when Matt and I got high just for the hell of it—weed, blow, shrooms—even Adderall.

There's no way he's still dealing. *Jesus, get a grip.* He's not twenty anymore. We're in our thirties now. We've got jobs, wives. He might even have kids. And what am I gonna do—walk up and ask if he sells painkillers?

I almost laugh at how ridiculous I'm being. I'm not some fucking drug addict. But still, maybe he knows someone. Just to get me through the week.

"Jensen."

My head jerks toward Matt. "Yeah?"

He eyes me, brows furrowed. "You alright? You've been distracted all night."

"Yeah, man. I'm good."

Matt doesn't look convinced. He studies me like he's trying to read between the lines. "I asked if you were planning to come with Kevin and me to the game next week."

"Oh... um, yeah. Sorry. What day is it again?"

"Thursday."

"Yeah, that should work. Let me check with Alley."

"You said you'd ask Alley yesterday and let me know tonight." Matt takes a sip of his drink.

"Right," I say slowly. "Sorry, man. I forgot. I'll go ask her."

"You don't have to right now. Just let me know by tomorrow."

I spot Seth in the kitchen, finally alone. Now's my chance for a casual run-in.

"I will," I say. "I'm gonna grab a drink. You want anything?"

"Nah, I'm good."

"Cool. I'll be back."

I turn and head toward the kitchen, forcing myself to act relaxed. I slide up beside Seth, reaching for the tequila like that's why I came over. "Hey, man. How's it going?"

"Oh shit, Jensen!" Seth claps my back like we've been tight all these years. "I almost didn't recognize you with that wig. You pull off a damn good Kid Rock."

I chuckle. "Thanks, man. Yours is great too."

I have no fucking clue who he's supposed to be.

Twisting the cap off the tequila, I pour a shot and wince slightly as I shift my weight to my bad knee. Seth catches it. His eyes flick down, subtle, but not missing a thing.

"Shit, man. You alright?"

"Yeah," I say quickly, brushing it off. "Just my knee acting up. I had surgery a while ago. I'm still dealing with the aftermath."

I hesitate, bringing the tequila closer to my lips. I took that half pill earlier, but it's been over two hours. I probably shouldn't mix, but it's just one.

I toss the shot back and exhale, the burn hitting my chest. "The doctor's got me on fucking ibuprofen and Aleve, like that's supposed to do anything."

Seth snorts. "Yeah, man. Docs always act like that shit's magic. You doing PT?"

I nod, eyes on the empty glass in my hand. "Starting soon. I've just gotta get through next week until I can get an injection." I rub at my knee. "It's been brutal, though. There's not enough liquor in the world for nights like this."

Seth raises a brow, then glances around, lowering his voice slightly. "Man, if you need something stronger, I might know someone."

I go still for half a second, keeping my face neutral. "Yeah?"

"Yeah," he says, taking a slow sip of his drink. "Nothing crazy. Just a couple to hold you over, if you need 'em."

I hesitate, just for show. I don't want to look too eager. I take a second to roll my shoulders like I'm mulling it over.

"Shit," I say, shaking my head. "I don't know. I've had a few left over from surgery, so I've been managing, but..." I let out a low, humorless chuckle. "I'm running low, and I can already tell the next few weeks are gonna be hell."

Seth shrugs. "I get it. No pressure, man. But I've got a buddy who can hook you up. Nothing sketchy. Strictly clean, prescription stuff. None of that street shit where you never know what you're getting. This is the real deal. You know, wealthy circles, high-end supply. Just guys helping out guys dealing with shit like this."

I pour another shot for dramatics, lifting the glass to my lips. But I don't drink it, I just nod. "I appreciate that, man." Setting the glass down, I pull out my phone. "Maybe I'll grab your number. Just in case."

Seth grins and rattles it off. I save it, and he clinks his glass to mine before walking off, leaving the offer floating in the air. The choice is mine.

I stare at the tequila for a beat, then push it aside. I'm not dumb enough to have another. Not when I've already crossed the line tonight. Rubbing my forehead, I exhale a long, slow breath. When I look up, Matt's watching me from across the room. He lifts a brow like he knows something's off.

Shit. Did he see me talking to Seth? It doesn't matter. Even if he suspects something—which he shouldn't, I didn't do anything wrong. I'm not going to call the guy. And even if I do, it's just for a week. That's it. It's not like I'm scoring coke like we used to back in the day.

I nod his way, dump my shot in the sink, and push through the crowd to find Alley, suddenly needing to get the hell out of here. I find her on the balcony with Jordan, and now Megan, who must've arrived when I wasn't looking.

I sneak up behind her, arms slipping around her waist as I press a kiss to her neck. "Is that Pam Anderson?" I murmur, my eyes dropping to her cleavage like a magnet.

"There's my rockstar," she says with a grin.

"Babe, you look so fucking sexy," I whisper.

"God. Get a room," Megan groans, rolling her eyes.

I chuckle against Alley's skin, glancing up at Megan. "When did you get here? Where's Kev?"

"Thirty minutes ago. No clue where Kevin is, probably upstairs at the bar." She shrugs, turning back to Jordan and their conversation.

We're interrupted by Jordan's boyfriend, Max—the definition of a douchebag. She's been seeing him ever since that ski trip, and I have no idea what she sees in him. The guy's dull. Kudos to Matt for inviting him, I guess. But we all know the truth. Matt can't keep Jordan at arm's length no matter how hard he tries, and she wouldn't have come without Max.

"Hey, I'm ready to go," he says to Jordan.

She hesitates, clearly stalling. You can tell she doesn't want to leave.

"How about thirty more minutes?" she asks, turning toward him.

"Nah. This party blows. Let's get outta here."

She exhales hard. "Let's go talk about it over there." She gestures to the corner, weaves her hand with his, and tugs him away from the group.

"Jesus," Megan mutters. "He's such a buzzkill."

Alley laughs. "He's definitely not *fun.*"

"Seriously. I'd rather read the dictionary cover to cover than have another conversation with him." Megan glances between me and Alley. "I'm gonna go find Kev, take some shots. Do something to shake off the Max energy."

Laughter bubbles up between them.

"Okay, I'll come find you in a bit," Alley says.

Megan touches her arm. "Sounds good. You two have fun."

"Don't get too drunk, Megs," I call after her, and she waves me off as she disappears into the crowd.

Alley spins around, her hands finding their place on my bare chest. "Have you had to fight off all the ladies tonight?" she teases. "Because I'm ready to rip the rest of these clothes right off you." Her nails drag down my abs, a smile playing on her lips. She slides her arms inside my open shirt, hugging me tightly. Rising onto her toes, she tilts her chin up, and I lean down, meeting her halfway for a kiss.

"Mmm," I murmur against her lips, eyes dropping to her chest again. "Jesus, babe. Can you wear this bra, and low-cut shit like this more often? It's such a fucking turn-on."

"I'll wear low-cut shit for you anytime," she says, biting the corner of her lip.

"You wanna get outta here?" I ask, voice low and husky.

"Already?" She glances at her watch. "It's only ten." Her eyes flick to my knee, then back to mine. "Is your knee doing okay?"

"Yeah, actually feels pretty good tonight. Just tired... you know I've been sleeping like shit. Plus, I've been eyeing this hot blonde I'm thinking about taking home." I raise my brows, and she laughs.

"Oh yeah? What's she look like?"

I pull her in closer. "Let's see... smoking hot, beautiful smile, big hair, nice tits, great ass. I caught her checking me out earlier, so I figured I might get lucky tonight."

She laughs again, pressing a kiss to my chest. "You were? We could probably arrange that. Too bad the big hair isn't mine. And that my tits don't really look like this."

"What are you talking about? You have great tits."

She shrugs. "They're okay."

I cock a brow. "You better give my wife a compliment right now."

"Fine. I have a great rack."

"That's my girl." My lips find hers again, my hand cupping the back of her head as I kiss her firmly. "Mind if I head out?"

Her brows pull together, her warm palm flattening against my chest. "No, that's okay. You want me to come with you?"

"Nah, you stay. Have fun."

"You sure everything's okay? It's not like you to bail early."

I want to tell her. That the pain's worse than I let on. That it never lets up. That it's fucking exhausting.

Instead, I force a grin. "Everything's fine. Like I said, just tired."

"Alright," she says softly. "Well, I'm gonna say goodbye to a few people. I'll be right behind you." She flashes a teasing smile. "Besides, it'd be a shame if Kid and Pam didn't hook up. I hear they had a wild sex life. So... " She walks her fingers up my chest, brows raised. "Don't go to bed without me."

My cock grows instantly hard. "Hell, yeah." I trace my fingers over the bare skin of her back and lean in, whispering in her ear, "I'm not really that tired. I just wanted pussy." I chuckle against her ear, kissing her jaw. "I'll see you in a few."

She feigns shock and slaps my arm, mouthing *bad boy* as I back away.

Turning, I weave through the throng of people toward the elevator, thoughts of sliding that red swimsuit off her shoulders flooding my mind. I think about all the things I want to do to her. *God, I love making her squirm.* Making Alley come is one of my favorite things in this world. My cock strains against my jeans, anticipation building, and I can't wipe the stupid grin off my face as I press the button for the lobby.

This Kid Rock's about to rock her fucking world.

Chapter Twenty-Six

ALLEY

THEN

THE ELEVATOR DOORS slide open and a smile sweeps across my lips as Jensen's hand grips mine.

I almost got stuck on call but Cindy saved my ass at the last minute and traded me for Christmas Day. I'm excited to be here, to see Michael and Stella, and the kids. Jensen's been hoping I'll be ready to see my dad. I'm nervous about it, and I'm not sure I'm ready, but I haven't stopped thinking about it.

Either way, here we are. New Year's Eve, and back in Chicago.

The last time I was here was Michael's birthday last year. Megan and I flew in a few days early to hang and have some girl time. Jensen came out later that weekend for the party.

I glance up at Jensen, watching him for a second. *Damn. He's all mine.* My lips curve into a smile as my gaze sweeps across the floor, landing on Michael and Stella talking to Leo and his girlfriend, Vivian.

I tug at Jensen's arm. "Come on, Michael's over here."

We weave through the crowd, and a grin spreads across my face when Leo's eyes meet mine. He grins and winks, his hand resting lightly on Vivian's back.

"Hey!" I call out a few feet away.

We all take turns hugging and saying hello. I've only met Vivian twice before, but she's stunning and easy to get along with. She and Leo live together now and have a baby—little Isla. They brought her to New York for the wedding, and she's honestly the most beautiful baby I've ever seen. But how could she not be with those two as parents?

I'm ecstatic for them. I've never seen Leo look happier. And holy hell, no one ever thought he'd settle down. But if he was going to, it makes sense that it's with Vivian. She seems absolutely perfect for him.

Conversation flows easily. Michael and Jensen head to the bar together, and my heart could burst just watching them. They don't know each other well. They've only met in person a handful of times, but it makes me so happy to see how easily they get along.

I ask Stella about the kids and her job, and Leo and Vivian fill me in on all things Isla—telling stories, showing pictures. Excitement bubbles in my chest at the thought of possibly being pregnant soon.

My last two periods were met with disappointment. I know it can take time, especially after stopping birth control—my body's still trying to regulate. God, my last cycle lasted fifty days. I started to get hopeful, taking test after test, only to get nothing. I guess that's normal too, though, post-pill.

Jensen's still at the bar with Michael, but now Adam's there too. We lock eyes across the room, and he smiles, lifting a hand in a wave.

I smile back, and lift my hand too.

Jensen spots me and waves me over, and before I know it, I'm clinking my water glass with Jensen, Michael, and Adam.

* * *

I'M AT THE BAR, refilling my water when Vivian and Stella make their way over.

Stella grins. "Vivian has a fun game to play," she says.

"What is it?" I ask, curiosity piqued.

Stella looks to Vivian, who laughs, and says. "Oh my God, they're going to think I'm crazy."

"Trust me, this game's right up her alley." She shoots me a grin. "No pun intended."

"Ooh, now I have to know," I reply.

Vivian hesitates, then exhales. "Fine. But please don't judge me. Alley, you have ten seconds to find someone to take home tonight, and obviously it can't be Jensen."

I laugh. She's right. This is totally my kind of game, even more Jensen's. I already know the two of them would get along great. But also, shit. Is she serious? Because if I can't pick Jensen, my next choice would be Adam. And I can't pick Adam—that's just a no. Leo's hot as hell, but he's Leo. He's like a Kevin to me.

There are plenty of good-looking men in the room, though. No surprise, considering many of them are Leo's friends. Which basically means: wealthy, well-dressed, confident-as-hell businessmen.

"Seven, six, five," Vivian counts, and I scan the crowd like I'm on a mission. My gaze lands on a guy who looks mid-thirties. He's got a decent build, dark hair, thick beard, tailored gray suit. Not my usual type, but he's hot in a rugged, put-together kind of way.

"That guy over there, I guess. In the gray suit with the beard."

Stella gives an approving nod, and Vivian grins. "Okay, yeah. I'm into it. Great beard."

"Who has a great beard?" Jensen interjects, amusement dancing in his eyes.

"Great," I blurt.

"Busted," Stella laughs. "Alley wants to bang Beard Guy."

My cheeks burn as I smack Stella's arm. "I do not." I turn to Jensen, laughing. "It's a game. One you would've crushed, by the way. But I swear, you're the only one I want."

"Wow. Jesus, babe. I didn't know you were into beards. Should I grow mine out?"

"No. Please don't. I don't think you have the genetics to pull off a thick beard like that anyway."

He puts a hand over his chest, feigning offense. "Whoa. Questioning my beard-growing abilities? Harsh. I'm gonna have to prove you wrong." He leans in, dropping his voice just for me. "Lola would like it against her soft skin."

He chuckles against my neck, the heat of his breath and that voice sending shivers down my arm. I press my lips together, trying not to grin, then spin around and kiss him.

"Hey," he murmurs against my lips, "you wanna get outta here?"

"Yes," I whisper, biting back a smile. I know what *'get outta here'* means. "But it's not even midnight."

"I know, but... I dunno." He shrugs slightly. "I'd rather take you back to Michael and Stella's and celebrate with you. You know, ravishing your body."

"But you love New Year's. You love parties."

I pull back slightly, brows pinching. I'm genuinely confused. This is the third time he's bailed early on a party since Halloween. And that's not like him.

He shifts his weight, wincing, and concern flickers through me. "Is your knee hurting again?"

He hesitates for a beat, then exhales in frustration. "Yeah. It's been giving me a hard time the past few days. But I can just sit the rest of the night. I'll be fine."

I reach for his hand. "No. It's okay. If you're hurting, we can go."

"Nah, babe, I don't want to ruin your night."

"You're not." I give his hand a soft squeeze. "All I really need is to be with you. It's fine."

He studies me for a second, eyes scanning mine like he's making sure I mean it. "You sure?"

"I'm sure. Let's say our goodbyes and grab our coats."

The relief on his face is immediate—subtle, but unmistakable. His shoulders ease, and his jaw unclenches as we turn to go.

We make our rounds, exchanging quick goodbyes and polite hugs, and grab our coats. As we head toward the elevators, I glance over at him, and I can't help it. Something in my chest pulls tight. This isn't just about a party.

* * *

As we head outside to wait for our Uber, my mind spins with worry. Jensen hasn't said anything about his knee in weeks. After

195

Halloween, he had an MRI, got an injection, started physical therapy. I guess it's been a few months since then, maybe the injection is wearing off.

It makes me anxious. I know he's a guy—wants to seem tough, doesn't like to complain or let anything slow him down. But God, it's concerning. For a while he was taking ibuprofen around the clock, and that's not exactly healthy.

Now, it's starting to affect his social life. That's what worries me the most. Jensen is the life of the party. Who am I kidding—he *is* the party. He thrives around people, and people are drawn to him.

It's New Year's Eve, and he wants to go home. I can't even wrap my head around that.

We slide into the backseat of the Uber, and his hand lands on my thigh, giving it a squeeze. He tips his head back against the headrest and closes his eyes.

I watch him, because *God,* he's handsome. His brows pinch together like he's in pain, and I want nothing more than to take it away. I reach for his hand, threading my fingers through his, giving it a squeeze. He squeezes back, a faint smile tugging at his lips, but he keeps his eyes closed.

The ride is mostly quiet, aside from the occasional question from the driver and soft music in the background. By the time we get to Michael's, it's eleven-thirty, and Jensen heads straight for the bedroom. I follow close behind.

The second we're inside, he's already digging through his backpack. He pulls out the bottle of ibuprofen and turns his back to me as he shakes some into his hand.

"Do you need some water?" I ask.

He glances over his shoulder. "No, I'm fine," he says, popping the pills into his mouth and swallowing them dry.

"Do you think you need another injection?"

"I'll be fine, Alley." His voice is sharp. Irritated.

I let it roll off me, even though it stings. He must really be hurting, because Jensen never gets short with me.

"Babe," I say softly, stepping toward him. "What can I do? How can I help?"

I come up behind him, placing my hands on his back and running them slowly over the broad, thick muscles, across his shoulders, and down his arms. I press a kiss between his shoulder blades, breathing him in, my heart cracking a little for him.

He draws in a deep breath and lets it out slowly. Then he turns, pulling me into his arms. He kisses the top of my head and rests his chin there. "Nothing... I'm sorry. I didn't mean to be a dick. You being here is enough." He swallows, hard. "I'm sorry I made you leave the party early."

"It's okay. I just want you to be okay. I'm worried about you."

He exhales sharply, the breath warm against my hair. "You don't need to worry about me. I'm fine. I'll be fine. Everything's good."

"Okay." I step back gently. "I think I'm going to take a bath, wind down a bit."

"Alright. I'll just be here."

I grab a few things from my suitcase and head for the bathroom. The guest bath has one of those freestanding tubs—big, with the perfect slope. I use it every time I visit.

I start the water and plug the drain, brushing my teeth while I wait for it to fill. Dimming the lights, I add some salts and light a candle before slipping out of my dress and stepping into the tub.

I sink down into the hot water, letting it wash over my skin.

"Oh, wow," I breathe. *God, that feels so good.*

I close my eyes and try to quiet my thoughts. In through the nose, out through the mouth—slow, long, meditative breaths. I count to four on each inhale and exhale. Every time my thoughts drift back to Jensen and the pain he's in, I force them back to the count.

Something feels... off. Leaving the party was unusual enough. But what really gets me is that he didn't get handsy on the way home— didn't slide a hand up my dress, didn't whisper something filthy in my ear. We've been home for a while now, and there's been no attempt to have sex. No playful teasing. Nothing.

I glance down at the edge of the tub, lips pressing into a frown. *I was wearing a short dress.* That's not Jensen. That's never Jensen. *How much pain is he in if he's not even thinking about sex?*

It almost stings. But I know it's not personal.

Damn. Stay focused. One, two...

The bathroom door creaks open, and I open my eyes. Jensen stands over me, a familiar smirk forming on his lips.

There he is.

The medicine must be kicking in. He looks better now, like the pain has eased. He pulls his shirt over his head, then pushes his joggers and underwear down, stepping out of them without a word.

"Room for one more?"

Warmth floods me, low and fluttery, spreading through my chest and down between my legs. Grinning, I slide toward the middle of the tub. Jensen steps in behind me and sinks down, his legs framing mine. He pulls me back against him, his arms wrapping around my body, firm chest pressed to my back.

His mouth finds the spot just behind my ear, lips dragging slow kisses along my neck. One hand cups my breast, his thumb circling my nipple in lazy, perfect strokes. I feel his cock throbbing behind me, hard and hot against the base of my spine.

His other hand trails lower, gliding across my stomach, inching toward that deep, steady thrum building between my thighs. Goose-bumps prick my arms, and I melt into him, body going pliant, like we're sinking into the same pulse.

When his fingers reach my pubic bone, my legs part instinctively, resting open against his. But instead of going where I crave, his touch veers slightly, brushing that soft, hypersensitive skin along my inner thigh.

The thrum turns into a steady pounding, like a heartbeat deep in my core, heat radiating into every inch of my body. My head falls back against his chest, lips parting as a soft sigh escapes into the air. My hips shift beneath me, aching for more of his touch.

A deep chuckle vibrates behind me, echoing off the porcelain walls of the tub.

He keeps teasing me. Tracing slow circles along my inner thighs, his fingertips barely dusting my skin. The heat of his touch blurs into the warmth of the water, sharpening my focus, pulling all my attention to every stroke.

My hands slide down to his thighs, gripping tight, nails digging in.

I press back against his hard length, and his arm tightens around me, pulling me flush against him—the same hand still cupping my breast, fingers toying with my nipple.

Then, *finally*, his fingers slip lower, gliding over my slit and circling my clit.

I gasp, melting deeper into him as my pelvic floor tightens, hips arching to meet his touch.

"You like that?" Jensen murmurs, his breath hot against my ear as he kisses a slow path along my jaw.

I moan in response.

His fingers have always been magic, pulling pleasure from places I didn't even know existed. Not until him. No one else has ever satisfied me the way he does, quieted my cravings like he can.

My gaze drops, drawn to the way the muscles in his forearm flex with every motion, his veins rising from the tension. Watching him work me, watching those hands—it's almost enough to push me over the edge.

They're big. Strong. Masculine. Capable of being both firm and impossibly gentle. The way they cradle me when we sleep. The way they hold me when I'm hurting. The way they pleasure me when I'm burning with need.

The way they make me feel safe.

God, I love him.

My throat constricts, thick with emotion, as my orgasm rises—gathering low and deep, a slow burn spreading like wildfire. The heat intensifies with every stroke, and I close my eyes, bracing for the climax that's about to take me over.

He slides his fingers lower, pushing them inside me as his thumb takes over. The pressure builds, pooling in the center of my thighs. My orgasm sends white-hot sparks shooting through my limbs, my hips tensing as I tighten around him, unraveling completely.

Gasps and moans echo softly around us as his fingers slow, and I sink back into him, melting—liquid and weightless in his arms.

His lips brush against my ear. "I love you so fucking much, Alley."

He draws his fingers from me and tightens his hold. His forearms flex around me, strong and steady. There's something about the way he's holding me—like he's scared to let go.

Like he's afraid of losing me.

"God, I love you." His voice cracks, rough and unsteady, and something heavy settles in the air between us—an undercurrent of fear I don't understand. It radiates off him, strong and suffocating, and I've never felt anything like it from him before.

I shift, turning just enough to see his face. The sorrow in his eyes, the quiet glisten on his cheeks. My heart lurches. His love for me is unmistakable, but it's tangled up in something else. Something I can't name. And it shakes me to my core.

"Hey," I whisper, turning to fully face him.

I kiss him softly, and he kisses me back, deep and lingering, drawing my lips into his. My fingers drift beneath the water, gliding down his torso until I reach his cock. I wrap my hand around the base and slowly stroke him.

His hands catch my wrist, gently stopping me.

He shakes his head. "No," he murmurs, barely above a whisper. "Not tonight, baby. Just you."

His hand cups the back of my head, and he crashes his mouth to mine, kissing me with a desperation that's hot as hell—and terrifying at the same time.

He stands abruptly, water streaming down his body, and steps out of the tub. Wrapping a towel around his waist, he walks into the bedroom leaving me satisfied, but deeply unsettled.

I'm warm and sated, but nowhere near at peace. Something about that moment didn't feel right, and I can't shake it.

I watch the candle flicker, shadows dancing on the wall, my heart pounding. He held me like he needed me. Like he was scared.

And then he walked away.

I stay there a while longer, letting the water cool around me, hoping clarity will come. It doesn't, and sitting here isn't helping.

Standing, I step out of the tub and wrap myself in a towel. I blow out the candle, and pad into the bedroom. The lamp is on. Jensen's already lying down—naked, one arm draped across his abs, the other tucked behind his head. His eyes are closed. His chest rises and falls in a steady rhythm, lips parted, hair still damp from the steam.

But he's not asleep.

And he's still mostly hard.

I let the towel fall.

Part of me wants to crawl in next to him, wrap myself around him, and drift off in the quiet comfort of his arms. But another part of me—it aches for that deeper connection. The part where he needs me too. The way that I need him.

I climb onto the bed and straddle him, my knees settling on either side of his thighs.

His brow twitches, eyes fluttering open slowly.

"Hey," I whisper.

He hums, low and quiet, looking up at me. His hands rise lazily, skimming up my hips. "Hey," he echoes, his voice thick and slurred with sleep.

I lean forward and kiss him softly. His mouth opens beneath mine, but there's no urgency. Just a response—a reaction, but not desire.

I reach between us, wrap my hand around him, still semi-hard, and stroke gently.

He lets out a breath through his nose. "Babe..."

But he doesn't stop me.

Once hard, I guide him to my entrance and sink down slowly, letting a soft moan escape my throat as he fills me. My hands brace on his chest, and I move—slow at first, rocking my hips back and forth. His hands slide up to my thighs, holding them lightly, but he's not taking control.

He lets me do the work.

His eyes are half-lidded, watching me, but there's a haze to them. It's like he's here, but not fully. His jaw clenches, like he's trying to focus, trying to feel it the way he normally would, but something's missing. He's disconnected.

I keep going. I grind down on him, finding the friction, even as my heart aches. It's good. It still feels good. But it's different—detached, quiet.

After a few minutes, I slow, leaning forward until my chest is against his. "You okay?" I whisper into his ear.

He nods, slow. "Yeah. Just tired. You feel incredible, baby."

I nod against his neck, biting my lip, and press a kiss to his jaw. I keep rocking my hips, gently, coaxing what I can from him. His breathing deepens, his hands squeeze my thighs once, and eventually, he groans low in his throat and finishes—more from the motion than the moment, or me.

His arms wrap around me after, pulling me down onto his chest. "I love you," he murmurs.

I swallow down the lump forming in my throat. "I love you too."

I can't help the tiny crack forming in my chest, because for the first time, I felt like I was loving him alone.

I glance at the clock on the nightstand and let out a sigh—12:03. *Happy New Year.*

* * *

We pull up to my childhood home, and Jensen shifts the car into park. The yard is dead from winter, but still well-kept, leaves cleared and weeds pulled. Everything looks maintained, just waiting for spring to bring it back to life. Already, it's a vast improvement from the last time I was here.

Jensen's hand finds my thigh, giving it a reassuring squeeze. I turn to meet his gaze. He seems different today. Better. More like himself, happy and focused. There's a light in his eyes again, bright and clear.

"You sure you don't want me to come up with you?"

"Yeah, I'm sure. I'll be okay," I say nodding, like hearing myself say the words will make me believe them.

"Alright. Well, I'll wait here until you're inside. I'll stay close. Just call or text when you're ready for me to come back."

I nod again, more firmly this time. "Okay..."

My fingers fumble with the door handle. I pause, glancing back at Jensen. "What if he doesn't want to see me?"

"He wants to see you. He reached out to Michael. He wants to see you," he says, steady and sure.

"Alright," I say softly, my pulse quickening.

He leans forward, kissing me fervently, like he's trying to kiss the fear right out of me.

Without another thought, I open the door, and before I know it I'm standing on the porch of my dad's house. My house. My mother's house.

I swallow hard, my fingers trembling. I take a deep breath and lift my hand to knock, my heart pounding so hard it echoes in my ears. Nerves crawl up my throat with every passing second.

The door swings open, my dad's expression shifting in an instant—shock melting into something soft. A ghost of a smile curves his lips, his eyes lighting up, and just as quickly, filling with tears.

"Alley girl." His voice cracks as the words leave his mouth, and his fingers fly to the bridge of his nose, pinching it as his eyes squeeze shut. He lets out an audible cry.

And then—he breaks. Right in front of me.

A love so deep bursts free from the cell I've kept it locked in for far too long. The space that's kept me safe for a decade. Kept me from shattering, from getting hurt. Every emotion hits me all at once, but it feels like a hug. And somehow, the storm inside me calms, warmth radiating through every inch of my soul.

My pulse steadies, and I step forward—into the first hug with my dad in over ten years. "Hi, Dad," I say, my voice shaky, choked with all that I'm feeling.

I let myself fall into his arms, and the dam breaks. Tears streak down my face, and every crack begins to fill with hope.

Chapter Twenty-Seven

ALLEY

PRESENT DAY

My tears finally subside as I sink into Matt's arms—a grounding force pulling me back to reality. I'm not alone in this. Not completely, anyway.

"Alley." Matt's voice is quiet, comforting. "What's going on? Megan texted me, said you couldn't find Jensen."

I swallow hard, my throat raw from crying and sore from screaming. My eyes are swollen, and my head pounds.

I don't answer.

"Is he using again?" he asks, gently. Just hearing him say it unleashes another wave of grief.

I don't want to say it. Not out loud. Maybe if I keep it to myself, like I've been doing for the past few weeks, it won't be real. But it is, and Matt's asking.

I squeeze my eyes shut, more tears slipping out. I nod, unable to speak. I hate how this moment feels familiar—deja vu in the worst way —a scene I never wanted to replay.

I tighten my grip like he alone can take the pain away. Like he can make it better, or fix this. Fix him. Fix us.

"Yeah," I finally admit, my voice barely audible.

"Shit."

"Yeah." I loosen my grip and sit up. "It's our anniversary..." My gaze drops to my hand, landing on a chipped nail I broke earlier. I pick at it, whispering, "He didn't call. Didn't text. Just didn't fucking show up." I clench my fist, lifting my eyes to meet Matt's.

He rubs my back, his own eyes closing like he's trying to absorb the blow with me. "I'm sorry."

"It's not your fault." I take a slow breath, then let it out. "Thank you for being here."

"Of course." He leans back and tips his head against the couch, dragging both hands down his face. "Fuck."

"That's what I said." A weak smile tugs at the corner of my mouth, but it doesn't quite make it.

A groan falls from Matt's lips, and he leans forward, elbows on his knees, head in his hands. "Fuck," he mutters again, quieter this time.

Then he looks at me. "I suspected. A few weeks ago. But I didn't want it to be true. God..." His voice cracks, the sound slicing through me, tightening my throat all over again. "I didn't want it to be true, Al."

I press my palm to his back, rubbing gently to comfort him this time, as he starts to break too. They're best friends, practically brothers. They've seen each other through everything. This doesn't just affect me. It affects *all* of us. But, at the end of the day, I'm not blood. I'm not his sister. I'm not his mother. I'm not his brother sitting next to me, breaking down because his best friend is disappearing.

I'm his wife.

And as much as I love him—*God, I love him*—I have something none of them do. I have a choice.

I can leave.

I don't *have* to stay.

Not anymore.

Chapter Twenty-Eight

ALLEY

THEN—A YEAR AND A HALF AGO

JANUARY

MEGAN'S UPDATING Christy and me about the kids while I pick at the bread in the middle of the table. I tear a piece off, slather it in an absurd amount of butter, and take a bite.

Oh God, that's good.

I'm only half-listening.

My mind's split in two—here, and with Jensen. He's been... I don't know. Different. I can't quite explain it. He's stressed, irritable, tired, withdrawn, late. Just off.

It's sporadic, too. I never know which version of him I'm going to get. He'll seem completely normal for a few days, and then—bam, something shifts. Last week, he said he forgot something at the office and disappeared for three hours. On a Saturday.

"Hello? Earth to Alley." Megan waves a hand in front of my face, her voice pulling me from my thoughts. I blink, jerking my gaze toward her.

"Sorry." I say as both their faces come into focus. Christy's watching me closely, and Megan's trying not to laugh.

"Where'd you go?" Megan asks, raising a brow.

I push the thoughts away. "Nowhere. Sorry. What'd you say?"

She nods toward Christy. "Mom asked if you and Jensen are coming to family dinner next week."

"Yeah, we'll be there. Can I bring anything?" I turn to Christy, doing my best to sound normal.

"Nope. I've got it covered. Just bring yourselves." Her eyes narrow slightly, her voice softening. "You okay? You've been quiet today."

I wave it off. "Oh, it's nothing. I was just thinking about a friend at work." I swallow, forcing a small, sad smile. "She had to get a biopsy on a mole. She's been really worried while she waits to hear back."

Cindy *is* waiting for results, but I don't know why I just lied. Maybe because there's nothing *technically* wrong. Or maybe because I don't want them thinking less of Jensen—or me. Voicing concerns about our relationship to his mom and sister doesn't feel right. What would I even say? *Things just feel off, and I don't know why?*

Besides, Jensen's amazing. Things are still great ninety-five percent of the time. We're probably just hitting a bump. Doesn't that just make us... normal?

"Oh, that's too bad. I hope everything turns out okay," Christy says gently. She means it. She's one of the most thoughtful, genuine people I know. It's no wonder Jensen turned out the way he did—well, all of them, really. They're all so great. I love every single one of them.

Our server comes by to refill drinks, and Megan launches into details about the surprise Disney trip she and Kevin are taking the kids on for Easter. I pull off another piece of bread and dip it into the ball of butter, practically scooping the whole thing.

We do monthly brunches the last Sunday of the month. Amber's out sick today, so it's just the three of us. It's always the same place: The Porcupine, Christy's favorite, where designer purses sit upright in their own chairs like honored guests.

It's a little fancy for my taste, but the food and coffee are incredible. In the summer, the outdoor patio is to die for—huge hanging flower pots, crisp white linens, strung lights. It's gorgeous, and one of my favorite ways to start the day. Jensen and I go often when it's warm, just us or with Matt and some of our other friends.

"Al, do you and Jensen have any trips planned? I know you mentioned Miami a few weeks ago. Did you book anything?" Megan asks.

I set down the piece of bread I've clearly been using to manage my feelings. "No. Not yet. We talked about April or May, but haven't booked anything. So far, just the Berkshires next week. Everyone's still going, right?"

"I think so." Megan takes a sip of her Bloody Mary. "I'm so excited to be going over Superbowl weekend. Maybe Jensen can teach Kevin how to make better bets. I swear that man will bet away the kids' college funds. He can't win to save his life, even if it's a fifty-fifty shot."

I laugh, grateful for the distraction. Jensen definitely has the good luck charm on his side. "Oh my God, poor Kev. I still can't get over the fact he was up five grand at Jensen's bachelor party, and then lost it all on red."

Megan scoffs, rolling her eyes. "Don't remind me. Seriously, what an idiot. I love him, but—*God.*"

"Well, I can't believe that after all these years your father and I *still* aren't invited to the Berkshires weekend," Christy teases. We all know she doesn't really mean it. She secretly loves that the kids have something just for them—that they're all close like this.

"I know, Mom. You give us shit every year. But we all know you don't really want to come. One, you hate skiing. Two, do you really want to be cooped up with all your kids, drunker than skunks, talking about stuff you definitely don't want to know about? And three, we can't talk shit about you guys if you're there." Megan sticks out her tongue and laughs, and Christy playfully smacks her arm.

I laugh along with them, my mood officially lifted. The server brings our checks, and Christy grabs it, of course. She does every time, and while I feel bad, I'm also not complaining.

We chat for another fifteen minutes before finally making our way outside. It's a cold January day, and I have zero interest in walking, even though it's not far. I'm looking forward to spending the rest of the day with Jensen. It's football Sunday, Conference Championship weekend. He and Matt will be glued to the game, a few beers deep, and the charcuterie I left for them will most likely be destroyed.

I'm *really* excited for the Berkshires trip next week, especially with it landing on Super Bowl weekend. I've fallen hard for football this season, and I'm not mad about it. I even joined two fantasy leagues: one with Jensen's family and one Michael started with our dad, Adam, Leo, and a few others. The leagues are over, but the trash talk hasn't stopped. Jensen won in the Adams family league, and one of Leo's buddies, Ryan, took the win in Michael's.

As we reach the exit, we all stop to hug goodbye. I push the heavy door open, walk to the curb, and hail a cab. I slide into the back seat for the five-minute ride home, watching out the window as it starts to flurry. I hate the cold, but I love the snow. I lean back in the cab, giving in to the smile tugging on my lips. It's going to be a great day.

* * *

Everyone's wearing a Bengals jersey. Everyone... except Matt, who just walked into the kitchen wearing a Rams jersey and the biggest smartass grin I've ever seen.

Jensen laughs when he sees him. "Bro. You've got to be kidding me. Wipe that shit-eating grin off your face and go change. That jersey's banned in this house."

Matt chuckles. "Fuck off. This is my house. You'll be wishing you had one in a few hours."

Kevin pipes in. "Seriously, dude. You don't like the Rams. You just did that to piss us off."

I can't help but laugh. They're absolutely ridiculous, arguing like it's life or death over a team they don't usually root for. Things are about to get heated. We all chipped into the Super Bowl squares pool, so the trash talk is only going to get worse as the night goes on.

"What are you talking about? I love the Rams," Matt says, rounding the kitchen island with a smirk. "You assholes are all going down. All my money's on Stafford." He leans in, lowering his voice near my ear. "I totally did it to piss them off."

I laugh again, slicing open another pack of cheese for the charcuterie board, the chaos around me oddly comforting. I couldn't tell you why the Adams siblings are all-in on the Bengals because they're die-hard Jets fans. I'm just along for the ride, but I was told it was *very* important that I wear a Bengals jersey. So, I did—though Jensen was deeply upset that I had to wear pants.

We're back in the Berkshires. We got here three days ago, and it's been a blast so far. I've needed this. *We've* needed this—time away to destress and reconnect. It's been really, really good.

And yes, I delivered my now-annual tradition of road head on the way up.

"You need therapy, Matt," Megan calls from across the kitchen. "There are other ways to deal with Jordan not coming." She pauses, realizing what she said. "Ha. No pun intended."

Kevin snorts while Jensen high-fives her.

"Oh, Jordan's coming, Meg," Jensen says. "She's just not coming with Matt."

Yep. That's my sweet, sweet husband. And I love him all the more for it.

"I mean, we're all here, Matt. We all came. What's wrong—you can't make Jordan come?" Jensen slaps him on the back, and Megan spits her drink out with laughter, wine spraying across the counter.

"Jesus, Megan. Get it together," Kevin says, cracking up.

Matt's face does it for me. I can't hold back either. He's a ticking time bomb, and I almost feel bad—almost.

"Ha. Ha. Ha. You're all *so* funny. She's with Dr. Douchebag again this weekend."

"Is every guy Jordan dates going to be a douchebag?" Megan asks, one eyebrow raised.

Matt scoffs, eyes darting to the side. "For the record, I made her come two weeks ago. Joke's on you fuckers." He flips both middle fingers up, grabs his drink off the counter and storms off to the living room, flopping onto the couch beside Jeff, who's glued to his phone.

Jensen raises his brows at me, grinning.

"That was mean, babe," I say, smothering my smile.

"He asked for every bit of it by wearing that jersey."

"You got that right," Megan adds.

"Besides," Jensen points to Megan. "She started it with the whole coming innuendo."

Megan grins proudly, dramatically rolling her shoulders and stretching her neck like she's gearing up for a fight. "He shouldn't mess. He knows better."

Megan tosses the salad one last time while I pull the wings from the oven, the heat warming my face as I set them beside the rolls. We've got quite the spread, and I can't wait to load up my plate, cuddle up next to Jensen, and watch the sibling banter.

Oh yeah, and the game.

* * *

At halftime, all the guys head into the kitchen for more drinks and food. Jensen grabs a beer and vanishes down the hallway toward our room.

I push up from the couch and head to the kitchen to throw my plate away, telling myself I *won't* pick at the food again, but as I pass the charcuterie, I can't help swiping a piece of cheese from it.

"Hey, Megan," Matt calls out to the living room from across the kitchen.

Megan turns her head. "Yeah?"

"Who's winning?" Matt's grin is so smug he might as well have "fuck you" tattooed across his forehead.

"That's tiny dick energy, Matt!" Megan fires back without missing a beat.

God, these two. They need their own show.

I park my ass back down on the couch, settling in for the halftime show. Snoop Dogg and Eminem, are you kidding me? This is going to be great.

My phone dings.

It's my dad. He's sent a picture of him, Michael, and Stella.

DAD

Miss you, Alley girl.

My heart swells. I could honestly burst just trying to wrap my head around having my dad back in my life. I'm grinning like a fool as I text back.

211

> I miss you too, Dad! All of you! Who you rooting for?

DAD

> The Rams, of course.

Michael chimes in. I didn't even realize he was in the thread.

MICHAEL

> The BENGALS. Dad's delusional.

I laugh softly, completely lost in the texts, the halftime show forgotten. I hold up my phone, snap a quick selfie in my Bengals jersey, and send it.

> But honestly, I'm just here for the food and the halftime show. Lol.

DAD

> Well, enjoy the show. Love you.

> Love you!

My eyes fill with happy tears. It feels silly that something so simple could bring this much joy, but it does. It's been too damn long. For so long, I felt like I was drifting, not really belonging anywhere. I had Michael, and sure, he'll always be my brother—my family. But without a parent, I felt like a stray—wandering, lost, always searching for somewhere to call home.

I found home with Jensen, but now with my dad back—it's tenfold.

My head snaps up. *Where the hell is Jensen?* He's missing the halftime show. I know he had a *lot* of wings, but he's been gone for ten minutes.

I rub my temples, a headache starting to creep in as I text him.

> Hey, everything okay? 💩 Haha.

JENSEN

> Jesus. I'm not taking a shit… Just lying down for a minute. Cum sit on my dick.

I shake my head, grinning.

What do I get out of it?

JENSEN

Is that even a question? Cum find out.

A laugh slips out of me.

Hmm. Idk. I'm not convinced yet.

JENSEN

I'll go down on you.

It's a no brainer, baby.

Get over here. I'll eat you out, then fuck you. And if you're a good girl, I'll hold you after.

Oh my God. Wow. I shift in my seat, already wet, anticipation fluttering low in my core.

Annnnnnnnd tsunami.

Cumming!

I hop off the couch, excited, needing him, and insanely turned on. He hasn't been this flirty in a long time, and *God*, I'm so here for it. I practically run down the hall, turn into the bedroom, shut the door behind me, and twist the lock.

Jensens propped against a stack of pillows, shirtless, a sexy grin resting on his lips. "I knew I could lure you in here."

I walk over to the bed and bend down, kissing him gently before pulling back. His hand wraps around my ass.

"Where's your ibuprofen?" I ask as he pulls me in for another kiss. "I've got a bit of a headache."

"Ah, that sucks. I'll get it for you." He starts to move, but I press a hand to his chest.

"You don't have to get up. I can get it."

He swings his legs over the bed anyway. "Yeah, but it's buried in my backpack somewhere. I'll find it."

Standing, he walks to the other side of the room and begins sifting through his backpack. He glances at me with a smirk. "Take your clothes off. I want you in your underwear when I get back over there."

"Yes, sir." I say, pulling my shirt over my head and tossing it aside, my eyes never leaving him.

He cocks a brow, then twists the lid off the bottle and dumps a few pills into his hand—some brown, others white.

"What else you got in there?" I ask.

"Tylenol and my muscle relaxer." His eyes flick to mine. "I just keep it all in one bottle so I don't have to carry three around."

"Makes sense." I peel off my leggings as he screws the lid back on, his gaze locking on me.

"Get on the bed," he commands. "And put your sleeping mask on."

My bottom lip rolls between my teeth. I love when Jensen goes all Dom on me. It's not something I ever expected to like, but I do. I love it. Crawling across the bed, I grab my sleeping mask and slide it over my eyes, anticipation coursing through me.

Seconds later, my legs are yanked from beneath me, and I'm dragged to the edge of the bed. He sits me up, his lips ghosting over mine.

"Open your mouth."

I do as I'm told, opening my mouth as he places two pills on my tongue. Then he takes my hand and wraps my fingers around the Hydro Flask I keep on the nightstand.

I take a sip, washing down the pills. Once I've swallowed, Jensen takes the bottle from my hands.

His breath warms my ear. "You're about to get a halftime show you'll never forget."

Shivers ripple down my spine as his lips brush against my skin, trailing slowly down my neck, each kiss intensified by the darkness behind my sleeping mask.

A gasp falls from my lips, and my hands instinctively reach for him, but strong fingers close around my wrists, guiding them down to my sides.

"Try not to touch," he says, his voice low and grave.

I force my hands to stay put, but I'm aching to pull him closer, to feel his skin against mine, to make him feel what I'm feeling.

A warm palm presses against my chest, guiding me back until I'm lying flat on the bed. He holds it there for a moment, and I savor the comfort of it.

Slowly, he drags his hand down my torso, over the curve of my stomach, until he reaches my waistband. His fingers hook around the sides of my underwear, dragging them slowly down my thighs, over my calves, until they fall to the floor.

He opens my legs, splaying them flat against the bed, cool air sweeping the center of my thighs, sending goosebumps down my legs.

"I'll be right back. Don't you move."

The door opens and closes, and I'm left here—legs spread, blindfolded, vulnerable—wondering what the hell he's doing. I almost laugh at the thought of someone walking in. What a scene that would be.

The door opens again a minute later, and I rely solely on my ears to piece together what's happening.

There's a soft rattling sound, then the shift of weight on the bed as Jensen hovers over me. His lips lightly sweep across mine, taunting. I lift my head, reaching for him, my mouth grazing skin.

He pulls away. "I said no touching."

I let out a dramatic whine, playing it up. He loves that—the need, the want, the desire.

A moment later, his mouth finds mine again, cold and wet.

Ice.

He drags an ice cube from his mouth across my lips, my tongue instinctively licking the moisture from my lips.

The cold trails down over my jaw, along my neck, across my collarbone. I shiver, breath catching as it continues lower. When the ice hits my nipple, I gasp, my back arching.

He chuckles wickedly, swirling the ice around the hardened peak. Then there's warmth, cooled heat, his mouth replacing the ice as he sucks my nipple into his mouth, his hand palming the other breast.

"God, babe, that feels so good," I breathe.

My hands slide up, gripping his shoulders out of pure habit, but his teeth clamp gently around my nipple—a warning.

"I said no touching." His voice is rough, heated, and it's so damn hot.

He moves again, trailing a line down my stomach. My hips shift beneath him, the chill of the cold mixed with pulsing desire, sending a rush straight to the center of my thighs.

He kisses, then sucks at the sharp edge of my hip bone.

Then, more rattling.

More ice.

The cold returns in an instant, trailing down my thighs, teasing all around where I'm aching with need. His fingers follow the path, tracing over my skin.

Then—nothing. No touch. No sound.

"Jensen?" I whisper, soft, needy.

"Shh."

Good Lord. He's so good at this.

Without warning, cold hits my clit, and I jerk, the chill mingling with my arousal in the best possible way.

"Holy shit. That's incredible," I breathe.

He teases me with the ice, alternating the shocking cold with the heat of his mouth, sucking my clit, lapping up the moisture.

His fingers plunge into me, and the rise of my climax builds fast, gaining strength, ready to crash through me. Gripping my hips, he gives me the best damn halftime show a girl could dream of—and then some.

My orgasm rips through me like a tidal wave, wild and all-consuming. My back arches, body trembling. He holds me through it, his mouth still pressed to me, working me through every last pulse until I'm nothing but a melted, panting mess.

When he's done, after doing exactly what he said he'd do, he holds me. I tighten my arms around his, savoring the feel of both our heartbeats. Mine pounds against my chest; his is steady against my back, spooning me. Eventually, they sync, settling into a steady rhythm, beating as one, and I forget about that five percent that's been off lately. The tension that's been creeping in more and more. I close my eyes, soaking in the warmth of his skin on mine—the closeness. It's beautiful, and it always has been. With him, it's always been easy. He gets me.

God, I don't want to move. I could lay like this forever.

* * *

We make it back to the living room just in time for the fourth quarter, and everyone gives us shit for being gone so long. They know what we were up to, obviously.

The Rams win, and Matt's celebration is exactly what you'd expect—loud, dramatic, and completely in-your-face.

Jensen pulls me into his lap, his arms tightening around me. I fold mine over his and let my gaze drift around the room. The love in this room wraps around me, and for a second, I could cry from how full my heart is.

I tighten my grip on Jensen's forearms and silently vow to never forget this moment, to engrave it into my memory.

Chapter Twenty-Nine

ALLEY

THEN

MARCH

"Hi, you've reached Jensen Adams. You know what to do."

"Dammit." I end the call as it goes straight to voicemail. My eyes sweep across the apartment, landing on the door. Like if I stare hard enough, maybe he'll walk through it.

He's over an hour late. This is so not like him.

I text him for what feels like the hundredth time.

> Babe, are you okay? Kind of starting to worry…

Panic flutters in my stomach, but I force myself to breathe, to not jump to conclusions. *If something were wrong, someone would've called.*

I glance down at what I'm wearing and let out a dry laugh. A brand new black lace push-up bra, matching panties, and a garter belt. I even bought the damn thigh-high's. *So much for a sexy surprise.*

I made his favorite dinner: roast, mashed potatoes, carrots, and picked up the freshest sourdough you can get from the bakery a few blocks over. I wanted to do something special, something extra to show I was thinking of him. I hoped he'd walk through the door after a long day to find his favorite meal, and his wife, waiting in practically nothing—ready to be devoured by him. This is exactly the kind of thing Jensen would lose his mind over. What man wouldn't love coming home to that?

I even bought a dozen of those tiny tea light candles, the battery-operated ones that seem to only last a few hours. They're scattered all over the apartment: mood lighting, candles, dinner, lingerie—sex. It's romantic as hell in here. And I'm sitting in it alone, like some abandoned fantasy.

I sink deeper into the couch, crossing my legs, my bare thighs rubbing together. I flip on an episode of *Gossip Girl*. Call me crazy, but I started the series for the third time two weeks ago. There's something nostalgic and comforting about it. And now that I know how my husband grew up, it feels wildly familiar in a weird kind of way.

My phone vibrates, and I scramble to grab it, swiping as fast as I can.

JENSEN

Hey babe, I'm so sorry. I got held up at work and my phone died.

That's ok... Are you on your way?

JENSEN

Yeah. I'm on my way.

Alright... ETA?

I take a deep breath. He's on his way. *Tonight's still going to be great.*

I picture him walking through the door, a cocky grin plastered on his face as he eyes me up and down. He won't even care about dinner when he sees me. He'll want me first. He'll run his lips along my skin, teasing and tasting until I'm all but *begging* for him, making me forget all about the meal I made. I press my thighs together as heat pulses through me. *Shit.* I'm turned on just thinking about it. *He better hurry.*

It dawns on me just then that I can check his location. I pull up the Find My app and tap his name. My brows furrow. That's weird. His phone's offline. The last known location shows him at work. I stare at the screen. *Offline?* Why does that feel like a punch to the gut?

Maybe it died again. He might have only gotten a quick charge, just enough to send that text.

I pause the show and call him again, but it goes straight to voicemail. *Yep, his phone's dead.*

I press play and position myself on the couch so I'm angled toward the door. I want to be the first thing he sees when he walks in. He's been so stressed lately, so uptight. Work's been extra busy, and he's been having to stay later than usual. Nothing a little seduction can't fix.

I finish another episode, and the credits start to roll. I glance at the time. *What the hell?* It's been forty minutes since he said he was on his way. I stare at my phone, willing it to vibrate.

But it doesn't.

With a sigh, I push up from the couch and head into the kitchen, glaring at the dinner I made for him. I left everything on warm, but after two hours... it's just not the same. I make myself a plate and return to the couch, my pride wounded. I flip on another episode. I need the distraction or I'll go crazy waiting. I feel stupid, sitting here like this—all this work, all this effort. He's not even here.

Another episode ends, and my stomach twists. My worry's no longer a four. It's an eight. Jensen doesn't just come home three hours late.

I try calling again, but it goes straight to voicemail. Again. My fingers drum against the couch cushion, the rhythm getting faster.

I text Matt.

> Hey, have you heard from Jensen?

He responds within minutes.

MATT

> No, sorry. I'm just barely getting home. Everything okay?

Yeah, was just wondering.

He sends a thumbs up, and I drop my phone beside me, my heart beating slightly faster.

It's almost nine. Even when Jensen stays late, it's never past eight, and he always keeps me posted. I bite my thumbnail, my leg bouncing with restless energy. *Something's not right.*

I shuffle into the kitchen in my underwear and start cleaning up, needing something, *anything*, to keep my mind from spiraling through the what-ifs. I'm sure he's fine, and worst-case, I can still surprise him. Even if dinner's put away and I'm no longer in the mood.

All I wanted was to take some of the stress off his shoulders. Help him unwind. Make him feel loved.

My phone dings from across the room, and I rush to the couch to grab it.

JENSEN

Babe, I'm so sorry. A coworker was having car trouble. I've been helping him. Be there soon.

I let out a sigh of relief. He's okay. He's helping someone. It sucks for me, but that's also so... Jensen.

Ok. Love you.

I make a plate for him, then pack the rest of the food into containers and slide them into the fridge. I wash the pots and pans and wipe down the countertops, determined to keep my mind busy so my impatience doesn't get the best of me.

By the time I'm finished, he's still not home and my frustration is turning into anger. I know I shouldn't be mad, but *God*.

Ten minutes later, I call him.

Nothing again.

Thirty minutes later, I blink back tears as I unclip my garter belt and bra, the lace I picked out for him now crumpling to the floor. I pull on one of Jensen's oversized shirts I love to sleep in, and crawl into bed.

Forty minutes after that I roll to my side, eyes on the clock. It's 10:30.

I blink once, then again. A single tear slips down my cheek, soaking into the pillowcase. And still, no Jensen.

* * *

I HEAR Jensen come in around eleven. He moves quietly through the apartment, slipping into the bathroom. Five minutes later, he's sliding into bed beside me.

"Where were you?" I ask, my voice clipped.

"Ah, sorry, babe. Did I wake you?" His arm slides around my waist, and he presses a kiss to my temple.

I squeeze my eyes shut. "Where were you?" I ask again, a little sharper this time.

"I told you... I was helping a coworker with his car. He couldn't get it started, so we waited for a tow, and then I drove him home. It took forever. By the time I got to my car and charged my phone, it was late. I didn't want to wake you if you'd already fallen asleep."

I don't have a reason not to believe him, but something in my gut's calling bullshit. And I don't know why—Jensen doesn't lie. Not to me. Not to anyone. I trust him with my life. But something's off, and I can't explain it. I have nothing to go on but a feeling.

Is he cheating on me?

No. He would never.

I roll over, my eyes meeting his, searching them. It's dark, but the sincerity is there. It's Jensen. He loves me. He wouldn't lie.

I sigh, a faint smile tugging at the corner of my lips. "Well, I guess he was lucky you were there to help."

"Yeah. We were the only two left in the building." His lips meet mine—warm, tender—and for a second, I almost forget that I waited for him in my underwear for three hours. "How was your night?" he asks, stroking his thumb over my cheek. "I'm sorry I wasn't here."

"It's okay," I say softly. "Um..." I swallow the lump forming in my throat, the memory of tonight rushing in. "It was fine. Just watched some Gossip Girl. Ate dinner." My fingers trace a path down his chest. "Pretty low-key."

"Hmm. That sounds nice." He kisses me again, then rolls onto his back. "I'm fucking exhausted, babe. Night."

That's it? Thats all I get from him?

His eyes close, and I watch his chest rise and fall with each steady breath.

It's fine. He was helping a friend. It's one of the things I love most about him. He's always thinking of others. Always willing to help.

His phone died. He had to wait for a tow.

But then... Why does this hurt so much?

Chapter Thirty

JENSEN

THEN

APRIL

FUCK ME.

I feel like I'm going to die. My insides might actually explode.

I squeeze my eyes shut and clench my jaw as a sharp pain rips through my core, twisting hot and tight inside my stomach.

"Gah! Fuck." The words scrape out of me, my voice strained.

I have to get through this. I have to get off these fucking pills. Alley still doesn't know, but it's only a matter of time. I'm a ticking time bomb. A goddamn terrorist in my own house, keeping secrets from my wife. Waiting to be discovered at any moment.

The last pill I took was Friday night. It's Sunday morning. If I can survive this weekend, I'll go into tomorrow's workday pill-free, pain be damned.

Yesterday, I was anxious as hell. I couldn't sit still. I was tired and restless. Every muscle in my body screamed in protest, and I was sweating like a guilty bastard who just fucked the preacher's daughter.

Then came the argument. It was so stupid. I left my breakfast plate on the coffee table, and all Alley did was ask me to take it to the dishwasher. She asked nicely. It's something I'd normally do. But my body was already screaming, and her request just set me off. You'd think she asked me to climb a goddamn mountain.

I snapped.

I grabbed the plate and chucked it into the dishwasher, muttering under my breath about what a stupid fucking ask it was. Then I asked her why she couldn't just do this one thing for me when I felt like shit. I stormed into the bedroom and slammed the door behind me.

God, I'm such an asshole.

Rolling onto my back, I scrub a hand over my face. *Jesus. I don't deserve her.*

That's why I'm powering through this. I'm gonna do it. I *have* to, for her.

This year's been a slippery fucking slope. Not long after New Year's, my two-a-day turned into three.

I need three pills just to feel normal. They don't even make me feel good anymore. Three just get me to baseline—a shitty one at that. They work better than anything else, though, and I'm only taking them to manage the pain. But still, I don't want to be on them.

Alley would lose her shit if she knew. She already suspects something. The arguments have become a weekly routine. I feel like she's always on my ass, always nagging. I know that's not fair. She's not. But Jesus, I'm just trying to survive the day. I have to provide, keep this life that we have together.

It's the pills. I know it is—because the second they wear off, I'm a fucking animal. Like a bear that's been poked too many times behind a cage. One wrong word and I snap.

I apologized later when she came into the room. I told her I didn't feel good, that it was the stomach flu or something similar. Of course she believed me. She was understanding. She even kissed my forehead and told me she loved me.

She's been waiting on me hand and foot since then. Made me soup yesterday. Rubbed my shoulders. Even laughed at my stupid joke when I was curled up on the couch like a fucking gremlin. She's taking care of me like I deserve it.

But I don't.

The door creaks open, and the voice of an angel drags me from my misery. "Hey," she says, her footsteps drawing closer. The bed dips as she sits beside me, but I can't bring myself to look at her. I'm too ashamed.

"How you doing?" Her fingers rake gently through my damp hair. "Can I get you anything?"

I shake my head as nausea rises, unexpected and fast. My stomach clenches, and bile surges up my throat, hurling me forward. Gripping the bowl beside me, I dry heave until splashes of yellow hit the bottom. Acid scorches on the way up, molten lava weaving through my gut, heat penetrating every nerve ending.

I clamp up, sweat beading down my forehead, my hair drenched. Alley rubs my leg—and it's sweet, thoughtful. I know she means well, but her touch feels like nails on a chalkboard against the tornado of hell thrashing inside me.

I try to air out my shirt, peeling the sticky fabric from my skin. It's soaked. I yank it off, tossing it to the floor. Wiping my mouth with the back of my hand, I push the bowl to the side, too weak to deal with it. Alley takes it, placing it gently on the nightstand.

I collapse back onto the pillow, chills setting in now, rattling through me. My bones ache. Every nerve feels like it's being sawed through with a dull blade.

It's pure fucking torture.

"I'm so hot, but so fucking cold at the same time," I mutter, my teeth chattering as I pull the comforter up to my chin.

Alley presses her wrist to my forehead, frowning. "That's weird, you don't feel hot. You're having chills?" Her gaze shifts to the bowl—foamy, yellow bile—and I see it in her face. She knows something doesn't add up.

Her hand falls to my shoulder, her thumb brushing gently.

"Fuck! Don't touch me!" I snap, grimacing.

She goes still, her hand slowly pulling back, but she doesn't move away.

"Sorry. I'm so sorry, babe. Please don't touch me. It hurts." My throat tightens. *Jesus Christ, I'm going to cry. No. Hell no—*

A sob wrenches from my chest before I can stop it, and I fucking hate myself for it.

"It hurts. Everything hurts."

My eyes flick toward her—and the look on her face guts me. Concern. Worry. Suspicion. Love.

But yeah... she definitely knows something's off.

"I'm so sorry, babe. What can I get you?" she asks softly.

"Nothing." My voice is barely audible. My breaths are short and sharp through my gritted teeth as another wave of indescribable pain crashes through me.

"This is pretty intense for a stomach virus. Do you wanna go to the ER?"

I squeeze my eyes shut, harder this time, like not seeing her will make the questions stop. Make her stop. Make her leave.

God, I hate having her see me like this. Fucking weak.

I manage to shake my head.

It's quiet for a moment.

Then the shaking starts. Fuck me sideways, the shaking. Dear God, it's like my bones are vibrating, like someone plucked a chord deep in my spine and now I'm shuddering with pain. Every part of me feels like it's been beaten with a sledgehammer.

A sound escapes my lips. *Jesus Christ. Did I just whimper?*

"Babe..." Her voice is low and steady, but I can hear the fear woven through it. "I'm getting worried. This isn't normal."

Her fingers move to my wrist, checking my pulse, quiet and subtle. I feel the weight shift from the bed.

"I'm getting you some water. You need to stay hydrated."

I barely hear her. I don't know which way is up or down. I just want this to end.

The bed dips again. "Hey. Jensen. Here. Take a sip."

She guides a straw to my lips, but I turn my head away.

"Babe, you're sweating like crazy and puking bile. You're going to get worse if you don't get fluids in you."

I still don't drink.

"Jensen," she says again, this time firmer. "You have to drink something."

Her voice cracks, and it's like a dagger to my chest. I open my eyes and force myself onto an elbow, just high enough to take the straw into my mouth and sip. The cold liquid slides down my throat, and immediately sends my stomach into convulsions. I dry heave. Tears sting as the burn threatens to rise.

"Shit," Alley says, grabbing the bowl and thrusting it in front of me.

The heaving worsens, and motherfucking God, it hurts more than anything I've ever felt. Every gut-wrenching spasm hits on a level I didn't know existed. Every centimeter of my body quivers with pain too intense to describe.

The tiny sip of water I managed ends up in the bowl.

And I break.

I fucking break.

A "fuck" bursts out, tangled in a cry. Gripping my hair, I pull tight as sobs tremble through me, each one ripping from my chest in a shudder through clenched, chattering teeth.

I collapse back against the pillow, wishing someone would just put me out of my misery. I don't want to die. I just don't want to do this anymore.

But there is something that can make it better...

My mind wanders to the ibuprofen bottle. *No. Jesus, no.* I'm not going through this shit for nothing.

"Babe," Alley whispers. "You need fluid. I'll get a cup of crushed ice. Sorry, I should've brought that in the first place. I'll be back."

It feels like an eternity before she returns, and even though I want her gone, I like when she's close by. It's less terrifying.

"Here. Try an ice chip."

The cold touches my lip, and I shake my head. "No."

"Babe, if you can't keep the ice down, we have to go in. You need fluids. If I had an IV kit, I'd do it myself."

I reluctantly open my mouth because there's no way in hell I'm going in. I let the cold liquid coat my tongue, sucking softly. I don't heave.

"Good, babe. We'll have another one in ten minutes, okay?"

I nod, and even though I'm not looking at her, I know she's crying.

"Do you want me to stay?" she whispers.

I nod again, tears soaking my cheeks as I reach for her hand. My fingers find hers, gripping tightly, holding on like she's my lifeline—like she's the only thing between me getting through this and dying trying.

She grips my hand back. "I'm right here," she says soothingly. And for a moment, I don't even care that it feels like a mother speaking to her child. Because I need her.

More than anything. I fucking need her.

* * *

I WAKE in a puddle of water. *No–sweat.* Somehow, I managed to fall asleep. But within seconds, reality slams back in. *This isn't over, dumbass.*

I'm shivering. Chills whip through me like a fucking storm, relentless. I curl into myself, trying not to cry like a goddamn baby.

I reach for my phone with shaky fingers, checking the time. It's 2:00 AM. My hell. When is this going to end? I have work today. I can't just not go.

I swipe up, fingers trembling, and open my browser.

How long do withdrawal symptoms from oxy last.

Fuck me. They peak at day three, then slowly subside. Day three? That's tomorrow night. I can't take work off all week. *And I can't fucking take this anymore.*

I try to be rational—tell myself I can take a few days off. It's only one more day. Then the worst of it will be over. But then, maybe not. This site says symptoms last five to seven days. I can't do this for five more days. I can barely do five more minutes.

I could try again next weekend. Take Monday off, and start Friday night. Prepare. I'll freeze electrolyte cubes. Stock Tylenol and ibuprofen. Prep everything in advance. Take my last pill Friday, work from home Tuesday.

I'll plan it better. I'll know what to expect.

Guilt comes crashing in as I push the covers off because I've

229

already made up my mind. I'm desperate—desperate for anything to pull me out of this fucking deathbed.

I sit up, barely steady on my feet. *God, I'm weak.* Everything inside me screams.

I shuffle to the door, stopping to rest against it. Making my way down the hall, I lean and bump into the walls with every step. My vision blurs. My knees buckle. I grip the wall like it might give me strength. When I round the corner into my office, my eyes lock on my backpack.

Dropping to my hands and knees, I fucking crawl to it. With trembling hands, I tug the zipper open, just enough to slide my hand inside. The fabric brushes against my skin, sending an aching chill up my arm, straight to the core of my bones. It takes everything in me to not cry out.

My fingers find the bottle, barely able to hold on. I pull it out and drop to my ass, slumping against the wall, head tipped back, eyes fixed on the label. My arms rest on my knees, feet flat on the floor. I swallow, blinking back the failure burning behind my eyes.

I've never hated anyone more than I hate myself in this moment. Right here. Right now.

I unscrew the lid, tilt the bottle, and let the little white pill fall into my palm. My fingers curl around it, clenching tight. My jaw locks. My breathing's heavy. Hands shaking. And that sting of failure slips down my cheek.

For the first time in my life, I'm fucking terrified. I've never come up against a fight I couldn't win. And this isn't just a battle I'm losing. It's one I've already surrendered to.

I've fucking quit.

I place the pill on my tongue, letting the now familiar, bitter taste seep into my taste buds.

I swallow.

The pill wins.

Chapter Thirty-One

ALLEY

THEN

MAY

Oh my God.

He's on something.

I had my suspicions, but I didn't want to believe it. I couldn't even go there. But now I know.

He's definitely on something. I just don't know what.

I wrack my brain, digging through everything I know about withdrawal—because that's exactly what's happening in our bedroom right now. Again.

It's Sunday morning. One week ago, Jensen woke up with the same symptoms—symptoms of withdrawal.

"Shit," I say aloud. I'm in the kitchen, coffee in hand, rooted to the spot. My brows pull together, cursing myself for not seeing the signs earlier, the sleepiness that started last fall, the irritability, him showing up late... his eyes.

But he didn't have a prescription.

It doesn't matter. I should've seen it. I should've freaking seen it.

Dammit.

I take a deep, shaky breath, my fingers trembling around the mug's handle. I set my coffee down before I spill it, and that's when it all comes crashing in—six months of memories flooding at once: leaving the Halloween party, New Year's Eve, the night he was "helping a coworker" with his car. The arguments. Our sex life. All those feelings I had that things felt off.

And I just ignored it. I pushed it down because I didn't want it to be true. It's not like pain pill addiction is my go-to when it comes to my husband. He's my person. The one I love more than anyone else. The one I trust with my life.

There's a mix of emotions brewing deep inside me—anger, confusion, sadness—and the one bigger than all the others?

Betrayal.

He didn't tell me. Not only did he not tell me, he *lied* to me.

My vision blurs as it all slams to the surface, and I gasp, realizing I've been holding my breath. *Calm down. Maybe I'm overreacting.* This may not be what I think it is.

I'm moving before I can even process, and a strange calm settles over me as I walk down the hall, barely aware of my own footsteps. I open the bedroom door and step inside.

Standing at the foot of the bed, nausea settles in the pit of my stomach as I take him in—shivering, soaked in sweat, dry heaving all morning. Aching. Groaning. Curled into himself.

It's Jensen. It's my husband, the man I chose to spend my life with. Except it's not *him.*

"What are you on?" I ask, my voice trembling, thick with emotion I can't seem to swallow.

His eyes squeeze shut, and he shakes his head.

"What are you on, Jensen?" My voice rises slightly, and I force myself to stay calm.

The agony is visible on his face. The pain, shame, torture—it's all there, etched in the way his forehead creases. The way he can't look at me. The way his lips press together.

The way a tear leaks from his eye.

I soften, torn between wanting to shake him and hold him simultaneously. "I can't help you if I don't know," I whisper.

He opens his eyes briefly, just long enough to look at me, then shuts them again, tears now streaming down both cheeks.

It makes me want to die. To wrap my arms around him and make everything okay. But I can't.

I won't.

This right here. This moment. It's one of the worst of my entire life—right up there with my mother dying.

He doesn't say anything. He doesn't have to. He knows I know. The look of guilt, the tears—it's basically a confession. And one I know all too well. One I've seen far too many times.

He promised me. God, he promised me.

Knowing I won't get anywhere with him right now, I turn on my heel, slamming the door behind me.

A volcano of rage erupts, abrupt and all-consuming. I storm into his office, determined to find whatever's been slowly killing my husband's soul. I yank open every drawer, ripping through the contents, tossing everything aside without a care for the mess I'm making.

I open anything that can be opened, my hands run along surfaces, over edges. I'm searching like a madwoman. From the corner of my eye, I see his backpack, tucked behind the open door. *The ibuprofen bottle.*

Remembering the other pills from the Berkshires, I dart for it, my hands moving faster than I knew possible. Unzipping the top, I reach inside, frantically searching. My fingers hit something hard that rattles. But it's not in this pocket—it's in the one behind it. I open the back pocket and pull out the bottle.

My hands are shaking, and I fumble with the childproof cap, struggling to open it. "God, come on," I whisper, my voice cracking with desperation. It takes three tries, but finally, I get the lid off. I squeeze my eyes shut, inhaling deeply—too terrified to look. Too scared for it to be true.

Finally, I muster up the courage to dump all the pills onto the desk, praying I'm wrong.

Even though I know I'm not.

There are only two kinds of pills—ibuprofen and one other—a

small, white, circular tablet.

I pinch it between my fingers and study the inscription—M 05 52.

Holy shit. My gut tells me it's Oxycodone, but I rarely see actual pills anymore, and I'm not about to guess. Not with this.

I bolt to the kitchen for my phone and pull up *drugs.com,* typing in the number. My stomach drops instantly, a knot forming low and deep. My chest tightens, and the air leaves my lungs like I've been punched.

I'm right.

Dammit. Why did I have to be right? My new reality crashes through me like a tidal wave, powerful and overwhelming.

Without thinking, I dump my coffee in the sink and chuck my mug against the hardwood floor, screaming through clenched teeth. It shatters on impact, sharp pieces scattering, and I welcome the sound.

I know too much about addiction to stay calm. I've seen it up close —watched the lies pile up behind familiar eyes. I know the mask the addict wears, the stories they sell to protect their secret.

Now my favorite person in the world is wearing it.

And I don't recognize him.

I sink to the ground, leaning back against the cabinets. It's too much. Everything swirls inside me, and an audible cry tumbles from my lips as I let myself fall apart.

My head tips back, and I feel the fear creep in—dark and black shadows of my past swirling into every corner of my mind, filling it with doubt and heartache.

The irony of it all—my dad finally coming back into my life just as I feel Jensen slipping away.

My reconnection with my dad was one of the best moments of my life. It was the first time I really listened to him, actually heard him. The first time I let the addict tell their story. It was heartbreaking.

It didn't take away the hurt, or the years of aching for him, or the tainted memories, but it helped me understand.

He didn't choose alcohol. Alcohol chose him.

As healing as it was, I still fear losing him again. It's a vulnerable place to be, like I've opened myself up for target practice, just waiting for the arrow. I never thought I'd need a shield in my own home.

My heart breaks into a thousand little pieces. For me, for my dad, and for Jensen—the man that I love even more than myself.

Anger stirs with everything else inside me. I'm *pissed*—at the doctors, at our medical system, at the pharmaceutical companies, at Jensen. But mostly, I'm pissed at myself, for pushing away the warning signs. I should have seen this. I should have known. Maybe then Jensen wouldn't be in there, going through hell.

I gasp for breath, my head pounding as I sit here, crying for what feels like hours until the sobs quiet. Until the sharp edge of panic dulls and a cold, heavy numbness settles in.

My head tips back, my chest rising and falling with each deep breath. Pieces of my last conversation with my dad resurface—how much he loved me and Michael. How much he loved my mom. That his addiction was never about us. We were what kept him going, kept him trying.

He told me if it weren't for us, he would've ended up on the streets long ago. Just like that man I stepped over months ago.

My eyes squeeze shut, silent tears falling down my cheeks. I won't let that happen to Jensen. I love him too much. And I know how much he loves me. He *needs* me. He's already trying to make it right.

God, he's already trying, and I'm out here instead of beside him.

I force myself into motion, picking up the broken glass. I run a finger along the chipped wood where the mug hit—a scar for this moment. One more mark left by addiction, carved not only into our home but into my heart, along with all the others.

I walk slowly toward our bedroom, my heart pounding, the tightness in my throat impossible to swallow.

I stop just outside the door, hesitating. Delaying the reality.

Once I step inside, there's no going back. The Alley and Jensen I once knew will be gone—because once I walk through this door, it becomes real. No matter what happens next, even if we make it out stronger, we'll never be the same.

Taking a deep, shaky breath, I steady myself and slip inside. The room feels heavier than it did before, the weight of the truth now lurking in the air. I walk over to the bed and lower myself beside him.

He winces, like even the subtle shift of the mattress sends an unbearable pain ripping through his body.

I bite down hard, trying to hold myself together. I have to be strong for him.

But it's so hard to breathe.

My chest feels like it's collapsing in on itself. Like my heart is being squeezed in a vice that won't let up. It's too much.

I reach for his hand, gripping it tightly—like if I hold on hard enough, I can keep him from hurting.

"I know it's Oxy," I say, the words catching in my throat, thick and strangled.

His eyes squeeze shut, shame spreading across his face.

"Babe." My voice breaks. "Look at me."

He opens his eyes, his gaze meeting mine. The sorrow in them is so heavy—it nearly breaks me.

"I'm here." My voice cracks, and I swallow hard. "I'm right... here." I'm fully crying again. There's no stopping it. "I've got you, okay? I'm not going anywhere. We'll get through this. Together."

His eyes fill, tears brimming, lips quivering as he whispers. "Promise?"

I sniff, snot running down my nose, and tilt my head back, trying to catch my breath. Trying to hold it together.

Finally, I nod. "I promise... What do you need?"

He squeezes my hand. "You," he says softly. "Just you."

* * *

I stare into the bathroom mirror at Jensen's parent's house, my tear streaked face looking back at me. My period just came. If there's one more thing this day needed, it was that—a final kick when I'm already down.

It's late again. Disappointment and relief flood through me at the same time. We've been trying for nine months now, and I'm starting to wonder if something's wrong with me. We agreed to give it a year. There's no rush, but if I wasn't pregnant by then, we'd look into it.

Every period's met with the same frustration. But today, it's different. The emotions are hitting harder because I don't know what I'm feeling. I want this—*we* want this. But now there's a fear tangled up in the sadness. A quiet voice poking at old memories of growing up with an alcoholic.

I won't do that to my kids. We'll have to put this on hold and use condoms for a while. Make sure Jensen can stay clean.

Stay clean. There's a sentence I never thought I'd have to say about him.

My head falls to my hands, elbows on the countertop, as I try to keep my composure. My world has fallen apart in a matter of hours. I take few deep breaths, and pat cold water under my eyes, trying to cover up the fact that I've been in here for several minutes crying.

I wasn't going to come tonight. I feel guilty as hell for leaving Jensen at home. Plus, I'm worried. He insisted, though—he didn't want to raise red flags with his family, and he didn't want me to sit there and watch him go through hell. He didn't want me to see him like that.

Reluctantly, I agreed, but only if he promised to stay hydrated. I took his vitals before I left and confiscated all the pills. They're in my car for now. I'll drop them at a pharmacy tomorrow. There's no way in hell I'm doing it at work. I don't want anyone asking questions. This is Jensen's reputation. I'd never risk that.

I worry he'll give in, but he wasn't well enough to even sit up earlier—let alone go looking for more pills. I doubt he'll get out of bed while I'm gone.

My stomach knots at the thought. I shouldn't have left him. He needs me. I need to get home to him, sooner rather than later.

I end up on the couch in the living room next to Kevin, where he and Matt are deep in discussion about the stock market. I tune them out, blinking rapidly, fighting the urge to cry.

Part of me never wants anyone to know about Jensen. But the other part of me wants to tell them all, just so I don't have to keep holding it together. I've felt on the verge of tears all night.

I glance around at the family that's become my own. Megan's in the kitchen with her mom. Amber, Jeff, Cole, and Jensen's dad are playing a game at the table.

Cole is Matt's godson—his cousin's kid. He visits a couple times a year over long weekends or when Cam, his dad, has to travel for work. Cole's eight, and he and Matt are surprisingly close. It's actually really sweet, watching them together.

Matt playing dad? Who would've thought.

"Have you talked to Jensen since you've been here, Al?" Matt's gaze meets mine, and I nod—even though I texted Jensen thirty minutes ago and haven't heard back. *What if he's not okay?*

Matt cocks a brow. "Yeah? How's he doing? Feeling any better?"

I muster a small smile. "Yeah. He said his migraine's finally lifting." Jensen has a history of migraines. He doesn't get them often, but when he does, they're bad—enough to make him nauseous, sometimes even throw up.

Kevin gets up, joining the next game at the table, leaving Matt and me alone on the couch.

"How's the nightclub with Leo going?" I ask, desperate for a subject change, and genuinely curious.

Matt runs an exclusive, members-only nightclub here in New York. He took Leo there the last time he came to visit. Leo was impressed and loved the idea of bringing one to Chicago, so they partnered up last year ago.

"It's going great. Leo's easy to work with."

"That's awesome." I try to sound excited for him, because I am. But my voice isn't cooperating.

Matt's eyes narrow, his expression thoughtful. "Is everything alright? You seem quiet. Quieter than usual."

"Yeah. I'm good. Just tired. I didn't get a lot of sleep last night."

His lips press together, like he knows I'm lying.

I realize the irony—lying to cover for Jensen.

"You sure? You know you can talk to me, right? Even if it's about Jensen."

I scowl. "Why would I need to talk about Jensen?"

Matt shrugs, frowning. "I don't know." He pauses, his eyes scanning mine. "He's just been a little... uptight lately." His frown deepens. "I thought maybe if there was tension or something..." He trails off, rubbing the back of his neck like the conversation he started is suddenly making him uncomfortable. "Anyway, I just mean—if you ever wanna talk, I'm here."

I sigh, a small smile tugging at my lips. It's sweet. And of course Matt's noticed. He knows Jensen almost as well as I do. They grew up together, went to the same college. They've basically lived in the same building their entire lives. They see each other nearly every day.

"I know," I say softly. "I appreciate that. He has been a little uptight. Work's been stressful, but we're good. Things are good. Promise. Thanks for looking out for me."

"You know I got your back, Al. I'd do anything for you guys."

"I know. You're probably the best thing that's ever come into Jensen's life."

"Bullshit and you know it. You are. Maybe I'm second—but not even close."

His comment hits me right in the feels, and I stand abruptly so I don't burst into another wave of tears.

I take a breath. "Thanks, Matt. I'm gonna head home, spend the rest of the night with Jensen."

Matt stands too, pulling me into a bear hug that reminds me of Michael. It's tender and full of love—brotherly.

"Bye, Al..." He pauses. "Actually, mind if Cole and I hitch a ride with you? We took an Uber here. We were with Jordan earlier at the park and came straight from there."

My brows shoot up. "You were with Jordan? Isn't she still seeing Dr. Douchebag? What's that about?"

He shrugs. "Yeah, but she loves seeing Cole when he's in town, so we did lunch and then the park."

"God, you two are basically married. Why don't you just seal the deal already?"

Matt laughs, doing what he does best—brushing it off. "Ha. That'd be something, wouldn't it?" Then he turns and calls out, "Cole! Time to go, buddy. Alley's giving us a ride home."

We all say our goodbyes, and as we head down the driveway, I toss my keys to Matt. "You drive?"

"Sure," he says, unlocking the doors with the fob.

Cole climbs into the back, and I slide into the passenger seat.

Turning around to make sure he's buckled, I hand him a cookie. "I snuck an extra one just for you." I give him a wink, and his smile stretches wide.

"Try not to get crumbs on the seat," Matt chimes in.

My gaze flicks to Matt. "It's fine. I don't care."

There's an ache in my chest as I say it. A quiet, hollow feeling—like I'd take any child making a mess in my backseat, because right now, the possibility of having my own feels a lifetime away.

* * *

THE WHOLE APARTMENT is dark when I get home. Not a single light's turned on. *That's good. He must be sleeping.*

Turning on the flashlight on my phone, I make my way down the hallway and slip into the bedroom as quietly as possible. Jensen's still in bed. It looks like he's asleep.

In the bathroom, I ready myself for bed, careful to open and close every drawer softly. Once I'm in my pajamas, I crawl into my side of the bed and assess him. I run my hand through his hair. It's damp, but not wet, not like before.

He's shirtless, breathing deeply—snoring, even.

Wow. He's really out.

I watch him closely. Slow, steady breaths. I place my palm against his chest. It's warm and dry, and his pulse feels steady. He's relaxed. And I'm glad, I really am. I know he needs the rest, but...

He seems... comfortable. Too comfortable.

He was sweating earlier and having chills. His whole body hurt. He said the pain was unbearable. But now? He's dry, snoring, and calm.

That doesn't just happen. Not without help.

My heart skips a beat. Maybe he finally turned a corner. Maybe it's nothing—but my gut won't let it go. It feels too soon.

I fall to my side, head sinking into the pillow, facing Jensen. I think about waking him, but I don't want to disturb the sleep he's finally getting.

Maybe he took an edible. He's got a stash of those. Sometimes he uses them to sleep. That would help. *Yeah. That's probably what he did.*

But the furrow in my brow won't ease, and my pulse starts to climb. There's a tug in my chest—a longing for him to pull me close, to hold me, to make love to me. To make everything okay. For both of us.

My eyes trace the details of his face, and the love I feel for him is so strong it almost hurts. I wipe at my nose, catching the tear that slips down my cheek. He's right here.

But I miss him.

God, I miss him.

Chapter Thirty-Two

MATT

THEN—ONE YEAR AGO

AUGUST

I TAKE a sip of my whiskey, licking my lips as I set the glass down on the bar top.

The place is packed—live music playing way too loud, sports high-lights flashing on every screen, and way too many damn people.

Guys night was Jensen's idea, since Alley went to dinner with Scarlett. I figured we'd have a few drinks, catch up, unwind. But instead, I can't stop watching him, and not in a good way. We've only been here twenty minutes, but something feels... off.

Jensen can't seem to sit still. He's twitchy, jittery, unfocused. It's almost like he's tweaking. I've seen it before, in college, sophomore year, when Tyler couldn't stop popping Percs. The exact same energy —not to mention, Jordan's dad was an addict. He spent her entire trust fund on gambling and drugs by the time she'd turned eighteen. I don't know what the fuck he's been taking, but Jesus, he's on something. He's acting like a complete wack-job.

I watch his toes bounce against the bar stool, his fingers tapping like he's Beethoven pounding out a fucking masterpiece, right here at the bar. Don't even get me started on the fact that he hasn't heard a goddamn word I've said.

He swipes a bead of sweat off his forehead, glancing down at his phone for the fiftieth time since we sat down.

Jesus Christ.

"Everything good, man?" I ask, trying to keep my cool—because *what the fuck?*

"Yeah, I'm good. Sorry, Alley was texting."

He doesn't make eye contact. It's not the first time he's acted off these past few months. And even though Alley swears everything's fine at home, I know better. I'm not stupid.

I know Jensen. Hell, I'd bet I know him better than she does. Sure, she's got me beat on the intimate stuff. But all the other parts of him? I fucking know this guy. And he hasn't been himself for a while now.

Jensen's fingers tap against his screen. This alone isn't like him. Sure, he's a social guy, but he's also the type to give you his undivided attention when he's with you. And Alley's not the type to blow up his phone while she's out with Scarlett. She's never been needy like that— *unless something's wrong.*

"You sure?" I ask.

He doesn't even hear me.

"Jensen," I say, louder this time.

His head snaps up.

"What the fuck, dude? You're distracted as hell. You got something you need to take care of? Because I didn't come here to watch you text all night."

"Fuck, I'm sorry. You're right." He flips his phone face down, finally looking at me—well, almost. His eyes never fully meet mine, they look past me. Toward the door.

I glance over my shoulder to see what's got his attention.

Fucking Seth.

Seth makes eye contact, surprised, and starts heading our way.

"Jesus," I mutter under my breath as he approaches.

"Jensen, Matt! How the hell are you guys?" He slaps me on the back like we're old buddies. I can't stand the guy.

Sure, I know him. He was at my Halloween party, but not by my invite. He came with a buddy of mine who, turns out, was later involved in some shady scam shit. He's not a friend anymore. I should've known. He was hanging out with Seth, after all. *Yeah, that tracks.*

"Hey, Seth," Jensen says, and maybe I'm seeing things, but I swear his entire demeanor shifts. He relaxes, and his fingers stop fidgeting for the first time since we got here.

I don't say a word. Not to Seth. Not to Jensen. I'm too busy watching this weird-as-fuck interaction.

Seth's the worst kind of person—slimy, dishonest in every possible way. He used to be the guy everyone went to when they wanted to party. Always had the hookups. Word on the street is he's cheating on his wife and has a second family in another state, and neither one knows about the other. I've also heard he's still playing middleman, only now it's not for cheap college kids. He's dealing high-end scripts and coke to suit-wearing execs with money burning a hole in their pockets.

He and Jensen exchange a few words, then Seth's eyes bounce between us—like he can tell he's not fucking wanted here. *Good.*

"Well, it was good to see you both. Catch you around."

Jensen says goodbye, and my eyes follow Seth as he wanders over to a large group of people across the bar.

"Can you believe that guy?" Jensen says, finally giving me his attention. "Heard he's been cheating on his wife for years." He scoffs and takes a sip of his beer.

"Yeah. Heard the same thing." I toss back the rest of my whiskey. The burn slides down my throat and hits just right as a solid buzz settles in.

Jensen takes another swig of his beer, and he seems... more relaxed. Maybe my suspicions are way off. Maybe he really is just stressed, and now that the alcohol's kicking in, he's finally able to chill.

He sets his beer down. "I've gotta pee."

Standing, he downs the rest of his drink, then makes his way through the crowd. As he passes Seth, I swear to God, their eyes meet —just for a second. Then Jensen disappears down the hall toward the restrooms.

No lie—thirty seconds later, Seth follows. Same direction. Down the same hallway. I'm either losing my mind or something shady as fuck is about to go down.

I stay put—watching, waiting. Seth reappears in under a minute. Not even long enough to take a leak.

Three minutes pass, and there's still no sign of Jensen.

I try to talk myself down. Tell myself I'm overthinking this. This is *Jensen*. He's just taking a piss, maybe even taking a shit—I don't know. But no matter how hard I try to convince myself otherwise... My instinct says something's not right.

Chapter Thirty-Three

ALLEY

PRESENT DAY

MATT SITS UP, holding it together better than I am. "What are you going to do?" he asks.

"I don't know," I whisper into the room. The words just... hang there, heavy and suffocating.

I thought we were done with this. I thought we'd won the battle. Things were good. They were actually *good* again.

I'll admit, there was damage, wounds we were still healing. But we were working on it. We were moving forward. I was happy. I felt hopeful. But now? Now I don't know what I am. I'm not sure if I feel anything at all. No, that's not true.

Anger. That's what I feel. Pure, seething anger. It's not even directed at a person. Not Jensen. Not Christy. Just... *life.*

I'm mad at life.

I guess I'm mad at myself, too. For not being able to help him. For staying, for leaving, for—I don't know. For not being enough.

"Is there anywhere you want to go to look for him? Anywhere you think he might be?" Matt's eyes lock on mine. "I'll go anywhere. Call anyone. Just tell me what you need from me, and it's done."

A self-deprecating laugh slips out, followed by a sigh of defeat.

"You mean check a back alley? The bar? God forbid he's at an AA meeting." I shake my head. "No. I don't want to waste anyone's time looking for him. All I can do is wait for him to come home, whenever that may be." I stand abruptly. "I'm getting some water. You want anything?"

"A beer," he says somberly.

I walk to the fridge, grab a beer, and fill a glass with water before heading back to the living room. I hand Matt his drink, then set my water on the coffee table.

Across the room, my phone lies face-down on the floor—right where it landed after my tantrum. I walk over and pick it up, inspecting the screen for any damage. None. *Good.* The last thing I need is a broken phone.

An unread message from Michael lights up on the home screen. I swipe it open, anxious to see what he has to say.

MICHAEL

> Dad's stable for now. They're taking him back for more testing. Try to enjoy your night with Jensen. I'll keep you posted.

Oh, thank God. He's stable for now. I let that soak in, a sliver of relief making it a little easier to breathe.

"Is that Jensen?" Matt asks as I start typing.

> Ok. Thanks for letting me know. And for being there with him.

"No," I say, lowering the phone. "It's Michael. My dad's in the hospital. Something's wrong with his liver. He called earlier, on my way to dinner, to let me know." I let out a dry laugh. "It's been a day."

"Ah, shit. I'm sorry, Al. Is he gonna be okay?"

I press my lips together, trying to force a smile. "I don't know. I hope so."

I walk back to the couch and fall into it beside Matt. "I should be booking a flight to Chicago, but I can't even find my fucking husband."

Matt huffs out a laugh. "Why does it make me feel better when you say the F word?"

His comment draws a small laugh from me too, and it feels... good. "I don't know. Because you're a bad influence?" I reach for my water, stealing a glance at Matt. His once-grim expression softens—just a little.

He chuckles. "Someone's gotta be. You're too good."

A small smile curves my lips. "Thank you," I say softly. "For coming over. For knowing I needed someone."

He tilts his beer toward me, and I clink my glass to it.

"Of course. I'll always be here for you." He takes a sip, then adds, "I'm sorry about your dad."

"Yeah." I exhale a long breath. "Me too."

Chapter Thirty-Four

JENSEN

THEN—ONE YEAR AGO

I WAIT for Seth to leave the bathroom, then rush into the stall, locking it behind me. The Altoids tin is right where he said it would be, tucked behind the toilet on the ground.

My hands are shaking as I reach for it, snapping it open like I haven't taken a breath in hours. I needed a pill six hours ago. I'm barely hanging on here—barely keeping it together.

Seth was supposed to meet me two days ago when I was running low, but he didn't show. I panicked and went ape shit on him. I only had four left at the time, and I was forced to space them out yesterday. This morning, I took one, then split the final pill in half—took one half at noon, the other two hours later.

It didn't do shit.

I needed a full pill. I had to duck out of work early today—couldn't focus, couldn't sit still. I was anxious as fuck and sweating through my shirt.

I wipe the back of my hand across my forehead, clearing another bead of sweat as I pull a pill from the tin. I set it on the toilet paper holder, then press my phone over it until it starts to soften. This is anything but sanitary, but I don't give a shit.

I need this.

Right fucking now.

I don't have twenty minutes for this to kick in. Snorting it hits faster.

I keep crushing the chunks until the pill's nothing but powder. Pulling my credit card from my wallet, I sweep it into a tight line, each side neat and controlled.

I press my finger against one nostril and lower down. Just as I'm about to sniff, the restroom door creaks open.

I freeze, listening. Waiting. Nothing.

Lifting my foot to the flusher, I press down. Water swirls, loud enough to mask the sound as I bend over and inhale the powder into my nose.

I drag my finger across both nostrils, sniffing again, sucking up and wiping away any excess. My fingers swipe at the toilet paper display, dusting away the remaining traces.

I sniff hard a few more times, then exhale, slow and steady. Leaning against the door, a wave of calm spreads over me, every part of me submerged in relief. The anxiety, the restlessness—gone. Washed away like sin at a baptism. A clean slate. It's fake as hell, but it feels real enough.

I take another breath, savoring the illusion of normal. Wiping off my phone, I tuck my credit card back in my wallet, grab the Altoids tin, and shove everything into my pocket.

I unlock the stall and step out. Fucking Matt's standing there. Arms folded. Eyes narrowed. Suspicious as hell.

And not at a urinal.

I try to play it cool. "Hey, bud. You gotta pee?"

His stare doesn't flinch. "What were you doing with Seth?"

Right. So he's going there. "Jesus, Matt. I had to take a shit. Not everything's a goddamn conspiracy."

"Bullshit." His voice is low, steady. "I saw Seth come in. Did he give you something?"

My blood boils. Heat rushes to my face, and my brows furrow. I'm pissed. "I don't know what the hell you think you know. But it's weird as fuck that you followed me in here. If you don't have to piss, then leave. And stop asking me stupid questions."

He scoffs, shaking his head. "Just talk to me, man. I'm not judging you. I'm trying to help."

"Yeah, well, I don't need help. I've got everything under control."

"You've got it under control? Dude, you were a fucking mess at the bar just now."

I don't say anything. I move to pass him, needing to get the hell out of here.

He grabs my arm. My first instinct? Swing. But then I see his face, and it's not pissed. It's scared. Worried.

"Jensen, come on. It's me. You can tell me anything."

Silence.

"Does Alley know?" he asks, his voice soft, full of concern.

Just hearing her name, here like this, it stings in the worst way. My eyes well up with fucking tears, and I blink rapidly. "Please don't tell her." My voice cracks, and I look past him, unable to meet his gaze.

He doesn't answer right away. The silence stretches. The tension between us is thick. Ugly. Foreign for us.

I might as well just admit it. But I can't. I still can't say it—*I'm an addict*. Not yet. I'm still working. Still social. Still functioning. I've still got it under control.

Alley knows. How could she not? The way she looks at me—or doesn't. The way she goes quiet when I come in late. The way she pulls away at night. She practically ignores me. She's distant, like she doesn't even give a shit anymore. Our marriage is barely hanging on. And it's all because of me—because of my selfishness. My weakness. My failures. I've become everything I swore I wouldn't.

I'm a fucking fraud.

Matt looks at me like he's trying to figure out where his loyalties lie.

"Okay," he finally says, quiet. "I won't tell her."

My shoulders sag with relief.

"But you have to promise me something."

"Anything."

"You stop. You get help. Or I tell her my fucking self."

* * *

I GET HOME BEFORE ALLEY, my night cut short for obvious reasons. I head straight to our closet and pull a pair of socks from the drawer. Emptying my pockets, I set my wallet on the dresser along with the Altoids tin.

I open the lid and count.

Thirty.

It's not enough. It will barely get me through the week. If I space them out, maybe I can make them last ten days. Maybe.

I push the pills to the side, revealing a small, clear plastic baggie of white powder.

Seth said it was clean—top shelf. Just something to pick me up. To balance the scales when I'm dragging.

I won't need it this weekend. But we've got a few things coming up —Megan's birthday party, our anniversary, Zach and Joey's wedding next month. I'm determined to show up for all of it. Not just be there —*be there*. I need to be present and fun. I need to be me. For Alley.

She needs a normal night out. She deserves to laugh, to dance. To have the version of me she married. I can't show up as a zombie.

The Oxy doesn't make me tired anymore, but it makes me bland. And unless I snort it, I barely feel anything. It just takes the edge off. Without it, I'm short. Irritable. Impatient. That's not me. At least, it didn't used to be.

My libido's shot to shit too, and honestly? I don't even care. I can't remember the last time Alley and I had sex.

I'm almost too chill. But the pills help me breathe. They help me make it through each day without pain.

Yeah. I'll definitely need this soon. Maybe I'll try it next weekend, test it out. Make sure it works.

I scoop the pills into my palm, then dump them into a sock and roll it tight. I shove the sock into a small, hidden pocket inside my backpack. Next, I pick up the bag of coke, flicking off the loose powder. I carefully tape it to the inside of my iPad, flat and secure. The cover conceals it completely. No one touches my iPad. Not even Alley.

I slide it into the sleeve of my pack and let out a slow breath. *Two grand.* Two fucking grand.

And I'll need more next week.

It's not usually this much, but Seth had to pull some strings. I don't know how long I can keep this up without Alley noticing. Thank God she doesn't pay attention to the finances. That's all me.

We're fine—really, we are. More than fine, even. But soon, I'll have to start pulling from other places, savings, investments. It's only a matter of time. I just need to get through the next two months. I need to be there for Alley. Then I'll get off them. I'll get off everything.

I just have to make it to the wedding. That's it. Then I'm done.

* * *

THE WEEK'S BEEN BRUTAL. End-of-month pressure has everyone on edge, scrambling to hit goals. I'm exhausted, and the last thing I want to do tonight is go on this double date.

Scarlett has a new boyfriend that she's eager to introduce to Alley and me. I've got to be on my A-game. Charming. Engaged. Present. And I'm just... not feeling it. It's important to Alley, important to Scarlett, and fuck, it's a lot of pressure.

Especially because I'm dragging. I could crawl into bed right now and call it. What I need is a serious pick-me-up.

I button the last button on my shirt and reach for my belt, my mind drifting to the iPad. To the powder tucked safely inside. *I could just do a little. Just enough to feel normal.*

I shake the thought off. *No.* I can't try that for the first time on a night out with people. I haven't touched coke since college. I hardly remember what it's like.

But I do remember it was fun—gave me confidence. Made me feel like I could take on the world. It also used to make me horny. And Christ, what I'd give to want to fuck my wife tonight. She'd probably appreciate that too.

It's not that I don't want to, I do. When we have sex, I enjoy it. I just... I don't think about it like I used to. I don't care if we don't. And

253

sometimes, when we do, it's harder to get there. Harder to get hard—or stay that way.

Alley walks into the closet wearing jeans and a fitted bodysuit—thin straps, tits out. She looks hot. I wait for something to happen down below, but...

Nothing.

Yeah, we can't be having that. I'm not some fucking old man. I miss that part of us. I miss her. I know I've failed her in more ways than I can count, but I haven't even been man enough to make her feel like a woman—desired.

And if there's one thing Alley is, it's desirable.

I can't keep showing up like this—dull, tired, and limp. Fuck no. I want her to have fun. Feel sexy. Laugh. But mostly, I want her to come home with me tonight because she wants to, not because she's my wife. Not because she has to. I want her to want to. And I want to want her again.

She gives me a half-smile—her attempt at pretending she's excited to go out with me.

But she's not. Not anymore.

"You look good," she says as she slips on her shoes.

"You look good too, babe." My eyes rake down her body. *Jesus. Where the hell have I been?* I've got this beautiful woman right in front of me, and we haven't had sex in what, a month?

She mumbles a thank you but doesn't look at me. She moves to her jewelry, and my heart aches at what we've become. What I've become.

Because this thing? It has nothing to do with her. She's still here. She didn't change. She's still perfect.

Except she has changed. She's quiet. Distant. And fuck, she looks sad all the time. And it's all because of me. I did this.

And that truth? It fucking stings.

"Hey," I say, reaching for her hand, gripping it tight. "Come here." I pull her to me, my hands sliding around her waist. "You look really beautiful."

Her eyes meet mine, searching, glistening with unshed tears.

I kiss her. Soft. Tender. She kisses me back—hesitant at first, then urgent—desperate. Like she's trying to find me in my mouth.

Her hands slide up my chest, one wrapping around the back of my neck.

She pulls back suddenly, a tear slipping down her cheek. "I miss you," she says, and it's like a knife to the chest—rips my fucking heart out.

"I'm right here," I whisper, sucking her lip back into my mouth. Her tongue strokes mine, her mouth crushing harder against mine. It's hot as hell, and my dick jerks in response. I wait for it to get fully hard. But it doesn't.

I kiss her anyway. I can feel how much she needs this, maybe even more than I do. My hand glides upward, sweeping across her tit, my thumb circling her nipple.

I grin against her mouth. "No bra?"

"I hoped you'd notice," she says, reaching for me.

I flinch, pulling back, but it's too late. Her hand finds my cock—half-limp. A pathetic excuse for even a chub.

She presses her lips together. The sound she makes is part scoff, part laugh—biting, humiliated, disappointed. "You're not here. You're never here. You're always on something with some lame excuse." Tears fill her eyes again, and she swipes them away as they fall. "You're not even half the man I married."

She slings her purse over her shoulder. "Let's go. And please be normal tonight." And with that, she storms out of the closet.

Fuck.

I'm such a fucking failure. I can't even get it up for my wife.

I head straight to my office and lock the door behind me. I rip the iPad from my backpack and peel off the baggie.

My heart pounds as I stare at the powder. Just a bump. Half, even. Just enough to wake me up, to pull me out of this hole, get my fucking dick hard for Christ's sake.

I haven't touched this shit in over ten years. I don't even remember what a normal bump looks like. But I know better than to overdo it. Just a sliver.

I tap out a tiny line. Barely anything. Just a push.

I grab my wallet, slide out my credit card, and a twenty-dollar bill. My hands shake as I press the powder back and forth, forming a clean line. I roll the bill, muscle memory taking over like I've done this a hundred times. I lean in, hovering—doubt creeping in.

What if it makes it worse? What if I can't keep my shit together?

Too late for that.

I snort it fast. A sharp, chemical burn fires up my nose and down the back of my throat. The rush is instant. My face tingles, eyes water, and my heart hammers like a goddamn drumline.

There I am.

I feel awake. Present. Capable.

My head buzzes. Everything sharpens. Colors are brighter. Thoughts are clearer.

A rattling at the door whips me back to reality.

"Jensen? What are you doing?" Alley's pounding on the door, trying to come in.

Jesus. Give me a fucking minute.

"Why is the door locked?"

My pulse spikes again, this time with panic. I scramble, folding the bill and sliding it back into my wallet, along with the card.

"Jensen. Open the damn door!"

"I'm coming!" I call back. I grab a Q-tip from the drawer and swipe each nostril, clearing the residue. I toss it in the trash, my hands steadying, thoughts aligning.

For the first time all day, I don't feel like shit. I actually feel good. Like I could sit across from my wife without disappointing her. Maybe even get it up.

I shove the baggie into my pocket, just in case.

In case the feeling fades.

In case I lose this edge—this version of me that might actually make her smile, that might actually fuck her like I used to.

Because I can't disappoint Alley any more than I already have.

Chapter Thirty-Five

ALLEY

THEN

MY EYES FLICK to Jensen in the back of the cab. I feel awful. I said some really hurtful things back at home. But he's here. He's with me. And he seems—happy. Which is rare these days.

He did run into his office before we left. I know what's in there. I know what he went in there to do. He locked the door so he could get high.

That's what he does now. It's not just about pain anymore. He's chasing something. A feeling. His new normal. He takes something every day. How much or how often? I don't know. It doesn't matter. What matters is that he's using.

Using. Something a drug addict does. And that's what he is. An addict.

Just like my father.

Alcoholic, addict—they're all the same. They lie, they manipulate, they cheat the system of life. Jensen taking something to get through tonight? Cheating.

How did the one thing I feared the most become my reality? How could he do this to me after everything I went through with my dad?

After his second attempt at detoxing, I really thought he'd done it.

I thought he kicked it. But he didn't. Two weeks later, he was sick again. Trying again. And the week after that.

He hasn't tried since, not that I'm aware of anyway. I'm not even sure he ever made it past two days. And I'll never know because I can't trust him anymore. He's always lying, stretching the truth, disappearing, locking himself in his office.

I sigh and turn my head, staring out the window as cars blur past.

That kiss in the closet? It was good. *God, it was good.* My fingers drift to my lips, brushing over them. It felt like he was almost there—*almost.*

Jensen's hand falls to my thigh, pulling me out of my thoughts. He gives it a light squeeze. "What's this guy's name again?"

"Mark," I say quietly, still watching the cars pass by.

"And where did Scarlett meet him?"

"Bumble."

"What does he do?"

I turn, my gaze landing on Jensen. He's... trying, and I appreciate the effort. I muster a small smile. "I don't know. She told me, but I can't remember."

He chuckles—an actual laugh, and the sound wraps around me like a hug. I don't even remember the last time I heard that sound from him.

"Don't worry, babe. I got you. I'll make sure to ask. She'll never know you forgot." He gives my thigh another squeeze, and it's... weird. Like he's already forgotten I stormed out and yelled at him to open the door.

But it's also nice because it feels—*normal.*

I place my hand on top of his, welcoming the touch as our fingers weave together.

He leans in, pressing a kiss to my temple. "I love you," he murmurs.

A lump rises in my throat, but I swallow it down. "I love you too," I whisper.

Because I do. *God.* I do. I love him so much.

* * *

Mark seems great. No red flags so far, and Scarlett looks happier than ever. He does something with insurance—I didn't catch the details. I stopped listening halfway through. I'm distracted.

I can't figure Jensen out tonight. He's been super attentive, talkative, happy, touchy. His personality is back, charming and fun—more like himself, but... not.

He hasn't stopped talking, bouncing from one topic to the next. It's like ADHD on steroids.

I watch him while he and Mark chat, slipping into my own world, trying to decode him. His jaw keeps flexing when he talks. I can't tell if he's anxious or angry, but the way he's half-talking through clenched teeth... it's disturbing.

He's also talking a mile a minute. His energy feels like it's vibrating off him. Like he's about to explode.

Scarlett and Mark haven't seemed to notice, thank God.

Our entrées finally arrive, and the server sets them in front of us.

"Oh my God, this looks so good," Scarlett says, eyeing her salmon.

"It looks *so* good," I echo, cutting into my steak. Jensen and I both got the ribeye. Mine's cooked to perfection.

Jensen cuts into his steak. "Dammit," he mutters. He drags a hand down his face, groaning under his breath. "These idiots overcooked my steak." He drops his silverware with a sharp clink. "I can't fucking eat this."

I freeze, completely mortified. This is so not Jensen.

Mark and Scarlett are deep in conversation, thankfully. Either they didn't hear or they're politely pretending not to.

I glance at his plate. It *is* overcooked—and yes, that's annoying— but *God*, what is his deal?

His leg starts bouncing, his whole demeanor shifting like a switch just flipped.

"Here," I say, picking up my plate. "Trade me. I don't mind medium-well."

"No, babe. This steak's a hundred fucking dollars. They need to make it right."

"Please. Just take mine." I try to lock eyes with him, but he won't look at me. Sweat's collecting on his forehead, and he rubs his hand over his face again.

"Please," I say again, quieter this time. *Don't make a scene.*

He grips the back of his neck, then exhales hard, dropping his hands into his lap. "Fine." He slides his plate in front of me while I pass mine over, painfully aware of Scarlett and Mark witnessing the unraveling of my husband.

"Everything okay?" Scarlett asks.

I force a smile. "Yeah. They overcooked Jensen's steak, and I like mine more done... You know what, babe? They probably just mixed ours up." I say, even though I know damn well we both ordered medium-rare.

Jensen stands abruptly. "I'm gonna take five. Gotta pee." He rubs a hand over his face as he leaves, and I watch in horror as he disappears toward the bathroom.

"Is he okay?" Scarlett asks, then lowers her voice. "Are *you* okay?"

"Yeah, I'm fine. I'm sorry. He just had a really stressful work week."

"I thought Jensen loved his job."

"He does, but he has a new boss, and he's kind of a dick. It's been a rough transition."

Great. Now *I'm* lying to my friends—making shit up, covering Jensen's ass.

It makes me feel sick.

"That's shitty. I hate when someone comes in and ruins everything for everyone else," Mark chimes in.

"It is shitty." I glance around, searching for a subject change. "How long have you been at your job, Mark?"

Seriously? That's the best I could come up with? He literally just talked about his job.

"Seven years," he says, and judging from the look on his face, I've officially outed myself as someone who hasn't been listening.

A moment later, Jensen slides back into his seat. "God, babe. You look so fucking hot tonight. Let's hurry with dinner. I'm dying to rip those pants off you."

Scarlett busts up laughing. It's not completely out of character for

Jensen to say something like that, but in front of Mark, who we barely know? It's a lot. It's too much.

Mark chuckles, and I gawk at Jensen. I don't know if I'm turned on or embarrassed. For a split second, I even wonder if he's drunk. But then I look at his drink. He's been nursing the same old fashioned all night, and it's still half full.

Jensen's hand finds my thigh again, his fingers creeping a little too high for comfort in public. He sniffs, then rubs at his nose, grinning.

"What'd I miss?"

What the hell?

Scarlett starts talking to him again, and it's like the whole steak thing never happened. He's back to being charming, flirty, easygoing Jensen.

He swipes at his nose again, sniffing.

My stomach drops. *Shit.* A knot twists tight in my core. He took something in the bathroom. But this isn't Oxy. This behavior is noticeably different. He hasn't been like this, not since he started taking the pain pills regularly.

Is he on some kind of stimulant? I wrack my brain. *Adderall? Ritalin?*

Then, the tiniest thought slips in—unwelcome and terrifying.

Cocaine.

No. *No.* He wouldn't do that... *Would he?*

I fix my gaze on him, watching. His fingers make their way farther up my thigh, and he strokes along the inseam of my pants.

Jesus. I jolt, sitting up straighter and quickly crossing my legs.

Suddenly, I don't know what Jensen would or wouldn't do anymore. All I know is this isn't Oxy.

And it sure as hell isn't Jensen.

Chapter Thirty-Six

ALLEY

THEN

The car ride home is confusing. Jensen's all over me—touching, kissing—I swear he'd do it right here in the back seat if I gave the okay.

Seven months ago I was begging for this—for him to touch me, flirt with me, *want* me. If this had happened on New Year's Eve, I would've stepped out of this cab blushing, satisfied, and with mussed-up hair.

That was before.

Before the Oxy.

Before the detoxing.

Before he became someone I hardly recognize.

This used to be in character for him, but now? It's not. In fact, it's so far off that I can't stop thinking about it long enough to just let go and enjoy this. And *God,* I want to enjoy this.

His hand cups my breast, his breath hot against my ear. "You're so fucking hot, baby. I can't wait to get you home so I can eat your pussy."

Holy hell. I shift in my seat, that tingly sensation spreading low in my core, a steady pulse building between my thighs.

I *want* this. I *want* to feel good. I want—*him.*

His hand glides down my stomach, sliding between my legs as he strokes me. I'm pounding with need, aching for him.

"You like when I do that?" he whispers in my ear. "Just wait until I get you naked."

He takes my hand in his and presses it against his bulging cock. "You feel that? Feel how hard I am for you? I want you so bad."

He trails kisses down my jaw, my neck, his hand moving with precision. I'm so turned on I can't even think straight. I know the driver can see us. He knows what's happening. Part of me doesn't care because I've been dying for this. I've been so lonely. Living with Jensen—without him.

I shove away the thoughts that tell me he's high—shut out the images of him locked in the bathroom, doing God knows what. I close my eyes and give in to the sensations storming through every nerve in my body.

I'm knowingly choosing ignorance.

Just for this moment.

Just tonight.

I can wake up tomorrow still married to my drug addict husband. But right now? It's just us in the back seat of the cab. And he's so hot for me he can't wait.

I tell myself everything is okay. He loves me. He wants me.

I love him. I want him. I *need* him.

But the way he touches me doesn't feel like Jensen. And I don't know what's worse—that I know it, or that I don't care.

His hand moves back to my breast, palm massaging, thumb brushing over the sensitive peak. His other hand cups my cheek, and his lips crash into mine in the most possessive, all-consuming, fierce as hell way.

A fire burns, deep and low, and I cry out—his mouth and the music in the car drowning out the sound.

"God, you feel so good," I breathe, panting.

He's on cocaine. I slam the thought away. I don't care. Not right now.

His mouth works its way down my neck, across my chest. He sucks at my nipple through the fabric of my bodysuit, the heat and wetness seeping through. He pulls it between his teeth, and a gasp escapes me, sparks tearing through every inch of me.

I don't know what it is—the cab, the soaked-through fabric, his primal hunger for me, or my own pathetic need to be wanted—but I've never been this turned on in my life.

The cab pulls up to our building, and the driver clears his throat, loudly.

Jensen doesn't seem to hear him.

"Jensen..." He keeps kissing, keeps sucking. "Jensen," I say louder, pushing him away.

He finally pulls back, chuckling, and grabs my hand, sliding out of the car and tugging me behind him.

He moves fast through the lobby, practically dragging me while I scramble to keep up—one hand clutched in his, the other trying to cover the wet fabric of my top.

We make out the entire elevator ride up. His hands are everywhere. There's no shame in his game. He doesn't care if we get caught, doesn't care if anyone sees.

By the time we get into our bedroom, my pants are undone and his shirt is off. He pushes me back onto the bed and yanks off my jeans, leaving me in just my bodysuit.

He flips on the lamp beside the bed.

"Jesus Christ. I love that thing," he says, grinning, his eyes raking over what's left of my outfit.

He lowers down and kisses his way up my legs, stopping at the snaps of my bodysuit. A low chuckle escapes him, his breath hot against me. I arch my back, hips lifting to meet him.

He bites the seam, popping the snaps open with the help of his hands. A finger plunges into me, and I moan loudly. "Oh my God."

Then, his mouth's on me—tongue licking, flicking—finger thrusting.

It feels incredible. My head spins, and I almost feel drunk. I get lost in the warmth spreading through my limbs, the pulsing against his mouth, the pounding of my heart.

I get lost in him.

He's not himself.

God. Shut. Up.

I push the thoughts away.

A delicious ache builds, hot and burning, teasing me. My orgasm's right there—so close I can taste it.

He curls his fingers inside me, hitting just the right spot.

A hurricane of pleasure rips through me. I cry out, my eyes squeezing shut, tears leaking from the corners.

He's on something. This isn't him.

I take deep breaths as I come down from the high, and quiet the thought again.

Jensen presses a kiss to my thigh, and then the weight on the bed shifts. I hear the zipper of his jeans and open my eyes. He's pulling off his pants and underwear. I bend my knees, opening for him.

My heart pounds wildly in my chest as he settles between my legs, his body hovering over mine. He pushes into me, slow and steady.

I study him, his face, his jaw. It's clenched again. His eyes are closed, and he looks lost in the feeling. He's tense.

He thrusts again, eyes opening.

The light hits his face and there's something in his eyes. A shadow. A darkness. Like an aura wrapped around him, embedded in his soul.

I blink. Am I imagining it? Am I crazy? Stuck in some euphoric haze? I blink again. No—I'm not crazy. It's there.

Jensen's gaze meets mine, and it's so unfamiliar, so far from him, it steals the breath from my lungs.

I don't recognize this person. I know logically that it's Jensen. My husband. But it's not him. He's not here.

Panic rises, sharp and fast. My pulse races, my chest tightens, and I'm suddenly locked in full-blown fight-or-flight. A crushing weight presses down as I realize—I'm having sex with a complete stranger.

Fear grips me, ripping through my chest and burrowing deep into the pit of my stomach.

I push against him.

"Get off," I say, barely above a whisper. I push harder. "Get off." My breath turns ragged. "Stop! Get off!"

Jensen slows, confused, his brows pinching together.

"Get the fuck off me!" I scream, shoving with everything I have.

He pulls out, stumbling back as I scramble away, tears already falling down my cheeks as I gasp for air.

My hands fly to my face, covering my eyes as I collapse, my sobs shaking through me.

I force myself up, swing my legs off the bed, and rush to the dresser. I grab the first pajama shirt and shorts I see and throw them on.

"Why are you freaking out?" Jensen asks, his voice baffled, completely unaware.

The sobs come harder, gutting and uncontrollable, spilling from somewhere deep I haven't let myself feel in months. I don't even know what just happened or why it broke me like this.

I don't respond. I can't. Shame claws at me. Grief swells in my chest.

I'm devastated. Heartbroken.

"Alley, what the hell just happened?"

I wipe at my eyes with both palms, still unable to look at him. I cross the room and grab a pillow from my side of the bed. I glance at him, just briefly. He's still hard. His expression twisted with confusion, hurt, and something that looks like irritation.

I take a shaky breath and hold it for a moment, just long enough to regain my composure. "I can't do this right now," I say quietly, my voice flat with defeat.

He rakes a hand through his hair. "Fuck. Come on. Talk to me, babe. What'd I do?"

A sound forces its way out, something between a laugh and a sob. "What'd you do? That's a great question, Jensen." My eyes fix on the wall. "I'm sleeping on the couch."

I walk toward the door, past Jensen. He follows me.

"Jesus. You're acting like I fucking hurt you."

I shake my head. The tears still fall, but more silently now. This is a different kind of pain. A new kind of pain. The kind where you no longer recognize the person you love the most, but they no longer see you either.

I throw my pillow onto the couch and turn to him. "Please don't talk to me right now. I'm sleeping here tonight. You can go do whatever the hell you need to do."

He takes a beat, his eyes flicking to me before he huffs out a breath. "Fine. Whatever. I'll be in my office."

He turns and walks away.

"Of course you will," I mutter.

I watch him storm down the hallway and disappear into his dungeon, the door slamming shut behind him.

I sink into the couch, my mind racing—questions I never thought I'd ask surfacing more frequently with each passing moment. *What am I going to do? What the hell was that?*

I let myself cry for a long time, staring at nothing, trying to make sense of my life and the decisions I know I have to start making.

Jensen has to stop using. I can't keep doing this. I can't live with him like this.

My heart explodes inside my chest, and not in the way love does.

This is a bomb.

Pure chaos.

Shrapnel.

A heartbreak so sharp I feel it everywhere. Like the heart that once beat for us just stopped. And now, there's nothing. No rhythm. No pulse. Nothing.

My shoulders tremble, and my head throbs with pressure so intense I swear it might burst. The salt of my tears burns my skin, and my chest aches so badly I can't breathe. I gasp for air, each breath followed by a groan.

Life has been so damn hard the past few months. I feel parts of myself slipping away, right along with Jensen. I'm not happy. I rarely laugh. I hardly even smile. I've shut everyone out. I'm quiet at work. I don't engage in conversations. I've completely withdrawn from my friends.

I keep it all inside because I'm scared to say it aloud. I'm embarrassed. I'm ashamed this is what my marriage has become. I'm afraid. I'm sad. And I'm so damn lonely.

But most of all—I'm angry.

Angry at Jensen for leaving me.

At myself for staying.

At God for destroying us.

Losing myself has been hard, but that's not the hardest part. I can deal with that. I can handle that.

The hardest part is watching Jensen lose. Watching him destroy his body. Seeing the parts of him that are so incredibly good slip farther and farther away.

Watching the light leave his eyes.

The smile leave his face.

Sitting by as the things he used to love no longer seem to matter. One of them being me.

I know that's not true. I know he loves me. I know I matter to him. That's what makes this such torture, for both of us.

I'm not ready to give up on him. Every part of me aches to be held in his arms. To have the old Jensen look into my eyes. To make me smile. To watch football together. To laugh at his stupid jokes.

God, I want him back.

I cry for what feels like hours. Breaking for everything we once had. For me. For Jensen. Even for my mom—for what she went through with my dad. For him drowning in a bottle when she left this earth. She didn't get to see the real him one last time.

I can't do that.

I won't accept this.

I need to see Jensen again. I know he's still in there somewhere.

Through blurred vision, I swipe up on my phone. Tears and snot mix together in a salty mess that hits my lips. I wipe it away and type.

AA meetings near me.

A list appears. Some are close, some farther out. Churches. Off-campus buildings. Offices. They're everywhere.

I find one for tomorrow night just a few blocks away. We have to go. *He* has to go.

The office door creaks open in the distance, and Jensen's footsteps move down the hall. He appears moments later, his eyes red and bloodshot, his whole body subdued.

As soon as our eyes meet, he squeezes his shut, pinching the bridge of his nose. His lips tremble, like he's trying not to fall apart.

"I need help." His voice cracks—and he shatters.

I'm on my feet before I can think, arms sliding around his waist. He wraps himself around me and buries his face into my hair, sobbing uncontrollably. We both tighten our grip, pulling each other closer, until there's no space left between us. We cling to each other, holding on for dear life.

We stay there, wrapped around one another.

Broken.

Shattered.

But somewhere in this dark mess, in the middle of all this pain, it feels like someone just lit a match. A spark glimmers in the distance. His spoken truth, a flicker of hope.

His chest shudders beneath me with every breath. My tears soak his shirt. His soak into my hair.

"God, I love you so much," he chokes out. "I don't want to lose you."

I can't answer. I'm crying too hard, strangled by the weight of everything I feel.

So I squeeze him tighter. I don't want that either. I don't want to lose him.

I'll fight.

With him.

For him.

For me.

For us.

I need more time. We're not finished. This can't be the end of us. Not today. Not tomorrow.

Not ever.

Chapter Thirty-Seven

ALLEY

THEN

THERE'S a fluttering in my chest as I look around the room. It's not set up like I remember from when I used to attend AA with my dad. There's no folding chairs in a circle. Instead, the space is small with stadium-style seating, a single podium front and center. I chose an open meeting, one that allowed family and friends, so I could be here with Jensen.

A man with gray hair, maybe in his fifties, stands. "Hello everyone. My name is Grant, and I'm an alcoholic and an addict. I've been clean for ten years and sober for two. Welcome to this Alcoholics Anonymous meeting. We're glad you're here. We welcome anyone recovering from alcohol, drug addiction, or any other substance use disorder. Let's take a moment of silence for those still struggling."

During the silence, I glance around the room, taking in the people seated near us. They all seem... normal. Sure, a few look like they've had a rough past, like life's beaten them up a bit, but most? They look like fathers, sisters, husbands, daughters, and friends.

They look like Jensen. Good people caught in a bad cycle. One bad choice. One accident. One surgery. One moment, and it swallowed them whole. Gave them a problem. A problem so many others can avoid, even with the same choices made.

Grant continues, "If you will all stand for the Serenity Prayer."

Fortunately, and unfortunately, I know it by heart. I've said it hundreds of times with my dad, my mom, Michael.

My eyes flick to Jensen, unsure of what's going through his mind. I don't know if he even knows the Serenity Prayer.

Everyone rises, and the room fills with steady, unified voices:

"God, grant me the serenity to accept the things I cannot change,

The courage to change the things I can,

And the wisdom to know the difference."

Jensen knew every word.

We sit, and Grant looks around. "Is there anyone new to recovery or returning?"

His eyes land on Jensen, holding for a second, but when Jensen doesn't move, he shifts his attention to the rest of the room, scanning for raised hands.

A man behind us lifts his arm, and Grant offers a warm welcome.

Jensen stays quiet, his hand sweating in mine. I give it a squeeze. *It's okay if he's not ready.* He's here. That's the first step, isn't it? Admitting you have a problem.

Grant continues, explaining the twelve steps before moving on to the sobriety chips. I listen quietly as people walk to the front of the room, celebrating their milestones—thirty days, sixty, ninety. Some get chips for staying sober just twenty-four hours. Each one earns quiet applause, and every hand that clutches a chip feels like a small miracle.

I drift into my thoughts when Grant invites people up to share.

I know addiction can happen to anyone. It isn't picky. But Jensen? He doesn't belong here. He's too good. Too kind. Too fun. A year ago he was almost too good to be true. We were almost too perfect.

But I guess no one gets through life unscathed. Eventually, something gets you. I guess this was our turn.

It's not fair. I did my time growing up with an alcoholic father, and losing my mom to cancer. I thought I finally caught a break.

I did all the right things. I went to college. I got good grades. Became a nurse. Built a career.

I didn't sleep around, or get drunk on the weekends. I never touched drugs. *I even fucking prayed.*

I stopped praying when Jensen stopped trying. When I realized the same evil that wrecked my childhood had crept into my home, even after all the pleading, all my faith.

Turns out, God doesn't care if you pray.

This whole thing has shaken my faith to the core. I'm not religious. I never really was. I went to church here and there with my mom growing up, but it never clicked for me. I had my own thing, though, my own relationship with God.

But now? It's dwindling. Sometimes I envy Jensen for not giving a damn about what happens after we die. He doesn't overthink it. He's never prayed. He just lives.

He says he's agnostic. He believes in something bigger than himself, but doesn't feel the need to define it.

One by one, people take turns at the front. Stories of failure, of hope, of wins. Every story's different, but they're all the same at their core—people trying their damndest to get it right. To rewrite their story. Some have relapsed again and again. Some have been clean for years and still keep showing up. Because this? It's a lifetime fight.

A woman around my age steps to the podium. She's pretty, even wholesome-looking. And when she speaks, my heart splits in two.

She talks about losing custody of her children. About being homeless, and chasing the next needle, the next high, the next moment of unconsciousness. She lost everything: her husband, her kids, her family. Everything.

She starts crying as she shares that she's been clean for one year today. Tomorrow, she gets to see her children for the first time in four years.

I sniff loudly, but I'm not the only one. There's not a dry eye in the room. Jensen wipes at his face with the back of his hand, and for the first time in a long time, a calmness settles over me.

This woman isn't a bad person. She's a mother. She loves her kids. She just got caught in the web. Most of those people out on the streets didn't start that way. They all had lives. People who loved them. Dreams. Homes. Families.

Addiction can steal even the purest of souls. It takes them slowly, piece by piece, until they can't remember where they came from, let alone how to get back. Their soul gets buried so deep, they forget where to even start looking.

She sits down, and Jensen stands.

He walks to the front of the room, and I swallow my shock as he takes center stage.

"Hi, I'm Jensen."

"Hi Jensen," everyone echoes.

"And I'm... an addict." His voice cracks. He swallows, staring out across the room. He exhales a shaky breath, trying not to break in front of everyone. "Sorry," he chokes out. "It's my first time actually saying that out loud."

My breath shudders as a well of tears rises, overflowing and streaming down my cheeks like a river.

"I'm so ashamed," he says. His voice breaks again, and he presses a hand to his forehead. "I wasn't gonna come tonight, but my wife... She saw me last night at my lowest."

His eyes find mine. I nod, encouraging him.

"I used two hours ago. So I don't even know if I belong here yet. Sorry. I don't know if I'm supposed to say that." He lets out a breath. "Anyway, I want to stop. I just don't know how. That's all."

He walks back and slides into his seat.

My hand finds his, and I grip it, tight and strong. *I'm right here.*

Jensen brings my hand to his lips, pressing a kiss to the back of it. I offer him a small smile. And right now, I believe we might actually be okay.

I love him. He's my best friend, and together, we can get through anything.

A few more people get up to speak and then Grant closes with a few remarks, then asks everyone to stand to recite the serenity prayer again.

"God grant me..."

Chapter Thirty-Eight

ALLEY

THEN—ELEVEN MONTHS AGO

SEPTEMBER

I STEP out of the shower, wrap my hair in a turban, and slide my arms into my robe.

After going through my skincare routine, I brush out my hair and tip my head forward, starting the blow dryer.

It's almost ten a.m., and Jensen should be home by one. He had to fly to Boston yesterday to meet with a potential client. He only travels for work a handful of times a year, but of course, this trip had to fall on Zach and Joey's wedding weekend.

He lands at noon. It's cutting it close, but we should still be fine. As long as there are no delays.

I flip my head upright, using the dryer and my brush, smoothing and adding volume.

He's clean. It's been six weeks. I was nervous about the trip, but I guess it's no different than him being at work here. He kicked it. It was brutal and ugly, but he did it.

After that first AA meeting, he went from four pills a day to three the following week. I helped him when he got home. He was grouchy, short-tempered, and didn't feel well. That Friday, he worked from home, and cut them cold turkey. I took the day off to be with him. To babysit him, basically.

By Monday, he was in the thick of it. Wednesday night, he finally started turning a corner. He worked from home the rest of the week. Matt stayed with him while I was at work. It was a nightmare. But we got through it.

Since then, things have been good. Not great, but good. Better than they were. We're still dancing around the hurt, and the broken trust. He's struggled with some depression since getting clean. Some days are harder than others. But more and more, he's becoming himself again, and I'm starting to lean back in.

We celebrated our one-year anniversary and him being one week clean on the same night. We stayed home, and ordered in. Jensen still wasn't one hundred percent, but we ate, watched a movie, laughed, cuddled. We even had sex. Nothing wild. We used toys to make up for the energy he didn't have.

He lost a lot of weight during those first two weeks. It's starting to come back now. Slowly but surely, Jensen's starting to look like Jensen again.

I smile at the thought. He really is so good-looking, and I can't wait to see him dressed up tonight. Jensen in a suit? That always does something to me. It reminds me of the first time we had sex after Matt's birthday party.

I turn the blowdryer off and reach for my makeup bag just as my phone lights up with a text.

JENSEN

Hey babe, they overbooked my flight and bumped me to the next one. Fucking bullshit. I'm trying to talk to the gate agent now.

Oh my God. No.

I snatch up my phone and call him. It rings, then goes to voicemail.

He texts me immediately.

JENSEN

I'll call you in a bit. Talking to the agent now.

"Dammit," I mutter under my breath. This night means so much to me.

Oh my God. When's the next flight?

I set the phone down, curl my lashes, and apply a coat of mascara with an unsteady hand.

Fifteen minutes later I still haven't heard from him.

Babe. Did you get it figured out? If you don't get on a flight in the next hour, we won't make it in time for the ceremony.

The ceremony doesn't start until four-thirty, but cocktail hour starts at three-thirty, and the wedding's in Long Island. With traffic and everything that could go wrong, it's not looking good.

I'm almost done with my makeup when he finally texts back.

JENSEN

It's not looking good, babe. I'm so pissed. They've oversold everything. Greedy fuckers. They can't get me on a flight until one. I'll be late. But then I just have to fly back tomorrow for a meeting Monday morning…

I try calling him again, but he doesn't answer.

JENSEN

Sorry, babe. It's chaos here.

"Ugh!" I grit my teeth, frustration building.

What are you saying? You don't want to come?

JENSEN

> You know that's not it, babe. I want to be there. It just doesn't make sense. By the time I get there, it'll be half over and then I just have to turn around and come back.

Is he serious? He's just... not coming? I've been looking forward to this wedding for a year. Zach's one of my best friends. This is so important to me. And God—a big, fat gay wedding? There's literally nothing better.

It's a small wedding too. They splurged on all the things. I'm honored to be invited. Joey's wearing a velvet suit, and Zach wrote a song for him. He's singing it during the ceremony. His voice is phenomenal. It's going to be epic.

> So you're not coming?

I drop my phone on the counter and take a second to steady myself.

Is he even telling the truth?

Goddammit. I hate that my brain just went there. Of course he's telling the truth. I saw him leave yesterday. His bag was packed, and he was wearing work clothes. I watched him walk out the door. He loves Zach and Joey just as much as I do.

But what if he took something while he was there? What if he's spiraling? What if he was in pain and couldn't handle the pressure?

Fear plants itself deep in my chest, and suddenly I'm a mess of nerves. My breathing turns shallow, my hands start to shake, and an overwhelming urge to play detective crashes through me.

My phone lights up again.

JENSEN

> I know this sucks, Al. I was really looking forward to it. I'll let you know if something changes. Call you later.

Doom and gloom settles over me. *Why won't he answer his phone? Why won't he call me now?*

This isn't some child's birthday party he's missing. It's a *big deal*.

I turn on my heel and storm into our closet, yanking open drawers, shuffling through shelves. Don't ask what I'm looking for. I don't even know. Pills, bags, a receipt, a clue. Anything to tell me he's full of shit.

I dig through pants pockets, shoes, boxes, the safe. I'm praying—begging that I don't find anything.

He's clean. He has to be. I *know* he is.

Next I'm in the office, tearing through drawers like I'm insane. I feel completely unhinged. The irony is almost laughable. I look like the addict right now—strung out, searching for a fix. The desperation is radiating off me in waves.

I'm crouched in front of the bottom drawer, everything pulled out and scattered on the floor.

Nothing.

I start pulling the drawers out again, one at a time, running my hands along the undersides. Nothing's off-limits. I know how this works—what lengths an addict will go to. I grew up with it. I've seen what my dad was capable of. I've read enough blogs and forums. I've heard the horror stories. You *never* underestimate an addict.

They are masters of deception.

I get to the top left drawer. I pull it out and run my fingers underneath. My fingers bump into something hard. *What the hell?* There's a container of some sort Velcroed to the bottom of the drawer. I rip it off and stare at it. It's black, small, and looks like a tackle box. I freeze, staring at it for a full ten seconds before I move. Like if I don't touch it, it's not real.

Popping the lid open, I almost laugh out loud when I see what's inside. Even though it's not funny.

Not even a little.

It's organized. I'll give him that: Q-tips, Neosporin, an old hotel key card, a razor blade, a metal tray with white residue, cut straws. All the paraphernalia you'd need to snort something up your nose.

And the worst part? The part that screams guilty? The pills. And the little baggie of white powder.

If those weren't here, maybe I could gaslight myself into believing this was old. Something he forgot to throw out.

But it's not.

He has drugs.

In the house.

Right now.

I grab the whole kit because *fuck him*. How dare he?

My entire body goes into some kind of shock. My hands shake so hard I nearly drop the box as I carry it to the kitchen. I toss it onto the counter, letting my head fall into my hands as I lean on my elbows, trying to breathe. Trying to stabilize.

The room spins, and I feel like I might pass out or throw up. Tears sting, threatening to fall.

Shit. No. I refuse to cry today.

I just did my makeup. I can't do this today. I won't let anything ruin this day for me.

I drift down the hallway, running trembling fingers through my hair. Back in the bathroom, I pick up my phone and text Jensen, already knowing I won't hear from him the rest of the day.

> I know.
>
> I found your stash.

God. I'm so mad I could take a sledgehammer to everything that matters to him.

My heart hammers between my ears, and I remind myself to take a deep breath so I don't have a panic attack or a nervous breakdown.

I text Matt.

> What are you doing the rest of the day. You busy?

Matt responds almost immediately. You know, because he's *not* on drugs.

MATT

> Just meeting a buddy for drinks later. What's up?

> I hate to ask this, but... can you cancel? Will you go with me to Zach and Joey's wedding?

My phone vibrates. Matt's calling, and I swipe to answer.

"Hey," I say, my tone flat.

"Hey. What's going on?"

"I don't know. Jensen was supposed to be home today, but then he texted me some bullshit excuse about flights being delayed and overbooked."

"He's in Boston, right? Work trip?"

"That's what he says, but..." My voice cracks. "I found drugs, Matt. Hidden in his office. There's a whole kit with Oxy and cocaine."

"Shit. What time do you want to leave for the wedding? I'll pick you up. No problem."

"Um..." My lips quiver, and my shaking hand knocks the phone against my ear. "Two o'clock, if that's okay? It's in Long Island."

"Sure thing. I'll be ready. I'll drive."

"Thanks, Matt." I tilt my head back, eyes squeezing shut.

"No problem. It's gonna be okay, Al. We'll have fun, alright?"

I nod, like he can see me. My silence says it all.

"What can I do?" he asks gently.

"I don't know," I whisper. "Find him?"

"I will. You need anything?"

"No."

"Try to relax, okay? I know you don't wanna mess up your makeup."

I laugh-cry into the phone.

"Take some deep breaths, alright? I'll see you at two."

I nod again. "Okay. Thank you. See you soon."

"See you soon."

I end the call.

It's noon now. My face is a mess, but I know I'm not done crying, so I put off fixing it.

I wander into the living room with my laptop, not finished playing detective. I need more information.

I open it and then pull up the FindMy app on my phone. Jensen's location is no longer even detectable. He turned off his sharing.

I scoff aloud. *Figures.*

I drop my phone beside me and navigate to my browser on the computer and log into our bank account.

I'm not sure what I expect to find. He uses his work card for most travel, but not everything is covered by his per diem. I just need some kind of proof—not even that he's lying, but that not *everything* he's told me is a lie.

Maybe the drugs are old. Maybe he's not using again. Maybe I'm just jumping to conclusions.

I'm surprised I even remember our login. I rarely check our bank accounts. Jensen handles all of that. I've never had to worry about paying bills or moving money around. He takes care of everything.

I navigate to our checking account, which has a good amount in it. Makes sense. It was payday for both of us this week.

I scroll through the transactions. Both paychecks deposited Thursday, and a large chunk was transferred to our savings. That's normal. We always save on payday. I know Jensen moves money around for investments, too. He's been working with a financial planner Matt introduced him to years ago.

A big credit card payment was made the day before. That also checks out. We use the card for just about everything.

I click into our savings next, expecting to see a solid number.

It has less than five thousand dollars in it.

That's low. Way too low. Especially since I know he moves thousands in every other week. Maybe he transferred it somewhere else? Maybe to the investment account?

I scroll through the savings transactions and stop cold, my breath catching.

There are large ATM withdrawals every few days. Three to five days apart. Going back months.

Six hundred dollars here. Nine hundred there. Sometimes a thousand. Every time. Over and over again.

Holy shit. Why would anyone need so much cash?

As soon as I ask the question, I answer it.

Drugs.

"Oh my God," I whisper into the quiet, my fingers going cold. I can barely feel the keys beneath them.

I pull up the calculator on my phone and start adding the ATM withdrawals. The last few months are steep. He's pulling anywhere from five to seven thousand a month. January through March were slightly lower, but it escalated fast. A direct correlation between how much he was spending and how deep he'd fallen.

I finish adding it up, my eyes locking on the number.

Forty-six thousand dollars.

My heart pounds, and my pulse is running a marathon in my chest. Forty-six *thousand* dollars. Withdrawn from an ATM. This year alone.

I wait for the emotions to come—rage, grief, disbelief. But I feel nothing. I'm numb.

How could I be so stupid? Who doesn't check their finances? How did I have no idea this was happening? If I'd just logged in months ago, I would've seen it. The evidence is right here.

I walk back to the bathroom to touch up my makeup and get dressed.

Forty-six thousand dollars.

I actually start laughing while I'm getting dressed.

"Forty-six thousand dollars!" I shout to myself in the closet.

Yeah—I might be losing it.

I laugh again.

"Holy shit."

But that last word catches in my throat, and a lump rises.

Nope.

I just redid my makeup. *Keep it together.*

I inhale slowly and hold it. Then exhale even slower, counting.

I repeat.

And repeat.

I keep going until Matt picks me up at two, and I finally have someone to distract me from the absolute shit show my life has become.

I didn't even do anything.

I just fell in love.

And now look at me.

* * *

THE WEDDING HAS BEEN BEAUTIFUL—PERFECT, really. Everything these two deserve and so much more.

Both grooms look handsome as hell. Zach is every bit himself—suave, confident, his signature blend of cocky and wild that makes you want to laugh, cry, and spill all your secrets at the same time. He's built like a model: six-three, abs of steel, strong jaw.

Joey is the yin to Zach's yang, the calm to Zach's chaos. He's rugged and built like a wrestler. Hairy, bearded, and stupid hot. Zach's got Cody Rigsby energy; Joey's more the unruly Viking who makes women irrationally upset the moment they realize he's gay. Yet somehow, they fit together seamlessly.

The ceremony wrecked me. I was determined to hold it together, but the second Joey started crying, I didn't stand a chance.

The worst of it was when Zach noticed me after the ceremony with Matt. The look on his face said everything. He knew.

I only just told Zach about everything a few weeks ago. He cornered me at work, said I'd been off. Quiet. Sad. He said he knew something was going on. I broke down and told him everything. It sucked, but it's been nice having someone to talk to besides Matt.

Matt's the best. Truly. In fact, he's so great it almost pisses me off that he won't settle down with someone. It feels like a backhand to the universe—like what's the point of being one of the good ones if no one gets to have you?

Then again, Matt would probably argue that if he's *that* great, it'd be selfish not to share. Which is so Matt.

I used to feel that way about Jensen. That's what makes all of this so damn hard. Jensen *is* one of the good ones.

I'm sure Matt has his own flaws, everyone does. The kind you only discover when you live with someone. He's not perfect.

For one, he kept what he knew about Jensen from me. Which, I guess, makes him a loyal friend to Jensen... and something different to me. I get why he did it. They've been friends forever. Still, I was so mad when I found out he knew and didn't tell me.

Jensen told me right after that first AA meeting. He said Matt had walked in on him at the bar the week before.

Matt told me later he *was* planning to tell me. He just didn't know how or when.

Turns out, Matt's easy to forgive.

I catch him weaving through the crowd in a suit that probably costs more than my rent, two drinks in hand.

Not gonna lie, I'm a little drunk. I never drink cocktails, but Matt's bringing back the third. After the first, my face was tingling, and now? I have to concentrate just to see straight. I can barely feel my mouth.

Guilty thoughts creep in, and I try to shove them down. The ones that say I'm a hypocrite. That I'm no better than Jensen. That I pounded a cocktail to numb the thoughts and dull the pain. That I'm drinking just so I can laugh and have a good time.

It's working. I *have* been laughing. And it feels so damn good.

But isn't that pathetic? That I have to drink to laugh—to forget? Does that make me any different than my dad? Than Jensen?

The intention is the same. Only the outcome is different.

Matt slides into the seat beside me, placing two waters in front of us.

My brows knit together. "Water? I thought you were getting us drinks?"

"I did." He flashes me a grin, the same cocky smile that gets Matt laid every time he looks at a girl.

"I don't want water. I wanted another mojito."

"I know." His lips press into a line. "But I also know you, Al. And you're already pretty tipsy. One more will ruin your morning. The last thing you need is a hangover. Plus, you're an amateur. Trust me, right now, you're at the perfect spot. Fun, relaxed... one more will push you over the edge. And I have to drive us home. So, water it is."

He lifts his glass and holds it in the air, waiting.

Reluctantly, I pick mine up and clink it with his. "Fine," I say, a hint of a smile creeping in.

"Should we go dance?" Matt asks.

I glance at the chaos on the dance floor. Zach and Joey's moms are out there showing everyone up.

A full grin sweeps across my lips, and though I'm smiling, the heaviest sadness settles in my chest. I wish Jensen were here. I want to dance with him. Laugh with him. Take pictures of us in the photo booth.

Don't get me wrong—Matt's been a great date. The perfect gentleman. He's made me laugh, and we had a really great talk on the way here. I'm grateful he's here with me. It's comforting having him by my side tonight.

But he's not Jensen.

I turn my gaze to him. "Yeah," I say slowly. "Let's go dance."

* * *

I'm still breathless from dancing when Matt checks his phone. He freezes.

"You okay?" I ask.

"Uh..." He glances at me, hesitating. "Megan just texted me."

"And?"

"Jensen's not in Boston."

Silence.

"He's at Tom and Christy's."

His parents?

I gawk at him, then grab my clutch. "Drive me."

I start walking, but when I look back, Matt's still standing there.

"Now," I snap.

He exhales hard and follows me toward the car.

Chapter Thirty-Nine

ALLEY

THEN

THE DRIVE to Tom and Christy's has been long and mostly quiet. I've managed to keep most of the rage storming through me bottled up. I ranted for a few minutes when we first got in the car. Matt let me do my thing. He listened, validated. But since then, I've just stared out the window, letting the silent tears that feel like a daily part of my life now streak down my face.

As we get closer, the anger starts to stir again, rising and bubbling up—ready to explode like a bottle of champagne shaken one too many times.

"Hey," Matt says gently, breaking the silence. His hand rubs my shoulder. "You sure you wanna do this now? I could drive you back tomorrow... after some sleep. After you've sobered up."

"Oh, I'm sure." My gaze stays locked on the blur of lights outside the window.

"Okay. If you're sure." He squeezes my shoulder once more and then turns into the neighborhood.

My stomach flips and twists, nerves coiling—the kind that make you feel claustrophobic. The kind that press heavy against your chest. The kind that feel like someone's hand is around your throat, squeezing and cutting off your air. The kind that make you wonder if you're having a heart attack because your pulse is so out of control, something has to be wrong.

I keep thinking I've felt it all. That nothing else can shock me. Jensen lying? I'm not surprised. Sadly, that's becoming routine. But his mom? That's new. Christy covering for him? I still can't believe it. And the thing that pisses me off most? She texted me last night. She asked when Jensen would be back from Boston.

It's worse than Jensen lying. He's an addict. I'm learning to expect that from him. He has a *reason*. What's her excuse? She's texting me, to what? Throw me off? That's a whole new level of low. And it's a gut punch to my pride I didn't see coming.

We pull into the driveway, and before Matt even fully shifts into park, I'm throwing the door open. I don't wait. I don't think.

"You're coming," I say over my shoulder firmly. I don't even look at him. I just keep walking.

I'm halfway up the walkway before Matt gets out of the car. I hear his door slam shut just as I reach the porch. I punch in the code for the lock, the sound of the deadbolt barely registering. The second it clicks, I shove the door open.

I storm inside—a tornado of rage, ready to blow through anything standing in my way. Christy's the first victim. She rounds the corner from the kitchen.

"Alley, what a pleasant—"

"Don't you fucking talk to me!" I shout. "Where is he?" I don't wait for a response. I'm already moving toward our bedroom, charging down the hall.

"Alley, stop. Let's talk."

I swing the door open. He's not there. Slamming it shut, I whirl past Christy, ignoring her like she's invisible.

"Alley. Please. Calm down."

Calm down? Is she serious?

I glance over my shoulder with a glare sharp enough to cut glass. "Don't you *dare* tell me to calm down!"

Charging into the great room, I find Jensen lying on the couch.

He's exactly how I expected. Sweaty. Shaky. Pale. Eyes sunken and dark. He looks like death.

The second I see him, everything inside me erupts. My body and soul split in two. It's out of body—like I'm watching this girl completely lose her shit. But it's not me. It can't be. I don't feel it. I'm not in control. I'm just a witness.

My eyes lock on Jensen, and my body moves before I even register it. "You lying asshole!" I grab the nearest throw pillow and hurl it at him. He winces, covering his head. I know even the slightest graze against his skin hurts like hell right now.

Good.

Because all I want to do is hurt him. Like he's hurt me.

"Alley..." His voice is raw, grated and small. His eyes squeeze shut, the way they always do when the shame creeps in. He starts crying. Again. And even though I know detoxing from opioids causes emotional waves—I don't care. Not right now. In fact, it only makes me angrier.

"You think you get to be sad?" I scream. "You think you get to feel bad?" I scoff. "Get up!"

His eyes open, finally meeting mine. They're full of moisture. Bloodshot. Glassy. We stare at each other—our pain staring the other down with full-on hatred.

But it's not hatred.

It's love.

A love so deep it hurts.

A love that's been shaken to the core.

Battered. Bruised.

A love that was too good to be true.

A love that broke us.

My soul slams back into my body, awareness settling like dust after an explosion. And when I look into his eyes—really look—it's me again. Me, Alley. His wife. Not just rage in a body. And the wall I've built to hold all this resentment comes crashing down.

The tears burst out of me, seeping through every crack that's formed over the past year. I cry so hard I can hardly breathe, let alone speak. I don't know how long it lasts, but I'm aware that Christy, Matt, and now Tom are all watching. Watching...

As Jensen and I break.

You know that part of the storm—when it gets worse right before it gets better? You panic, rushing outside to save whatever might blow away or break.

Then, moments later it's over. Just like that, it's gone. It calms. The sky clears, and the quiet settles in, like nothing ever happened. But the wreckage is left as evidence. Furniture tipped over. Debris scattered. The damage is done.

That's us.

That's me.

A heavy numbness settles in, erasing all emotion like it was never even there. But the mess proves otherwise. It's a fucking disaster.

And so am I.

A breath fills my lungs as my eyes look past Jensen, my voice flat. "Get up. We're going home." It's not soft. There's no comfort. Just duty.

I avoid all eye contact as I turn to leave. Passing Matt, I whisper, "Matt, get him in the car."

Christy follows me to the door. "Alley, please."

"Don't," I snap, without even looking at her.

"Alley, can we just talk?"

I shake my head, the fight in me gone. "You said enough when you lied." I reach for the handle. "You're just as bad as he is, only you have no excuse." I turn, facing her for only a moment. "And I won't forgive you."

Pulling the door open, I walk to the car to wait for Matt—and Jensen.

* * *

MATT HELPS JENSEN INSIDE, and I head straight to our bedroom, barely looking back as I say, "I'll get his pillow."

Grabbing it off the bed, I walk to the hallway and toss it out the door before shutting it behind me and locking it. He can sleep on the couch tonight, because he sure as hell isn't sleeping with me. It won't matter anyway. He's not going to be comfortable anywhere.

Guilt tugs at my chest. *Am I being too cruel? Too hard on him?*

No. He's earned every bit of the pain he's in.

I do feel bad about Matt, though. It's not his job to carry this. To help Jensen or be there for me. To pick up the broken pieces of our marriage.

Matt's voice echoes down the hall through the door—not quite yelling, but raised and heated. "Goddammit! Man the fuck up! I swear to God, if I ever have to watch her break like that again, I'll beat the shit out of you." There's a beat of silence. Then his voice softens. "What do you need?"

I press my ear to the door. I don't hear Jensen's response, his voice is too muffled between his emotions and the closed door. Maybe it's for the best. I'm not sure I can even handle hearing his voice right now. I'm too fragile. Too broken.

I'm so angry, but... the sadness? It's so much stronger. It overshadows everything else that's stirring inside me.

I go through my nighttime routine on autopilot and fall into bed a few minutes later. Leaning back against the pillows, phone in hand, I stare at the screen. I need someone to talk to. Someone who gets it.

I need help, too.

I swipe up and scroll through my messages until I find Leo's name, and click into our thread. The last text was six months ago—a photo of him and Vivian at their wedding in Turks and Caicos. I sent a quick congratulations. That was it.

Leo's an extremely successful businessman, but first and foremost, he's a psychologist. He's been a professor and therapist for years, and he's always been a sounding board when I've needed one.

I type out a text.

Hey... can you talk?

I stare at the message, my thumb hovering over the send arrow. I haven't told anyone in Chicago about Jensen. They're *my* people. I need them... but I know they don't have to love Jensen. They choose to. Jensen's family and Matt? They love him no matter what. The only other person who knows is Zach. He loves Jensen too, but he told me to get the hell out.

I know Leo would never say anything if I asked him not to, not even to Michael. But if I text him—if I talk to him right now—I risk changing the way he sees Jensen forever. And if Jensen gets clean, I'll have made it harder for Leo to respect him. To even *like* him.

I swipe out of the message thread. Not because I don't trust Leo. But because I still want Jensen to be worth trusting.

The front door shuts a few seconds later, and a text from Matt pops up.

MATT

He's on the couch. I made him as comfortable as I could. Lmk if you need anything. I'll stop by in the morning to check on him... And you.

Thanks, Matt... for everything. I really appreciate you.

MATT

Anytime.

I look up, my gaze landing on the bedroom door. It's locked. Like that alone could keep out the pain. I wish I could do the same with my heart. Slam a door over it. Keep it guarded. Keep it safe.

Wanting to be numb always scares me. The thought of just turning something off inside me—not feeling anything at all—it's dangerous. But it's easier that way. It's what I did with my dad. I buried every feeling, good and bad, and just walked away. I chose numbness. I chose avoidance. I didn't want it to control me anymore. I didn't want to be codependent.

And yet here I am. Letting someone else's choices steal my happiness again. I won't let it happen forever. I can't.

I told myself the first time I discovered Jensen's addiction, the day I realized he was detoxing, that I'd give him one year. One year to get clean. He deserves that at the very least. He's a *good* person, and we have too much history to just throw it all away. Everyone deserves a second—or even a third—chance. Time to prove themselves. Time to fail. Time to win.

But how many chances do I give him? I don't want two or three to turn into twenty years of trying—like my mom gave my dad.

No. One year. That's all he gets to prove himself. To get clean, and to stay that way.

Until May.

I do the math. That's seven months. Seven months of trying, waiting, and hoping.

God, that feels like an eternity.

I don't know if I can do this for that long—if I'll make it. But I have to try.

I never asked for easy. But damn. It shouldn't be this hard.

My gaze drops to my phone again. I'm going to need something or someone to lean on. And it can't be Leo, not yet anyway.

I open my browser and type: *Al-Anon NYC.*

I scroll through the meetings. There are plenty to choose from. I add a Thursday evening one to my calendar. There's an AA meeting at the same time, in the same building.

Good.

We can go together. Get the help and support we both need.

Chapter Forty

ALLEY

NOVEMBER

I PLACE the last ornament from the box on the tree and step back, assessing my work. There's a cluster on the bottom right—too much of the same. I pull off one of the medium round snowball ornaments and find a new home for it on the opposite side, where things look a little bare.

Sinking onto the couch, I take it in. The twinkling lights cast a glow across the room, spreading a warm happiness through me I haven't felt in a long time.

This is my favorite time of year.

It's the Sunday after Thanksgiving, and this has become a tradition for Jensen and me. Football's muted in the background, soft holiday music floats through the air. Jensen helped me put the tree up, but the decorating? That's my thing. I like it a certain way.

He's in the kitchen now, making the wassail for our first holiday movie of the year, *Just Friends*. It's our favorite.

The past few months have been confusing. I honestly don't know where Jensen stands right now. He says he's clean, and maybe he is.

But sometimes—sometimes I feel it. I can sense that he's off. Like he's hiding something, but he always swears he's not. I don't know if I believe him. And he's here, so...

I can't help but wonder if he's just getting better at hiding it. Better at lying. Better at dosing. Better at finding the right upper for the downer. I hate that I can't be sure, and what's worse is that I don't fully trust him yet.

I want to, though. *God,* I want to.

"Hey babe, this is ready. Wanna pull up the movie?" Jensen calls out, stirring the pot one last time.

"Yep." I navigate to Prime, rent *Just Friends*, and queue it up. A minute later, Jensen settles in beside me and hands me a steaming mug of wassail. "Thanks, babe."

I blow on the surface, take a careful sip, and let the warmth spread through me. I savor the blend of sweet and spiced—it's Christmas in a cup. I set the mug down and snuggle up beside Jensen. His hand finds mine beneath the blanket now draped over both our laps.

Thanksgiving was different this year. We stayed home, just the two of us. I didn't want to be around Christy. I know it's petty, but I can't forgive her. I cooked dinner, and Jensen helped with the sides. It was... fine.

I debated inviting Matt or a few other friends, but it didn't feel right asking Matt to choose between us or Jensen's family. Most of our friends already had plans, anyway. Honestly? It was for the best. I was worried Jensen would have a bad day or not show up at all. But he managed to be there *and* keep his shit together. It was a small win.

I haven't spoken to Christy since the night of Zach and Joey's wedding. And Megan hasn't spoken to Jensen in almost as long. The two of them had it out the same week.

Megan came over to check on him—and me. But the second she saw him, and saw what it was doing to me, she snapped. She couldn't handle it. She started yelling, screaming at him, called him a piece of shit husband. She was hysterical. I almost had to kick her out.

She apologized to me later, and we still talk almost every day. But she still hasn't said anything to Jensen. And he hasn't tried to fix it either.

I understand why it triggered her. It's *hard*. It's so hard to watch someone you love destroy themselves. To waste their potential. To wreck every relationship they have for something they didn't exactly choose— but still keep choosing anyway. It's no easy feat.

Basically, the last few months have sucked. I even had to cancel my trip to Chicago for Michael's birthday. I couldn't leave Jensen. I couldn't trust that he wouldn't spiral if I was gone. I had to lie about not being able to get time off work.

We're five minutes into the movie when Jensen's hand drops to my thigh, giving it a gentle squeeze. He presses a kiss to my temple. "The tree looks great, babe." His thumb brushes back and forth over my Christmas pajamas.

"Thanks," I say, leaning into him, letting my head fall onto his shoulder. I take what I can get while he's here—being present, being normal.

The corners of my lips curve slightly, melting into his touch. *God, I want him to scoop me into his arms.* To kiss me, touch me—make love to me.

But he won't.

That's one thing that still isn't normal—not since that night. The night I pushed him off of me. Things haven't been the same since. Whether Jensen's scared to try, or just not interested... I'm not sure. But a sadness tugs at my chest when I'm near him like this. A longing. A thirst I can't quench.

I tilt my head, looking up at him. "I love you," I whisper.

He glances down at me. "I love you too." His hand squeezes my thigh again, and I hesitate.

Do I just... make a move?

I search his eyes. He looks normal. Like Jensen. Is this just his new normal, though? Do I even remember what the old Jensen looked like?

My pulse quickens. It's pathetic, really—being nervous to make a move on my own husband.

What if he's not clean? What if he doesn't want me?

I steady myself with a deep breath and climb onto his lap, straddling him. His hands find my ass instantly, a slow grin stretching across his face as our eyes lock.

"Hey, baby," he says, his voice low and deep, seconds before he crashes his mouth to mine.

My God.

I've missed him.

I drink in the warmth of his lips like they're the air I need to breathe. My heart thunders in my chest, and a fluttery sensation spreads low and hot in my core. I'm instantly wet. Heat pools between my thighs, and butterflies stir in my stomach.

He groans into my mouth, one hand sliding up to cup the back of my neck, pulling me even closer as he devours me. I grind against him, and I feel his length hardening beneath me.

There he is.

Chapter Forty-One

ALLEY

PRESENT DAY

MATT STANDS AND STRETCHES, grabbing his phone off the coffee table. "You sure you're gonna be okay?"

I nod, though I'm anything but. "Yeah. I'll be good. I'm just gonna go to bed. I'm tired."

He gives me a long look. "You call me if you need anything, alright? I don't care if it's two in the morning."

"I know."

Pulling me into a hug, he says, "I'm serious. Promise me."

"I promise," I reply, squeezing him tightly.

"Okay." He pauses at the door. "See you, Al."

"See you." I lock the door behind him, then wander the house like a ghost—restless, searching for anything to distract me from my thoughts. I'm exhausted, but there's no way I'll fall asleep. Not without knowing where Jensen is and that he's okay.

I end up in bed with my laptop, apparently in the mood to torture myself. I've pulled up our wedding video. Pressing play, I quietly sob as the day unfolds, our favorite music playing in the background.

We were so happy. Until everything fell apart.

Part of me can't believe we're back here—right where we were not long after we got married. I don't know what happens next. I don't know if we'll make it.

But I do know that I wouldn't trade the past few months for anything. Being married to Jensen. Watching him get clean. It showed me what marriage could be. What it's supposed to feel like when both people are fighting for the same thing.

It's wild how it takes two committed people to make a relationship work, but only one to tear it apart. One person not committing. One person getting sidetracked. One person becoming an addict.

One person to fuck it all up.

The video ends. I hit play again, and it almost feels like surrender. Like I'm finally admitting to myself that I may never have this again— what we had on that day. Not even what we had a few weeks ago. And it hurts. More than I ever thought possible.

I'm losing him again. He's losing me.

Hitting play for a third time, my cries are no longer quiet. They come in waves—loud, ugly, gut-wrenching—as I break once more. Still alone. The ache is indescribable. Jensen's face. His smile. The way he looked at me like I was the only woman in the room. Like his eyes were made only to see me. The old Jensen always looked at me like I was the only thing he needed to live.

Not water.

Not food.

Not air.

Not Oxy.

Just me.

Chapter Forty-Two

ALLEY

THEN—FOUR MONTHS AGO

APRIL

I POUND my fists on the office door. "Jensen!"

I'm met with silence.

I've been standing in the hallway for five minutes, and I'm losing my patience. It's been a day, and I'm not in the mood for this bullshit. I don't even know if he's home. For all I know, he's passed out in his car somewhere.

It's six p.m. on a Thursday, and I just got home from one of the worst shifts I've ever had. Normally, I love my job. But not today. A patient coded coming out of anesthesia, and it scared the absolute shit out of me. It was the first time I've ever dealt with something that intense. He ended up being okay, but still had to be transferred to the ICU. My hands shook for an entire hour, and the charting, the debriefing—it was mentally and emotionally exhausting.

The last thing I'm capable of right now is playing the patient, loving wife to my addict husband who's been MIA for weeks. I feel extra defeated.

"Jensen!" I slap the door again, harder this time. A sharp sting spreads through my hand. "Dammit!" I drag my palm down the frame, teeth clenched.

He hasn't responded to a single one of my texts today—which tells me one thing: he's higher than usual.

What blows my mind is how he still manages to keep his job. He's a fully functioning addict at work, and a complete mess at home. Like a child who holds it together all day at school, only to fall apart the second they walk through the door. Except in this scenario, he's a grown-ass man with a successful career... who either shuts me out of his office or avoids me completely by not coming home at all.

I've had it. Rage boils up like a volcano—pressure building, seconds from eruption. I'm so damn tired. Tired of the not knowing. Tired of the lies. Tired of this life.

And I'm sick of this door being locked. My eyes land on the hinges. *Bingo.*

I pull up YouTube and search for the easiest way to remove a door. I watch a two-minute how-to video, dig Jensen's tools out of the utility closet, and get to work.

It takes longer than I expect. One of the pins is jammed, and I wrestle with it, cursing under my breath. But with effort, and the last shred of patience I have, I finally get the damn thing off.

Jensen isn't in his office, and his location is turned off, per usual.

I haul the door to our storage closet, rearrange a few things to make space, and lean it inside before shutting the closet door. Then, I return to the hallway to gather the pins and hinges.

I take the elevator down to the lobby and step outside. The cool, spring air hits my face as I drop the hardware into the nearest trash can. I walk away with a slight, satisfied smile, like this one small win somehow made up for the nightmare of a day I've had.

I don't feel like cooking or making a mess just to eat alone, so I wander a few blocks to my favorite Mediterranean restaurant. If I'm going to eat by myself, I might as well enjoy it.

* * *

At dinner, I pull out my phone and glance at the last text I sent to Jensen.

> Can you just let me know that you're okay?

That was over an hour ago. My vision blurs as I stare blankly at the screen.

It's almost been a year. A whole year since I realized what was happening—since Jensen first tried to detox. A year of living in hell, watching the love of my life slowly destroy himself... and our marriage.

My timeline is almost up, and I start to seriously wonder what I'm going to do. Am I really going to leave? Where would I even go?

The thought of trying to find a place to live in this economy makes me physically ill. I had great rent at my old place, but that was before prices exploded. Now, even *looking* for something decent feels impossible, especially without Jensen's income. And the thought of being single? That feels scarier than not having a place to live right now.

God, I don't want to be divorced.

I squeeze my eyes shut and take a deep, steadying breath, trying to quiet my mind. I hate when it gets like this, when I fixate on everything that could go wrong. But sometimes the weight of it all gets so heavy, my thoughts go to the darkest places. There's even a part of me that wishes I'd just get a call—right now—telling me he overdosed. Then I wouldn't have to deal with this anymore. I wouldn't be the wife who left her husband when he needed her most.

Holy shit. Guilt sweeps through me, gripping my subconscious in a way that makes it hard to breathe.

What the hell is wrong with me? When did I become such a monster?

My phone buzzes on the table beside me.

JENSEN

> Sorry, babe. I was at an AA meeting.

I stare blankly at the message, then swipe out without responding.

That's his new go-to: *Tell her I'm at an AA meeting so she can't get mad—can't question it.*

Except I *am* mad. I *do* question it. And I *don't* believe him.

I take a sip of my Guinness, because it's been a day, and text Leo.

> Hey, I know this is random, but I was wondering if I could come stay with you and Vivian sometime in the next month for a few days. I'm needing a visit home and Michael's got a full house…

Michael and Stella have three kids now, one more than the last time I stayed with them. They'd still welcome me in. The kids are little, they'd happily crash on the floor, and they'd love to have me. But I want my own space. And if I'm being honest, I want to pick Leo's brain.

He replies a few minutes later while I'm signing for the check.

LEO

> Of course. When you thinking?

> I don't know. Maybe in 3–4 weeks? I need to check my work schedule. I'll let you know in a few days. You sure? You checked with Vivian?

LEO

> I'm sure. And I don't need to check with Vivian to know she's more than okay with it.

> Okay… Well, I'll keep you posted. Thanks, Leo!

LEO

> Sure thing, love.

I can hear Leo's British accent in my head as I read it, and a grin spreads across my face, full and involuntary, lifting my mood just enough to break through the fog.

This will be good. A few days away to clear my head. To talk to someone rational. Someone who knows me but isn't too close. Leo might be a little biased, but not like my family or Jensen's.

* * *

I DON'T GET HOME until close to eight. Jensen must be here because the kitchen lights are on, and I remember turning them off earlier. I fill up a water bottle to take to my room, then turn to head down the hall, and stop dead in my tracks.

A dozen emotions slam into me at once—anger, frustration, sadness. But mostly? Defeat.

My breaths go short and shallow. A drum pounds in my chest as I stare down the hallway at the door that's been removed from our bedroom...

And reattached to the office.

I'm moving on instinct, without thought. My hands connect with the door before I know what I'm doing. The banging. The screaming. It doesn't even feel like me.

But I've lost myself in this—just like Jensen has. I'm not proud of who I've become. But it's been necessary. Guard up. Shield on. Ready for battle. Ready to fight. Every day.

Every. Damn. Day

Because I have to survive.

But so does he.

Chapter Forty-Three

JENSEN

THEN

"Jensen!" Alley's voice comes sharp from the other side of the door, the pounding insistent and unnecessarily loud.

Jesus Christ. Can't she just knock like a normal person?

I'm agitated. On edge. I stayed late at work, then hid out in my car, snorted some Oxy, and took a nap. I had to chill out from the stress of the day before I could face her.

It's getting too hard to be around Alley. I avoid her at all costs. I can't mask it anymore—can't control it. I've spiraled further than I ever thought I would.

It's starting to show at work. I can barely focus. It takes everything I've got to appear present. My boss is noticing—small things, but I'm slipping. Thank God he likes me. I've got years of success with him under my belt. I've proven myself, that's for damn sure.

But how long before that's not enough?

He cornered me today. He said I seemed off, and asked if I was okay. I told him shit at home with Alley wasn't great. I blamed it all on my marriage. Sure, we're hanging by a thread, that part's true. But it has nothing to do with Alley.

It's me. It's all fucking me.

I did this.

I fucked up.

I ruined us.

The banging grows louder, adding fuel to the dumpster fire of my already-shitty day.

I'm losing everyone else too. Matt's starting to avoid me. Megan won't talk to me. Jeff treats me like I'm fucking twelve. It's awkward as hell with Kevin because of the whole Megan thing. My dad's pissed.

My mom's the only one I can still talk to. She's the only one who doesn't criticize every little thing I do. She doesn't mention my problem every time she sees me. Doesn't treat me like an addict. She just... lets me be.

Coming home and finding the door off my office, when all I wanted was some privacy to take a hit, was a slap I didn't see coming.

Unfuckingbelievable.

I had the door switched out in fifteen minutes.

"Jensen! Open this fucking door right now!"

Damn. She's really mad. I move fast, stuffing everything away. The hit I took ten minutes ago is settling in fully now—and *God,* I needed it. I can't do evenings at home without it anymore. The day drains the life out of me, and it's the only thing that lets me even pretend to be present.

I shove my kit into my backpack. I have to keep it all with me now. Alley thinks she's the fucking CIA.

She's kicking the door now, screaming at the top of her lungs, and I snap. "I'm fucking coming!" I yell, my patience gone two hours ago. My pulse spikes—coke and adrenaline—a toxic combination. I already know I'm not in complete control here.

I unlock the door and swing it open hard, coming face-to-face with my wife. Her face is red and tear-streaked, eyes wild.

She shoves past me and darts for my backpack. I reach for it, but it's too late. She has it.

"Babe, give me my backpack."

She doesn't even look at me—just storms past and into the closet, yanking down a suitcase and tossing clothes into it.

Panic shoots through me. "Jesus. What are you doing?"

She doesn't respond. And to be honest, I prefer screaming, shouting Alley to this—this version that won't even look at me. It's like she's already gone. Like she doesn't give a fuck anymore.

I watch her pack, my eyes flicking to my backpack lying on the floor near her. I could grab it, take it to my car. Get it out of the way before she—

What the fuck is wrong with me?

I'm actually debating saving my stash over my marriage. Like I'd rather watch her walk out that door than lose my drugs.

That reality hits like bricks to the chest.

I've lost it.

I'm completely gone.

She's a hurricane of rage—all that built-up hurt and resentment ripping through her. Drawers slam shut. Her breathing's loud, fast and sharp—exhaling in ragged huffs, cries bursting between each one.

I stand there, completely dumbfounded, at a total loss for what to do. My brain and heart aren't aligning. Part of me wants to stop her. To pull her close. To tell her to stop crying. That everything's going to be okay.

That I'll stop. I'll fix this—I'll fix us.

But the other part—the part overtaken by the coke—is *seething*. How dare she take my stash. Ignore me. She thinks she's just going to walk out of here without saying a damn word?

Fuck that.

Alley zips her suitcase and slings my backpack over her shoulder, heading for the front door.

"Babe, what are you doing? Where are you going?"

She keeps walking.

"Alley, I'm speaking to you," I say, louder this time. "Alley!" I shout. "Don't you walk away when I'm talking to you!"

Nothing.

She reaches for the handle.

"Give me my fucking backpack!" I'm yelling now, and I regret it the second the words leave my mouth.

She stops, turns suddenly, and shoves my pack into my hands. "Fuck you, Jensen!"

She backs toward the door, tears falling hard with every step. The look on her face rips my goddamn heart out, gutting me alive.

"No, Al." The words rush out—shaky, desperate, full of fear. "Don't go. Don't fucking go."

Her hand trembles as she opens the door, and I hate myself—more than I ever have.

The door slams shut.

She's gone.

My jaw clenches, and the tears sting like fire behind my eyes. "Fuck," I grit through my teeth. I grip my backpack, holding on to the only thing I have left.

"Fuck. Fuck. Fuck."

I chuck my pack across the room, yelling out another "FUCK," and drop to my knees. My hands wrap around my head, and I fold to the floor, sobbing.

And I pray.

I fucking pray.

I'm not even sure to who—or what. Anyone. Anything that'll listen.

God. Buddha. Allah. Motherfucking Earth. I don't know. I've never prayed before.

Please.

Don't let me lose her.

She's all I've got.

She's the only thing that matters.

Please.

Help me.

Chapter Forty-Four

ALLEY

THEN

THE COMFORT of Leo's kitchen feels grounding compared to the chaos I just came from. He's making me a cappuccino. The smell of coffee fills the air, and the quiet sound of him moving around is the first thing that's felt normal in weeks.

After my fight with Jensen, I went to Matt's. I slept in one of his guest rooms and caught an 8:00 a.m. flight to Chicago. So much for figuring things out with work—or giving Leo time to prepare. I texted him late last night and asked if I could come in the morning. I called my boss first thing and took the next few days off. I told her it was a family emergency.

It's 11:00 a.m. now, and I'm exhausted. I didn't sleep at all last night. I just kept replaying everything in my head. The things he said. The things he didn't. The way he chose his backpack over me. The way he didn't stop me. Didn't say anything. Didn't fight.

I left.

I had a suitcase, and he just... watched me leave.

My heart feels shattered. Like it's been split into a million pieces. And I don't know if it'll ever be whole again.

Leo doesn't say anything as he works the espresso machine, giving me space. I'm sure that showing up on his doorstep ten minutes ago, sunglasses on, bloodshot eyes, tear-streaked face, wasn't what he expected. It's obvious that I'm not okay.

I still haven't told anyone in Chicago, not even Michael. Because how embarrassing is that? *Hey, you know how dad was an alcoholic and I knew all the signs? Yeah somehow I ended up in the same situation Mom was in.*

Leo sets the cappuccino in front of me, then leans back against the opposite counter, arms crossed. He studies me quietly, assessing, feeling out the situation. "Do you want to be left alone?" he asks, cautiously, one eyebrow cocked.

"No," I say softly.

He nods, then says, "Do you want to tell me why you don't want Michael to know you're here?"

I force myself to look at him. "No," I whisper.

A Mickey Mouse song plays behind me on the TV. Leo glances toward the living room, where Isla's singing along, shouting the lyrics the best she can.

He puffs out a laugh, a small grin tugging at the corners of his mouth. I peek over my shoulder, then turn back to Leo—and the look in his eyes breaks me. It's like every hope and dream I ever had with Jensen comes tumbling down all at once. Every wall I've built to block out the pain and denial crumbles, hitting me like a ton of bricks.

I let out a sob and then gasp for air. Leo's arms wrap around me in an instant, pulling me up from the stool.

He hugs me tight, and I cry for everything I thought I'd have—a future with Jensen, kids, a family. For the man I believed would be the best dad in the world. He's so good with kids. They love him. For everything I've lost, and for who we've become—a sliver of who we once were.

I soak Leo's shirt, trembling in his arms. He rubs my back and tells me it's okay, to let it all out.

God, this is embarrassing. He doesn't even know why I'm upset.

I finally pull back, swiping at my eyes with both index fingers. "Sorry," I manage, my voice shaky.

"Don't be sorry, love. I'm glad you feel comfortable enough to come here." He scrubs a hand over his chin. "You know, you're the closest thing I have to a sister. I've always felt like you filled that space for me after I moved here. Filled the void Chloe left when she died."

Chloe is Leo's twin sister. She died from Leukemia when they were seventeen.

He looks at me, steady. "You're family, Alley. Whether you talk or not. Stay as long as you like. Whatever you need."

I nod, choking out, "Thanks. I want to talk. I need your advice and your perspective."

"You have my undivided attention."

We move to the table, where he can still keep an eye on Isla but give me his full focus, and I tell him everything.

He listens, occasionally asking a question—soft, steady, patient.

There's no judgment. No telling me what I should or shouldn't do. That's not his role. And while I know this isn't a therapy session, he'd never take me as a patient anyway, it's comforting to talk to someone who gets it. Who gets me.

Who won't hate Jensen.

When I finally finish, Leo leans back in his chair, dragging a hand over his face.

He exhales sharply. "Fuck. I'm so sorry, Alley."

"What do I do?"

He chuckles softly. "You know I can't tell you what to do—whether to stay or leave. I can't do that. But I will say this... your pain is real. And you can still love someone and decide they're not good for you right now. What's your gut telling you?"

"I'm not sure," I say, staring at my hands on the table. I force myself to meet his eyes. His expression is kind and understanding. "I'm not ready to give up yet. But I can't—" The words catch in my throat. "I can't do this anymore. It's slowly killing me. I'm not fun anymore. I barely laugh. The joy's been completely sucked out of me."

Leo's voice is quiet. "What do you miss the most?"

"I don't know. Just... us. Me with Jensen. Being able to do nothing at home and still feel totally satisfied and happy. Before, my cup was always overflowing because it was so full." I laugh softly, tears clinging to my lashes. "It sounds stupid, but we could literally be doing nothing and laugh our asses off. You know?"

He nods with a sad smile. "Oh, I know exactly what you mean."

"I used to be so excited to see him at the end of the workday." I wipe at my nose with a tissue. "Sometimes I think it would be easier if he were cheating on me, or hurting me. If he made me hate him. At least then I'd have a reason to walk away that made sense to everyone, including me."

Leo stays silent, letting me speak.

"But this?" I gesture helplessly. "He's sick. He didn't ask for this. And I keep telling myself I can't leave someone in their worst moment. I can't abandon him the way my dad abandoned my mom when she was dying... You know what I thought the other day?" I pause, debating whether I should say it out loud.

Leo gestures for me to go on, and somehow, I know he won't judge me.

"I actually thought to myself... I wish I'd just get a call that he overdosed, so I wouldn't have to deal with this anymore. I wouldn't have a choice. I could still love him... and not have to leave him." A sob bursts out of me, and I shake my head. "God, what kind of person thinks that? It's so selfish." I try to breathe through it the best I can. "I don't really want that. I would never want that. I love him so much. I just... it's so hard."

Leo's voice stays calm and steady. "You're not awful, Alley. You're human. And the mind does some pretty crazy shit to protect us. It's normal to think that, considering what you're dealing with. It's not Jensen you want gone, it's the addict inside him. You want him back. You love him. That's obvious. Don't beat yourself up."

I cry so hard now I can't even look at him. I can't speak. I can't do anything but cry.

And I'm so *tired* of crying.

I nod. I know he's right, but it doesn't make me feel better. Those thoughts... they're part of what I hate most about this. They're not me. The good in me feels lost, buried somewhere deep inside. The part that used to trust easily, forgive quickly, and see the best in people— that part of me is gone.

Now I'm the cynical wife who wishes her addict husband wouldn't come home, just so I don't have to deal with all his problems anymore. It's such a mess—a mess that's spilled into every part of our lives and touched everyone around us. Everything Jensen touches is affected by his addiction.

Leo lets me cry for a while before he speaks again. "Have you thought about what staying would look like?"

"Yes."

"And what does that look like?" he nudges, patient as ever.

"It looks like hell... if he doesn't get clean." I pause. "And hard if he does." I grab another tissue from the box Leo set out earlier, my pile embarrassingly high. "But eventually, I know we'd find our way back. Maybe we'd even be stronger. Better. Is it ignorant of me to think that?"

Leo frowns. "Not at all. That actually sounds realistic. You're not denying it'll be hard. You're not romanticizing it either." He hesitates this time. "And what would it look like if you left?"

I squeeze my eyes shut. "I don't know. I can't get past the part where I'd have nowhere to live." I open my eyes again, my voice small. "And even when I do picture myself moving out, I don't see myself any happier than I am now. It looks like hell too. Hard. Sad." I pause. "Lonely."

"You're right. It probably would look like that... for a while," he says quietly. "But time's the one thing that always passes. That's guaranteed. And with it, things get easier. Not right away, but eventually." He pauses, watching me carefully. "You'd figure it out. You'd be okay. You'd find joy again. The pain might still be there sometimes, but it won't rule you. I know that firsthand." He exhales slowly. "Eventually, other things get bigger. Life gets louder. The grief is still real, but it becomes more of a memory. A sad one, yeah, but memories only carry the weight we give them. Over time, they get lighter. They just become part of the story."

I swallow hard, my eyes burning. "But I don't want him to be a memory. I don't want to live a life without him in it."

The door downstairs opens and closes, followed by footsteps on the stairs. Vivian walks into the kitchen moments later, giving us a quick once-over before smiling. "Hi, Alley!"

I wipe my face and force a smile. "Hi, Vivian."

She glances at Leo as she walks past, her small baby bump visible under the dress she's wearing. "I'm just going to grab Isla and take her to lunch with me."

"Thanks, love." He pushes up from his chair, meeting her on her way back with Isla in her arms. He kisses Vivian, then presses his lips to Isla's forehead. "Bye, princess. Have fun at lunch with your mum."

His hand rests briefly on Vivian's belly as they exchange a few more words, then Vivian calls out, "Alley, it's so good to have you. We'll catch up later, okay?"

"Sounds great. Thanks, Vivian."

"Bye!" she calls over her shoulder, Isla's little voice echoing a tiny "Bye!" behind her.

Leo settles back into his seat. "Can I ask why you haven't told Michael?"

"Michael would tell me to leave. He'd hate Jensen for it. You know what we went through with my dad."

Leo's brows draw together. "I don't think he'd hate Jensen. He might surprise you. Look how great he's been with your dad all these years." He pauses, chuckling softly. "But you're right about the leaving part. He probably would say that."

"It's different. He's great with my dad now, but he told my mom to leave all the time."

Leo tilts his head. "And did you?"

"Did I what?"

"Did you tell your mum to leave?"

"No," I say quietly. "I selfishly just wanted my dad to get better. I never wanted him gone. Even though I hated him half the time..." I pause, picking at my cuticles, sitting in the discomfort of my thoughts —of my reality. "But I also swore I'd never end up in a marriage like my mom's."

Leo nods, letting that sit for a moment before he responds. "Look, ultimately I think it's important to trust your gut. Follow your instinct.

It doesn't sound like you're ready to give up on Jensen, or your marriage right now. You'll know when your time is up. Even if it's not today. But I also think it's smart to have a plan, even just a loose one. Give yourself a timeline. Otherwise, you might find yourself ten years down the road, stuck in something you swore you'd never live through, just like your mum." He pauses, thinking. "Maybe you could... try some automatic writing. Write a letter to yourself. Say everything you're feeling right now, what you'd want your future self to hear when things are hard. Be honest. Seal it up, and pick a date to open it, no matter where you are by then. You might be surprised by what you needed to hear."

I nod slowly, considering it. "Yeah... that's a good idea. I could do that."

It's quiet for a moment as I process everything we've talked about. It doesn't feel right to leave. Not yet. Not today. No matter what anyone else says or thinks.

I know this could be a long road. I know some people never get better. But I've seen miracles happen, too. And even though this feels like a nightmare, it hasn't been enough time to throw in the towel.

"I know you can't tell me what you think is best, but..." I pause. "What would you tell Vivian? Or Chloe?"

His eyes sparkle with amusement, a soft chuckle slipping between his lips. "Ah, the old *ask me what you should do without asking me what you should do*." He shakes his head. "I can't tell you that. One, it's irrelevant. Vivian is my wife, so for her to be in this situation, I'd have to be the one putting her there. And two, even if Chloe was alive, I'd be looking at it from a brother's perspective. It's different. It's easy to pass judgment from the outside and say, *Yeah, I think you should leave*, because I care about you more than I care about Jensen." He pauses, then looks at me, honest and raw. "But I'll tell you this... if it was Vivian in Jensen's shoes? If *she* was the addict?" He exhales hard. "Fuck. I'd walk through fire for her. Fight like hell before I gave up. I'd probably destroy my entire soul trying to save her."

A bitter smile pulls at the corner of his mouth. "And I don't know if that makes me fucking stupid... or a hero."

I hold his gaze for what feels like minutes before finally saying,

"Thank you for saying that, Leo." Because I've never felt more seen, more understood for staying, than I do right now.

He gives me a soft smile. "It's only the truth, love... And Alley?"

"Yeah?"

"You always have a place here. Should you ever need it."

* * *

I PAUSE the show I'm only half-watching—*Dead to Me*, too emotional to sit through another story about grief. I can't focus.

Hugging my knees to my chest, I stare blankly at the TV in the dark of Leo's guest room. I do feel better—if only a little. Getting my truth out. Being able to speak my deepest, darkest thoughts out loud. Admitting what I'd been too ashamed to say, and not being judged for it.

Leo's confession of what he'd do if it were Vivian? That hit hard. He's one of the most logical, emotionally intelligent, reasonable people I know. Hearing someone like him say he'd destroy his entire soul to save the person he loves? It shook me.

I feel that too. Jensen would do the same for me. I know he would. The Jensen I fell in love with would move mountains. He'd go full-on Moses and part the red fucking sea for me. That's what makes this so hard. I know he's still in there, buried under the addiction and the chaos—drowning beneath the surface—and I'm the one holding the life jacket.

Talking to Leo didn't fix anything, but it helped... more than I thought it would.

This is just what I needed. Aside from Al-Anon, it's been the most helpful thing I've done for myself. Al-Anon's been great too. I don't make it every week, but almost. It's been the only place, besides here, where I don't feel alone. Where I don't feel crazy. Where other people get it.

I've connected with another wife in a similar situation. Her name's Jenna. She's a couple years younger than me, but her husband was in the military. He came home and somehow wound up right where Jensen is.

There's nothing more validating than meeting someone who understands. Someone who's been there. Someone who can relate.

I've finally told Scarlett. But her and Zach? They love Jensen, but they'll always be team Alley. And while I appreciate that, they don't really get it. They tell me I should leave all the time.

That's why Leo's words hit even harder. He's team Alley, but he still found a way to relate and make me feel seen—to validate why I've stayed.

I open my messages and re-read the last few exchanges between Jensen and me.

JENSEN

> I'm sorry, babe. I don't know why I did that. I don't know why I didn't stop you. I love you.

> Please come back. I know I'm a fuck-up, but please don't leave me.

Those were from late last night. I didn't respond until a few hours ago, after I spoke to Leo.

> I'm not leaving you, I just needed space. I'm in Chicago for a few days. But I can't do this for much longer. You NEED to get help.

JENSEN

> I know.

> I'm packing a bag right now. Checking myself into the closest detox center.

> I'm getting clean. For good this time. I can't lose you, babe.

> That's good. I love you too. I'll see you in a few weeks then. Call me when you can.

I haven't heard from him since that last text an hour ago.

Maybe leaving and coming here was the right thing. Maybe he really went to the detox center. Maybe it scared him enough to take action.

Detox centers are brutal. I remember my mom taking my dad

once. He checked himself out after two days because it was hell. But if it were easy, I guess people wouldn't be alcoholics or addicts.

I keep thinking about what Leo said—about writing myself a letter. It might actually help. I've done automatic writing before. I wrote a letter to my dad, back when I left and moved to New York. I never gave it to him. I ripped it up. But it felt good to get it all out, to say what I needed to say, even if no one ever heard it.

I've never thought about writing one to myself.

I pull a notebook and pen from my backpack, and think about what I'd need to hear if Jensen relapses again.

Dear Alley,

Chapter Forty-Five

JENSEN

THEN—TWO MONTHS AGO

JUNE

"All right, you ready? Three, two, one!" I shout, wading toward Matt in the pool with my niece, Sierra, on my shoulders—Cole, my nephew, on his.

Sierra locks hands with her brother, and they start battling it out in a chicken fight.

She's won four of the last five rounds. She's two years older than Cole, and I've gotta give Cole props—he's not backing down without a fight.

Matt ducks under the water, then launches up fast, knocking Sierra off balance and pulling her into the pool with a splash. When she surfaces, she glares at him. "Not fair, Matt! That's cheating!"

Matt just laughs as she scowls, and then turns to me, fire in her eyes. "C'mon, Jensen, let's kick their ass!"

"Whoa! Language, young lady. Does your mom know you talk like that?"

She rolls her eyes. "My mom says that word all the time."

"I bet she does," I say, laughing as Matt and I exchange a look.

I dunk down so she can climb back onto my shoulders. She's a sassy one. Just like Megan.

It's Sierra's ninth birthday, so naturally we're having a big family party at Matt's.

We play three more rounds before the kids are summoned for pizza. Sierra and Cole hop out of the pool and take off running. Alley sits on the edge, her feet dangling in the water, smile wide. She and Amber have been cheering the kids on.

Amber stands to go inside with the others, and I swim over to Alley, sliding between her legs in the water. "Come swim with me."

My hands graze her thighs as I grin up at her, mischievous and playful. She presses her hands to my shoulders and slips off the edge, wrapping her legs around me as her mouth finds mine for a quick kiss.

"That was really sexy," she says through a smile, brushing her lips against mine again. "Watching you with the kids."

"Yeah?" I cock a brow.

"Yeah."

Our lips meet again and again. "Keep it up, and we're gonna get kicked out of the birthday party."

Her head tips back as she laughs into the sky. She brings her smiling face back to mine. "I don't even think I'd care."

God, it's so good seeing her laugh like that.

I chuckle against her neck. "I'll have you on your back and naked in four minutes. We're just two short elevator rides away from our bed."

"Hmm. That's tempting," she replies. "But I think we'd be shunned by the entire family if we bail on a nine-year-old's birthday party to have sex."

Her expression shifts, voice softening. "I love you." Her eyes search mine with a tenderness that makes me feel like the luckiest bastard on earth.

"I love you too, babe." *God, do I love her.*

"Thank you for being here. I know I say it a lot, but—" She pauses. "I'm really proud of you."

I never know what to say to that. Because there's nothing to be proud of. It's not like I deserve a medal for not being a fuck up.

"Thank you," I say anyway, and kiss her once more.

"Ew!"

I turn to see Sierra glaring, her face scrunched with obvious disgust.

I chuckle, and Alley's warm laugh skims my ear as her legs drop back into the water.

"Party's over," I whisper, leaning in. "You sure you don't want to sneak out?"

Alley shakes her head, grinning. "How's the pizza?" she calls.

"Good. You better hurry if you want any, it's almost gone."

Alley flashes me the *let's go* look, and I reluctantly follow her out of the pool and into the kitchen.

Things are almost back to normal—*almost*. My relationship with Megan is still a little strained, but hey, I was invited to her daughter's party. I'll take what I can get at this point.

We've talked it out, but Megan's never been one to forgive easily. You have to earn it, and I'm not mad about that. It just sucks. She and Alley are so close. And when we double with her and Kevin, which isn't often anymore, it's not the same. There's still tension.

Megan told me, even though I'm her brother and she loves me, that Alley and Amber are the sisters she never had. She'll go to bat for them, always. And she should.

Alley deserves nothing less.

She also told me if she ever loses Alley because of me, she'll cut my balls off. And honestly? I believe her.

I've been clean for ten weeks now. Truly clean. It's the longest I've ever gone. Before this, my record was three weeks.

It's still tough. Every day is a challenge, and I wonder how long it's going to feel like this. It's nowhere near what it was two months ago, but it's still a fight. Every goddamn day.

When Alley left for Chicago, I checked myself into detox. That place is rough. I felt insane for signing myself up for it. It's like walking into a medieval torture chamber and asking to be strapped to one of those iron stretchers—or whatever other nightmare they used to inflict pain.

But I did it.

Every minute, I had to think of Alley. If I didn't, I knew I'd give in —and I almost did.

On the third day, I had my discharge paperwork filled out and ready to go. But when they handed me the phone to call for a ride, I froze. If I walked out, that was it. No coming back. No second shot. They don't stop you from leaving, but they don't make it easy either. Especially when you're a fucking mess.

I stared at my contacts. Who the hell was I going to call? Alley? My mom? Matt?

They'd all be disappointed. And I knew if I called any of them, I'd lose everything.

Alley would be done for good.

Ripping up those forms and turning back around was one of the hardest things I've ever done. Detoxing is hell. But doing it like that? Without the comfort of your own bed? Without your wife by your side?

It was brutal.

When I got out, I came clean to my boss too. I told him everything. I even said if he needed to fire me for using on the clock, I'd understand.

I'm working the steps they teach you in AA: admitting your faults, being honest, making amends, and being ready to face the consequences. It's all part of the process.

I know it's hard for Alley. Hard to trust me. Hard to just flip the switch back on after spending the last year in hell.

I've hurt her. Plain and simple. It's punishment enough just knowing that.

"Alley, honey, what kind of pizza do you want?" my mom asks her, like Alley can't get her own slice.

Alley glances up, meeting my mom's eyes for a split second. "Um... I'll just have a pepperoni," she says, gaze dropping.

I know she's trying, but this thing between Alley and my mom is one of the hardest parts of being sober. I'm fully aware of the tension— the elephant in the room—and I'm the one who put it there. It's heart wrenching.

For so long, Alley looked to my mom as her own. She was someone who filled the space her mother left behind.

My mom still loves her; I know she does. But Alley can't seem to let it go. It's awkward as hell for everyone. Kudos to Alley for even showing up today. She's only seen my mom a handful of times since that night—almost a year ago.

What's crazy to me is that she can forgive me after everything I've put her through. But when it comes to my mom? She's just not ready, and I'm not going to push it. She's been through enough.

Alley takes her pizza and sits on the couch—far from where my mom sits with her plate.

I glance around at my family. Alley's on the couch beside Megan. My mom and dad sit at the table with the kids, Jeff, and Amber. Kevin and Matt are leaning against the bar. From the outside, it probably looks the same as it always has.

But it's not. It's different. *We're* different, and it's all because of me.

And I miss the way things used to be.

* * *

MEGAN'S LAUGHTER carries across the patio, the sound of screaming kids and splashing echoing from the pool in the distance.

My hand rests on Alley's smooth skin, her legs draped across my lap. We're sitting in the same spot we were the night I brought her here for Matt's birthday party. The night we first slept together.

We've sat here a hundred times since, and it always feels a little nostalgic. I remember how I couldn't stop thinking about her. How I couldn't wait to get her alone and tear her clothes off. The way I tried to hide how fucking hard I was while she sat next to me—then had to walk through a crowd of people back to my place, trying to act normal.

But tonight, it feels different. We've really been through some shit. We've earned this spot—sitting here, five years later. Still fighting like hell. Still in love. Still each other's person.

"What do you think they're talking about?" Alley asks, nodding toward Matt, Megan, and Kevin. They're the last ones here. Everyone else has gone home, and Megan's laughter is practically bouncing off the walls.

Matt and Kevin together after a few drinks? That's a guaranteed comedy show.

"Oh, Matt's definitely telling one of his sex stories."

We watch them from across the room like hawks, trying to read lips from too far away. Alley leans forward, squinting like it might help her hear better.

"Her eyes rolled back into her head, and I swear to God she passed out when she came!" Matt yells, and both of us crack up.

Alley holds out her fists for bones, and I meet her halfway with mine.

"Well played," she says grinning.

I lean in, mouth close to her ear. "Now Megan's gonna try to one-up him with a story about how she actually did pass out once. And Kevin'll get pissed when she says it was from some guy in college."

Alley laughs, nudging me. "You're so mean," she teases. Her hand drops to mine, and our fingers thread together like it's the easiest, most natural thing in the world.

Megan turns toward the pool, calling out to the kids. "Alright, time to go!"

Then she heads over to us. "We're gonna head out," she says.

Alley stands, meeting her with a hug. "Bye, Meg. Love you."

"I love you, too."

I stand as well, and Megan gives me a quick, half-assed hug. "Bye, little brother."

"Bye. Love you."

She doesn't say it back. And I get it. But it still stings. She doesn't linger either, just turns and disappears inside.

"She's still so fucking mad at me."

Alley shrugs. "It's gonna take time."

She walks over to the pool, sits down on the edge, and then slides in. "Come in," she says, raising her eyebrows, a smile playing on her lips.

I cannonball in, and when I come up for air, she's laughing—pure joy ringing in my ears.

I scoop her into my arms and crush my lips to hers. Holding her tight, I pull her close like I might lose her if I let go—even for a second. She kisses me back with a hunger that has my cock hard in an instant. I press against her, backing her toward the wall.

Anticipation surges through me, my pulse quickening. Her fingers rake through my wet hair as she moans into my mouth.

Why is everything so damn good with her?

It never gets old. She's just as exciting now as she was that first night five years ago. Her slick skin slides against mine, and it's hot as hell—her tiny swimsuit, her tits pressed against my chest, her breath mingling with mine. The heated pool water against our bodies, the cool night air around us—it's perfect.

She's perfect.

A knock hits the glass behind us, followed by Matt clearing his throat. Alley's lip slides between her teeth, eyes wide with embarrassment, and I glance over my shoulder.

"Hey, I'm hitting the hay. You two lovebirds stay as long as you want. Just lock up when you leave."

"Thanks, man," I say, turning back to Alley with a slow grin, waggling my brows.

She laughs softly. "Night, Matt. Thanks for hosting."

"Night, guys."

And just like that—it's only us.

Alone.

In the dark.

In the pool.

The pool lights flicker across the water, casting ripples of light over her skin. Behind her, the city lights glow in the distance. It's dark enough that no one can see us, but there's just enough light for me to see everything I want.

As soon as I'm sure we're in the clear, I reach for the strings of her bikini top and tug, freeing her tits. The water laps against them as I cup one in my hand.

She's so fucking sexy.

"You're so naughty," she whispers, eyes dark.

I chuckle against her jaw. "Only for you, baby."

Pulling back, I run my thumb over her nipple, my eyes locked on hers. For a second, I just take her in—really take her in. That smile? It's the most beautiful thing I've ever seen.

Reality hits me hard. I almost lost her.

"Fuck," I mutter, closing my eyes for a beat. Nope. I'm not going to cry. I've done enough of that to last a lifetime.

"What?" she asks, her hands roaming over my chest—slow, explorative, sensual.

"I just love you," I say, still trying to wrap my mind around what a jackass I've been, and how fucking lucky I am to have her. "That's all."

She cups the back of my neck and presses her lips to mine, slow and tender. No tongue. Just emotion. "I love you," she whispers. "More than you could ever know."

I wrap my arms around her and pull her closer, our bare chests flush, and I kiss her again.

And again.

And again.

My hand slides lower, gliding down her stomach, fingers grazing the edge of her bikini bottoms. I dip inside, and she lets out a quiet groan, pressing into me. I roll my hips into hers—the friction perfect, sparking a desire that's deeper than just sex.

Her hips roll against my hand, a soft whimper escaping her lips. I curl my fingers just right, and she gasps—one hand flying to my shoulder for balance.

"Jensen…"

God, the way she says my name—like it's the only word she knows.

I kiss her again, savoring it this time, my fingers still moving inside her while my other arm wraps tight around her waist. The water shifts around us, but all I can feel is her—how her body trembles, how she grips my wrist, how her nails bite into my shoulder as she gets closer.

"You feel so good, baby," I whisper against her mouth. "You always feel so good."

She moans and continues rocking against my hand, chasing release. I shift slightly, giving her more—curling, pressing, drawing another gasp from her lips.

"Don't stop," she breathes.

Like I could.

"I'm almost there."

I kiss her jaw, then her neck, letting my lips trail across her skin as her body tightens beneath my hand. Her thighs tense around me, and I feel the moment she unravels, her pussy clenches around my fingers, and she trembles in my arms. Her breaths come in short spurts, gasping in my ear.

"That's it," I murmur. "Let go for me."

Fuck, she feels like heaven—her breath hitching in my ear, her body trembling. Somehow, everything around her fades. It's just her. Just us. She's all I see, all that matters. And the way she looks at me? It makes me feel things I never thought possible.

Her body slowly relaxes against mine, chest rising and falling, and I can't help the grin that tugs at my lips. She leans her forehead against mine, still breathless.

"Holy hell," she whispers.

"Yeah," I say, cocking a brow. "Also... minor problem."

"What is it?"

I press my hips into hers. "I have a boner."

She laughs, full and unfiltered—and there it is.

That fucking dimple.

Instantly, I'm taken right back to the first time I saw her. When I confessed my "problem" to my hot nurse. That dimple stole my heart before I even knew her name. The first time I kissed her, I knew I'd never get enough.

The first time I made love to her, I knew—without a doubt—I wanted her forever.

I'm an addict, after all. But I'll never forget my first addiction.

Alley.

Chapter Forty-Six

ALLEY

PRESENT DAY—TWO MONTHS LATER

My phone dings, and a message from Megan syncs to my computer screen.

MEGAN

> Hey—just checking in. Jensen home yet? How are you?

I don't have it in me to respond. Mostly because I don't know what to say. I'm not good. Jensen's not home. He's been more MIA these past three weeks than he's ever been. Nothing makes sense. And this time... it's worse. I've never been more scared for his health than I am right now.

I remember what it was like when my dad would relapse. He'd spiral fast, drinking himself into blackouts. And when he came out of them, he was grumpy and mean. He'd deflect all the shame onto us just so he didn't have to sit with it himself.

Opioid relapse is even more dangerous. Most addicts go straight back to their old dose. That's how so many overdoses happen. The craving hits just as hard, but their bodies can't handle it anymore. There's no longer a tolerance. No build-up. Just... overdose.

It's just one more emotion I have to sit with. Fear. Real, paralyzing fear.

Is my husband lying dead on a street somewhere? Am I one phone call away from being a widow?

My thoughts race, dragging me into the darkness of the past year. It's been a constant struggle—a brutal push and pull of get clean and relapse. Jensen would stay clean for two, maybe three days. A week if we were lucky. Then he'd relapse. But most of the time, he never even made it to clean. He'd try to detox, only to give up three days later. Every weekend became a cycle of misery. Another failed attempt to get better.

Most of the time, I didn't even know if he was clean or not. He'd go through detox, disappear, then show up just enough to convince me he was okay. Just enough to make me question my instincts.

Our lives had gotten so chaotic, and my expectations for him had gotten so low; I honestly couldn't even remember what *normal* looked like anymore. In the middle of all that madness was the real destruction. The lying. The stealing. The sneaking.

I had to take Jensen off every financial account I could. Some were originally his, and I didn't have the authority to remove him, so I did the only thing I could. I transferred the money out—into my own account. It had to be where it was safe.

It was never about punishment. I had to protect what was mine—what was *ours*. We'd both worked so hard. I wasn't about to watch everything we built get lost to drugs.

He always found a way, though. He'd steal my credit card or debit card when I wasn't looking, or when I was sleeping. He found an old checkbook and drained it in a matter of days, writing out checks to cash.

Then it was the little things that started to go missing—the GoPro, the expensive art piece from the guest bedroom. Things I wouldn't notice right away. Things he could pawn, like he was some desperate stranger on the street. It was heartbreaking—and pathetic. Still, I stayed. Through all of it.

I decide to message Megan back, just to let her know, though I'm sure she's already talked to Matt by now.

He's not home yet. I'm worried about him.

She calls immediately.

I don't want to answer, but I feel like I should, so I swipe to pick up.

"Hey," I say, my voice flat.

"Hey. What's going on? Do I need to come over there? Do you want me to kick his ass?"

I force a laugh, but it's dry and humorless. "He'd have to be here to kick his ass."

"God, Al. I'm so sorry. What can I do?" Her voice is warm and loving, full of concern.

"Nothing..." I pause, swallowing the lump forming in my throat. "There's this part of me that doesn't even want him to come home. Because when he's here, I don't think rationally. I turn into this codependent version of myself. He manipulates, gives me some sob story that smells like bullshit a mile away, and for some reason, I eat it up." I scoff, bitter. "I'm sorry. I shouldn't be telling you any of this."

"Why? Because he's my brother? That doesn't make him any less of an asshole."

The tears come again—and I'm so—God. Damn. Tired. Of crying.

"But he's not an asshole," I whisper. "He's Jensen."

Megan doesn't say anything. She's good at that, just sitting in the discomfort with me.

"Do you think your mom knows where he is?"

"She doesn't. I talked to her about an hour ago."

I scoff.

"She really doesn't. I know you don't trust her anymore, but... I don't know, I feel like I'd know if she was lying to me. I know she babies him. Trust me, I know. I grew up in that bullshit. But she sounded worried."

"I'm sure she did," I say sarcastically.

She also sounded real curious last year when she asked what time Jensen was getting home from Boston. Turns out, Christy's quite the actress. "You know she picked him up from the detox center last month?"

Megan goes quiet.

"Are you serious?" she finally says. "When did Jensen relapse? I thought this was all new."

"Yeah. Me too," I say. "I started suspecting about three weeks ago, but I wasn't sure. Then Jensen told me he couldn't go back to detox—that they wouldn't take him. I didn't understand why... until he finally admitted he checked himself out a month ago, and your mom picked him up."

I exhale, biting down a wave of bitterness. "She brought him home. Tried to detox him herself. He disappeared, of course."

I glance toward the window, shaking my head. "I sent her a nasty text. She replied and said I could never understand because I don't have kids. And you wanna know the ironic thing about that?" I add, my voice sharper now. "I'd love to have kids. But I'm married to her son, who can't keep his shit together."

"Seriously?" Megan groans. "That's so my mom. That makes me so angry for you." She pauses, then continues. "Why didn't you tell me? I told you, you don't have to do this alone."

"I know. But it's not your problem. You've got your own life, a family to worry about. You shouldn't have to deal with this."

"Stop. My life is so fucking easy. I'm here for you. Always."

She goes quiet, and I can hear it in her breath. She's choking up. It takes a lot for Megan to cry, so when she does, it means something. "God, I'm so *fucking* mad at him," she says finally. "I want to tell you to walk away. To stop putting up with his shit. But goddammit, Alley... I don't want to lose you as my sister."

It goes silent, both of us too overwhelmed to speak. The tears spill again, soaking the neckline of my shirt.

"I don't... want to... lose you either," I manage to choke out.

"Listen," Megan says gently. "I'm gonna do what I can to find him, okay? I'll call around. I know people who know Seth. Maybe that dickwad has a clue where he is."

"Okay."

"I'll call you if I find anything."

"Thanks, Meg."

"Don't thank me. I love you."

"I love you too."

"Bye."

I end the call, and press play on my show. Maybe it will help me fall asleep. It won't—but it's something.

Chapter Forty-Seven

JENSEN

PRESENT DAY

I DRIFT in and out of consciousness, my eyes fluttering. Blurry shapes move around me, and every sound feels muffled and far away.

Jesus, my heart is pounding. But it's slow, methodic—loud.

"Oh, good. You're alive," a voice says.

Is that... Alley?

What the hell is happening? Did I have surgery again?

"You dropped these."

I feel something land on my chest, and I force my eyes open. My vision sharpens just enough to make out a woman stepping into a skirt, pulling it up around her hips. She's in her bra, eyeliner smudged beneath her eyes.

She's pretty, maybe. Hard to tell beneath sunken eyes and hollowed-out cheeks, her hair a tangled mess.

I groan, head fuzzy, my gaze shifting down to the little plastic baggie she tossed on me. I'm shirtless—and my pants are undone.

Panic surges, nausea rising fast. "Fuck," I rasp. "What the fuck?"

Her eyes flick to me. "Relax. We didn't sleep together. You got up to piss, came back with your pants halfway down, then passed the fuck out on the floor." She lets out a dry laugh. "Classy."

She bends to grab something off the floor, her tone flippant. "Good thing, too. Jake and I went to town after. That could've been awkward... unless you're into watching. Are you?"

Her words bounce around in my head like bumper cars, slamming into each other while I try to make sense of what she just said.

What? I passed out?

I try to lift my head, but it's too heavy. My neck gives out halfway. "What?" I ask, my voice scratchy.

"Are you into watching?" she repeats, way too casually. "Better yet, are you into threesomes? Because Jake's still here, and you're hot, so..."

"No. Jesus. Fuck no, I'm married."

She laughs as she pulls a shirt over her head. "Right. You know, you were passed out for a whole thirty minutes. It's not like you're a saint. That shit'll knock you on your ass. Especially the first time smoking it."

"I smoked something?" My mind is spinning, trying to dig through the fog, to remember what I did, what I took.

Where the fuck even am I?

I can't remember. I don't know where I was earlier tonight, or how I got here. Shit. I can't remember the last fucking month.

My relapse hit hard. I spiraled fast. Worse than ever before. I don't remember it ever feeling like this.

She hums but doesn't answer. "You gonna be alright?"

"What did I smoke?" I ask again. I try to sound firm, but it comes out groggy, slow and slurred.

She looks down at me—her expensive heels just a few feet from my face. "Oxy."

I'm half-slumped in the corner against something soft. A chair maybe... or a chaise? I don't know, but it feels expensive. Everything in here does. The bed across the room is wrecked—sheets tangled, something black hanging off the edge. The air reeks, too, a thick mix of perfume, sweat, sex... and something burnt.

There's some kind of fancy silver tray on the table with wax hardened on it. Ash is scattered on the floor, foil crumpled around it. A wine bottle's tipped over in the corner—red, I think. Or maybe it's the lighting—honestly, it's all kind of a blur.

"Listen, I don't know you, but Seth vouched for you," she says. "The party's still going, so take your time. If you need a bump to get you going, I can get you one."

I force a nod and squeeze my eyes shut. My stomach lurches, and cold sweat beads along my hairline.

"Yeah? I'll be back in a bit." She slings a Yves Saint Laurent purse over her shoulder and walks out, the door clicking shut behind her.

A whimper escapes my throat. "Fuck."

Jesus, did I take something else? Seth said it was Oxy. But—what if it wasn't just that?

I smoked it? I've never done that.

I vaguely remember coming to the party to meet Seth. He handed me pills and told me if I needed it to hit faster, there was a setup in the back. He said nobody would bother me.

But I had a drink first, and I think I took a benzo before he even showed up. My anxiety was through the fucking roof. And now—

I guess that's how I ended up here.

The girl's words slam back into my skull. *You passed the fuck out.*

My stomach twists tighter. Everything inside me swirls like a storm—loud, violent, sick.

I smoked it? I fucking smoked it? Jesus. What the hell is wrong with me?

My head throbs. My limbs feel heavy. My pants are undone, I'm half-dressed on a stranger's floor, and I can't even remember how I got here.

Wait.

Alley.

I suck in a breath. *Shit. Was I supposed to meet her tonight?*

My mind grasps for the memory, but it's slippery.

Fuck. Our anniversary. *Was that today?*

Panic surges, swallowing the nausea whole.

My whimper turns into a cry. "God. No. Not today. Please, no." The words tear from me, desperate and broken, begging my own mind to believe them.

A sob rips through me, raw and full-body, and I curl onto my side —because my limbs are fucking useless.

"Alley," I whisper. "God. No. Alley."

I'm a piece of shit.

I don't deserve her.

She'd be better off without me.

I wish I would just fucking die.

My gaze drops to the baggie that slid off my chest, now lying on the floor in front of me. I reach for it, my fingers wrapping around the plastic. I grip it tight, like it might save me from my choices—from myself.

Relief ghosts through me, filling the corners of my mind, body, and soul.

I scan the room. My eyes land on the foil and a candle.

Fuck.

I push myself to my knees, crawling toward it like it's my Savior— like it will give me life—or end me. Maybe both.

Fuck it. I've already ruined everything anyway. I've already lost. It's just a little more. Just enough to forget. I'll deal with dying later.

Besides, I'd be putting Alley out of her misery.

I drop back on my heels, whispering the lie I always start with. *"It's the last time."* My hands shake as I hold the bag, and the second I make my decision—they stop.

And I stop fighting.

* * *

I STUMBLE into the side of my building.

No. Not my building.

Mine isn't brick.

Shit. How much farther?

I fix my gaze on the street sign at the corner. *Goddammit.* I can't make it out. I squint, trying to bring the letters into focus, but everything's spinning. The streets swirl around me. The noise of the city feels louder than usual. Sirens, voices, and tires on wet pavement all bleed together into one haunting sound.

"Almost home. Just get home," I whisper, my teeth chattering. "Youcanlaydown. Just... gethome."

My shirt's soaked through, and I wrap my arms around myself, rubbing up and down for warmth. I wipe my face. Rain—or sweat—I can't even tell. Everything's wet.

I focus on a nearby building sign, lit up like a beacon, but it's too bright. I flinch, squeeze my eyes shut, and press my hand to the wall. My knees buckle, and I slide down, my body giving out beneath me. "I jus'wanna lay down," I mumble.

"You have to keep going," a voice says.

"No. Need to rest."

"Keep going."

My head snaps up. "Who said that?" My voice comes out cracked, weak. I look around, trying to make sense of what's happening—of where the fuck I am.

Someone's following me. I know they are. I have to get home. *I think I'm close. I have to be close.*

A blonde flashes through my mind—distorted, lips parted, fuzzy like a dream. *Alley. Was she at the party?*

I stumble farther down the road, feet dragging. There are people around me—I can hear them, feel the movement—but they all blend together.

I press my fingers to my brow and swipe at the sweat dripping down my face. *God. I'm gonna be sick.* Nausea whips through me, sudden and sharp. It knocks a groan out of me as I clutch my stomach and double over, crouching low until it eases just enough to breathe.

"Just get home, you piece of shit!" I yell, voice echoing down the street.

Fuck. What did Seth give me?

This feels different.

Was it the benzo? Was it the smoking?

Alley.

"Get to Alley."

If I can just get to her...

"If I can just—"

Home.
I just need to get home.

Chapter Forty-Eight

ALLEY

PRESENT DAY

THE FRONT DOOR SLAMS, jolting me awake. A second later, there's clattering.

My body bolts upright, heart racing.

What the hell?

I look over at Jensen's side of the bed. It's empty.

I press my palm flat to my chest. *Oh, thank God.* It's just him. He's home. I take a few deep breaths, trying to slow my pulse. *It's just Jensen.*

There's a loud bang, followed by a "Shit."

Of course he's messed up. *Great.*

"No. You be quiet!" Jensen whisper-shouts.

My body stills—frozen in place.

Did he... bring someone here?

Goosebumps crawl up my arms, and the hair on the back of my neck stands straight.

"Just go away!"

Why would he bring someone to our home at—

I grab my phone. It's 1:26 a.m. Something about this feels very... creepy.

I get out of bed and move slowly toward the door. I make my way down the hallway, each step deliberate and quiet, ears straining to hear who he's talking to.

"You saw her?" he says.

I stop again—cold.

Saw her? Who?

"Fucking liar."

I round the corner, my eyes adjusting to the darkness. My gaze lands on Jensen, then scans the rest of the kitchen and living room.

No one else is here.

A barstool lies on its side a few feet from the counter. That must've been the noise. Jensen's leaning over the counter, staring down at his phone.

I let myself relax a little. He must've been on a call. But still, it's 1:30 in the morning.

"Hey," I say.

He jumps, setting his phone face down on the counter, like he doesn't want me to see it.

My brows knit together. "Who were you talking to?" I take a step closer.

"Nobody," he mutters.

It's dark, but I can tell just by the way he's standing that he's high.

"You were talking to someone." I snatch his phone off the counter. "Open it," I say firmly. There is no room to argue.

He swipes up, unlocking it with Face ID. Gripping it tight, I pull up his call history. The last call he made was hours ago, when he was still at work.

"Jensen." My voice rises. "Who were you talking to?" I don't mean to be confrontational, but—*my God*, he owes me an explanation.

He lets out a short laugh—like it just dawned on him. "Oh, that... it was Amber's sister. She was right over there." He points toward the living room.

"What?" I ask, softly. "What are you talking about?"

"Amber's sister," he repeats. "She was here. She was talking to me." His voice shifts—uncertain now—like he's afraid. His brow furrows, like he's just now realizing that what he's saying doesn't make any sense.

You know that feeling when you watch your first scary movie—when chills race up your spine and creep across your skin?

That's what's happening to me now.

"Jensen," I whisper, my voice barely there. "There's no one there. Amber's sister died years ago. She couldn't have been here."

"No." He shakes his head hard. "No, you're wrong. She was right there! Right there!" he shouts, pointing wildly. The sudden outburst sends a fresh surge of fear through me.

I stare at the dark, empty living room, squinting—like if I look long enough, I'll see the ghost he swears he saw.

It's chilling.

"Okay," I say gently. "She was there."

He nods, relief breaking across his face. "Okay. You saw her, too. That's good."

"Let's just get to bed, okay?" I loop my arm through his. His skin is clammy, sticking to mine. "Come on, babe. Let's go. This way."

My chest swells with heartache, and a tear slips down my cheek as I hear my own voice. It's the same voice I used back when I was a CNA in the old folks' home—the one I used with Alzheimer's patients when they were lost or confused.

And it cuts like a dagger to my core.

"I just wanna lie down," he murmurs.

"Okay, babe. Let's go lie down."

I help him into bed and slide in beside him, my thoughts racing.

What is he on?

This is *different.*

What did he do? Where was he?

Minutes later, he's out of bed, stumbling into the bathroom. I hear drawers and cupboards slamming shut and more crashing sounds.

"Fuck!"

I sit up fast. "What are you doing?"

"Nothing," he says quickly. "I'm just... I need a Q-tip. I can't find them."

I grab my phone and step into the bathroom, lighting the floor with the flashlight. The Q-tips are everywhere.

"God, I can't find the Q-tips."

"They're right there," I say, pointing.

He starts yanking drawers open again, slamming them shut.

"No. I need them. Fuck! I just need them, okay?"

"Jensen..." My voice shakes, and my pulse picks up. "You're scaring me."

He doesn't hear me.

"Will you please just go back to bed?" I whisper. "Please." I close my eyes. "Please?"

He freezes. Then turns like nothing happened. "Fine." He walks back to the bed and lies down.

I settle in next to him—sort of. My body's tense, and my heart is pounding.

Two minutes later he's up again. "I need a damn Q-tip!"

He's back in the bathroom. Drawers open. Cupboards slam. Again and again.

"They're right there!" I call out.

"Where?" he snaps.

"On the floor. You spilled them."

"No. That's not what I need."

More cupboards. More frantic searching.

He's not looking for Q-tips anymore?

I don't know what he's doing. But I do know that in all our years together—even when he's been high—I've never been scared of Jensen.

Until now.

And I'm fucking terrified.

My brain spins with headlines—stories of wives killed by their husbands, only to find out later they were high. A psychotic break. A relapse gone from bad to worse.

I know these are crazy thoughts. Jensen loves me. He'd never hurt me. But this stranger pacing through our bathroom, whispering and slamming drawers, and talking to ghosts?

That's not Jensen.

This man could literally kill me, and not remember a second of it.

A fear so deep wraps around my throat, cutting off air. I'm on my feet before I even register moving. I flick the light switch on.

"Jensen, stop!"

He turns to face me. His eyes are sunken, the skin around them dark and hollow. And that shadow—the one that scared the hell out of me once before—it's back. It's here.

An evil presence you can actually see.

My lips tremble, and fear claws at my throat. "You're scaring me," I whisper. "I'm going to sleep at Matt's tonight, alright?"

"No!" he cries out. "Don't leave. Don't leave me, babe." His face crumples—grief, terror, all of it—and then he's sobbing. Not crying.

Sobbing.

"Please don't leave me with them."

Them?

I look around, my heart feeling like it's going to beat right out of my chest. "Who?" I ask, barely able to get the word out.

"Them! They're everywhere." He grabs my hands, pleading. "Please don't leave me with them. I'm scared. Please, babe. Please. I'm so scared."

I know he's hallucinating, but whatever he's seeing *feels* real. Like his demons are now mine—thick as fog, settling over everything, suffocating, and all-consuming.

The fear in his eyes tugs at my heart. I can't leave him like this. I search his face, desperate for a flicker of Jensen. Even a shred of him. He *has* to be in there. But I can't find him.

He's gone.

And it breaks my fucking heart.

Because I feel it—deep in my bones—in my goddamn soul. This is it. This is the last time.

This is the end.

I want so badly for him to come out of it. To fight for me. To say something—*anything*. But he doesn't even know where he is. He doesn't know his wife is standing here, scared out of her mind. That today was our anniversary. That he missed it.

That he left me sitting alone at dinner.

He quit.

He gave up.

On me.

On himself.

On us.

And now he's losing me. Because *I can't do this* anymore.

I inhale deeply, trying to steady my trembling body. "I'll stay if you lay down and go to sleep," I say. My voice is low and stern. "I'm serious, Jensen. Not another word. If you get up or speak, I'll leave."

He nods, collapsing against me. His arms wrap tight around my body, his cries muffling into my shoulder. "Thank you. Thank you. I love you so much."

I rub my palm up and down his back, tightening my hold around him as a quiet sob shakes through me—one I try to hold in but fail. "I love you too," I whisper.

I hold him for as long as I can, for as long as my heart can take it. Knowing deep down that this might be the last time he holds me like this—even if he's just clinging to me out of fear, holding on for dear life.

I don't want to remember it this way, so I force my mind to the memories that matter. All the tender ways Jensen's touched me over the years. The way his hands made me feel loved. The way they always made me feel safe. Protected.

They never made me feel like this.

I pull back, cupping his cheek, and kiss his forehead. "Go lay down, alright?"

I flip off the light, and climb back into bed, hoping it's for the last time tonight. Jensen slides in next to me.

He doesn't get up again. He doesn't speak. And eventually, he falls asleep.

But I don't. My mind won't shut off. And one thought keeps playing, over and over: no one should ever have to witness what I just did. No one should have to go through this.

What happened tonight—in our home—is not normal.

Tossing and turning, I finally give up.

I slip out of bed, walk into our closet, and turn the light on. My hands move quickly, pulling open a drawer with keepsakes.

After digging through a few items, I find what I'm looking for—an envelope—the letter I wrote to myself at Leo and Vivian's four months ago.

My breath catches as I stare down at it. I know what's inside. I know what it says.

And I promised myself I'd only open it if I ever found myself here again.

I slide down the wall, envelope in hand, and trace my thumb over the date:

April 14th.

I swallow the lump rising in my throat. I told myself if Jensen got clean, I'd wait. I'd give it time. But if he relapsed—I'd read it.

Otherwise, the plan was to wait until December 31. To give it everything I have. To give *him* everything I have.

I have.

God, I have.

I've given him everything. And then some.

With trembling hands, I slide my thumb under the edge of the envelope, breaking the seal, and pull out the letter.

Dear Alley,

I'm writing this letter the way I'd write it to Scarlett, or Megan, or Amber. Even Mom. The women I'd fight like hell to protect. The ones I'd want to be strong, and more than anything, happy.

I know you love Jensen. I know it. I've seen it with my own eyes. And I know he loves you, too.

You two have something special. Something not very many people are lucky enough to find.

But Jensen's sick.

And it's not something that can be cured with a pill, or a doctor, or even love. It's not something that patience or kindness or time can fix.

It's something only Jensen can do. And he has to do it for himself.

Not for you. Not for Matt. Not for his mom. Not because he's scared to lose you. He has to do it because he wants to get better.

For him. And him alone.

For so long, I've watched as you've stayed by his side, hoping, wishing, even praying for him to get better. To get the help he needs. But you can't do this forever. You deserve more. You deserve better. You deserve a life with someone who can show up for you. To celebrate life with you. To laugh with you. Grow with you. Build a life together.

You know this is a lifelong illness, even if he gets clean. It's still a battle, a cancer sitting in the corner, waiting patiently for the right time to pounce. To take over again.

You've seen it with Dad.

And even though you know it's possible for Jensen to get clean and stay clean, you also know this fight does not go away.

It's not yours to fight anymore.

You've done enough. You've done all you can.

I know you don't want to. But you have to. It's time.

You can love Jensen, and still leave him.

Let Jensen fight his own battles.

No more questioning. No more what ifs. No more.

You promised. Do it for your future self. Your future children. Your future happiness.... For Mom.

Because sometimes, we have to lose the things we love the most in order to find ourselves again in the chaos.

It's time to move on. Time to be happy. Time to remember who you were before all of this, and who you still are.

I gasp for air, the tears coming so hard and fast they blur and soak the words on the page.

"God," I sob—loud, guttural, wrecked. "I can't do this." I drag in a sharp breath, my chest aching, my lungs desperate for air. "I can't do this."

I hang my head in my hands.

And I cry...

One last time...

For us.

* * *

I WAKE TO DARKNESS, my sleeping mask still in place. I don't feel rested—not even a little.

Pushing the mask to my forehead, I force my eyes open, letting the brightness blind me.

Jensen's side of the bed is empty.

Guess he had to get his morning fix.

He probably doesn't even remember last night.

I wait for the emotion to hit—the sadness, the panic, the guilt. But it doesn't come.

I grab my phone, open the Delta app, and book a flight to Chicago for this afternoon. *It's now or never.* I need to see my dad anyway.

Silently, numbly, I move through the house, packing whatever I can fit into a large suitcase and a carry-on. Clothes, toiletries, just the essentials. Only the things I need for now.

I keep waiting to cry—to feel something. But it's like the well of tears has gone dry, emptied out by everything that came before.

Zipping my suitcase closed, I roll it to the front door, pausing for a moment to take one last glance around the apartment.

Our apartment.

My eyes land on the couch—the first place we ever made out. The corner of my mouth tugs up, just a little, at the memory of him trying to focus on a work call while he stripped my shirt off.

My gaze shifts to the dining table, where I took a chunk of skin out of my hip bumping into it so hard. Jensen wanted to kiss it better—and then it led to more. The kitchen counter, where he ate me out after a Sunday football day full of drinking and laughing.

My eyes squeeze shut. *God. Football.*

There it is. The emotion. The sadness. The overwhelming feeling that I might actually die right now from a broken heart.

He's everywhere.

I fell in love with him here. In this place. In this life we built. This apartment is us. It's full of our love, our history... our dreams.

But it's also where he broke us.

A shudder rises in my chest, my throat swells, thick with everything I'm about to lose, everything I'm about to walk away from.

My hopes.

My home.

My love.

Jensen.

I can't wait for him to come back this time. Because right now, it's him or me.

I choose me.

Opening the door, I step into the hallway, unsure of what my future holds.

I'm scared as hell. I'm dreading it. But it's like Leo said: *Time is the one thing that always passes.* It's guaranteed. And with time, things will get easier.

Eventually.

I close the door behind me... and pray for strength to keep walking.

Chapter Forty-Nine

JENSEN

PRESENT DAY—THREE DAYS LATER

SHE LEFT.

She really left.

I don't blame her, though. I'd leave me too.

I lean back into the sofa, the pillows swallowing me up. My eyes are heavy, breathing slow—relaxed.

I stare at the candle and the foil on the coffee table, my thumb rolling over the lighter switch, flicking it again and again.

Football's on in the background.

But I'm not watching.

I *can't* watch it. It reminds me too much of her. It makes me think.

And I don't want to think.

Thinking always leads to the same thing: There's nothing left for me.

No Alley.

No hope.

Nothing.

I take a swig from the beer in my left hand, trying to numb the pain, to erase it completely.

It won't work. She's everywhere. Her presence lingers in every room—in the furniture, the art. Fuck, even the air still smells like her.

I take a slow, broken breath, my attention drifting back to the candle on the table.

I have nothing left to lose.

I lean forward.

Rip the foil with shaking hands.

Flick the lighter.

And give what's left of my fucking soul to the devil.

A Note from the Author

Dear Reader,

Alley and Jensen's story doesn't end here. While this ending may have left you mad, frustrated, or devastated, don't lose hope. Their Happily Ever After is coming in Book Two of the Broken and Bound duet (Book Four of the Chicago Series).

I've wanted to write this story for eighteen years. It's close to home because it's partly mine. And I had to give this book the ending I felt was necessary for them in this moment. My ending.

The last few chapters—the ones that made you say *"holy shit"*?

Those are my stories. Pieces of my real life from my first marriage.

Yes, some of the details and settings are different, and the characters are fictional. But the experiences? The feelings? Alley's thoughts?

Those were real. Those were mine.

This book was brutally hard to write. I found myself avoiding it because it brought so many buried emotions to the surface. You know how readers often avoid books with their trigger warnings? Yeah, I decided to write one—and then I had to live in it.

I cried and sobbed more times than I can count. Chapter Thirty-Six wrecked me. My heart was racing, and my hands were shaking for a good thirty minutes after I finished writing it. The hardest part wasn't reliving the pain, though. It wasn't the trauma itself.

It was ruining Jensen.

Because Jensen is loveable. He's kind, and funny, and full of life. The kind of man who'd give you the shirt off his back. Watching someone like that disappear into addiction? That's the heartbreak. That's the grief. That's what makes it so damn hard.

My story ended differently. I did get my Happily Ever After, but only because I left. That chapter where Alley finds Jensen hallucinating and whispering to ghosts? That was the final night of my marriage. I slept in that house one last time. I woke up, and I left. I filed for divorce that day.

Everything Jensen said and did in that scene wasn't exaggerated for the story. It wasn't dramatized. That's what happened. That was my moment—the one that made me realize that my marriage wasn't normal. That no one should have to live like that.

And still, I love Jensen. It killed me to destroy him. But I knew I had to. I knew if I wanted to give him his redemption, I had to take him to rock bottom first. Because that's where real healing starts. And once I finished this book, I couldn't wait to write the second—his comeback, his reckoning, his love story. And let me tell you, it's worth every tear we shed getting here.

I'll be honest. When I started writing this duet, I planned for Book Two to be about Alley finding happiness with someone else. That was the arc I envisioned—her healing, her growth, her new love story. But somewhere along the way, everything shifted. I wasn't excited to write the second book anymore because I'd fallen for Jensen. Hard. And not just him, *them*. Alley and Jensen. Their friendship. Their history. Their chemistry. I couldn't walk away from that.

I couldn't ask readers to either.

But I also felt like I needed to honor *my* story. That's when I realized I could have both—this ending, my ending, right here. And their Happily Ever After in Book Two.

Even after everything Jensen has done, and all they've endured, I still wanted them to find their way back to each other. Once I admitted that, I couldn't write any other ending.

As you move into Book Two, I hope you'll open your heart. Because forgiveness isn't for them. It's for you. And Jensen's about to show you how much he's willing to earn it.

I've never felt resentment toward my ex since leaving. It sucked. But I was lucky. I found my now-husband, who helped pull me out of that hole. Together, we've become the best versions of ourselves.

And because I know some of you will want to know—no, I don't keep tabs on my ex. What I do know is that he got clean six months after I left. As far as I know, he's been clean since 2008.

And if he is, I couldn't be happier for him.

Thank you for reading this story, and for seeing the humanity in it. I hope it meant something to you.

~Erin~

Resources and Terminology

This story includes themes of addiction, relapse, and recovery. If you or someone you know is struggling, please know you're not alone. Support is out there. Below are a few terms used in this book, along with organizations that offer help and information.

Common Terms:

- **Oxy** – Slang for Oxycodone and OxyContin.
- **Oxycodone** – A powerful prescription opioid used to manage pain, often misused for its euphoric effects.
- **OxyContin** – A brand-name, extended-release version of oxycodone. It's designed for long-term pain relief but often abused due to its high dosage and longer-lasting effects.
- **Coke** – Slang for Cocaine, a fast-acting stimulant drug.
- **Benzos** – Slang for Benzodiazepines, prescription medications often used for anxiety or insomnia; dangerous when combined with other depressants like opioids or alcohol.
- **NA** – Narcotics Anonymous, a 12-step program for individuals recovering from drug addiction.

- **AA** – Alcoholics Anonymous, a 12-step program for individuals recovering from alcohol addiction.
- **Al-Anon** – A support group for friends and families of people struggling with addiction.

Support & Crisis Resources:

- **Suicide & Crisis Lifeline (U.S.)** – Dial 988 or visit 988lifeline.org
- **SAMHSA National Helpline (U.S. Substance Abuse and Mental Health Services)** – 1-800-662-HELP (4357) – Free, confidential help 24/7
- **Al-Anon** – al-anon.org – For families and friends affected by someone else's drinking and drug use.
- **Narcotics Anonymous** – na.org – Meetings and resources for those recovering from drug addiction.
- **Alcoholics Anonymous** – aa.org – Worldwide fellowship and resources for those recovering from alcoholism.

Note from the Author:
Recovery is not linear, and relapse does not mean failure. Whether you're seeking help, supporting someone, or simply holding space for healing—your journey matters.
You matter.

Acknowledgments

As always, I owe everything to my husband—my real-life book boyfriend and best friend. He is, without a doubt, my biggest cheerleader. Babe, thank you for always believing in me and my crazy dreams, for picking up the slack around the house when I get too caught up in writing to pull away, and for just being you.

To my amazing kids—thank you for letting me get away with some questionable mom moments, for manifesting in Target and airport bookstores with me, and for loving me unconditionally. I love you both more than you could ever know.

To my beta readers—thank you for your support, excitement, and friendship, and for always being willing to read just one more chapter. This book wouldn't be what it is without your feedback. The text messages, FaceTimes, endless GIFs, and inside jokes have been some of my favorite parts of this whole process. In no particular order: Nikole Allred, V.L. Williams, Shauna Haddock, Hannah Wells, Derrian Whetton, Paige O'Neill, Bree Sleater, Kallie Street, Lauren Andrew, and Leah Richmond. And to Kyle Carsey and Tyler Allred, for providing valuable feedback from a male perspective.

To my alpha readers, Bree Dodge and Courtney Summers, and my PA, Gina Rinaldo—thank you for all your feedback and for being my daily therapists. I genuinely don't think I could've finished this book with my sanity intact without you.

A special thank you to my editor, Celia Killen, who once again worked her magic in perfecting this book. You have a gift, and I'm so grateful for your patience, insight, and the suggestions that helped shape Alley and Jensen's story.

Thank you to my Bookstagram community. Damn, you ladies are

the best. Thank you for taking a chance on me, for reading and reviewing my books, for supporting me, posting, sharing—the list goes on and on. I will never forget you and the role you've played in this journey.

Music is a huge inspiration when I write, and this section wouldn't be complete without thanking the incredible artists whose songs helped shape this book. To every artist who contributed to A Love That Broke Us playlist—thank you.

A shoutout and thank you to some of my favorite authors who have inspired me in one way or another: Meghan Quinn, Sarah J. Maas, Elle Kennedy, and Colleen Hoover.

And last, but surely not least, to you, the reader. Thank you for picking up my book.

About The Author

Erin Cornia lives in Austin with her husband, two children, and two mini golden doodles. She rediscovered her passion for reading after a long break when *It Ends With Us* by Colleen Hoover fell into her hands. Now, she has a deep love for romance novels—contemporary, fantasy, and historical alike.

Some of her favorite authors include Sarah J. Maas, Colleen Hoover, Meghan Quinn, Tessa Bailey, Judith McNaught, and Rebecca Yarros with *Throne of Glass* by Sarah J. Maas holding the spot as her favorite series of all time.

When she's not reading or writing, she enjoys playing pickleball, working out, traveling, and spending time outdoors. You can often find her watching *Schitt's Creek, Sex and the City, Friends,* or *Emily in Paris*—with a bowl of homemade popcorn, of course.

For updates on new releases, ARCs, and bonus scenes (or to scream about the book and share your feels) come join Erin's Facebook Reader Group—Erin Cornia: Romance, Heartbreak, Healing & Hard-Earned HEAs

Follow Erin on Instagram and TikTok:
https://www.instagram.com/erincornia_author/
www.tiktok.com/@erincornia.author

www.ingramcontent.com/pod-product-compliance
Lightning Source LLC
Chambersburg PA
CBHW020227010826
48973CB00006B/1400